I0692838

THE SIGNING

Robert Banfelder

Broadwater Books

BB

~ ~

Broadwater Books
141 Riverside Drive
Riverhead, New York 11901

Cover Photo: Tom Tietz

Printed in the United States of America

10 9 8 7 6 5 4 3 2 1

ISBN: 978-0-9915912-2-0

In Memory of Richard Tchilinguirian

PRAISE FOR THE NOVELS OF

ROBERT BANFELDER

"A MASTER OF HIS CRAFT! . . . Banfelder captures the essence of the serial killer." [re *Trace Evidence*]
~ Linda L. Chase, Forensic Anthropologist Specialist

"BRAVO! As a forensic psychologist specializing in psychopathy, I have been researching authors who write fiction in the field of forensic psychology. I am impressed with Banfelder's well-researched, credible, and unique plots regarding the criminal mind." [re *The Teacher*]
~ Dr. Jason Dunham, Forensic Psychologist

"CUTTING PROSE, FAST PACED, INTRIGUING. Banfelder's descriptions are detailed, novels well plotted, and his imagination without bounds." [re *The Author*]
~ Donna L. Gestri, author, *Sweet Figs, Bitter Greens, For Jenny, Time Takes No Time*

"UNRELENTING IN HIS ABILITY TO MOVE YOU ALONG AND INTO HIS PAGES. You are running fast, and just when you think it might be safe, Banfelder hits you with another curve." [re *The Author*]
~ Patti Ann Bengen, author, *Sex, Danger in the Tulip Fields, The Devil's Dance, New Beginnings*

"THRILLERS THAT TAKE YOU AWAY TO A DIFFERENT PLACE, LIKE GOOD THRILLERS SHOULD. Just when you think you have figured out where the plot is going, Banfelder pulls out the rug from underneath you with heart-pounding effect." [re *Knots: A Justin Barnes Thriller*]
~ Russell F. Moran, author, *The Time Magnet Series*

Titles by Robert Banfelder

Fiction

Dicky, Richard, and I

The Good Samaritans

Knots: A Justin Barnes Thriller

Trace Evidence

The Teacher
Winner Best Suspense Book 2006 ~ New Book Reviews

The Author
Winner Best Suspense Book 2007 ~ New Book Reviews

Nonfiction

The Fishing Smart <u>Anywhere</u> Handbook for Salt Water & Fresh Water

Acknowledgment

My heartfelt gratitude to my soul mate, Donna Derasmo, for her exemplary formatting, being my sounding board, and forever giving me encouragement. You are my anchor.

THE SIGNING

CHAPTER
——>
1

It was a matter of course for Richard Geist to remain silent of tongue, for he had lost the ability to speak some years ago. It was, however, a different sort of silence he sought today: the ability to move stealthily across the dry terrain without as much as a single, solitary sound. Never a noise from the snap of a twig under heel or the crunch of crisp autumn leaves beneath the ball of his boot. Ne'er the careless rustle of clothing, but rather the careful selection of full Fall Predator camouflage. Nary ever the sudden removal of an aluminum arrow from quiver to quake, but rather its deft withdrawal, locked precisely upon the bowstring preceding a full fluid draw.

Of course, Richard couldn't completely mask the muffled sound of string-release as the shaft sped two-hundred-plus feet per second upward toward its target. Additionally, one couldn't help but hear the sudden *whomp* followed by the form falling noisily forward from its perch, a platform hanging fourteen feet above the ground. The figure toppled out of the tree stand, stopped suddenly by the safety harness, much like a parachuter caught short of his mark.

It was a clean kill. Relatively quiet. Quick. The quintessence of excellence in execution, from the selection of gear and equipment, right down to the scrutiny of the tiniest painstaking detail. Preparation, patience, and practice were the hallmarks of the archer's success.

Oh, the endless hours endured in having placed thousands upon thousands of field point arrows into paper plate targets at twenty, thirty, and forty yards, then repeating the process until he could consistently group three out of three missiles into a bull's-eye the diameter of a dime, Richard reflected. Only after years of practice did he come to know the bliss of delivering deadly broadheads to their mark at fifty yards with razor-sharp precision, tightly grouping every arrow or even splitting their plastic nocks with subsequent shots— before it was time for fun afield.

Chapter
——>
2

It was a brisk, crisp fall November morning on Long Island's South Fork. Real estate magnate Arthur Field, husband of Broadway's darling of stage and screen, Margaret Austin Field, owned over 100 acres. To Margaret's friends as well as fans, she was Maggie. Beautiful. Rich. Put upon that proverbial pedestal by the public, yet actually quite down to earth and devoted to her two daughters, her husband, and their dog.

Guests would come and guests would go, but Arthur's most recent arrival had departed earlier than expected—in a body bag, straightaway to the morgue. Ironically, a bag filled with hunting paraphernalia that Suffolk County District Attorney Barry Altman had carried into the guest cottage that Friday morning was practically the same sized bag in which the man's body had been carried out by police to a waiting van late that afternoon, the killer chortled with a wide grin.

Over the years, D.A. Altman had been one of several guests who ingratiated himself with the Fields for the privilege of hunting the prime acreage in Bridgehampton, land overrun with deer so surprising in size and number that hunting enthusiasts in the area would gape in awe.

Arthur Field would never permit gunning on his estate. Strictly bow and arrow. Woe be it to any hunter who trespassed let alone carried a firearm onto the man's property, out of season or otherwise. Poachers were dealt with harshly, the letter of the law fully enforced by the game warden. No first offense warning, but rather an immediate arrest of the perpetrator followed by an overnight visit to the local jail.

Only a select few of Arthur's friends and acquaintances were accorded the privilege of stalking or patiently sitting in a tree stand from dawn to dusk for the elusive whitetail deer. It was probably the primary reason why the district attorney had apparently felt safe and secure, although concerned colleagues protested vehemently.

Reluctantly, Altman had agreed to check in hourly with his retinue at the guest cottage via the VHF Horizon/Hand-Held, just so long as his associate and longtime friend and part-time bodyguard, Deputy Inspector Bill Lancing, Suffolk County Police Department—on the threshold of retirement—did not engage the district attorney in any lengthy conversation, for to Altman, the sport of bowhunting deer was serious if not sacred.

Early morning through noon had been uneventful. It was only when Altman failed to call in or answer after the second hour that his deputy inspector and two detectives put aside their card game to investigate, leaving the guest cottage to cross a ravine and a fifteen-hundred-yard meadow, fast approaching the wooded area where they had helped their charge prepare his tree stand a week before the hunt.

It had turned relatively warm that afternoon. Three men stood frozen, staring up wide-eyed into the pale face of their fallen, actually suspended, angel. The D.A.'s compound bow, bow quiver, several arrows with brightly-colored fletchings, along with lots of blood, covered the woodland floor, giving a surreal brilliance to the midafternoon matinee as Richard demurely lowered his Nikon field glasses.

Chapter
——>
3

District Attorney Altman certainly had lots of enemies. Defendants who vehemently swore bloody revenge. Some of whom simply swore under their breath. Still, there were others who had adamantly demanded an apology for Altman's misdeeds. Two such souls immediately came to the deputy inspector's mind. Cotler. Terry Cotler. The other was Clarence Kallace. Both men had been released from state prisons after DNA tests excluded them as rapists for which they were imprisoned, having served twelve and six years, respectively—but not before Altman had challenged his own scientific community, thwarting the prisoners' freedom. The D.A. had other enemies, too: powerful political factions who wanted him out of office. There had been two big scandals. Brian Cooper's column in *Newsday* had covered the stories extensively, along with the Kallace and Cotler cases. If the deputy inspector knew he could have gotten away with it, he would have framed Cooper himself for murder for all the grief the columnist had caused the office.

Cotler and Kallace and a score of others were investigated. Nothing. In a lighter moment, Lancing gave his colleagues ten-to-one odds that it was a Democrat behind the murder of his boss and lifelong friend, Barry T. Altman. On a more serious note, the deputy inspector privately avowed that he would avenge his friend's murder, that there would be no opportunity for trial by jury. None whatsoever.

Lancing continued his own investigation by personally visiting sporting goods stores on the East End of the Island that sold Easton's XX78 Super Slam aluminum arrows and 100 grain three-bladed Muzzy archery broadheads, like the one that had entered just below the D.A.'s ribcage, collapsing a lung and continuing through the man's heart before shattering the collarbone. Lancing, an occasional waterfowl hunter, was amazed at the single arrow's destruction. One Riverhead sporting goods store owner graphically explained how a customer of his who hunted whitetail from a tree stand with a bow and arrow had made a shoulder entry shot the diameter of a quarter before it blasted open the animal's lower extremity to the size of a sixteen-ounce soup can. Lancing was equally amazed at a precision bow's accuracy at distances far greater than he ever imagined.

"Well, most kills are made by the average bowhunter at fifteen to twenty yards," the sporting goods proprietor explained. "But an expert can drop a bull moose at fifty to sixty yards with gale winds whipping by at thirty-five miles an hour," the frail man continued quite seriously, eliminating himself from either category. "Me. I'm no archer. Strictly rifle. Hunt and fish upstate. Esopus. Got some mighty fine trout up there. Gonna retire there soon. Let my son take over this shop. Now, *he's* the archer. Shoot the bull's-eye outta paper at forty yards as sure as I'm standin' here. Don't hunt none, though. Strictly target. Fishes some. Mostly fools around with them bows and the ladies."

Deputy Inspector William Lancing glanced over at several photographs on the wall behind the counter. All were of the same young man over the course of several years. "That him?"

"Yeah, twenty-nine now, and about as settled as a chicken hawk. Good boy, though." The owner smiled broadly.

The detective studied one picture in particular: the focused figure in hip boots standing in a shallow pool, bow at full draw, aimed downward into the murky water. "Thought you said, strictly target," Lancing challenged.

"Oh, that. That was the last of it. Used to bow-fish for carp during the March thaw. 'Like shooting fish in a barrel,' he'd say. Couldn't miss 'cause they'd be in great masses. But I'll tell you what picture hangs in a cluttered corner of my mind," the man emphasized through a chuckle. "Saw him snap-shoot a bottom feeder that decided to go airborne at twenty-five yards out. Hit 'im dead center! Saw it with my own eyes. Fourteen years old he was at the time. Turned to me smiling and said, 'No challenge, Dad.' Been shootin' paper targets ever since. Rated number three in the state," he added proudly.

"What's his name?"

"Darrin. Darrin Ellis, and I'm Chuck."

The two men shook hands warmly and talked for a while before Lancing left the store. Frustrated. For almost every sporting goods store sold Easton's XX78 Super Slams along with Muzzy broadheads. Everyone on Chuck Ellis' Sporting Goods customer list who had purchased either item was a suspect. And the number of names throughout the area, especially when added to the number of customers ordering through mail-order houses around the country, was growing rapidly.

Lancing's investigation, tied mainly to lab report analyses, was not limited to the XX78 shaft and formidable broadhead. They included other elements such as bonding cements and fletching: the back formation of the arrow made up of either three plastic or feathered vanes—never a combination of the two materials. Yet the arrow the forensic boys had removed from D.A. Altman's body was uniquely fletched with two olive-green vanes and one black feather, all set in a left helical fashion. It was the killer's personalized signature.

CHAPTER
——>
4

R obert Redler, adjunct lecturer for local colleges and freelance writer, wrote part time for *The North Shore Towers Newsletter* of Great Neck, New York; actually, a registered local newspaper, which the journalist jokingly referred to as 'the prestigious rag.' Although it reached a readership of unimpressive number, it nonetheless was read by an impressive group of influential sorts who resided in the posh North Shore Towers. *The Towers*, as it was commonly called, bordering two counties, housed some of Nassau's and Queen's most powerful practitioners: judges, lawyers, and prosecutors as well as a collection of other professionals: bankers, engineers, dentists, and surgeons.

Through a series of scathing editorials involving the Queens district attorney's office and an innocent young man imprisoned for attempted rape, Redler had managed to incur the wrath of those most responsible for having put the Bayside man behind bars. After a relentless legal battle between Queens prosecutors and Manhattan defense attorneys, the presiding judge reluctantly reversed himself, overturning the guilty verdict and releasing John Lightfoot shortly before the Christmas of 1991. Redler's caustic criticism of Queens District Attorney David Black had been second only to that of *Newsday* reporter Brian Cooper's venomous attack of Suffolk D.A.

Altman and his regime. As a matter of record, Redler, too, had blasted Altman and his cronies for blocking the release of Cotler and Kallace.

And now, one week after Altman's murder, during dusk, Nassau's District Attorney Gregory Howe had been found fatally shot before the front steps of his home as he apparently stooped to read the cryptic message scrawled within a premature yellow chalk outline of a body. His own. The arrow had hit the D.A. on the left side of his ribcage with a *smack* that sent the next-door neighbor's dog yapping away insanely within the confines of an electric fence. Back and forth it ran as Richard Geist disappeared around the corner of the hemorrhaging man's home. A moment later, the sound of the barking dog was diminished only by the screams of a hysterical and disbelieving wife.

The evening news report focused primarily on the mysterious message, downplaying the often sensationalized coverage of Tony Giordano, a Long Island man convicted of statutory rape. An unconfirmed report had said that the words printed within the chalk outline read, Dances with D.A.s.

Robert Redler sat in shock as he listened to an update. Substantiated by police sources, the words repeated were, indeed, Dances with D.A.s. *Dances with D.A.s* was the headline of Redler's first of nine editorials concerning the John Lightfoot matter. It had nothing to do with District Attorney Howe or his office. The Lightfoot case concerned the Queens district attorney. Still, the police would be sure to come calling, Redler believed. The writer's mind was racing faster than a mad dog could cover ground.

He recalled one of his pieces concerning Nicholas Maldonado, the reputed Brooklyn Mob boss. Robert had thought the authorities would be coming for him then, too. Events from the spring of 1992 resurfaced in flashback.

Nicholas Maldonado's good friend, Wallace Keating, (dubbed the don's adopted son), had read Redler's front-page story, which assailed the federal government's handling of the case against Mr. Maldonado. Redler had numerated in print, point after point, as to why the defendant had not received a fair trial. Keating was impressed. Unbeknownst to Redler, Keating had made thousands of copies of the cover story, which were distributed to Maldonado supporters shortly before the man's sentencing. Redler had been present in the courtroom that morning but left the building before the real commotion erupted.

That very evening, one of Redler's students at Queensborough Community College had asked him if he had seen Channel 2 News. Redler had not. All too familiar with his Maldonado piece, which the instructor had handed out to his class the week before for discussion, several students related what their English professor would probably catch on the eleven o'clock news later that night. He did. Copies of the story carrying his picture and that of Nicholas Maldonado wound up on the windshields of official vehicles surrounding the Manhattan Federal Courthouse. A camera panned several overturned cars. One vehicle belonged to a marshal, it was reported. The lens zoomed in on the front page, capturing both photos affixed beneath the wiper blade. Filling the TV screen were two smiley faces: Robert Redler's (the writer of the story) and Nicholas Maldonado's (the crime figure who had hours earlier received life in prison without parole). Oh, they would surely come for him, Redler had believed. But they never did.

The following morning, the *New York Daily News* carried a front-page picture of demonstrators displaying placards as well as copies of Redler's article, holding them high for the world to see. *New York Newsday* had similar pictures on page 3. Now they would surely come for him, the writer reflected. They did not.

Today, however, was quite different, Redler realized. Two district attorneys had been murdered within a fortnight. Although he had no knowledge of those murders, he nonetheless ran scared. And there was good reason for it. Aside from the *Dances with D.A.s* editorial he had written, many of his other pieces attacked the district attorneys of all five boroughs.

In 1989, The State of New York, County of Queens, had gone after Robert Redler with charges of sexual abuse of a minor: the daughter of his domestic partner, Liza Downs. Just prior to the accusation, both Redler and Downs had forbade the rebellious teenager from seeing her drug dealer beau—attested to by two attorneys for whom the daughter interned as part of a work/study program through John Jay College of Criminal Justice. Redler had been arrested, indicted, and spent a day and a half locked up in the Queens Detention Center as well as Rikers Island before being released on an unsecured bond of $25,000. The following semester, he was fired after twelve years as a "gifted teacher."

Redler was reinstated, but the proverbial handwriting was on the wall. It read: *Get rid of him.* The following year he was out for good—blackballed by the City University of New York for the *unauthorized* use of his first published novel in the classroom, which was a blatant lie made by the chairperson of the English Department. For years, and with the *express* permission from the chairperson, Robert had excerpted from his novel while it was in manuscript form, presenting it to the class on an overhead projector. As a matter of fact, the chairperson was present and had evaluated Robert and his presentation as a matter of course, writing up the adjunct lecturer as a "gifted teacher." When the book was published by Hudson View Press in Manhattan, it went into the college bookstore and was permitted for sale to students; it was listed, along with required readings, on Professor Robert Redler's syllabus. However, when Robert taught a freshman composition course at Queensborough Community College's satellite school in Far Rockaway, the same chairperson claimed that she had no knowledge of, nor had she ever given Robert permission to use the text. Through the teacher's union, Robert had made the case that the chair had been present in his classroom not only when he used the text in manuscript form on an overhead projector, but that the woman was also present after the novel was published and available through the college bookstore, listed on his syllabus, and carried to class by students during a subsequent teacher evaluation. Robert offered to line up thirty-two students to give testimony that the chairperson was indeed present in the classroom when he was being evaluated and that she unquestionably knew that he excerpted lessons from the text.

His battle with both bureaucracies—the college as well as the courts—had cost thousands of dollars. Still, he continued to crusade, writing and fighting against injustices. His focus was now solely on the criminal justice system. He wrote about prosecutors who withheld evidence that would tend to exonerate defendants; cops and detectives who lied and railroaded innocent people; and judges who denied defendants a fair trial. With regard to his own plight, he had been put through the proverbial mill before all charges against him were eventually dropped. But he wouldn't let go; years later still sending around his thirty-four page packet, detailing the event to anyone who could possibly help right a wrong by punishing those responsible. All to no avail. Presently, he was busy exposing a prosecutor who not only hid exculpatory evidence from the defense, but went so far as to suborn perjury from the state's key witness.

Redler's thoughts returned to the moment and The *Dances with D.A.s* message scrawled within the chalk outline along D.A. Howe's walkway leading to his home. Still, there was something far greater in scope than the murders and the message that unnerved him.

CHAPTER
——>
5

Captain Eugene Cally of the 111th Precinct in Queens was perusing Robert Redler's packet. It read, in part, like a surreal play, yet had the ring of truth to it. Actually, it had been written by Redler and his girlfriend, Liza, in alternating voices. The treatise was Redler's and Liza's cry for help. The pair was relentless. Cally recalled their names surfacing several times over the years. Redler and Liza claimed that he had been railroaded, a vendetta by her daughter and *that* side of the family who had it in for him. A connected family at that. The whole thing smacked of impropriety from the get-go, Cally thought. But a vendetta involving the complainant's family and boyfriend, a lawyer, a bureau chief in the Queens district attorney's office, a police captain, a detective with the Sex Crimes Unit, a female prosecutor? Not to mention John Jay College of Criminal Justice where the state's witness and her boyfriend had both attended. What probably happened, Cally believed, was that Redler, as usual, had pissed people off. Many people. Plain and simple. It was amazing what could follow, and did.

Cally put down Redler's packet. "Civilians," he sighed annoyingly. One thing the captain assured himself. Mr. Redler certainly knew how to make enemies. Lots of enemies. Enemies of old and enemies of new.

After a preliminary check, Robert Francis Redler came up clean.

For now.

Chapter
——>
6

Throughout his years of teaching and writing, Robert Redler was respected by his colleagues, well-liked by his students, and loved by Liza. In that regard, the forty-seven-year-old felt blessed and, in effect, fulfilled. And as Liza was surely the love of his life, writing and teaching were positively his passions, too. Liza's daughter, however, was the bane of their existence. A student of evil. And he knew evil well, for he once knew Richard Geist. Studied him. Wrote about him. Wanted mankind to wake up and pull the proverbial plug on the Richard Geists of this planet by sending him and his kind into the next world.

"But why Richard Geist and not Nicholas Maldonado?" a bright female freshman sitting in the front row of Redler's class had questioned. "Where's your humanity now, Professor? Civilized man doesn't go around 'pulling the plug' on crazy people. Sounds to me like you're flirting with a contradiction of terms," the student challenged respectfully.

"Perhaps not as much a contradiction as it is a paradox, for maybe it only *seems* the uncivilized thing to do," Professor Redler offered evenly, playing devil's advocate in preparing his English 101 group for a composition on the death penalty.

As the period was about to end, he asked his class to hold that thought and to look up several terms for homework over the weekend: *civilized, crazy, retarded,* and *mental illness,* jotting the words on the blackboard with a new piece of yellow chalk that shrieked along with the shrill of the resonating bell. Addressing the young woman in the first row, he smiled and politely told her to be prepared to kick off the discussion for Monday evening.

At semester's end, Professor Redler's freshmen knew how to put sentences together smoothly, punctuate with utmost confidence, move through a composition logically, and conclude intelligently. Additionally, they had learned how to express themselves orally.

In end-term evaluation reports, most of Redler's students wrote that they learned more about themselves and the writing process during sixteen weeks than they had in four years of high school. They learned respect and discipline. Redler demanded it. They learned not to prejudge; hence, they truly learned about prejudice. Robert Redler fought against it in any form. Yes, Redler's students liked him, to say the least. That was the professor's reward. He felt as rich as a Rockefeller, yet somehow remained as humble as a starving beggar on a street. And when a few initially shy students approached him toward final days, as they always did, confessing that they had never ever read a novel on their own until he had *inspired* them—well, he could have shed tears of joy.

"So, tell me. What novel did you read?" Professor Redler had asked a lad enthusiastically.

"*Anna Karenina.*" The young man grinned.

"Prevaricator," the instructor bantered back. "Come clean, now, Carlos."

"James Dickey's *Deliverance,*" the young man whispered as though he were speaking to his confessor, which in some capacity the professor seemed to serve. "And yesterday I started *The Godfather.*"

"Finish it?" Redler had asked with a straight face.

"No!" said the student with some astonishment. "It's this thick, man!" he declared, indicating the breadth between thumb and forefinger.

"Then I'm surprised you're even in school today," Redler

teased.

"I know. I know," repeated the excited young man, smiling broadly. "That Corleone family's a ticket. Yeah?"

"Yes," Redler enunciated flatly.

"I mean, *yes*," Carlos corrected himself.

"No. You mean, *yeah*! And yeah's okay for now. Now, you go finish that first-rate fiction. Then we'll talk about it if you like."

"All right!" Carlos agreed emphatically. "Listen."

"I'm listening."

"I don't want this to sound queer or anything." He paused. "I love you, man. I mean as a teacher," he added, bordering on embarrassment.

Robert Redler grinned from ear to ear. "I love you back, man. I mean as a student."

Carlos could have melted away right there. All two hundred and forty pounds of him.

Those precious moments seemed like they had happened a million years ago. After his termination at the college, Robert Redler went deep inside himself, writing feverishly about the criminal justice system, his innocence, the innocence as well as the guilt of others. He watched the guilty walk away without remorse. He heard the finality of the prison cell door slam shut on the pure and the poor. He lectured and wrote about those travesties, pointing an accusatory finger at bureaucrats who bungled cases because of incompetence, or others who simply concerned themselves with the political climate rather than the facts of the matter. He lambasted law enforcement officers who contaminated evidence and twisted testimony and the very truth.

Robert Redler was fast becoming . . . prejudiced . . . to a degree.

Chapter
——>
7

R ichard Geist was busy preparing for another grand slam. It would be sensational, he promised himself, watching and listening carefully as the news crew stood at a respectful distance from the unhappy home of the deposed sovereign of Nassau. District Attorney Gregory Howe. A reporter gripping a microphone anxiously stated that someone had shot and killed the district attorney moments after he had been dropped off by his driver at 5 p.m.

"Five-0-Two, precisely," Richard mumbled and signed with flashing fingers, shaking his head disgustedly at the figure on the screen. *"The day was drawing to a close, dope."*

The reporter dramatically explained that the district attorney had been shot with a single arrow.

"In the same fashion as the district despot of Suffolk," Richard emphasized when the picture suddenly shifted to the newsroom where a commentator explored the similarity to last week's killing of District Attorney Barry Altman.

To Geist's disappointment, there was no mention concerning any of the *important* particulars. Next, the Tony Giordano/Alice Ziegler business was being bantered about, delivering the viewing audience into the courtroom to hear Tony's attorney plea for leniency for his client prior to sentencing. What an inept performance, the killer thought. Alice Ziegler had given her prepared statement. Then on to Tony's admission of guilt for statutory rape. Flashbacks to Alice's earlier admission of critically wounding Tony's wife with a handgun on the back stoop of the couple's home.

"*Upstaged by Long Island's dastardly duo!*" Richard blew in an incomprehensible and angry tone. "*Just wait.*" He'd make Alice, Tony and a host of others—who were giving Long Island an infamous reputation—seem like truants by the time he finished his business at hand, he swore silently, fletching the final black feather firmly in place upon the aluminum shaft.

Chapter
——>
8

Doctor Angelo Bianco, the director of the King Foundation in Suffolk County, sat in his office watching a follow-up report of the second district attorney to be shot and killed by a single, lethal arrow. Something gnawed away at him. Something from the distant past. The boldness of the act, perhaps. Having practiced as a young psychiatrist, Bianco had seen and treated patients sustaining mild forms of mania, formally labeled manic depressive illnesses, now more commonly referred to as affective bipolar disorders. Through the years, he worked with those suffering from severe cases of schizophrenia, characterized by features such as emotional blunting, intellectual deterioration, social isolation, disorganized speech and behavior, delusions and hallucinations—including some who exhibited tempers of a volcanic nature. The more volatile were those committed to Suffolk's North Shore State Hospital for the Criminally Insane in Havenwood.

"Dances with D.A.s," Doctor Bianco said aloud. "Hmm."

It was the succinct alliterative ring that riveted the psychiatrist. Alliteration! He once had a male patient—or more specifically his predecessor had—who swam in a sea of it. It was never more evident than during the young man's angry yet eloquent tirades, for he could string words together that surely sang. A language both paradoxically pure and foul in tone as the poor soul's most profane deeds. A voice that could seemingly sound off in some distant corner when it was, in fact, railing right in front of you. Or most eerily, voices in concert which could blanket a room with chortling while bemoaning the dead . . . simultaneously . . . without the slightest trace of trickery, Doctor Bianco recalled.

But that devilish instrument had been altogether silenced by a detective who literally tore the patient's tongue out of his head almost a quarter of a century ago, the psychiatrist calculated, running his fingers through a thinning black head of hair. Richard Geist would be forty-two years old if he were still alive. And why wouldn't he be? "Why wouldn't pure evil prevail?" he announced most pessimistically. Doctor Bianco contemplated that thought with the strictest of religious respect and the soundest of mind.

Richard Geist had escaped from the state hospital in Havenwood seven years after his transfer from the King Foundation, the private psychiatric institution that the late Doctor King (Richard's biological father) had headed until the late sixties. Richard was the most cunning and dangerous of psychopaths that Doctor Bianco had ever met—*not treated*—for there was no cure for Richard Geist. He was cursed. Plain and simply put, Richard was sheer genius and pure evil, packaged and delivered up from the depths of hell, the good doctor quite seriously entertained.

The gift of spoken language ripped from Richard was somehow salvaged, though, through his writing. Oh, but it was so much more than a salvaging. It was as though a sinister savior had simply swapped his facility of speech for sheer verse. So, while committed to Suffolk County's oldest state-run hospital, Richard Geist wrote his autobiography of celebrity status. In it, he had sorted out his multiple personalities. With it, he had convinced state psychiatrists that he was on the road to recovery. The model patient. Deeply remorseful he was for having murdered his own mother as well as a nine-year-old female patient of Dr. King's. Completely repentant was he for having killed or maimed others. Then came his daring escape while being escorted from his father's graveside in November of 1976.

Never to be heard from again.

The camera zoomed in on the enigmatic message scribbled upon the pavement of the dead district attorney's home.

Yes! In addition to the killer's message was that hasty hand, Doctor Bianco thought. Childlike. Like the helter-skelter printing and drawings Richard had scrawled on the dresser mirror in Bianco's own home seventeen years ago while he and his wife slept peacefully.

Chapter
——>
9

The two interim district attorneys for Suffolk and Nassau, along with the D.A.s for the boroughs of Queens, Brooklyn, and Staten Island, in addition to every assistant district attorney in all five boroughs, talked, squawked, and balked about the bow and arrow business. It became their main topic of conversation at arraignments, in chamber conferences, plea bargain discussions, pretrial hearings, jury selections, and sentencings. In brief, these servants of the people were running scared.

Security was extremely tight. Court officers, police, and personal bodyguards were now escorting many of the officialdom in, out, and around their respective homes and offices, as if someone might dare desecrate or trespass through the latter hallowed halls of justice with a stringed instrument of destruction and drop a D.A. in his tracks or pin him to an office wall.

Two Queens court officers who worked and bowhunted together argued over whether the killer had used a recurve bow, a contemporary compound bow, or the traditional type, commonly called a longbow.

Jurors had no trouble in abiding by a judge's edict not to discuss their pending case with family members, friends, or anyone for that matter, for their discourse centered around the actions of court officers, gossip, and rumors that flew through the building like so many cops

and robbers in a Mack Sennett silent-film slapstick comedy—
only no one was laughing.

Months before the murders, Richard Geist approached two
attorneys in an elevator, handing one of them a note as the trio
was about to leave the Queens Criminal Court Building. One
counselor was busy shuffling through a set of papers while the
other read Richard's message:

> I am a mute. I may require the services of a criminal
> lawyer. Do either of you gentlemen practice? If so,
> may I have your card? I'll have my secretary call
> your office and explain. My name is Richard Archer.

The attorney nodded and smartly withdrew a business card
from his wallet, giving it to Richard along with the note. The two
shook hands then parted. Richard left the building and walked
west along Queens Boulevard, smiling handsomely. It started to
drizzle. Richard put a hand deep into the pocket of his coat,
fondling the card, being careful not to *fold*, *bend*, or *mutilate*; he
giggled deliciously.

"*Fucking dumb*," he mouthed and signed, his fingers
tapping away excitedly within the garment. "*So fucking dumb.*"

Authorities as well as the general public speculated daily about
who the killer or killers might be. Almost everyone had a theory;
that is, everyone from the cop on the corner to the descendants of
Cochise. Nicholas Maldonado's crew was a favorite target. Only
no one knew anybody in the Mob who settled things these days
with a bow and arrow.

Of course, there were those who were interviewed on the
streets of our towns and cities who lived life in a vacuum, those
who heard little or next to nothing about the ambushings. One
pedestrian, when asked about the two D.A.s, said that he knew of
no one who worked for the Department of Agriculture.

Chapter
--->
10

Richard was home in his basement rental. Safe and sound. He stretched his six-foot frame across the open sofa bed and, reaching languidly for the remote control, switched on the TV. It was 5:55 p.m. The newscaster told his viewers to stay tuned for further developments involving the *Dances with D.A.s* story. The man promised "new and startling details" in the case. In an exclusive interview with a spokesman from the D.A.'s office in Nassau County, Suffolk County's Channel 12 News Brief would be discussing "illuminating information" which positively linked the two murders. Richard couldn't wait to be *startled* and *illuminated* as he lay there in semi-darkness.

It had all proved most disappointing. The "new and startling details" put forth were that the arrows' fletchings had been oddly arranged with two plastic vanes in addition to a feathered third, affixed to aluminum shafts which carried razor-sharp broadheads. The spokesman would not elaborate when asked about the projectiles' characteristics, except to say they were identical. Nor would he confirm or deny whether any significant progress was being made in the case. The spokesman concluded the interview by saying that the district attorney did not suffer, that he had died instantly, and that when ready, justice would be just as swift. Several others in the background nodded in agreement.

My, my, Richard mused. *What an angry lot* . . . remembering well that he had once been angry, too, as when his tongue was gnashed then ripped from his head by a Lieutenant Lark. And for the period involving convalescence at the state hospital, he had howled away insanely, effecting unearthly sounds that emanated from the hellish depths of his being.

At any rate, confinement had certainly been a lot better than the uncertainty of death. *How extraordinarily stupid the state is*, he entertained and laughed as he had a thousand times before. One could take a life or the lives of many and be parading down Fifth Avenue on an Easter Sunday in as little as 1.8 years to just under a decade. The key? The *cure*, Richard soared, flapping his arms and flying about the space like a great bird. *"How incredibly stupid they all are,"* he roared through a throated garble.

Through those speechless years, Richard had learned to communicate via his writing. Rather well, too, the doctors thought. But lofty expressions confined to a page or pages certainly had its limitations. And although the psychiatrists believed their patient was making progress by leaps and bounds, Richard knew early on that he was going to remain confined with the cuckoos for quite some time to come. Longer than he had anticipated. Therefore, he designed an elaborate plan of escape, made good.

On the outside, Richard's freedom had been threatened daily, for a massive manhunt was under way. On the inside, he had known really very little liberty. So in his silence, he swore that he would make full use of borrowed time while it lasted. Working his way out west had worked out rather well. First, south along the eastern seaboard went without a hitch. Several stolen cars and only one body later wasn't exactly a hot trail for authorities to follow. Then from Tallahassee to Tulsa and on to *Timbuktu*, he giggled and gloated.

In often quiet and secret places, Richard practiced the silent arts. Skilled early on with handguns, he somehow believed a bow would be a breeze, but it was a sudden breeze that would occasionally blow his shot, let alone an angry wind. So he had trained vigorously under all kinds of adverse conditions until he grew proficient. Judging distance, trajectory, and wind velocity became a snap, consistently hitting the bull's-eye at fifty-plus yards with ease. Having studied martial arts as part of a brief military stay, he could wreak havoc at close range also. He was a natural. At age seventeen, he dealt devastating blows to two orderlies at the hospital in Havenwood. Killing one and maiming another. *They* must have been crazy to mess with him, Richard reckoned. But having mastered the bow and arrow gave him the added edge he needed from time to time. Indeed, the silent arts made him deadly both at close range and just beyond. Sniper adept, too, he was—up to a thousand yards. However, up close and very personal was so much more to his liking.

The junior detective who had worked with Lieutenant Lark literally prayed for the day that he would find Richard, Richard surely knew. But prayers are not always answered straightaway, if ever at all. Yet, in those seventeen years, Captain Grear, now serving as Riverhead's chief of police in Suffolk County, had never stopped investigating. He uncovered nothing until now. Although he had nothing concrete, he had a strong feeling. Something beyond the parameters of a hunch. It was a sixth sense, a sense which he developed in the early years while working with his close friend and mentor. It was a sense he had honed daily on the streets of Suffolk County. And although a Suffolk cop's turf was considered a country club of sorts by many a carper, those boys in blue nevertheless saw their fair share of crap and corpses, too.

Grear, a young sergeant during the days he had worked with Lark, was now Police Chief Grear. Achieving an undaunted reputation not unlike that of his predecessor, Grear quickly climbed the ranks. Adept at playing the political game, he avoided the pitfalls which had so often plagued his no-nonsense mentor. Lieutenant Lark had died of cancer in 1974. It had been a painful period for a man who kept his large frame fairly fit. By the time Lark finally succumbed, he had gone from 210 pounds down to 90.

In 1969, Lieutenant Lark had paid Richard a visit to the

infirmary at North Shore State Hospital shortly after the patient's transfer from the King Foundation, intent on murdering the man in his bed. In fact, he almost did. Instead, the cop had finished giving the vicious killer a lecture before forcing open the killer's mouth and gripping the foul tongue, drawing the organ forward from behind a set of stubborn, angry teeth, gnashing the fleshy flap with the heel of his hand while the lunatic lay helplessly restrained.

Not exactly case closed. Not by a long shot.

Chapter
——>
11

A long shot was precisely what Richard Geist needed in order to take out district attorney number three, the killer planned well over a year ago, making sure that everything was finally in place on what promised to be an eventful morning. Preparation had been crucial. Police and civilians milled about the Queens Criminal Court Building. People were everywhere. Along the busy boulevard pedestrians paced or walked with purpose. Up and down the steps they came and went. Richard watched them through a window on the fifth floor. In back of him, several lawyers were busy on phones or scrutinizing the court calendar taped to the wall across the hall and to his left.

In short order, all the pieces were about to come neatly into play. The takedown bow had been relatively easy to conceal. Getting it into the building months before the murders posed no special problem. Unlike his own single-cam magnesium bow, the specially designed straight-limbed selection was constructed of laminated wood and glass. It hadn't set off any beepers or bells to alert the security officers downstairs. And as the weapon of destruction was a simple but powerful seventy-pound pull instrument, void of complex wheels or fancy gadgetry, assemblage would be a breeze.

On a subsequent visit, Richard surreptitiously brought in and planted the graphite arrows as he had the bow, simply by walking the straight and narrow, moving stiffly but steadily with seven carbon shafts taped beneath a pant leg. As a matter of fact, a sympathetic female court officer waved him around the checkpoint when she saw the cripple limping horribly at the rear of the long line. A male security guard told Richard to place his loose change, keys, watch, and any other metal objects into the gray plastic tray on the counter, then searched his canvas bag for contraband, giving no particular thought to a silver dollar tucked away in a corner. Richard remained relaxed while another court officer had him raise his arms as a wand-like instrument was passed over and around his body.

What Richard had given considerable thought to early on was the type as well as the number of deadly arrowheads he'd employ. A single arrow—which was all he actually needed—wasn't exactly high theater, he ruminated with a degree of frustration. Even if he'd gotten the traditional broadheads through security, having to assemble a dozen razor-sharp blades within the confines of a dark closet could prove difficult, for utmost dexterity and good light were required to set and lock together the scalpel-sharp, high-grade aircraft aluminum heads. Besides which, he couldn't run the risk of doing something as stupid as cutting himself. Suffice it to say, there would be enough bloodshed. Therefore, with regard to the issues concerning safety and concealment, uniformity of the act notwithstanding so as to remove any doubt that a single soul was on the warpath, Richard, with a bit of reservation, had decided from the onset to utilize BloodTrailers instead of Muzzy Broadheads, the latter of which he favored over all others. Still, upon contact, BloodTrailers' mechanical winged wonders promised to open without fail, assuring devastating results.

One arrow in particular, however, would carry a blunted head for a truly special purpose. Richard knew he was on the cutting edge of calamity, so to speak.

Passing those missile-shaped BloodTrailers through security without creating a scene had been a trick. But Richard was full of them. Anyone who knew him knew that for certain. Sleight of hand (of which he was a master) or some other distraction simply wouldn't prevent the buzzer from sounding. What to do?

Obviously, the two-inch projectiles had to be perceived as something other than for what they were intended, still sounding an alarm for certain, yet somehow allaying concern.

And so they did. A month before the first two murders.

A steel-gray plastic model fighter-bomber with its six missiles contained within the belly of the warplane played rather well one busy afternoon immediately following lunch as the alarm sounded and the box within a boat bag came off the conveyer belt and onto the counter. A security officer removed then examined the toy from the cardboard / cellophane package. Tiny trap doors beneath the aircraft released a tightly clear-taped air-celled bundle while the guard nostalgically flew twenty years back in time.

"I used to stand bomb watch alongside one of these . . . aboard an aircraft carrier," the man reminisced.

Richard smiled and nodded politely.

Scrutinizing the wrapping, the officer finally put the bundle back into the plastic belly, the model into its box and bag then passed Richard through. Hobby cement for a fast fix of gluing inserts into the arrow shafts was contained in the nose of the aircraft as was the single blunthead.

A place for everything, and everything in its place. Richard had placed things ever so carefully over a period of time.

Timing today would be the final test. District Attorney David A. Black and his driver would be entering the basement level from the rear of the building at approximately 10 a.m. as they did most every weekday morning. Once inside, Black would step from the vehicle, heading toward a private elevator to take him to the second floor while the retired detective / bodyguard drove off to park the car. The D.A. would walk a distance of thirty feet past a secured stairwell before reaching the elevator doors. However, Richard would be waiting in the wings a good forty yards away. He'd have about a four-second window to make the first well-placed shot. Having used bluntheads in the field for practice on small game when penetration was hardly the point, the blunt-headed arrow would not only have to stop the

D.A. in his tracks, it would have to wallop him without killing him and without having the poor soul utter a single sound. If Richard could accomplish that, he'd gain a good minute and a half in which to dramatize the event before the D.A.'s driver returned from the parking area. Of course, Richard had every detail planned out carefully.

Taking his bag off a window ledge, Richard left the sanctity of the fifth floor courthouse to make his duly appointed rounds. It was practically showtime.

He took the staircase down to the first floor after having gathered up the necessary accoutrements. Within a pitch-black closet at the back of a courtroom in Part Three, Richard screwed six BloodTrailers into miniature thimble-like cups set at the front of carbon shafts, adding a seventh, a blunt-headed arrow into an accommodating canvas duffel bag. He disappeared down another stairwell leading to the basement. Behind a heavy cabinet, he found and assembled the dusty sections of his takedown bow. With a silver dollar and special wooden screws, he joined two laminated limbs to the handgrip. Next, Richard drew a deep breath and waited, silently allowing the air to escape his nostrils before filling his lungs anew. Calmly, he waited.

Not five minutes elapsed when the D.A. and his driver rolled in below the building. Seconds later, along the basement corridor came the D.A. with elevator key in hand. From the opposite stairwell, Richard suddenly appeared. Committed. He brought the bow to full draw before the man realized something was amiss. Richard's release was on the mark as the shaft sped to the center of the man's neck. *SMACK*. The D.A. instinctively dropped his briefcase and clutched his throat. His eyes lit with terror before he toppled.

Richard moved steadily toward the quivering form, immediately withdrawing a BloodTrailer from a slit in his sleeve, nocking and locking the orange plastic groove precisely upon the well-waxed bowstring. He took another deep breath as the D.A. fought for his. *You're a lame duck*, Richard reflected most satisfactorily, sending a second shaft through the man's leg. Another through the other. David Black wanted to scream his lungs out but could not utter a sound. The fourth arrow struck him in the buttocks as he somehow found the strength to crawl and cower into a corner. A fifth missile pierced the side of his ribcage, collapsing both lungs he tried so desperately to fill with such sweet air. It was almost over. Practically standing over his target, Richard propelled the sixth arrow smartly into the man's spine. Turning the D.A. over, Richard stepped back and planted the seventh and final missile into the middle of the man's chest, watching ecstatically as a new bright red river quickly ran from the man's body.

Richard's adrenaline could have sent him soaring to the roof. Setting an attorney's business card upon the bloody body, the serial killer suddenly disappeared.

Chapter
——>
12

Whereas Robert Redler's style of writing was something akin to that of Richard Geist's, Robert had been formally trained in college, while Richard was self-taught. Still, the formation of certain phrases and syntax was, in several respects, remarkably similar. There was, however, a certain tone that told the two apart, as if anyone had ever cared to do so—that is, up until now. And as Redler wore on with his futile battle against the criminal justice system, a distinctive manner of expression, not unlike Richard's, came oddly enough to light. Both danced their metaphors and other forms of comparisons most magically across the page. Both told a tale of pain.

No incriminating connection between Robert Redler and Richard Geist had been drawn as yet. Captain Cally sat in his Queens apartment contemplating Redler's articles and other writings. Police Chief Grear sat home in the suburbs of Suffolk rereading Richard Geist's autobiography, published in 1975. The two men were completely absorbed when their respective phones rang but minutes apart.

A third D.A. was dead.

By 5 p.m. that evening, the news channels carried the story in great detail, comparing the slaying of Queens District Attorney David Black to those of the murders of the district attorneys in Nassau and

Suffolk counties. The similarities as well as the contrasts were, indeed, stark: three D.A.s murdered by bow and arrow, carbon shafts employed in lieu of aluminum this time out; different types of broadheads, identical fletchings; seven arrows instead of one —inclusive of a single blunthead generally used for small game.

There were questions galore. Was this a copycat murder? Or were there two killers working in concert? Were these the acts of a single serial killer? And certainly the big question:

Why?

Queens officials did not drag their feet in releasing many of the facts to the reporters. An expert in weaponry elaborated that the bullet-shaped heads were the newly designed conical points put out by BloodTrailer Corporation of Lorten, Virginia. Puckett's BloodTrailers. A cutting diameter of 1.25 inches. The man dramatically explained that the blades of the broadheads flew toward their target in closed flight, opening upon forcible contact with a deadly four-blade punch.

Reporters and journalists from the five boroughs were having a field day. Would an attempt be made on the Manhattan and Bronx D.A.s? "Did Staten Island even have one?" a housewife in her eighties wanted to know. And what about an attorney's business card found on Black's forehead? Information leaked to the press by a, quote-unquote, highly reliable source.

Richard bellowed from the depths of his being, unable to articulate the satisfaction he felt as he brought a closed fist down hard in triumph upon the coffee table. Twenty-five years ago, he could have thrown his voice across a room or filled a hall with the flutter of beating wings. From an early age, he had been an accomplished ventriloquist. Now, all he could do was vent garbled sounds of anger or delight. He conserved the latter for special moments like this morning and tonight. Rarely did he sound his anger. But when he did . . . .

Over the years, Geist had come to terms with a life sentence of silence, taking immense pleasure in reading or writing verse, executing katas, or practicing his marksmanship with several types of weapons. Secret places, although temporary, gave him ample opportunity to exercise and execute his art. As a matter of sheer fact, the simple release of a bowstring was music to his ears. Tuning a compound bow was tantamount to the personal satisfaction a musician might derive in bringing a fine instrument into accord. And although it could be argued that Richard's instrument of death produced no appreciative tone, he, nonetheless, felt that they made beautiful music together. *The perfect accompaniment for a mute,* he grinned. The perfect score.

Spokespersons for both the Suffolk and Nassau County district attorneys' offices would neither confirm nor deny that the type of broadhead used to kill D.A.s Altman and Howe were in fact Muzzy broadheads, unlike the six BloodTrailers found in Queens D.A. David Black's body. Surely the police had concluded that the killer of all three men had to be one and the same, Richard presumed. Although the arrow shafts recovered in Queens were different, their weight and draw-length remained a constant. And of course the signature fletching said it all. Perhaps not conclusive evidence, but too coincidental to assume that there was a copycat killer pussyfooting around, Richard meowed insanely. Latent fingerprints on the bow, arrows or the lawyer's business card might have told them what they wanted to know. But they wouldn't find any. Not this time around, he glowed exuberantly.

Chapter
――>
13

Gary Crane, a Queens County defense attorney, certainly had to have been asked a score of questions a hundred times over by police. One of the leading questions was how his business card wound up on David Black's body.

"I don't know, I told you," the attorney said defensively. "I give my card out to hundreds of people."

"Is there anyone you can think of who might have it in for you?" a junior detective asked.

It was a loaded question and a dumb one, too. The answer? Just about any witness for the state whose testimony he'd torn asunder. Any defendant whose lies he'd brought to light while serving as a prosecutor for the Queens D.A.'s office years ago. Every disgruntled client he'd ever disappointed for that matter, of which there were many.

"What you mean is, is there anyone in particular who might want to stick it up my ass? Someone capable of committing something like this. And the answer is yes. But they're all locked up last I heard," the attorney answered.

"Have you met anyone suspicious recently?" a senior detective's partner chimed in. "Anyone strange? Anyone you might have given a second thought to?"

Gary Crane immediately thought of the mute he had met some months ago. What was his name? Arthur or something. The man's secretary never did call his office. The middle-aged fellow had simply inquired as to whether he or his associate were criminal lawyers and that he might be needing one. Nothing strange or unusual about that. "No one I can think of offhand," Crane replied.

"You're sure?"

"Yep, but if I do, you'll be the first to know," he assured them.

Gary Crane had a reputation of being very bright. A real shark. Strictly out for the bucks. After the police left his office, he thought about Robert Redler and the sexual assault matter he had handled for the writer several years ago. He recalled the arguments over who was handling the case; he or Redler. He couldn't help but remember Redler's indefatigable pursuit of justice even after the charges were dropped by the Queens D.A.'s office—or more specifically by Liza's daughter who initially filed them subsequent to Robert having had her boyfriend arrested for death threats and destruction of property. A family feud ensued tantamount to the Hatfields and the McCoys.

Liza's sister and brother-in-law, two prominent podiatrists philanthropically revered throughout the city, had been the supportive force behind their niece. Crane recollected many articles and editorials that Redler wrote concerning the injustices found within the criminal justice system. *Power, Politics and Cronyism* headlined several of his pieces. He wrote about his plight and the plight of others. Robert Redler was a strange one, all right. But the man was no more capable of premeditated murder than he was of molesting his girlfriend's daughter—or anyone for that matter.

At the 111th Precinct in Bayside Queens, Captain Cally reread the first of a series of Redler's editorials concerning the Lightfoot case, titled *Dances with D.A.s.* It covered the imprisonment of John Lightfoot, a Bayside man, accused and convicted of attempted rape. The victim was the daughter of a high-ranking retired police detective. Cally was absorbed:

> *If ever there was a name reserved for this writer by the great American Indians of our nation, it would be Dances with D.A.s, for I have been dancing with these renegades since 1983. And I would probably adopt the namesake on behalf of John Lightfoot and his family who have been buffaloed by the savagery of the district attorney's office during the*

past four years to the tune of approximately sixty thousand dollars. That's certainly something to shriek about . . . .

The police captain knew the Lightfoot case well. Initially, the victim had claimed that her attacker stood five-foot-eight, weighing approximately 180 pounds. John Lightfoot stood six-foot-four and had weighed 240 pounds at the time. That was for openers. Cally read on, digesting the last sentence of Redler's editorial.

> *. . . And if I might be so bold as to make a suggestion to that worthy defense team, it would be, "Take scalps!"*

Redler was referring to the office of a renowned Manhattan lawyer whose partner had handled the appeal pro bono. Cally considered what might have happened had Black been found scalped. *Now, that would have been hair-raising*, he entertained.

Was Robert Redler in some way connected, or was someone pulling the writer's chain? the police captain wondered.

Chapter
-->
14

Robert Redler had been under surveillance since the night after Black's murder. Captain Cally wanted to know why the Queens Detective Bureau hadn't had him under the microscope earlier. Police Plaza and the Queens D.A.'s office had a file on him as thick as a phone book. A good comparison in that Redler had called and written everyone in the directory whom he thought might be of help in his single-minded cause. Councilman Sidney Bromer was one of the few who wrote on his behalf. D.A. Black had reviewed the file and sent a letter back to Bromer, concluding, "There is no basis at this time for any further action by this office." Bromer copied Redler, and Redler tried to speak with Black. The D.A.'s spokesperson stopped Redler cold.

It appeared that Robert Francis Redler had literally spoken with or written to every agency up and down the chain of command, including the feds as well as the President of the United States. Everyone! Reports and phone calls were coming in referencing Redler as a suspect at the rate of several per hour, all morning long.

One call, however, was somewhat different. It pointed in a direction other than where everyone else was jumping. The call came from Doctor Angelo Bianco, director of the King Foundation in Suffolk County. The psychiatrist stated that he had what he believed could be pertinent information pertaining to the three murders. Deputy Inspector Lancing listened intently and arranged a four-way conference call among Police Chief Grear of the Riverhead Police Department, Suffolk County; Captain Cally of the 111th Precinct, Bayside Queens; the King Foundation's director, Doctor Bianco, and himself. Although Lancing candidly admitted that what he had initially heard from Bianco amounted to nothing more than a hunch, the deputy inspector felt that shared information, no matter how tenuous at this point, was absolutely essential. If what the psychiatrist had could be shaped into anything at all, fine. If not, nothing was lost. Lancing was unofficially the man in charge.

"Cooperation is the key," Lancing announced evenly.

Captain Cally liked Lancing's candor and directness and was certainly anxious to hear what Doctor Bianco had to say, too. The call was set for 1:00 p.m. Cally wondered why Lancing hadn't arranged a face-to-face meeting to include the acting district attorneys from Nassau and Queens, choosing a four-way conference call instead. Perhaps Lancing felt that neither the Queens nor Nassau D.A.'s offices would give him the time of day, taking down his information for sure, but sharing nothing. Teamwork around there boiled down to independent teams of two: a cop and his partner, a prosecutor and the one he or she was screwing, Cally knew. The two offices trusted no one beyond that boundary. Not even their own families.

The next thing that came across Cally's desk was a copy of an invoice from a mail-order house in Sydney, Nebraska: bowhunting clothing and equipment ordered in the past from a Cabela's sporting goods catalog. Full fleeced camo, fanny pack, tree stand, and much more. The MasterCard number was issued in the name of Robert F. Redler of Fresh Meadows, Queens.

"Pick 'im up for questioning," Cally ordered flatly.

"Can't just yet," Sergeant Hennesey said.

Cally looked up from the copy of the invoice. "What do you mean, you can't?"

"He's out deer hunting. Been sitting in some fucking tree stand in Suffolk since six a.m."

"Where in Suffolk?"

"Villa Immaculata, on the North Fork."

"What the hell is that?"

"Convent or some kind of fucking retreat. A prayer house I think they call it."

"What's he got, asylum?" he joked. "And watch your mouth."

"Redler packed his vehicle, grabbed his gear, and went off into the woods before dawn's early light."

"Who's on him?"

"O'Shea."

"Oh, shit."

"He's been tailing him since three this morning. Took the Long Island Expressway out east to the end, then followed Redler north, then east again to the Villa."

"What town we talking?"

"Riverhead, I think."

"You think?"

"I'll check it out. Lot of overlap out there," Hennesey explained. "Sheriff's office, county boys, Riverhead P.D., and the state troopers," the sergeant expanded. "So you want them or O'Shea to bring 'im in when he comes out of the woodwork?"

"If it's Riverhead, I want you to get me their police chief, Grear, on the line. I'll try and get a warrant for the house from Judge Weinstein."

"You better have that chief get you one also."

"What do you mean?"

"He's got a home out there, too."

"In Riverhead?"

"Yep. On the river."

"You're on top of things, Hennesey."

"Yes, sir." Hennesey smiled.

"Fuckin' A if you ain't." Cally smiled back.

No warrants were forthcoming. A surreptitious search of Redler's Queens residence turned up squat. The Riverhead home, however, contained evidence with which any prosecutor worth his salt would have wagered big bucks and won an open-and-shut case. Carbon and aluminum arrow shafts cut to a specific length stood upright in a box against a basement wall. Feathered and plastic fletchings, along with bottles of bonding cements and other equipment, lay strewn across a narrow workbench. Muzzy broadheads and Puckett's BloodTrailers were tucked away in a plastic archer's box atop a worktable. In a corner, concealed within a metal closet, stood another box of arrows, each fletched with two olive-green plastic vanes and one black feather.

Bingo!

A small study on the first floor contained cartons of files concerning criminal cases dating back a decade. Copies of angry letters to various state agencies sat in separate folders on the desk. One letter was to the White House. Another file, labeled ACTIVE CORRESPONDENCE, held well over fifty letters to various law enforcement agencies and politicians. Other folders filled with personal correspondence stood behind them.

Deputy Inspector Lancing's one o'clock conference call had been rescheduled to 5:00 p.m. After introductions, it was Police Chief Grear who began the discussion:

"It was as though Richard Geist had disappeared off the face of the earth seventeen years ago—seventeen long years," the Riverhead chief of police emphasized. "In the late eighties, I hit on something. It was a murder involving a rookie cop who had infiltrated a cult called the Inner Circle of Friends. A splinter group of an Abyssinian Baptist Church here in Riverhead. It had Geist's signature all over it. Karate chop to the cop's throat. A witness told authorities about a man in his late twenties. A man who showed no fear. Six feet tall. Thin frame. Red hair. A mute.

"There's this well-known private investigator slash deprogrammer who had sent the undercover cop into an apartment building in Jersey City to bring out a fifteen-year-old female runaway," Grear continued. "The cop was found dead an hour later. The girl had been raped and sodomized. The stories she told even made the forensic boys wince. The cop's murder was of course covered in the local papers, but with no mention made of the cult or its connection to the Baptist sect. A month later, Redler came out with an article in a Jersey paper brazen enough to publish the account.

"Several months ago, this investigator/deprogrammer was sent to a federal prison on trumped up kidnapping charges according to Redler." The police chief sneezed and excused himself. "His story's in that Great Neck paper."

"The *North Shore Towers Newsletter*," Cally stated flatly.

"Right," Grear said.

Deputy Inspector Lancing explained that his own investigation clearly linked Redler's girlfriend's teenage daughter and the boyfriend directly to the Jersey cult, now deeply entrenched in the Washington, D.C. area near where the supposed kidnapping took place.

Doctor Bianco spoke next. The picture he presented, detailing Richard Geist's psychiatric profile, made a solid impression on Captain Cally. The psychiatrist calmly but matter-of-factly related the brutality of Richard Geist's early deeds. His cunning. His genius. Lancing realized that the doctor had been modest when he first said that he had something along the lines of a hunch. Things were beginning to fit.

Grear and Cally, along with Lancing, thanked Doctor Bianco profusely, and the psychiatrist took his cue, hanging up the phone. The three policemen agreed that it would be premature to bring Redler in, just yet. The plot was only beginning to thicken. Lancing, Grear, and Cally formed an alliance and a plan.

Chapter
––>
15

For days the talk was of Colin Ferguson and his rampage aboard the Long Island Rail Road. The body count had jumped from five to six. Richard Geist shut the radio and parked the stolen vehicle off Lumber Lane, bordering Arthur Field's property. Richard walked leisurely along the snowy tree line so as not to work up a sweat. He carried a portable tree stand over his right shoulder and a bow with an attached quiver filled with arrows in his left hand. Although the temperature was in the low teens, it wouldn't take much energy to break a sweat beneath the articles of clothing he wore. Thermax sock liners and long underwear worked well in wicking moisture away from the skin. A wool-blend turtleneck and denim pants lined with flannel formed a second layer. Special Gore-Tex/Thinsulate footwear between sock liners and rubber bottom boots with leather uppers kept his feet warm and dry. Silent-Stalk fleeced parka and matching pants in Treebark camouflage completed the third and final barrier from the cold. A fanny pack for accessories sat strapped at the small of his back. Fleece and foam camouflage mittens with palm slits provided dexterity while protecting both hands.

Richard took his time selecting a tree just several yards east off an oak-lined dirt road before working the climber-stand up, up and away, sawing obstructive branches as he ascended, stopping at about thirty feet. Field's wife and two daughters wouldn't be arriving at the rustic woodland cabin for another hour. Time enough to make himself comfortable and run through his master plan, for he was master of all he surveyed.

The wind was picking up, with sudden gusts to thirty miles per hour. The sun would be setting in a half hour, and the wind chill factor would make the mercury seem as though it had fallen well below zero. Lifting his bow gently off the ground with a haul line, Richard raised his weapon to his perch. Shifting the fanny pack to his hip, he seated himself snugly against the tree. He was comfortable except for his hands. Unzipping the fanny pack, he removed two disposable chemical hand warmers from a cellophane package and slipped the paper packets through the mitten's slits and into the palm of each hand. Toasty warm they'd be in a minute. Taking a wool/polypropylene balaclava from the pack, he pulled the cap down over his head, face and neck, exposing solely his mouth and eyes to the elements.

Eighty percent of body heat is lost through the top of one's head, he recalled his mother scolding whenever he'd run out of the house without a hat in the dead of winter. Actually, she couldn't have cared if he'd gone outdoors in the nude, as she once threw him in the backyard naked as a newborn in the middle of February for more than an hour. Another time in his underwear. Before the age of four. Punishment for talking back.

Richard adjusted the hood and drew the drawstring snugly, taking in the snowy, wintry world around him. He was high on life, especially before he was about to claim it. He took the cold, crisp air deep into his lungs and nocked an arrow upon the bowstring, resting the weapon flatly on his lap.

The wind sounded through the woodland, and a bevy of quail rose along a ridge. Soon the end of day would whittle the wall of woods away to nothing, and the last shavings of light would be perceived through the tops of shadowy trees. And then the trio would come like clockwork. Mother and two daughters. He felt the sway of the tree against his back as a steady wind ran its course. High and mighty, the majestic oaks and elms bowed ever so slightly to the invisible force at play. He squeezed the paper packets of heat for added warmth and waited.

Finally, fifty minutes later, in the distance, Richard saw beams of light move off the main road and along the quarter-mile tree-lined rugged path. Slowly, the vehicle approached. As the headlights drew nearer, he could see the Lab running from the main house toward the Cherokee, as it always did. Black as a moonless night, Pucky turned sharply about, keeping pace beside the bumpy wheels. Five miles per hour they moved. He could see the blonde heads of Maggie Field and her two children as they neared: Margaret, twelve and Melissa, fourteen. Maggie was thirty-four. Tall and trim and strikingly beautiful she sat staring and steering straight ahead. He watched her intently before she passed beneath him. Moments later, he saw the taillights signal their arrival at the remote woodland cabin, the boxy back of the vehicle momentarily bathed in a red glow. He heard three doors open and two close—then another. The woman's husband was away for the weekend, Richard knew.

Maggie's young daughters dutifully held pairs of packages in their arms as their mother unlocked and swung open the dwelling's rough-hewn wooden door. Richard held a special whistle between his lips. Pucky froze for an instant before bolting back into the dark woodland, making a noisy path in Richard's direction through the crunching layers of leaves. The Lab suddenly stopped short several yards north, near the base of the predator's tree. The lanyard around Richard's neck caught the silent whistle he let fall free. Silent, that is, to all but Pucky. The dog raised his head high as the archer set the illuminated sight pin slightly above and to the rear of Pucky's shoulder for a heartfelt shot. Richard quietly released his breath and let fly the arrow which sped swiftly downward and through the animal, instantly pinning the dog to the ground. Pucky felt no pain. Richard promised to tell that to the woman and her two rug-rats-in-waiting. Putting the whistle back into his mouth, he silently played taps for poor ol' Pucky.

By the time Richard descended the tree, Maggie was calling Pucky through a ripping wind.

"Pucky. Come on, boy," she called as the treetops seemed to point the direction of command. "Pucky. Come on, fella."

Pucky felt nice and warm to the touch as Richard pulled the

arrow through the dead animal before wrapping the haul line around its neck, dragging the dog toward the cozy cabin.

"Pucky," she continued calling.

Pucky's coming, Maggie, Richard wanted to shout, trailing the line and black lump of purebred through the virgin white snow. *Puppy's on his way, my dear*, he mused amusingly. He thought about how he'd finally take her. Over the back of the couch with her legs spread wide as her two daughters watched and whined. That thought excited him. *Watch how mommy winces when she takes it up her butt, my little darlings. Watch ever so carefully because one or the other is going to be next. Over mommy's dead body if need be*, he promised himself. Or maybe he'd begin with the youngest daughter, having her take his throbbing member in her little mouth as mommy fully undressed. They could scream all they wanted to, but no one except the woodland creatures would hear.

Maybe he'd go easy on them and have Maggie's eldest simply get undressed and masturbate him until he came all over mommy's face. That would be fun, too. Of course, he'd do what damn well pleased him at the moment. The spontaneity of it all would be the thrill. He had planned so carefully up to this point. The rest of the evening would be extemporaneous, he knew. Still, it was a thrill just thinking ahead. Perhaps he'd fuck all three on the cabin floor before the pot belly stove. First Maggie. Then Melissa. And finally, little Margaret. Maybe the other way around, he grinned excitedly.

Yes. Back to Bridgehampton for sport. Who'd have thought? Certainly not the authorities, for they were all too busy wondering and worrying about district attorney number four. He giggled uncontrollably, watching the trail of smoke billowing from the chimney while dragging the dead dog.

Richard was perspiring profusely by the time the pair reached the cabin. Down on his hands and knees he whined and scratched away well below the doorknob. It was Melissa who answered the call, opening the front door fully. Confusion turned to sheer horror as the fourteen-year-old took in the big picture at the threshold. Richard grinned up at the girl while Pucky lay still as stone. She suddenly brought both hands to her pretty mouth when Richard shot through the door on all fours, ripping the balaclava from his head, the static electricity standing the crop of flaming red hair on end.

"*Rufff*," he barked loudly, smiling up handsomely as Maggie stood momentarily frozen. It was as the mother made a move toward the back room that Richard sprang to his feet, grabbing Melissa by a shoulder. The girl screamed, and Maggie stopped dead in her tracks.

"Please. Don't hurt her. I have money in my purse," Maggie said evenly, pointing to the pocketbook lying on the couch. Richard did not take his eyes off Maggie Field. She stood five-nine in a taupe whipcord skirt, matching sweater and brown high-heeled boots. Her blonde hair hung long and perfectly combed.

There was the sound of a toilet flushing, and out from the bathroom came little Margaret Field. Cute, curious and concerned, dressed in jeans and sweater like her sister. "Why's it so cold in here?" she questioned before realizing the door was wide open. "Who's that, Mommy?" Margaret inquired, looking up. "Why did Melissa scream like that?"

"Something bad happened to Pucky," Melissa answered in a frightened tone, staring at the entrance.

What's wrong with this picture, Richard thought. *Three well-groomed, pretty females all alone in a rustic two-room shack. But certainly cozy enough, indeed*, he conceded as he looked around approvingly, relaxing his grip and guiding Melissa back to the doorway.

"What are you doing?" Maggie Field demanded as the trespasser led Melissa a step beyond the cabin door. "Where are you taking her?"

Richard paused and put a finger out to arm's length, indicating that he would be but a moment. Moving Melissa roughly along, he reached down and grabbed the haul line, pulling Pucky up and inside the room for all to see his handiwork, slamming the door closed behind him. Melissa dropped to her knees beside the bloody black dog and began sobbing. Margaret moved closer to her mother. Maggie began to shake, losing all color.

49

Richard signaled for Maggie to move behind the couch as he removed his parka and boots. His eyes said that he was quite serious. Maggie stepped back with Margaret clinging to her skirt. Richard came forward and took the little girl by the hand, pointing to a chair beside the fireplace. Margaret shook her head.

"Be a good girl and sit," Maggie told her instinctively.

Richard gestured for the older daughter to do the same, pointing to another chair. Sobbing, the girl went over and sat.

"Please take the money and keys," Maggie pleaded. "I have over two hundred dollars in my purse. Please don't hurt us."

Richard raised two fingers in mock surprise. He motioned for the mother to move closer to the couch as he crossed the room, switching off an overhead light then turning on a lamp in the corner for atmosphere. Stretching an arm around a wall without taking his eyes off of her, he closed another light.

Maggie began to tremble.

"My children," she whispered and wept. "Please. Take whatever you want. Just take it!" she snapped, pulling off a marquis diamond ring and golden wedding band. "Just take these and leave us alone," she shrieked.

Richard took the frightened, angry woman roughly by the neck and slowly but forcibly pushed Maggie's head down until she was bent over the back of the couch. He stepped in close behind, slowly raising her skirt, bunching the material up around a trim waist, pushing the shivering body further forward, gently passing a palm along her inner thighs. He kneaded her buttocks before carefully working the pantyhose down around the pair of highly-polished boots. The intruder pressed himself firmly against the actress's body, knowing full well she could feel his hardness.

"I'll go inside with you," she whispered. "Don't do this in front of my daughters. I beg you. I'll show you a nice time if you promise to go and leave us alone," Maggie assured him as she shook.

Richard thoroughly wet a middle finger in his mouth, withdrew it then inserted it between her buttocks. Maggie gasped.

"I'm scared, Mommy," Margaret shuddered.

"Why don't you say something, you filthy bastard?" Maggie managed in pain, her face covered in blood.

Richard opened wide his eyes and hellish grin and signed that he was mute, driving his thick member deep down Melissa's throat. The girl gagged and Maggie dry-heaved inches above the polished pegged floorboards.

"Oh, Mary, merciful mother of God," Maggie pleaded between gasping breaths. "Please make him stop . . . I beg you, please." Maggie rocked in supplication as Richard moved his pelvis steadily back and forth in ecstasy, level with her daughter's face. "Why in God's name doesn't he stop?" she questioned hysterically then sobbed.

And as if her prayer was suddenly answered, Richard did stop, withdrawing his penis. He beckoned for Maggie to approach, pointing deliberately to his penis.

"Why won't you go?" she moaned.

Richard removed a small notepad and pen from his shirt pocket and scribbled down a message, ripping it from its spiral holder and handing it over to Maggie.

Maggie reached for and read the note:

> Because I have staying power. Cooperate and they'll
> live. I want you to lick, lap, and like it. And then I
> want you to take it up your ass.

He put away his pen and pad and again pointed to his erection.

Maggie crawled over and took it in her hand.

"Please," she begged. "Take me inside. Not here. Not in front of them."

Richard raised his hand and hit Maggie hard across the face. Margaret winced and Melissa lay there motionless.

"Please," Maggie repeated, refusing to flinch as he struck her across the face again. Maggie suddenly took him into her mouth with a vengeance, pounding her face back and forth against his pelvic bone, swallowing him whole, pulling his buttocks toward her with both hands. Richard moaned and groaned, pulling up her top and seizing her lavish breasts, thrusting himself deep within her throat before exploding wildly.

Maggie swallowed every drop of Richard's semen rather than spill and chance offense. She knelt before him, staring up into the face of the madman who might or might not keep his word and spare her two precious children. *Cooperate and they'll live*, kept racing through her shaky state of mind. God, *she* didn't want to die either, she shuddered. A pitiful battered face with a broken bloody nose and puffy blue eyes pled mercifully. And again she began to cry. She couldn't bear to look at Melissa lying there on the floor. She gave Margaret a brave little look although she wasn't sure about anything except their survival.

Her husband's Walther sat in a nightstand drawer in their bedroom. Loaded. It was what was foremost in her mind the moment the stranger had crossed the threshold. It was what was in her head when she tried to lure him into the bedroom. If only she could have led him there. No! Negative thinking, she told herself. If only she could lead him there *now*. *Please God, give me courage,* she prayed.

"I want more," Maggie swore, standing and stepping out of her skirt, pulling off her bloody sweater and bra. "I want what you wrote on the paper," she affirmed, displaying her sensuous backside. Maggie moved toward the bedroom in just her boots. "I want you from behind. The children aren't going anywhere. Keys are in my bag, and it's a mile hike back to the main road. There is no phone there—or here. Let them be."

Richard looked around. Perplexed.

"I want you up my fucking ass!" Maggie screamed at him. "You wait out here, you little bitches," she brought herself to say. "You hear me?"

Richard stared at the two girls. He picked up Maggie's bag and followed her into the bedroom. She was standing naked alongside the bed, the tips of her fingers touching the very edge of the nightstand.

"Take off all your clothes," she demanded. "I want you to fuck me silly. I want to blow your mind," she said, forcing half a smile. "I want you climbing the bloody walls."

Richard came over and moved her away from the night table. He gently stroked her hair. Smiling, he opened up the drawer and slowly shook his head in disappointment.

Maggie now knew she should have made a mad dash for the drawer the moment she entered the room but figured she needed a split second to grab the gun and send a round into its chamber in the blind instant the man would take to pull his turtleneck over his face. Too late, she realized. Trancelike, she saw herself in slow motion emptying a full clip of ammunition into the rapist's chest, wishing to take back the moment and start afresh. Craving the moment.

Richard lifted the automatic and put the muzzle to her head.

"I don't believe my husband keeps that loaded," she lied.

He watched her expression as he squeezed the trigger. CLICK. Angrily, sliding back the action and slamming it forward, he pressed the cold steel barrel against her temple. He studied her intently.

"Pl-please d- don't hurt them anymore," Maggie stammered in the moment before Richard squeezed the trigger anew.

It was as though she had suddenly nodded off. But the sound of the shot surely would have wakened the dead. Maggie fell quietly to the floor.

Richard immediately returned to the front room. Margaret was holding her older sister in her little arms with Pucky lying at their feet.

Margaret looked up. "I think you shot our mommy, but I was praying it was you she shot. I know all about bad men like you. You're the very bad people that grown-ups don't want to tell little girls about until they're big. You hurt me and my sister. See?" she said bravely, lifting a bloody armchair cover from between her skinny legs. "My heinie hurts, too. And you killed my dog." Margaret could no longer hold back the flood of tears. "Wh-when I get bigger," she sobbed, "I'm going t-to find you if my da-daddy or the police don't find you first. And if my mommy's de-dead in there, I'm going to cut your insides out with the biggest butcher knife I can find. And the devil ca-can take my soul and I won't care."

Margaret held her stone-faced sister even closer as Richard

aimed the pistol. The shot hit Melissa in the chest, and her body jerked back instantly.

"And yo-you're a scuzzbucket, too," Margaret concluded, squeezing her dead sister with all her might while closing her blue eyes tightly, biting down hard upon her bottom lip.

The final shot struck little Margaret in the forehead, and she slumped down next to Pucky.

Three blondies and a black mutt, Richard sighed satisfactorily to himself. Not bad for an early evening's hunt, he thought and stretched, consulting his watch. *Oh, by the way, Pucky felt no pain*, Richard signed before the two dead girls lying on the cabin floor.

The Southampton police reported the deaths of Arthur Field's wife and daughters as a multiple homicide. Suffolk officials neither confirmed nor denied any connection between D.A. Altman's body found on the property weeks earlier and that of Arthur Field's family executed in their cabin retreat, acknowledging only the indisputable fact that the murders took place within a mile of one another on the family estate. The discovery of the note found between the bolsters of a couch in the Field's woodland retreat told that Richard Geist had, indeed, been there. Handwriting samples taken from Richard's file at the hospital in Havenwood matched accordingly. Additionally, scores of Richard's prints had been found throughout the cabin. The business of the family dog being shot with an arrow was kept from the press as were several gruesome details concerning the rapes. Deputy Inspector Lancing made sure of that.

The audacity of Richard Geist's return to Bridgehampton had baffled the deputy inspector. Maybe the killer had simply spotted Field's family on the day the lunatic murdered his close friend and colleague, Barry Altman, deciding to return for fun and games. Maybe he'd get lucky and find Geist before the others, Bill Lancing prayed earnestly. Maybe. But the fact of the matter was that he hadn't a clue as to where to begin to look.

Richard, on the other hand, certainly had given them solid leads. Sure as the broken nose on Maggie's face, let alone the hole in her head, he reveled in delight. Three D.A.s. The Robert

Redler contrived connection. Then coming full circle for the evening's escapades back in Bridgehampton, practically to the scene of the initial crime for a little R and R. Richard Geist was only a stone's throw away, across the Peconic River. A mile away from police headquarters in Riverhead. Holed up in a basement apartment where the North and South Forks of Long Island meet. Had been for some time, too. Around the time Robert and Liza bought the house on Riverside Drive.

As for Arthur Field, the man suffered a nervous breakdown and was hospitalized.

Chapter
——>
16

Richard Geist sat twenty feet above the snowy depression off Sound Avenue in Baiting Hollow, waiting to down a deer coming through the ravine. Large, fresh tracks leading from a nearby field wound their way fifteen yards from the base of the tree he picked to ambush the wary, noble creature. Rarely did he or his followers buy meat. Fish and fowl were primarily the group's mainstay, accompanied by corn or potatoes along with a variety of fresh vegetables picked daily and sold at farm stands along Long Island's North Fork. When the stands closed down in the late fall, the group virtually lived out of large well-stocked freezers. Richard, like Robert Redler, enjoyed hunting and cooking game. No human heads for Richard or disgusting body parts as with Jeffrey Dahmer or the fictionalized character, Hannibal the Cannibal in Thomas Harris', *The Silence of the Lambs*. Nothing as sick as that. But deer hearts and livers were a delicacy that Richard Geist enjoyed immensely.

At dusk, Richard knew the deer would be returning to the field to bed down for the night. More importantly, he knew which trail funneled from the wood lot to the field. With a full December moon on the last day of bow season, Richard decided to put down one more trophy buck. He had already taken several for his troops. At ten minutes past five, a family of four deer silently made their way, single file, along the winding trail. Twilight, reflecting off a light covering of snow that had fallen the day before, extended the evening's hunt. The four passed just beneath Richard, one directly behind the other in size order, a rich putty-brown color to their coats. As if on stilts, they moved stealthily forward, heading toward the field from which they had come early that morning. Richard let the last one, a good-sized seven pointer, step several yards beyond him. In one fluid motion, he rose, came to full draw, released his arrow, and watched the two hundred-plus pound prize drop in the spot it stood. A well-placed spine shot had taken the legs out from under the animal.

The buck stops here, he grinned.

Richard enjoyed deer hunting from a tree stand, which put him well above the whitetail's line of sight. Most importantly, height diminished the likelihood of human scent, which he guarded against with oil of tarsal gland fox wafers placed strategically on twigs and branches around the kill area. Still, other endemic cover scents were sprayed on his boots, clothing, and gloves.

Whereas other hunters utilized several sight pins set for different yardages, one illuminated pin was all that Richard needed. During low-light conditions, when deer tend to appear out of nowhere, the importance of a lighted pin could make the difference between success and failure, Richard knew. That pin had proven invaluable. He had used it successfully at dusk on his first deer of the season, then again, rather sensationally, on Nassau's D.A. Gregory Howe. However, not exactly under the Rules of Fair Chase as stipulated by the North American Big Game Award Program.

Not remotely, the killer smirked.

Some years ago, Richard had made a poor shot, wounding a nice doe because he could not clearly discern the tip of his conventional sight pin, having to track the animal for miles before recovering it. Following the blood trail at night with a mini-light proved to be a chore. His second mistake was that he had been bloody anxious. Not having waited the required half hour or so before tracking his quarry had caused Richard considerable grief. Following in hot pursuit only drove the worthy opponent onward. Richard soon realized that death from a deadly broadhead was generally the result of massive hemorrhaging. So a half-hour nap, prior to pursuit, would allow his prey (be it animal or human) to pace its doubtless death. Moot point, for Richard had since learned to drop everything in its tracks, even in *very* low-light conditions—be it a hollow or a hallway.

Chapter
——>
17

It was January. Two months into the investigation of the murders of three D.A.s and Arthur Field's family, and authorities were no closer to finding Richard Geist or putting together the pieces of a puzzle that purportedly connected him to Redler. Nor were they able to locate Liza's daughter, Ann, or her boyfriend, Ricardo, both of whom had vanished along with several other members of the Inner Circle of Friends.

Whenever Robert Redler sank his teeth into a story, he'd write a series of articles. Lancing found it odd that Redler had only tackled a single editorial concerning the cult in all those years. Maybe it meant nothing. Or perhaps it was something significant. In any event, Redler's movements were under a microscope. The Inner Circle of Friends and how it related to the writer remained a mystery to police.

If ever anyone needed a scapegoat, a fall guy, they wouldn't have to look further than Fresh Meadows or Riverhead. Lee Harvey Oswald would have nothing over Robert Redler as patsy of the century, Chief Grear believed, for the man was firmly convinced that the John F. Kennedy assassination was a conspiracy by definition; that is, more than one person involved in the shooting of the president.

Although the sexual assault case was dropped and court records sealed, the FBI as well as the Justice Department maintained a file on

Redler as thick as a donkey's behind. After he had sent his thirty-four page packet off to Albany and Washington, who had in turn passed it on to the New York State Commission of Investigation and the Justice Department, Redler was finally widely read. Not the audience he wanted. What he wanted was justice. Pure and simple. He wanted those who accused him of a crime he did not commit *punished*. Period. He wanted those who had followed through as part of a vendetta *hurt* as he and Liza had been hurt. He wanted those who refused to launch a full investigation metaphorically *lynched*. In short, Redler was obsessed.

While authorities were busy collecting information in connection with Richard Geist, Robert Redler, and the Inner Circle of Friends, the writer was busy with his own investigation, which paralleled that of the police. Richard Geist was, of course, busy with the games he loved to play and played so well. The game of cat and mouse. The game of life and death. It afforded him the opportunity to match wits with the best minds in law enforcement as he had with doctors at the King Foundation and North Shore State Hospital, twenty-five years ago.

Whereas Robert Redler sought justice for wrongdoings, Richard Geist had found a way of exacting revenge for all the writer's meddling. Richard had come far in eighteen years and worked too hard to allow this freelance investigative reporter to undermine his achievements.

Recently, Richard Geist had successfully managed to rid himself of a rival ring of racketeers, so charged by the federal government in the United States District Court for the Western District of Alexandria, Virginia. Under the banner of benevolence, Geist was able to free himself from the ruling hierarchy. In the government's multi-count indictment charging conspiracy, structuring, along with wire, bank and mail fraud, the prevailing force behind the scenes bid good riddance to five felons. Of the five, four had fled. Fugitives from justice. One upper echelon female lieutenant in the Inner Circle of Friends was friendless, left holding the proverbial bag after having successfully set up a private investigator/deprogrammer in a kidnapping scheme. Richard had her immediately replaced with a loyal companion. Although the female fugitive had been credited as the Circle's mastermind, it was Richard who undermined the coordinator's operations, exposing and flushing all of them into oblivion. Assuming absolute and, therefore, autonomous control, Richard Geist had reorganized the splintered faction of namby-pamby followers who would, given the proper motivation and guidance, develop the sense of character and *espirit de corps* necessary to do his bidding. The group had gone underground, organizing and extending its network across the land.

Religion was on the rise.

Chapter
——>
18

Barbara Giordano had arranged a meeting with Robert Redler. It would be a clandestine encounter, for it surely would have been against the advice of Tony Giordano's counselor, against the wishes of Tony's family and—most assuredly—against the wishes of Tony himself. Nevertheless, she contacted Redler and suggested that they meet out east. He had written several pieces concerning the Giordano/Ziegler matter, and she liked the way he wrote. With conviction. Recently, he had hit a nerve in her. She had met him briefly once before. It was not solely his editorials or their earlier encounter that prompted her to contact Redler and offer him a deal. Her decision ran more along the lines of his thirty-four page treatment which she had first heard about in Albany, coupled with the fact that she, too, had gotten caught up in the criminal justice system. She saw certain similarities between her husband's plight and his, along with the empathy she felt toward Redler's girlfriend, Liza, who co-authored the account. Hence, it was a combination of several factors that motivated the housewife.

The night before the scheduled meeting, Barbara read Redler's packet for a third and final time.

At 1:00 p.m., with her housekeeper in full swing, Barbara Giordano finished dressing and drove out to Eastern Long Island to meet the author. Making certain that she wasn't being followed, she got off Sunrise Highway, heading north to the Long Island Expressway, then east again to Exit 71. She reduced her speed to thirty miles per hour while nearing the County Center in Riverhead. Large, official-looking signs loomed out at her: Sheriff's Office, Correctional Facility, Supreme Court, Surrogate Court, Criminal Court. The array created an unsettling feeling in the pit of her stomach.

At 2:30 p.m., Robert Redler was waiting for Barbara in the dining room of the Osborn Inn. It was a place void of any ambiance, but he had assured her that the food was good. He picked it not only for the wholesome meals they served but because the place was low-key, both of them hoping that no one would recognize her, for she had been the talk of Long Island, her picture plastered in newspapers and on news channels everywhere. Practically everyone lunching at the Inn had returned to work by two; the place was virtually empty.

Redler saw her as she entered the dining room, her features concealed behind a pair of dark glasses and a print kerchief. He got up from his chair, took her coat and seated her.

"Are you sure the food here is edible?" she remarked when she reached the table. There was nothing condescending in her tone or manner. Simply a fair question in light of the lack of customers and general surroundings. Unimaginative would be an understated description of the place.

"Delicious," he swore. "Liza and I come here regularly. No worse for wear," he assured her, smiling and tapping his gut, pushing in her chair then sitting back down. "The absence of patrons and moderate prices may suggest a rather dubious fare, but I believe you'll be pleasantly surprised. I brought my editor here last month, and she absolutely raved about the place. She wants me to write a review."

Barbara nodded and smiled. "Janet Kramer."

"You actually read that rag?" he teased.

"Cover to cover. Reaches some very influential folks. Quite a looker Janet Kramer is," she added.

"Ah, you mean that photograph. Well, the picture is

actually some twenty years younger than she. Vain creature that she is. Things aren't always as they appear, Mrs. Giordano."

"Please call me Barbara, Robert."

Barbara liked Redler the first time they met, and he liked her, too. Even in the press, he liked her. You pulled for her recovery rather than pitied her because she was strong-minded and a fighter.

"You're staring at me," she said.

"Why don't you take off those glasses and that babushka? If anyone recognizes you, we'll tell them everyone has a look-alike. Who'll argue that?"

Barbara Giordano removed her scarf but kept her glasses. The waitress came over and took their drink order then disappeared, knowing that Redler liked to relax a bit before deciding what to eat.

"I may be leaving Tony," Barbara said evenly, staring past him. "Not immediately and not because I don't love him— because I do. I have to think about the kids—what affect this and other business will have on them."

"What other business?"

"Family business."

"Like in none of my business?"

"Maldonado business."

"Nicholas Maldonado?"

She nodded.

Redler sat silent.

The waitress returned with their drinks and said to wave her down when ready.

It was no secret that Nicholas Maldonado's son lived next door to the Giordano's in Oceanside. It was no surprise that they broke bread occasionally.

"You're telling me Tony's connected?"

"Like in New York Tel-a-phone," she quipped quietly in sing-song fashion.

"What's he's involved in?"

"You mean, what isn't he involved in? Everything but his *own* family."

Redler realized that the sensationalized Barbara/Tony

Giordano/Alice Ziegler saga was somehow going to be diminished to a mere prelude, previewing a much larger picture. "Are we going to be discussing that involvement?"

"Are you going to be true to your word regarding the handling of the material I'm prepared to lay on you?" she questioned anxiously.

"Far greater in scope than I ever imagined, I have a sense you're about to tell me."

"You have no idea, Robert. You couldn't begin to imagine."

"Why come to me? Why not the authorities?"

"Because they're all connected like in New York Tel-a-phone," she chimed again coyly. "I'm supposed to be dead. Not sitting here talking to you. If I don't wake up one morning because of this bullet in my brain, which they can't remove, I want *you* to tell *my story*—a nonfictional version—remain the honorable person I believe you are, and get rich in the bargain. But first things first."

Redler said nothing for a moment. They just sat together, sipping their drinks.

"Did Tony put Alice Ziegler up to killing you?" he asked bluntly.

"No."

"How do you know?"

"Alice Ziegler was sanctioned by the Mob to kill me, unbeknownst to Tony. He's a pawn who believes he's an important piece."

"How do you know that?" he asked, putting down his glass of burgundy.

"All in good time, Robert."

If what Barbara was saying was fact, time was a luxury Robert Redler did not believe that this mother of two should squander.

"Rich, you said," Redler said and smiled, staring up at the ceiling. "See, I don't have to be rich to come here. A dollar seventy-five for a glass of wine, six ninety-five for a delicious full course lunch, same prices for delectable dinners—on Terrific Tuesdays—eight ninety-five at all other times, and a few dollars for scrumptious appetizers."

"And last year you lost your job at the college for a second time and couldn't put your boat back in the water because of financial difficulties. True?"

Robert stared across from her fixedly. "How do you know that?"

"Because you mention it in your thirty-four page discourse. That's how. And you also told Tony when the two of you were discussing boats. Remember?" she asked and nodded the answer for him.

Redler nodded in the affirmative, recalling the conversation along with the picture of Tony's boat hanging on the wall in his office: *Double Trouble.*

"You'd like being rich, Robert," she teased, noting that the talk of big money made him somewhat uncomfortable.

"Real money changes people. Sometimes for the better, and sometimes for the worse. But it changes them."

"For Tony, it was for the worse," she stated flatly.

"Do you talk to him? I mean like we're talking now?"

"Serious talk?" she asked and smirked. "You can't talk seriously to Tony. He's more concerned with his so-called friends than he is his family." She lowered her eyes. "He doesn't see that, but it's a fact."

"Who instructed Alice Ziegler to murder you, Barbara?"

"Are you wired, Robert? Do you have a tape recorder in that bag of yours?"

"No. I'm not wired. And yes, I do have a tape recorder in my bag. But it's not on. Care to see?"

"No. If you tell me no, then it's so."

"Tell me who."

"Junior."

"Nicholas Maldonado's son?"

Barbara nodded. "Are you beginning to understand why your *initial* story has to be presented in the form of fiction, Robert?"

"Rob. I hate being called Robert."

"Are you beginning to get the picture, Rob?"

"How do you know it was Maldonado, Jr.?"

"Because Alice told me so just before she pulled the

trigger. "'Junior told me to say good-bye to you, Barbara,'" she said.

"Why?"

"They're tearing down the old regime."

"Who's they?"

"The government. Federal and state level that filters on down through the ranks. There's a new order in force. A body of centurions with good manners, management, and ivy league educations. And lots and lots of new money. They're not the tired old lot of hired, high-caliber lackey lawyers on a gangster's payroll. They're not the governors, senators, congressmen, judges, district attorneys, and police brass in some capo's hip pocket whom he controls at whim like in *The Godfather*, Rob. But rather the governors, senators, congressmen, judges, district attorneys, police brass, and ivy league lawyers who *are* the new regime."

"And you say you can prove all this." It wasn't framed as a question.

"I can, indeed."

"And you can't take it to—"

"To whom?"

"If not the police, then perhaps the newspapers. Let them see and expose what you have," *if anything at all*, he wanted to add.

"Oh, the journalists are going to save the world and protect me in the bargain," she said sarcastically.

"Not every governor, senator, police official, et cetera, is corrupt, Barbara."

Barbara removed her glasses. "But the ones who are, are presently in control," she said with serious eyes.

"Back to my earlier question. Why did Nicholas Maldonado, Jr. order you shot?"

"I didn't say he ordered it. I said he told Alice to say good-bye to me."

"I had asked you who ordered it."

"You asked who instructed Alice Ziegler to murder me. You better start listening carefully, Rob. You tell me you don't have a wire and that your tape recorder is off. I suggest you start taking notes," she said evenly, taking another sip of wine. "There's a big difference between who ordered my death and those instructed to carry it out."

Redler was losing patience. "Did Maldonado, Jr. *instruct* Alice Ziegler to shoot you?"

"Yes."

"And who *ordered* Nicholas Maldonado, Jr. to do that; in other words, who put out the contract on you?"

"Joseph Scalla."

"A former Queens D.A.?"

"A *deposed* district attorney."

"And who put Scalla out of office?"

"Daniel Russo."

"*The* Daniel Russo? Our governor?" Redler asked incredulously.

Barbara Giordano nodded.

"Why?"

"Guilt by association."

"What's the connection?"

"The connection?" she echoed. "Let's see, now," she reflected as if considering the question for the very first time. "How about the fact that every heavy-duty player's name ends in a vowel?" she offered amusingly.

"Seriously. What's the connection?"

"They're *all* connected."

"How so?"

"Through Senator Demeco."

"What about Senator Demeco?"

"Senator Demeco serves as an intermediary between Russo's people and Scalla's group."

"Group?"

"Can we order? I'm famished. And I could go another glass of wine, too."

Robert Redler called the waitress over and placed their order. The two started with shrimp wrapped in bacon for appetizers then worked their way through savory seafood bisque, fresh fish, more wine, followed by coffee and homemade bread pudding for dessert. Barbara had done most of the talking through lunch, while Redler's mind reeled in wonder.

Chapter
——>
19

After lunch, the inn's pleasant owner came over and offered Robert and his guest complimentary drinks. She did not recognize Barbara Giordano. The housewife and the unemployed college lecturer enjoyed their amaretto straight up; she, resuming discourse; he, finally taking copious notes and ruminating over her allegations of Albany's covert day-to-day, behind-the-scenes operations while overtly dispensing daily doses of over-the-counter diplomacy to its constituents. The gospel according to Barbara Giordano.

"I want you to go back to that infamous fourteen-hour luncheon with Joseph Scalla and Maldonado," Robert insisted. "What year was that?"

"Nineteen eighty-three."

"Eleven years ago."

Barbara nodded.

"And you're telling me that the former district attorney for Queens County, Scalla, knew of the plot to cover up one of Maldonado, Jr.'s murders and did nothing?"

"He did plenty. He allowed his chief investigator to receive a ten thousand dollar bribe from Nicholas Maldonado himself."

"And this investigator was District Attorney Black's top investigator, too, you said."

She nodded. "And for the time being, he's still the interim D.A.'s right hand. Birds of a feather, Rob. They're all a flock of falcons ready to swoop down on one another in order to protect their own skins. They're all corrupt. Right on up to the very top. The sour cream always rises, too, you see. We were no better. Tony helped run prostitution in Nassau. We were protected. That's why deals were cut."

"Did your husband run that escort service as first reported in the papers, paying the utility bills or whatever?"

"Owned and operated, Rob. Not on paper, of course. We backed it with profits from the carting concern."

"Complete Cartage, Inc.," Redler said.

"Complete in every way. Attracting all the garbage in the community. Servicing judges, lawyers, police, politicians, doctors, actors, musicians, businessmen. Even a clergyman. You name it."

"You can prove this?"

"You're looking at one of the madams."

Redler dropped his eyes to the table. "How did Alice Ziegler fit into all this?"

"She was one of our part-time party girls."

"Why did she agree to shoot you?"

"Agree?" Barbara laughed. "You do what you're told to do. But I think she also *wanted* me out of the picture. Wanted Tony for herself. His lifestyle. To a seventeen-year-old, Tony is a god."

"And to you?"

There was a pause. "He's a good Joe. Not out to hurt anyone intentionally."

"But people did get hurt. You almost got yourself killed in the bargain."

Barbara raised her eyes to the ceiling before setting them back on Redler. "He's not as bad as the others. Believe me. I'm as much to blame as he. I allowed things to happen. Probably would have happened anyway. But I allowed myself to become a part. A very big part."

Barbara and Robert watched as a group of young men and women walked into the dining area, stopping to study the menu written on the blackboard off the entranceway. Dressed in modified western garb, they stood staring intently at the choices, discussing and deciding what to order then and there. The men wore boots and jeans and thick leather studded belts; western shirts with collars were open at the neck. The women stood in boots and skirts, coats buttoned at the throat. Each had stepped into the role of country dude or doll as surely as her husband Tony had played the part of suburban wise guy, Barbara entertained somewhat sadly. Fugitively connected and therefore ephemerally empowered.

She couldn't help but laugh as the soundtrack emitted Billy Ray Cyrus's *Achy Breaky Heart*. Here she was, sitting across from this virtual stranger, pouring out a part of her sordid past in a honky-tonk tavern while Tony sat in a Nassau County jail.

"To what extent was your involvement in this operation?"

"Well, Rob. Before I madamed, I hooked. I screwed some of those judges and lawyers, police and politicians, actors and even an actress—if you care to picture that. That's when I was doing drugs and drink, doctors and even a deacon. Darling of a man, though. He'd have me kneel in the first pew while he'd grope and take me from behind. Loved to put a plastic bag over my head while he recited scripture in my ear just before orgasm. His. Not mine, mind you. Paid me right from the collection basket on Sunday evenings. Dropped me like a bad habit when he became a priest. I felt as though I'd been excommunicated."

Redler sat in shock at her bluntness.

"Well, aren't you going to write that down? Or do you trust that you'll remember the good parts?"

Redler looked hurt.

"I'm sorry," Barbara said sincerely. "It's a defense, I guess. You don't know how hard it is to let this all out. And when I do, it's irretrievable. I can't grab it back or pretend it didn't happen."

Robert nodded. "You want to stop here?"

Barbara shook her head. "I'm not as ashamed as I am scared. That's the sorry business of it all. I'm more afraid of going straight to hell than I am of what they can do to me. It's the curse of being raised Irish Catholic, I guess. That's the cross I bear. But first and foremost, I'm afraid of what they can do to my children."

"Wouldn't my writing your story, even in a fictitious vein for openers, jeopardize you and your family?"

Barbara fixed her eyes confidently on Redler. "No."

"How do you know that?"

"Because you're going to explain it to them. You're going to show them the very thin line between fiction and fact. They're going to dread you, Rob Redler. They're going to fear you as I fear retribution for my sins."

"But what's to prevent them from eliminating what they fear?"

"Full disclosure."

"Supported by?"

"Full documentation."

"Which I will see?"

"Which you will see."

"And who will hold this documentation over their heads?"

"Others will."

"What others?"

"That, you will not know."

"And what if the *others* believe that *I'm* the threat?" Redler reasoned. "I mean solely."

"They won't."

"What guarantee do I have?"

"My promise to you."

"And suppose I decide at some point to abandon this business?"

"I'll find someone else."

"Do you have a backup in mind?

"Yes."

"Who?"

"Brian Cooper."

"*Newsday*? I thought you said you didn't want a mainstream journalist."

"I don't. I want someone I can trust."

"Think he'd do what you're asking of me?"

"I'd have to wait and see."

"And what if he said yes to you and went ahead—"

"You mean what if he double-crossed me and wrote the story as fact instead of fiction from the get-go?"

"That's exactly what I mean."

"He'd wind up dead."

"By who?"

"*La Mano Nera.*"

"Who?"

"The Black Hand."

Redler looked at her in disbelief. He knew little of the secret organization formed in Italy in the late nineteenth century and supposedly disbanded.

"And why would they kill him?"

"Because serious damage would be done, and he would be expendable."

"And what if this faction you're so concerned about happens to get to those who hold this documentation, regardless of any guarantee or promise you might extend? Then what? Shit happens, you know."

"Won't happen."

"Why?"

"They're impenetrable."

"Like the City of Troy?"

"You must take me at my word on this or bow out."

"And at what point must I make this definitive decision?"

"At the point you view the documentation."

"What kind of documents?"

"Photographs, written records, and audio tapes."

"When will I be able to see and hear this evidence?"

"You'll see soon enough."

"You seem to have things worked out."

"Oh, I do, Rob. I really and truly do."

"You know, generally speaking, there really is a thin line between fact and fiction."

"Your fiction will be membranously thin, Rob. Only the names and dates will be changed to protect the guilty and save my kids and Tony's behind."

"What about yours?"

"Hopefully."

"And if not?"

"Then other documents will be released for publication, and an expendable part of the Mob will go down the crapper as a warning that if my children or husband are hurt, they'll *all* be flushed."

"If they do hit you, why would your children, Tony, or even I, for that matter, be immune to a vendetta?"

"When your book comes out, Rob, they'd have to be insane to try something. They'll know it was me who fed you information. Not Tony or anyone else."

"How so? Give me that much."

Barbara hesitated. "I know things no other person in the world could possibly know."

"Because?"

"Because I'm a woman, for one thing. That's all I'm going to say for now on that point. If they take me out, they'll pay a dear price, at which point you'll turn fiction into fact with a second book."

"What if they take out one child to teach you a lesson?" Redler was filling up his notepad.

"Total war. I told you; I'll flush them all."

"How will you make that clear?"

Barbara smiled. "Keep writing," she nodded. "You're doing just fine."

Redler looked up from his notes and laughed. "I like your style, Barbara."

"I like yours, too, Rob. You make things oh so clear."

"How do you know the right people will get the message?"

"Oh, the right people will get the message all right. Your publicist will see to that."

"My publicist?"

"And the movie will be ten times bigger than *The Godfather*. That I promise, too."

"The movie?"

She nodded her head. "Of course you'll be invited on every talk show in America. And that's where the problem will arise."

"Problem?"

Barbara nodded assuredly. "You're going to have to become an actor as well, Rob dear. Especially when they ask you, 'Mr. Redler. How did you come up with the idea for this magnificent story?' You're going to have to be convincing in front of millions of people. And in the process, we're going to keep a handful of those viewers literally on the edge of their seats."

"The Mob."

"A very organized and orderly mob, Rob. Run by your government and our tax dollars at work." Barbara leaned forward and removed a Manila envelope from her bag, handing it over matter-of-factly. "This does not leave with you. You're to give it back to me momentarily. If our waitress or anyone else approaches the table, you're to put the materials back in the envelope." Her tone and manner changed dramatically.

He opened the 8 ½ x 11-inch envelope on the table and removed a large grainy black and white photograph along with several others. An instantly familiar face loomed before him. Standing there in the nude was the governor of New York with an erection the size of his ego, propped for action. Leaning over a desk was a black male in his early twenties, also balls-ass nude. Redler flipped through the series of photographs. What he saw shocked and revolted him. What he was privy to momentarily made him want to rush to the phones to call in the story like he had seen in many a movie.

What Redler held in his hands was gold. A story he could sell. A story that would put him on the map. A story, in short, that would somehow begin to even the score for the injustices brought against him and others. The governor of New York caught with his pants down. No. Off. He studied the pictures for fakery. A superimposition perhaps. He focused on the lighting in the foreground. The shadows. The angles cast. He was so busy analyzing the photographs and attaching headlines to the story, he almost missed something. A figure obscured in the background in one of the shots. He stared down in amazement. Stewart Weisman, New York State's convicted chief appeals judge, was standing in the shadows in the back of the room, fully clothed. Redler went through the photos again.

"Who's the black guy?" he asked.

"An aide."

"And where was this picture taken?"

"Albany. Capitol Building. The director of criminal justice's chamber."

"When?"

"December of 1990. Around the holidays."

"Is he *crazy* to allow pictures like this to be taken? He's got to be nuts."

"He was very drunk. He's a very violent drunk."

"How would you know that?"

"Let's just say I'd rather be getting buggered with a plastic bag over my head by the deacon I mentioned than by dear old Daniel."

"Judging by this scene, I don't think you'd have much to worry about."

"Oh, he's quite the ladies' man when sober. Liquor changes his personality and sexual proclivity."

Membranous, and now *proclivity*, Redler thought. Certainly not the way the woman seated across from him was portrayed by the media. "Tell me more about our governor and this violence."

"The aide you saw. Disappeared that same evening."

"You were there that evening?"

"I didn't say that."

"Who took these pictures?"

"Can't say."

"Can't or won't?"

"It's not important," she snapped. "Look. Please try and understand that I can't tell you everything. All right?"

"I have the distinct feeling that you could author this book yourself."

"You're giving me way too much credit, Rob. I can think on my feet, put a sentence together, and hopefully get my idea across. But I'm not a writer who can capture a nuance, or the quintessential quality of a thing."

"I think you just did."

"I think you're sweet to say so. But I know you know what I mean. I also want you to know that I've read every article you've ever written. Including that packet you sent around—not to mention your first book, which followed Richard Geist's."

"Tough act to follow. That was a long time ago. I didn't think anyone remembered it."

"Well, they won't forget this next one."

"I used a pseudonym back then. How did you know it was me?"

"I make it my business to know everything about a person I do business with, my dear. As one reviewer said, you're brilliant. But only a handful of people know it. I'll be the storyteller up to a point, Robert. Excuse me. Rob. After that, you'll be the craftsman. The architect of a novel that's going to rock this government on its heels. Mark my words."

"From your lips to God's ears."

"As I said before, I need someone who can put this so-called fiction before a powerful faction, have them chew on it a spell, before they finally spit it out in one another's collective faces—before they try to run and hide—knowing full well that there will be no such place save an early grave. Again, the right people are going to get the message, Rob. They're going to crawl under a rock. You won't believe what I'm going to give you," she said, gathering up the photographs. "This is nothing compared to what's coming."

"Being able to label the governor of the State of New York a bisexual with a cover-up involving a murder while Weisman stands smiling in the background is nothing compared to what's coming?"

"By George, I think he's got it," she declared through a widening grin.

All Robert Redler could do at that point was to nod his head in agreement, not at all fathoming the depths to which he would descend before emerging from the likes of hell.

"So, let me hear you say it. Do you agree, at this juncture, to tell my story the way I insist it be told? The way that we discussed? It can't be told any other way, Rob. Not without jeopardizing innocent lives."

"I agree," Redler said. "Yes."

"Good."

Chapter
——>
20

Shortly after Nicholas Maldonado had received a life sentence, a sketch artist for law enforcement made a series of drawings showing how the don would age through his years of imprisonment. A major New York newspaper picked up and published the photo progression on their front page. As there was no recent photograph of Richard Geist, the same artist added approximately two decades to the serial killer's features by working from the back cover of the author's book jacket. Richard's assumed likeness appeared everywhere. Newspapers. Magazines. Television. Wanted posters. Many mainstream newspapers in nearly every major city carried some account of the killer's background: a bizarre childhood, a short-lived military stint in the Marine Corps, his institutionalization at the King Foundation as well as the psychiatric facility in Havenwood. People from around the country were beginning to think that the inhabitants of Long Island were somehow possessed. Some said it was the drinking water. Others believed it had to be something in the air. Richard's escape from the institution had been covered extensively. Now, a new generation of readers wanted to know where they could buy Geist's book.

Following Geist's 1975 publication, the publisher of a small press had contacted and convinced Robert Redler to write the madman's unauthorized biography. Few knew that Redler had interviewed Geist early on and at length. But after the killer's escape from a state mental hospital, the public wanted the genuine article, not the imitation, so Richard Geist's autobiography went into its second, third, then fourth printing. A sensationalistic public could not get enough of Richard Geist. Redler's publisher, on the other hand, had turned cautious and only printed two thousand copies of Geist's unauthorized biography in paperback. Initially, Redler thought it was a good beginning, but the book was dead in the water. As it turned out, it was the beginning of the end.

Chapter
——>
21

Barbara Giordano was fast becoming fascinated by the way Redler presented his fiction, cleverly incorporating the indisputable facts she had provided. The early chapters of his new novel explored a corrupt and lethal government on the rise to ruination, a blueprint for the destruction of a democracy. Redler's revelation might soon be a lesson in learning, she entertained . . . perhaps shaking and waking the world to sheer madness in the making. What better way to personify that possibility than through the symbol of insanity itself, for Richard Geist, Robert Redler's antagonist, was rapidly becoming a household name . . . a name connected with everyone's worst nightmare. The irony being, of course, that Robert Redler's *fictional* character was as real as real could be.

Surveillance teams reported that Robert Redler and Barbara Giordano were traveling east. He drove, and she read with the overhead light.

"Pure genius," Barbara stated genuinely.

"Pure madness," Redler retorted. "I have a bad feeling about all this. They're not stupid. And from what you tell me—"

"I've got it covered, Rob. You're just going to have to trust me on this. They won't touch you, I said. If they come after me or my children or Tony, they're dead meat—and they'll soon know it for certain. Those near the top of the heap will shit their pants before they drown in their own diarrhea."

"Suppose Tony comes after you?"

Barbara shook her head.

"But they may put him up to it, or find themselves another Alice Ziegler. It happened once. Remember?"

Barbara was still shaking her head. "I told you time and time again that I hold the trump card. Let any of them fuck with me, and their first line of defense goes down whether I'm alive or dead. Fuck around thereafter, and they *all* go down the shitter. It automatically goes into play. Foolproof. Fail-safe. Get it?"

"All right. Fine. You've got you and your family's asses covered. Tell me the part about why they won't go after Liza or drop me off some goddamn bridge in a pair of cement shoes. Tell me the good part."

"I can't tell you anything except that you're in the tractor's seat even though you don't know how the whole fucking farm operates."

"And you do." Redler shook his head.

Barbara sat silently, staring out the windshield of Redler's four-wheel drive vehicle.

"Let me ask you this. What happens if that bullet in your head suddenly causes your death and you don't wake up tomorrow? Then what?"

"For the final time, Rob. Five organized crime families go down the crapper, beginning with the New York Mob, for openers, followed by other families around the country. Then comes *La Mano Nera*. That's your government at work. If anything happens to me or *my* family, they will all suffer *full* disclosure. But feel rest assured that nothing is going to happen. Your book will be fair warning. There won't be a second chance," she said wearily.

"And the hierarchy is just going to stand around and let that happen without retaliating."

"Retaliation will mean their destruction."

"You keep saying that."

"So when is it going to sink in?"

"Your story. My book. How is that going to save the day?"

"A few good men in power will take a good look," she equivocated.

"And?"

"And a dismantling will take place."

"A dismantling?"

"Power is a balancing act, Rob. Between good and evil. No one side has ultimate power. But the evil in our land has the upper hand at the moment. Decidedly so." Barbara looked as though she carried the weight of the nation on her shoulders. "Just look around you. Look on the streets. Look at our schools. The economy. The criminal justice system that you write about. Look at the six, the ten, and the eleven o'clock news. Look at the neighborhoods. Look at the agencies from which you seek some sort of silly justice. They're laughing at you. But in short order, they're going to bow down before you. That's what you really want, isn't it? Revenge. Punishment. Pure and simple. What you euphemistically refer to as justice. Nothing wrong with that. But you have to know who *all* your enemies are, Rob."

"And you do."

"By name and by face. And I give them a slow death."

"Like who?"

"Joseph Scalla."

"*You* had him put down?"

"More like out of office."

"Who else?"

"Nicholas Maldonado, Sr."

"*You* had *him* put away?"

"For life without parole. You were at the sentencing."

"Yet it was his son who told Alice to shoot you, you said," he tested.

"He does nothing and is nothing without his father. I want to see Junior squirm. He'll dig his own grave shortly. Mark your written words," she said and smiled benignly, looking all around her. "Rob, where the hell are we?"

"Greenport. Who else did you tangle with?"

"Judge Weisman. Our people set him up."

"How? He was one of the nation's most powerful judges."

"He's a wimp, Rob."

"The papers said it was his mistress who'd blown the whistle to the feds because he threatened her and her daughter when she broke off their affair."

"True enough, but it was yours truly who sent copies of those incriminating photographs off to mommy. Weisman *still* believes it was his girlfriend's doing to send one photo in particular off to Demeco's secretary as a warning." Barbara grinned and winked.

"Weisman's up for parole soon."

"Yeah, we also let him know that if he doesn't stay in line when he does come out, we'll send that and other photos of the governor off to the media with his blessings."

"Is that why he tried to take his own life in prison?"

"Showboating, Rob. He'd no more take his life than discontinue masturbation. Oh, I didn't tell you *that* story. Perhaps another time. Anyhow, he's slowly losing his mind and lots of sleep, and that sits very well with me."

"What would happen if those pictures ever were released?"

"The same thing that happened to Russo's aide. Weisman would suddenly disappear."

"Are the media going to be getting those pictures anytime soon?"

"I hope it doesn't come down to that."

"Does Russo know the photos exist?"

"No."

"Then where's your trump card?"

"Russo knows that we can link him to organized crime quicker than you can say Nicholas Maldonado."

"Jesus Christ."

"We're working on that, too," she joked mischievously with laughing eyes.

"You're one tough lady, Barbara."

"You complain that you spent part of a day on Rikers Island. I was left for dead on the back porch of my own home. My children almost wound up without a mother. There are some tapes I want you to listen to. Scalla. The Maldonado faction. Weisman and Russo. I guarantee you you'll have an Excedrin headache before you're finished. I'll play them for you on the way back after dinner. Where are we eating?"

"The Rhumb Line."

"They have a clam bar at the end of a pier?"

"You're thinking of Claudio's, right around the corner. They're closed for the season."

"Yes. That's the place. Tony and I were there with another couple on our boat several years ago. Would you mind if we drove by there for just a moment?"

"Not at all. In our last meeting, you said Senator Demeco was a go-between for Russo's people and Scalla's group."

"Yep."

"And that Russo had Scalla put out of office."

"Yep."

"But a moment ago you said that you put him down."

"No, you said that. I said, 'More like out of office.'"

"Here we go again. You wanted Scalla out. Yes?"

"You're slow on the uptake, but you're getting there, Rob."

"You're telling me Demeco carried *your* order to the governor."

"The governor's people."

"Just like that?"

"Just like that."

"But not because of the pictures, but because you can link him to Maldonado?"

"And others."

"*You* ordered Scalla's *and* Maldonado's fall!" Redler said in amazement.

"That I did."

"And Demeco carried the orders to whom, exactly?"

"To those in charge is all you need to know for now."

"And what about Weisman?"

"Russo tried to use him to discredit Demeco and his brother."

"And so you ordered Weisman's fall from grace, too."

"Yes."

"How does Demeco fit in all this?"

"He's another one of the good guys, Rob."

Redler drove past the Rhumb Line and made a right onto

85

Main Street, down to the water's edge, stopping between Preston's and Claudio's.

"I remember that marine store," she said, giggling like a little girl. "Tony kept driving a salesgirl crazy, wanting to know why they didn't carry cowboy boots with nautical soles. 'I'm scratching up my gel coat and almost broke my neck with these goddamn leather soles,' she mimicked Tony, relating how her husband had walked around town in ninety-five degree heat in a tank top, shorts, and high-heeled snakeskin boots. 'I see you got Sperry Topsiders here in suede and all kinds of crap,'" she continued imitating Tony in a mocking Italian accent. "'If and when I come back to this store, I wanna see shit- kickin' high-heeled snakeskin-stompers with *these* here kind of soles, darlin','" Tony went on and on, holding up a pair of boat shoes," Barbara bellowed in reminiscence. "Some guy with his date said something about loud-mouth Italians, so Tony pulled him out of the store, threatening to throw him into the water over there." She pointed toward the wharf. "Well, his girlfriend, or whatever she was, went running for the Greenport police. We never did get to have those clams on the half shell out there on the pier. We barely finished getting gas and ice before the cops arrived, waving us in like crazy. Tony waved good-bye, shouting to them that the real crime was Preston's selling boat shoes for more than twice what he could buy a good pair of boots which came up to his *cojones*. Quote, unquote. And away we sped."

"*Cojones*?"

"Balls, Rob," the woman clarified and couldn't stop laughing.

"Sounds like a fun day," he remarked through a frown.

"You had to be there."

"You said there was another couple with you."

"Maldonado, Junior and his wife. Junior had wanted to kidnap the girl before she ran off for the police."

Redler smiled uncomfortably, following the circular drive past the pier and Preston's, heading back to the Rhumb Line.

Chapter
——>
22

As soon as Redler and Giordano were seated in the restaurant, she handed him the set of papers along with a file folder of insurance records. He reviewed the contents of the first folder, denoting subscriber coverage. All the folders contained similar information concerning men and women over the age of 55. Robert returned to the initial document and carefully examined the particulars, which presented a detailed report of a Cornelius Barret's family medical history, indicating the man's projected life expectancy: 80.3 years. Probably one of those confidential in-house reports that companies reviewed periodically to make sure they didn't over insure someone who might drop dead on them tomorrow, Redler thought.

Redler glanced across at Barbara who had her head buried in the early chapters of his manuscript. He leafed through the set of other papers, staring oddly at one page in particular, noting that the sheet was one large bar graph. At the top was Cornelius Barret's name. Redler noted that the descending names were those whose medical histories he had just perused. It took him a moment to realize that the men and women were retirees who never made it to the first plateau of their anticipated longevity; for the chart, with a bold red line running through the bars, terminated all those approaching age 60.

What Robert Redler digested next was an attached report that had nothing to do with any insurance company, per se. What it had to do with, insofar as he could ascertain, was an independent outfit that surveyed medical findings, which targeted certain pension fund programs, both large and small. It was the company's name that had thrown him off track. Term Life, Incorporated.

Again, Redler reviewed the set of folders and papers. The company did not appear to discriminate between blue and white collar workers, for steam fitters, teachers, engineers, truck drivers, maintenance workers, doctors, and lawyers comprised the list. He felt her eyes on him and looked up from the documents.

"Interesting?" she asked.

"Is this what I think it is?"

"What is it that you think it is?"

A waitress came over, but Redler rudely waved her away.

"Call me when you're ready, sweetheart," the middle-aged woman said sarcastically.

"Well?" Barbara asked him as soon as the woman disappeared.

"Terminating retired employees before departure time?" he both asked and answered in a disbelieving breath.

Barbara nodded knowingly. "The company pays out paltry sums of a few thousand dollars in pension payments over several years. And that's it. It's a lot cheaper than having someone collect till he or she is seventy or eighty."

"Yeah, but who benefits?"

"Term Life, Inc.," she assured him.

"I mean on the other end," he pressed, knowing she was toying with him. "I'm not very good at interpreting these kinds of things," he confessed. "I have no head for business."

"Oh, you're doing just fine. I saw those papers in Tony's closet for years before I realized what was going on. You caught on almost immediately."

"Well, I *knew* I was supposed to be looking for something, but I'm not getting the full picture yet. Wouldn't the payments go to a beneficiary upon death?"

"Only if the employee elected to take a reduced pension.

With full pension," she paused, "retirement benefits stop. Get it?"

"Is Tony involved in this?"

"No," she stated firmly. "What he was and still is involved in are viatical settlements."

"Via what?"

"Viatical settlements."

"What's that?"

"Financial services that provide payment for people with severe illnesses. Aids. Cancer. Heart disease and such. The companies enable those poor souls to sell their life insurance policies for cash. Ten cents on the dollar in some cases—but to do with what they want *now* instead of having it go to a beneficiary when they croak. All completely legal. Except that some institutions are more reputable than others. Tony's people, of course, are not. They're greedier. This other business? He's only holding these records for Junior."

"Nicholas Maldonado, Jr.?"

"Yes. Nicholas Maldonado, Jr., for Christ's sake," she said in a strained, impatient tone.

"Not in the same sentence, please," he joked, trying to put the documents in proper perspective.

Barbara sat pensively, unconsciously stroking the scar beneath the wisp of blonde hair that covered her temple. "You see, you know about writing and such; I know about all kinds of schemes and scams."

"You're not still keeping this in the closet?"

"No, these are copies that must be destroyed along with the tapes. Remember *Mission Impossible*?" she questioned through a smile. "Poof! Right after dinner. The originals are in good hands, though," she offered reassuringly.

"Listen," they both said simultaneously then laughed.

"What?"

"You first," he insisted.

"I think this is great stuff," she said, tapping his manuscript.

"You had it all of twenty minutes."

"Yeah, but what I read is great. Honestly."

"Tell me what you really think the next time we meet."

"I'm going to read every word. Believe me."

"Some of it's going to hurt."

"I know."

"You wanted me to be honest, you said."

"I do."

"That's what you told me."

"I did."

There was brief silence between them.

"What were you going to say?" She took and put the papers and files away.

"Oh, I was just wondering if we're ever going to get our waitress back, now that I pissed her off. I could use a stiff drink," he decided, scanning the room for their server.

Barbara took in the nautical setting, the pictures and items along its walls and ceiling. "The name of this restaurant, Rob; the Rhumb Line. What does Rhumb Line mean?" she asked, deciding to make small talk while they waited.

"What's the shortest distance between two points?"

"A straight line, I guess."

"Not on a sphere, such as the earth's surface. The shortest distance is a rhumb line, which is a curve that cuts all meridians at the same angle."

"What's a meridian exactly?"

"Well, it's an imaginary circle on the globe that passes through the poles."

"What poles?"

"Either end of the earth's axis."

"You mean like in the North and South Poles?"

"Bingo! Yes."

"Are they imaginary, too? These poles?"

"Well, they're not really poles. They're fixed points of reference."

"So they're imaginary."

"Yes."

"Are these rhumb lines imaginary, too?"

"Uh-huh."

"Let me see if I've got this straight."

"Not straight," he teased. "Curved."

"Shut up."

Robert bit down on the inside of both lips to keep from grinning.

"These rhumb lines are imaginary."

He nodded.

"The poles are imaginary."

He nodded again.

"And these meridians are imaginary, also."

"Yep."

Barbara fixed her eyes on Redler rather playfully. "You know, Rob. I imagine you got to be pret-ty smart to know where you're going in a boat. It's no wonder Tony always got us lost," she concluded, holding back a laugh.

"Well, you really don't worry about rhumb lines over short distances. It's when you circumnavigate— What?"

Her laughter was immediate and infectious, waving away his curiosity while recalling happier days gone by . . . days and nights with Tony, cruising the East End of Long Island . . . its bays . . . crossing the Sound.

Redler couldn't help but laugh, too. Lightly. A good minute passed before he, unlike she, composed himself and spoke. "Do you think we might navigate through dinner without making any more waves?" he asked, unable to either understand or share but a moment of her mirth.

Barbara nodded then waved him off again before she was finally able to catch her breath. "Remember I told you in the car that the Greenport police were flagging us down after that incident at Preston's?" she asked and tittered. "Well, Tony thought he was making a bee-line for the Shinnecock Canal, only we wound up in Connecticut. He didn't even realize we had crossed the Sound. He believed it was Peconic Bay," she said through a guffaw. "I told him the police were going to nab us. You know what he said? 'How the hell can they find us when I don't even know where the fuck we are,'" she strained, lowering her voice and laughing hysterically as the tears rolled down her pretty face.

People throughout the restaurant were staring at the pair.

"Finally, when we stopped for gas, some marina guy told

us we were in Connecticut. So Tony asked him where we could find snakeskin Topsiders. You should have seen Tony's face when the man told him that the 'darndest thing just happened,'" she continued through a snicker. "'Some fella in Greenport was looking for a pair of snakeskin Topsiders, too. Just like you, Captain. Heard it over the marine radio no more than thirty minutes ago. Coast Guard's out right now lookin' to accommodate him.'"

Barbara was practically doubled over the table, unable to contain herself any more than the people sitting in the dining room could ignore her uproarious behavior.

"What happened next?" Redler inquired politely.

"Junior gave the man fifty dollars to keep his mouth shut, and we headed north. Tony said that if he was going up the river, he was going to do it his way. So up the Connecticut River we crawled, obeying the No Wake Zone for miles. Five miles an hour. Drove Tony nuts. Finally, we tucked into a secluded spot and went skinny-dipping. Junior and his wife. Tony and I. Oddly enough, it was one of the most wonderful days we shared."

Barbara finally settled down, and the people around them were buzzing like busy bees.

Redler heard Barbara's name whispered at a nearby table as she handed him an envelope.

"This is for you," she said. "Open it. Read it. Then put it away. Dinner is on you. I'm famished."

"Well, I hope they take MasterCard because they canceled my American Express."

She watched him as he lifted a corner of the sealed envelope, running a forefinger across its top, removing and unfolding several sheets of paper and a bank check.

Redler stared down in disbelief.

"What's the first thing you're going to do with the money, Rob?"

Robert looked up at Barbara then back at the check. "Have snakeskin boat shoes as well as boots with nautical soles made up for Tony when he gets out," he said in a quiet, even tone.

"Size ten-and-a-half, triple E," she told him through a giggle.

"I'll make a note of that."

"You can sign those contracts after dinner. Is Simon and Schuster a suitable publisher, Rob?" she questioned and smiled.

Redler nodded trancelike. "They rejected me when I tried to get my biography on Geist reprinted."

"Virtually everyone rejected you, Rob. But now they're going to reprint it in hardcover as well as publish your new novel. But first things first. Read."

He started thumbing through the contract.

"Of course, if you wish to consult a literary lawyer and/or have an agent represent you for ten to fifteen percent—"

Redler suddenly raised his hand as if to halt an oncoming car. "This is the *advance*?" he questioned as quietly as he could.

"Well, sure. You have to have a little something to keep you going until your masterpiece is completed. But if you're to be buying me dinners as well as custom made, hand-crafted footwear for Tony, I guess I could go back to Simon and see what I can do," she offered in deadpan.

"A five hundred thousand dollar advance?"

"Well, you're not exactly high caliber yet. You've got to start someplace, Rob," she teased.

"A five hundred thousand dollar advance?" he repeated.

"Some hacks are never satisfied."

"On a novel that isn't even written yet?"

"I saw the first draft."

"You saw some fifty pages."

"So I lied to Simon a little," she said holding up a thumb and forefinger with the tiniest of space between them. "Or was it Schuster? I always get those two mixed up," she kidded.

"I can't believe this!"

"Believe it. You're going to make a fucking fortune, Mr. Robert Redler."

He looked up at her, beaming.

"See? You don't even mind my calling you Robert, now. See what money does to people?"

Robert Redler was shaking his head.

"See? What's in a name, anyhow? Tony always says it's what's in your pocket that counts. The pages of a bankbook are the only kind that Tony likes to turn. He could look at numbers all day long. Hey, are you going to buy me a drink and dinner or what?"

"I think I can afford dinner and maybe buy this restaurant."

"When we're finished, you could buy this town, Rob."

"Maybe I will," he stated deliriously.

"See? See? You're already drunk with power. Just buy me a drink and dinner, Mr. Big Shot. I told my kids I'd be back before eleven."

"Eleven? Won't they be asleep?"

"I promised I'd wake them up and give 'em a second good-night kiss."

"You know, I worry about you driving alone at night. I really do. You must have a million enemies."

"You must have millions on your mind. Get a guy a half a million dollars for openers, and he falls all over you. Better watch it, or I'll tell Tony about you," she needled.

"I'm serious."

"I know you are. And I appreciate that. And I'm going to work through all this crap. You're my winning ticket. Better than any witness protection program," she said half seriously. "You're going to earn that money, Rob. Believe me. Here comes our waitress, thank God."

"Are you ready this time, sweetheart?" the waitress asked Redler abruptly.

Redler smiled lamely as Barbara put out her hand.

"Hi." The happy housewife smiled brightly, taking hold of the waitress's hand. "I'm Barbara, and this fellow here feels he owes you an apology. Right, Rrrr-obert," she said, rolling the ars around the paralyzed yet pretty part of her mouth.

Robert extended a hand awkwardly, expressing an apology for his rudeness earlier.

"No big deal," the waitress said, shaking his hand briskly.

"Robert has a lot on his mind of late and left his manners back home along with his American Express Card," Barbara beckoned, lowering her voice and leaning closer to the woman. "Actually, they canceled him months ago. But since the time you tried to take our order, Robert's learned that he's come into a good deal of money," she whispered and nodded energetically.

"We accept all major credit cards, and I'll expect a big tip, preferably cash, in light of Robert's good fortune." The waitress winked at Barbara. "May I get you both a drink?"

"One Scotch sour, straight up," Barbara answered.

"Make that two."

"You're Barbara Giordano, aren't you?" the waitress inquired quietly.

"Yes, I am," Barbara answered straightaway.

"How are you doin'?" she asked with genuine concern.

"Doing just fine," Barbara said in all seriousness. "Thanks for asking."

"Say hello to Tony from all of us out here in Greenport, Mrs. G."

"I will," Barbara promised as the woman went to get their drink order.

Chapter
--->
23

It seemed as though everyone in the country believed they had seen Richard Geist. Many were kooks. Most of the others were well-intentioned people who wouldn't recognize their immediate family in a line-up, Captain Cally pessimistically considered as he and his people followed up lead after endless dead-end leads. Deputy Inspector Lancing and Police Chief Grear certainly would have agreed with that sentiment, too. A sweep through Queens neighborhoods, virtually door to door, went down the day David Black's office received a handwritten note from Richard, promising Acting D.A. Byrd's downfall within the week. The single sentence read:

Going to kill me a mocky-Byrd before the next full moon.
Richard Geist

A full moon was one week away. Solomon Byrd's picture was enclosed, clipped from *Newsday's* Queens Edition. Richard had no intention of killing the acting D.A.; he just wanted authorities to focus on the inner borough while he was busy setting Robert Redler up for the fall.

Richard Geist's sudden departure from his Riverhead apartment was not involuntary by any means. If he had learned anything in life, it was that timing is everything. Timing was the key to his plan. If the police wanted a scapegoat, they'd only have to haul in Robert Redler's butt, at least as an accomplice. The evidence, of course, was manufactured but nonetheless compelling. At the very least, it could put him away for years.

For the next several weeks, the authorities wouldn't recognize Richard Geist if they fell on him. And if they did fall on him—figuratively, that is—they would do nothing less than extend their apologies: 'Excuse me, ma'am,' they'd reply politely. And he, unable to resist the magic of the moment, would give them a flirtatious glance, perhaps sauntering away with a seductive stride or other solicitous sign to put them off guard. For he could be as handsome a woman as he was a man; consequently, he could turn heads as well as split them open at will. Richard was successful in his endeavors because he could be all things to all people. One secret to the killer's success might lie in his salient approach to a situation. Perhaps an alluring moan to lull his victim into a state of calm or, conversely, a compelling deep-throated cry so as to startle an adversary. Always gaining the upper hand. Richard worked with what he had, and what he had was a winning way.

Ironically, Richard Geist's Suffolk residence had been discovered toward the tail end of the Queens sweep. However, it wasn't police efficiency that netted them their prize. No, indeed. It was a phone call from an old woman who lived in the apartment above Richard's. The nonagenarian had been complaining of strange sounds emanating from the basement studio beneath.

"Thump! Thump! Thump!" she sounded to one of the two officers standing before her. "Like a fist striking something. Day. Night. Back and forth he goes. Thump! Thump! Thump!" she repeated.

"The thumping was maybe from the man's walking around?" the police officer questioned.

"Not from walking around," the old woman said with obvious irritation. "Maybe from a punch or a kick it sounded like."

"Did anyone cry out?" the second cop asked.

"Huh?"

"Did anyone cry out after this thumping sound?"

"How can anyone cry out if they're dead?" the woman declared with annoyance.

The older cop glanced at his partner. "You're saying someone's dead down there?"

The tenant considered the question carefully before she answered. "Has to be."

"Why?"

"He's been kicking her for months and months." The old woman nodded anxiously.

"But you didn't hear anyone scream or cry out. Nothing like that."

The woman looked from one face to the other as if in shock, then she began to cry.

"What's the matter?" one of the officers asked.

"I told you. How can that poor woman scream when she's been lying dead down there for God only knows how long?" the old woman wanted to know, stamping her foot upon the linoleum floor above the apartment in question. "How? Tell me that!" she demanded, shaking uncontrollably as the two officers led her to a couch and calmed her down, promising to investigate the matter immediately.

There was no dead woman lying in Richard Geist's rather large studio apartment. What there was, though, was an indoor/outdoor target for bow and arrow practice. What there was were many clippings from three mainstream newspapers, all relating to the murders of the three D.A.s as well as the murders of Arthur Field's family. What there was, throughout the room, were old photographs of Richard Geist, recent snapshots of Robert Redler, as well as a photograph of a woman with her arms around the writer. A handsome woman at that.

If the basement in Robert Redler's home, but a mile away from Richard's Geist's basement apartment, had at all resembled a hobby shop of sorts, Geist's studio resembled a small but well-equipped warehouse for bow and arrow accessories. Hundreds of unopened cellophane packages displayed from sheets of Peg-

Board hung everywhere one looked: bow squares, string silencers, arm guards, commando head nets, bow rests, fletching cement, knife sharpeners, folding saws, sheets of adhesive-backed moleskin material, bowstring wax, slings, self-adhesive arrow holders, deer calls, scents, illuminated sight pins, kisser buttons. But why would Richard Geist have left behind that kind of inventory? An unfinished letter from Richard to Robert explained it all.

When Police Chief Grear and others arrived, they noted that none of Geist's clothing was to be found. No footwear, gloves, hats, shirts, coats or pants. Neither was there any primary hunting equipment. No bows or arrows. Only those accessories, newspaper clippings and photographs. So very strange.

The apartment was leased under the name of Gary Fletcher. And when Grear and his team questioned the tenants about their reclusive neighbor, they all had the same things to say:

"Very quiet." "A nice fellow." "Kept to himself." "Never a peep out of him." "Quite polite; always a big smile."

"A musician," the old woman who had called and complained earlier told the chief, standing at her door.

"A musician?" Grear echoed.

"You deaf?" the woman snapped with blatant exasperation. "Musician," she repeated, raising her voice several decibels.

The police chief smiled. "You know, you sound just like my wife when she's angry."

"Huh?"

"I said, how do you know he's a musician?"

"Goes out of there with a harp case every now and then. That's why."

"A harp case." Grear nodded in understanding. "But of course."

"Never heard no music, though. Just that thump-thump-thumping sound," she demonstrated, stamping her foot at the doorway.

"Did you ever see him with anyone?" the cop inquired.

"What do you think I am, a big busybody? Huh?"

"Maybe a *little* busybody?" he questioned and grinned. "Huh?"

She laughed. "I never saw him with anyone. But I did see a woman come and go once or twice from there."

Grear showed her a photograph found in Geist's apartment. A picture of a man and a woman.

"This woman?"

"Why, yes," she said without hesitation.

"You're sure?"

The old woman looked at him with annoyance once again.

"Just double-checking," he said. "I've got one more question."

"Shoot."

"Did you ever see the man in the picture anywhere before?"

The old woman shook her head. "Nope. And, yes I'm sure."

"Good," Grear said and smiled satisfactorily.

"Well, I have a question," she shot back.

"Shoot."

"Would you like to step in for a cup of tea?" she asked invitingly.

Grear glanced at his watch and wrinkled his brow.

"I'll bet you'll have another question or two to ask me," she said convincingly.

"I probably will at that," he agreed with a wide grin, stepping into the apartment.

"You know, my brother-in-law was a cop," she began, closing the door behind them. "Absolutely hated him. When he'd come over on Thanksgiving Day . . . ." she went on and on.

Chapter
——>
24

Police Chief Grear, attired in civilian clothes, drove his wife's station wagon up the driveway and around to the rear of Robert Redler's and Liza's residence on Riverside Drive in Riverhead. Redler happened to be standing in the kitchen, rinsing dishes at the sink. Liza was drying. Grear parked, stepped out, and admired the view of the Peconic River, the writer's boat and private dock.

"Somebody's here," Robert told Liza, stepping into the vestibule then out the back door.

"Nice setup," Grear said, showing his credentials and explaining politely that he came by unofficially, asking Redler if he'd accompany him to headquarters voluntarily. Redler practically laughed in the cop's face, knowing from personal experience how the police work. He flat-out told the cop to either show him a warrant or take a hike.

"I'd like you to come in to headquarters and look at some pictures," Grear said, ignoring the comment. "Please."

They were the same words the police in Queens used to lure John Lightfoot to the precinct before his arrest.

"Please?" Redler smirked, recalling the sound advice of his attorney: 'Guilty or innocent, you do not talk to the police without your lawyer present—period,' was Gary Crane's sound pronouncement.

"Yes. Please," the police chief repeated. "We can do this thing cordially, or I could be back within the hour with warrants from three counties if you'd like. I could line this street with Queens, Nassau, and Suffolk County vehicles inclusive of the sheriff's office, state troopers, and the highway patrol if push comes to shove," the man threatened quite seriously. "Stewart Weisman's arrest on the Long Island Expressway by the feds would look like a boy scout outing compared to the motorcade I could arrange if that's the way you choose to go."

"Screw you," Redler said, wondering and worried, but refusing to yield an inch. "I'm going to call my lawyer."

As Redler turned away, Grear asked him if he would like to use his car phone, knowing that the writer had no telephone in his Riverhead home.

Redler faced about. "Why do you say that?"

It was a silly question, and Grear couldn't help but smile. "You'd crap in your pants if you knew what we had."

"What's that supposed to mean?"

"It means you're in deep shit. And I would suggest that you do call your lawyer. But I'd like to talk to you first. Unofficially, like I said."

"Yeah. I've heard that kind of crap before."

"I know you have, Rob."

Liza stepped out from the vestibule. "Hello, there," she interrupted.

Redler turned around abruptly. "He's a cop. You don't talk to him or anyone," he snapped. "Remember? You know what we've been through."

"Seems you're being very rude, Robert," Liza frowned.

"I want you back inside, now!"

"Do you know who he is?" she asked.

"A cop, I said."

"Not just any cop," she stated evenly.

"What the hell is going on here?" Redler demanded.

"One of the police officers right out of your first book is what's going on," Liza answered. "Standing right before you. Sergeant Grear, promoted to lieutenant then captain, and now Riverhead's chief of police. Lieutenant Lark's protégé."

"A few gray hairs and thirty pounds heavier," Grear confirmed and smiled.

"Jesus Christ," Redler remarked, stepping off the deck. "Is it really you?"

"In the flesh."

"Been seventeen—eighteen years," Redler recollected. "You granted me a telephone interview for the book."

"Right. We spoke but never met. I'm surprised Liza even knows me."

"From the papers of late," she explained. "The *News Review* ran that story last week."

"I see," Grear nodded courteously.

"See nothing," Redler said, returning to the moment. "This man's still a cop, Liza. Building a case for the D.A. Plain and simple. All right?"

"Let's look at reality, Mr. Redler. Three D.A.s and a Bridgehampton man's family are dead. The D.A. here would love to add a feather to his war bonnet before the next election. They'd like to do it quickly, too. From what we have, I'd say they'd have enough ammunition to put you away for a long, long time."

Liza came right up to Rob's side, tears welling in her eyes.

"Oh, that's beautiful. Go ahead. Upset the hell out of her." He took an angry step toward the cop.

"That's right, Mr. Redler. Get violent with me so I can hand you over for the slaughter. The prosecutors would just love that. Wouldn't they? You'd play right into everyone's hands. Including Richard Geist's."

"Go back into the house," Redler commanded Liza.

Liza shook her head. "No. I want you to listen to what he has to say."

"I said go back inside."

Liza stood firm.

"I don't believe this," Redler blew, glaring at the two of them.

Chief Grear spoke quietly. "I came here, as I'm saying for the third and final time, unofficially. In my wife's car. Dressed like this. Civvies. Not in uniform. Because I'm betting you're going to keep your cool through this whole business. I'm here waging that you'll cooperate with us. The others want Richard Geist and anyone else connected to him. They want blood. So I'm asking you again to come with me voluntarily. I read everything you wrote regarding Geist. I read everything concerning your battle with the criminal justice system. I know better than most what you've been through, and what you're trying to accomplish. I've been on a crusade myself. An eighteen-year crusade. I swore over Lieutenant Lark's grave that I'd find, or help find, Richard Geist. And I intend to do exactly that."

Liza took Rob's hand. "He's different than the others," she told him quietly.

"I want my lawyer present," he told Grear.

"You can have a battery of lawyers if you want. What I suggest is that you hear us out beforehand."

"Who's *us*?"

"You'll meet them shortly. We'll do the talking. You'll listen."

"Listen?"

"Just listen and look at some pictures. After that, you may call whomever you like."

"Why not beforehand?"

"Because if you agree with what we have to say, you may not want an attorney to know what we've discussed."

"I'm going to keep things from my attorney?"

"You may want to."

"And if not?"

"Then you won't."

"And if I tell him whatever it is you're going to tell me—"

"We'll probably deny it," Grear said with a straight face.

"But I'll have a witness," Robert said calmly, pressing Liza close to him.

The cop shook his head.

"You mean she can't come."

"She can't come."

"When is he going to be back?" Liza wanted to know, the tears running down her cheeks.

Grear shrugged his shoulders. "May not be coming home right away, Liza," he answered quite honestly.

Chapter
——>
25

Police Chief Grear, Deputy Inspector Lancing and Captain Cally sat across from Robert Redler in a back room at police headquarters in Riverhead. Cally was to have been in on a conference call but decided to drive out from Bayside, Queens. Redler appeared nervous and could do little to relax, especially when at a loss to explain who the woman with him in the photograph was, which Grear had shown him at the start of the meeting. The figure had both arms wrapped affectionately around the writer's neck, the two of them posing cheek to cheek.

"I can't speak for these two gentlemen," Grear said to Redler. "But I think you've been set up. I think Richard Geist wants us to believe you're an accomplice in all this. Partners in crime as it were. If we don't get him, and we haven't in all these years, we've got you. That's what I believe he wants."

"Why me?"

"I think we both know the answer to that."

"Vengeance for the unauthorized biography I wrote."

Grear nodded his agreement. "Geist's is an autobiographical account of the insanity he supposedly suffered. Your work is a skillfully crafted account of his soundness of mind, portraying him as one slick son of a bitch. Slick not sick. And while it's argued by defense attorneys in courtrooms throughout the country that someone who commits heinous acts such as Geist's has got to be crazy, prosecutors are arguing that an insanity defense, in most cases, is simply a sham to save one's own skin. You bring that dilemma into sharp focus. You paint Richard Geist in a very poor light."

"I want the state to wake up and pull the plug on the Richard Geists of this world. The Charlie Mansons. The Jeffrey Dahmers. That's why I wrote the book. Geist is a killing machine."

"But civilized society has a big problem with capital punishment. Doesn't it, Mr. Redler?"

"That it does."

"Yes, indeed."

"Still, a civilized society has a responsibility. A responsibility to rid itself of a disease that permeates and threatens its well-being," Redler stated firmly.

"I think the three of us sitting in this room agree with you there," Grear said.

"It's the liberals that are taking us down the tubes," Cally chimed in matter-of-factly.

Lancing sat in silence, his eyes penetrating Redler's.

"Anything to add here, Bill?" Grear asked.

"I don't like one goddamn thing he wrote in his editorials. He sounds like one of the liberals you're talking about," Lancing said, addressing Cally. "He defended Nicholas Maldonado in one of his articles. Felt that Maldonado didn't get a fair trial," he sneered, looking at Grear and Cally, then back to Redler.

"Maldonado *didn't* get a fair trial," Redler barked. "Nor did John Lightfoot, or Kallace, or Cotler or—"

"Whoa, now," Grear interrupted, declaring himself referee. "Let's focus here on Geist, not Maldonado or anyone else. I'm sure we all agree that Richard is, to use your own words, Mr. Redler, a 'killing machine.' A killing machine that must be stopped." Grear paused and looked around the table. "Well?"

Lancing and Cally, of course, agreed.

"Good. Now, let's propose how we can go about that. First off, I'd like to tell Mr. Redler what we have and where we'd like to go from here. All right?"

Robert Redler could not believe he was part of this discussion. There could only be but one reason, he reasoned. They'd use him. As sure as he was sitting there, they'd use him. But how? What did they have exactly? *Who was the woman in the picture they seemed so concerned about?* he wondered. Why couldn't he remember her? *What did Grear and his cronies have in mind?* he pondered. Would he be spending his five hundred thousand dollar advance on lawyers' fees? Should he be calling one right now? He tried to settle back. He could always say no if he wanted out. He'd hear them out and at least have some idea of what was going on. Maybe he should call Barbara Giordano instead of a lawyer. Maybe he'd be finishing his novel in a jail cell. Maybe he'd just go crazy altogether.

"You with us, Mr. Redler?" Grear asked.

Robert put his concerns in abeyance. "Yes."

"Well, as I indicated to you before, we can link you to Richard Geist."

"That's insane."

"He's left a trail that beats a path right to your doorstep on Riverside Drive."

"Is that a fact?"

"And you to his."

"You found his apartment?"

"What makes you think it's an apartment, Rob? May we call you Rob?" Grear asked.

Cally scribbled something down on a piece of paper.

"I'm just assuming. A person like that can't have permanent roots. What the hell is he writing?" Redler demanded, gesturing toward Cally.

"He's taking notes," Grear replied. "Note that you have a pad and pen in front of you also. So does Inspector Lancing. Feel free. I may think of something while Captain Cally is speaking, so I'll jot down a reminder. Any problem with that?"

"You said this meeting is off-the-record," Robert Redler reminded them. "I've been to one of these so-called off-the-record meetings before. I must be crazy sitting here. Anything I say 'can and will be used against me,' regardless of any promises. Any lawyer will tell you that. You'll twist what I say into what you want it to mean. And what doesn't fit, you'll shape to suit your fancy. You're building a case for the D.A. right now. I want to see what the captain wrote on that piece of paper before I say another word," he demanded angrily.

Captain Cally's face turned beet red with anger.

Police Chief Grear was afraid that Redler was going to explode at any moment and demand the presence of a lawyer.

"Why don't you just sit there and say nothing," the police chief said, taking and turning Captain Cally's pad around and pushing it across the table directly under Redler's nose, hoping the situation wouldn't escalate into something that would set the short-fused suspect off prematurely. He wanted Redler's fury directed toward Geist and no one else.

Redler looked down at the pad. "You see," he blasted, reading Cally's note aloud. *Knows it's an apartment.* What the hell is going on here?"

Realizing that he had nothing to lose at this point, Grear went for broke. "Now, listen, you little shit. I didn't ask you to open your mouth. You did that all by yourself. I told you that back at your house. You just listen. We'll do the talking. That photograph set your mouth to running. You started asking questions before I had a chance to give you any answers. So the format changed, Redler. You changed it. You engaged *us* in conversation. Richard has set you up big time, I'm afraid. He's left a Dear Rob letter behind. So naturally Captain Cally is going to pick up on your comments."

"No, you're trying to—"

"Shut up and listen to me, Redler. You're just digging a deeper hole. We found a letter in Richard's apartment breaking off your relationship. Understand what's going on here?"

"I never—"

"An apartment, Redler. Understand? And you expect Captain Cally to just sit there twiddling his thumbs when you implicate yourself like that?"

Redler sat in silence.

"Now, do you want to hear how bad this thing really gets and how we may be able to save your butt? Or would you like to call your lawyer now? Your call."

Redler's mind was racing along a footpath with a fork at the far end of it. When he reached that juncture, his thoughts marked time. Finally, he spoke. "I want to hear what my lawyer has to say. You guys lay out what you have in front of us. I'll take what he says under advisement. I'll listen to your game plan, weigh both sides, *then* make a decision."

Cally laughed. "He thinks this is *Let's Make a Deal*."

"What's so unreasonable about that?" Redler wanted to know.

Grear was losing ground. Not patience. "Look, I'll level with you. You listen to your lawyer, I may lose you. We want Geist so bad, Rob, that we're prepared to do some very unorthodox things to get him. But we're going to need your help to pull it off. The politicians are going to demand a warm body. Yours if need be. A half a loaf is better than none, they'll feel. We can help you. Your lawyer is going to get paid whether he saves your ass or not. We're not talking alleged molestation here."

"Give it to me straight."

"As straight as an arrow, Rob. First-degree murder," Police Chief Grear set forth.

"Accessory before and after the fact," Captain Cally added somberly.

Deputy Inspector Lancing nodded his head, not saying a word.

"Take out your keys a minute, Rob," Grear said. "Go on."

Robert Redler numbly took a ring of keys out of his pocket and started to hand them across the table.

"Just tell us what each key is for."

Redler went through the set one by one. "Truck. Riverhead home, which also opens the side door to the garage. This one is for the front door to the garage; different key." He paused with the fourth key. "Oh, the key to the cap on the truck. Crook Lock." He forced a silly, nervous smile. "You know, The Club, which you boys endorse." Robert stared at the remaining sixth key, turning it over between his fingers.

"And that last key?"

"I'm not sure."

"Key to your gun cabinet, perhaps?"

Robert looked up in surprise. "No. It's in the gun cabinet. I don't lock it."

"Maybe your Fresh Meadows residence or your Camry?"

"No. Those keys aren't on this ring. I keep them on a separate leather key holder."

"I see. So you can't account for that last key."

Robert Redler shook his head. "It's got to be for something," he offered inanely.

"Oh, it definitely is," Grear assured him, taking a small clear plastic evidence envelope with a key suspended in the middle of it from his shirt pocket. "Mind taking the mystery key off your ring for a moment?"

Redler removed the brass key, handing it to Grear.

Again, Grear declined, handing Redler the transparent envelope with the single silver key.

"Without taking this key out of the plastic, I want you to put those two together and tell me what you see," the police chief instructed.

Redler took the tiny envelope, lining up the teeth of the two keys side by side.

"Well, what do you think?" Captain Grear asked.

"They appear to be duplicates."

"Indeed they certainly do—and *are*. And where do you think we found that key?"

Redler was afraid to ask.

"On the bureau in Richard Geist's apartment is where we found it," Grear said, taking back the sealed silver key.

Robert Redler wanted to close and lock the door to a nightmare and stand under a canopy of light forever, but a dark cloud of suspicion covered him completely. "Look. This is all nonsense. I was never in, nor do I have the foggiest notion where his apartment might be."

"Right here in Riverhead," Grear stated. "Not but a mile or so from your home. Right across the river."

"Well, I'm sure you checked that key for fingerprints. And mine aren't going to be on it."

"They don't have to be. This silver key is not your key. It's

Richard's key. That brass key you're holding fits the front door to Richard's apartment. Now put your keys away."

"This here is not my key," Redler insisted, slamming the golden mystery key upon the table.

Not that you'll be needing any of them, Lancing wanted to say, but didn't.

"Are you beginning to see the seriousness of this situation, Rob?"

"What else did Richard do to me?" he asked, looking into their faces.

"You mean besides labeling you his homosexual lover and accomplice? Lots more, Rob. Lots more, I'm afraid."

Redler didn't know whether to laugh or cry or live or die right there.

"You want to make that phone call now? Or do you want to hear the rest of it?"

"I want to hear the rest of it, and I want you to tell me what you have in mind to bring that sick, perverted son of a bitch down once and for all. You've got my attention, and you've got my full cooperation."

Captain Grear came around the conference table and tapped the tops of Robert Redler's shoulders. "That's good, Rob," he said, staring directly across at Lancing and Cally. "That's very good. We'll go through all the evidence first. You don't have to say anything. After that, I'll tell you our game plan. Not everything. Just what you'll need to know. Then you can make your decision as to whether you want to work with us or spend your money on attorneys."

Redler studied the trio. "I'd like to ask you a question before we go any further." He hesitated. "You introduced me to Deputy Inspector Lancing who you said earlier is heading up this investigation for Suffolk County, as you obviously are here in Riverhead. And Captain Cally is from Queens. How come there's no one here from Nassau? How come Howe's people aren't represented here?"

Police Chief Grear looked at the two cops. "Good question, Rob. Quite astute, in fact. However, let's just say that it is not in our best interest to be dealing directly with Nassau at this time.

You'll understand things better if and when you agree to cooperate; that is, after we go through everything. All right?" He didn't wait for a reply. "Would you like to order in anything before we get started? I can have Mary call in for Chinese."

Redler got the idea that it was going to be a long night.

"Oh, one more thing, Rob. The woman in the picture?"

Redler looked up.

"It's Richard Geist."

Robert Redler looked nonplused. "How do you know?"

"Image processing. Computers. Fascinating technology."

"*Richard* has his arms around *me*?"

"She, Rob. She has her arms around you."

"Jesus fucking Christ."

"We're working on the background in the photograph. Blowing it up for a clue to location. I'll let you know when it's ready. Maybe you'll remember something."

Redler nodded nervously.

Several hours later, Redler was taken into protective custody at an undisclosed facility. Precedents were being set, and politicians were demanding answers. When none were forthcoming, people in Howe's office in Nassau were demanding the immediate resignations of several of Suffolk County's law enforcement figures, citing a conspiracy and a cover-up. Suffolk authorities took Nassau authorities to task.

By nightfall, TV networks and newspaper reporters were literally camped outside the homes of Robert Redler, both in Bayside, Queens and Riverhead. By morning, staff writers and politicians converged at the Riverhead police station as well as the Suffolk County Courthouse.

"No comment," were the two words echoed by high-ranking Suffolk County officials who were accosted whenever they entered or exited the sanctity of their office buildings or homes.

Twenty-four hours later, campers and vans and camera crews crowded the lawns and driveways and sidewalks of anyone connected with the case. Cub reporters were busy on boulevards and in bars, virtually begging veteran journalists and officials for a lead. Leaks were not forthcoming, so rumors ran like cascading water in their stead. Captain Cally of the 111th Precinct in Bayside Queens had miraculously gone unscathed.

It was as though those invested with power in Suffolk held an impoverished nation at bay. *Newsday's* Brain Cooper *demanded* that Suffolk authorities tell their tale. And one of Suffolk's most prominent judges practically told Cooper to go to hell. The story of the decade was brewing, but practically no one had a clue. It was as though someone had clipped the tongues from the mouths of washerwomen who'd otherwise hang anyone's and everyone's dirty laundry out to air. But with no one to explain the rub, newspapers as well as the networks were left in the lurch to circulate innuendo, speculation, and such. The stage was a chaotic circus of empty rings, zoo-like rather than rich and refined. The information hounds were drying up like shriveling corpses. An amazing thing was taking place in a small corner of America. The integrity of several well-intentioned public servants and good Samaritans seemed intact.

Barbara Giordano was going mad trying to locate Robert Redler. She really didn't care that he was being held as much as the fact that he was being held incommunicado. That worried her considerably. Redler was her insurance policy, and a healthy premium had been arranged and paid for by her benefactors. But all their influence proved negligible outside of Nassau County. So at least they knew where he wasn't. He wasn't in—or at least hadn't been processed in Nassau. And although her associates' tentacles reached far into the dark corners of other boroughs, no one seemed to know anything whatsoever about Robert Francis Redler's whereabouts.

Thank God she had picked the perfect patsy just in case he was foolish enough to talk to the wrong people and make some sort of deal with authorities outside her realm of control, she ruminated.

The unassuming housewife managed to keep a low profile while her people blatantly blasted and charged that the clandestine tactics of Suffolk officials were tantamount to the actions of the KGB.

Chapter
——>
26

Robert Redler sat caddy-corner to Deputy Inspector Lancing and Police Chief Grear, the three seated at the large mahogany desk in Doctor Bianco's office. It was their second meeting that week. The psychiatrist was busy in the outer office dictating a letter to his secretary.

"Liza's been told you're in a maximum security facility," Grear began. "I told her you're all right and that she can come to visit you at the end of the week."

"Visit me where? Here?"

"Upstate," the police chief said.

"Upstate where?" Grear and Lancing held Redler's stare. "You're not *actually* sending me upstate," Redler gasped incredulously.

"Yes, we are," Lancing stated.

"Have to," Grear agreed.

Redler looked positively perplexed.

"It'll just be for several days," Lancing assured him. "There's nothing to worry about. You'll be in protective custody."

"Several days?"

"Maybe a week," Grear hedged.

"And how is Liza going to get there? She doesn't drive."

"Everything's been arranged. Not to worry."

"How far upstate does she have to travel? Where is this place?"

Grear looked at Lancing.

"Malone Correctional Facility," Lancing said.

"What? That's up by the Canadian border," Redler realized, raising his eyebrows along with his voice. "In a maximum security *prison*? It's where they had John Lightfoot before they transferred him to Clinton State Prison in Dannemora!"

"I'm sorry," Grear offered apologetically. "You'll be doing something constructive to help draw Geist out for us, Rob. Not just spinning your wheels writing editorials about a faulty criminal justice system, which have gotten you nowhere fast."

"You're talking about an overnight trip for Liza. I don't want her in some motel—"

"We're flying her up. She'll be back home the same day."

"Why does she even have to go at all?"

"We have to break a story."

"A story?"

"We can write fiction, too," the deputy inspector interjected.

"I don't know," Redler pondered, staring blankly at a wall.

Lancing wanted to tell Redler that he didn't have a choice in the matter, that what he wanted or didn't want was of little consequence. But the inspector refrained. What Suffolk authorities expected was Redler's full cooperation. Nothing less.

"As Grear explained, this is a temporary move," Lancing continued. "A one-shot deal. We want the media to believe you're in Malone indefinitely. But as the police chief said, you'll be back here before you know it."

"A one shot-deal," echoed Redler. "I've been dealing with you guys for two days now, cooped up in this booby hatch. And now you tell me I'm trading in polka-dot pajamas for orange prison garb."

Grear held back a grin. "Well, as far as this booby hatch goes, you can't say that Doctor Bianco hasn't extended every courtesy to make your stay here comfortable."

"Comfortable? My stay has been highlighted by patients literally climbing the walls at night, urinating in their pants during the day, or losing their marbles at any given moment. And now you want me to take a trip to Malone."

"Sounds like great material for another book," Lancing suggested with a smirk.

"We'll have you back here and in pajamas in no time," Grear

assured their reluctant prisoner.

"How long will I really be there? No bullshit."

Grear and Lancing exchanged glances again.

"I see," Redler said. "As long as it takes."

"Two weeks, max," Lancing swore. "Then you're coming back here to help us draw Geist out of the woodwork."

"And when you get back here, you can tell Liza what the deal is. That's a promise," the police chief pledged.

"And you'll allow her to visit me here?"

"As often as we can."

"And the media are going to believe I'm still up in Malone."

"Correct."

"But somehow Richard Geist is going to learn I'm back here," Redler said intuitively. "I'm the bait. Right?"

Grear deferred to Lancing.

Lancing looked up at the ceiling.

"Yes," the chief affirmed.

"How are you going to manage that?"

"We're working on it," Grear responded cryptically.

"Don't let it concern you," Lancing declared. "We'll have our men near you every minute."

"Thanks again, guys. You really assuaged my worries and fears," Redler said sarcastically. "I just don't like you involving Liza. I understand this whole thing has to look real and all, but I feel like crap putting her through this charade. I know she's worried sick about me. Probably thinks I'm in a world of trouble."

"You are, Mr. Redler," Lancing assured him. "We're just helping you find a way out."

"You know goddamn well that I'm innocent, so don't give me any—"

"All right," Grear broke in. "Enough of this. We've all got to work together. Doctor Bianco has some advice for you before you leave. So I think we ought to give this a rest. Anything else before we go?"

"Yeah. Tell me how you're going to explain away no arrest, no arraignment, no lawyer, and no bail when they see me sitting upstate in a maximum security prison. How are you going to sell them short regarding due process? How are you supposed—"

"Whoa!" Grear enjoined. "Let us worry about all that. Okay? You have no idea of the latitude we've been given. Three D.A.s are dead and a prominent family from Bridgehampton was all but wiped out by this lunatic. The public and the press believe we have Geist's accomplice. You. We're not worried about John Q. Public gunning for you. Our own people want you. Law enforcement at large. They've got the manpower, and they've got the motive to take you down. We can't risk that, Rob. You are one of the best kept secrets of the decade. Probably the century. You're going to help draw Geist out for us. *Us* is a handful who are holding back the long arm of the law just long enough to lure this madman into the light."

"*Us* must be pretty powerful, Chief."

Grear nodded. "We have seized the power, Rob. And we have perverted the law. There will be a price to pay at the end. But hopefully, we will put an end to this evildoer who, in your own words, is a killing machine."

"And it will all be worth it?"

"It will all be worth it."

"Well, it's late," Lancing said, glancing at his watch.

Grear nodded. "That's about it for now, Rob. And don't worry yourself about Liza. I'm handling everything tactfully. Promise. I've made sure that she knows but doesn't know, if you know what I mean," he made clandestinely clear through a sincere bright smile, putting Robert's mind somewhat at ease.

Robert nodded his thanks, gradually gaining a new respect for this Riverhead police chief. Liza was right; Grear was somehow different from the rest. How perceptive she was. How remarkably insightful. "Good night, gentlemen," Redler offered quietly.

"Good night," the two law enforcement officials replied.

Doctor Bianco was called in from the outer office.

Chapter
——>
27

Richard Geist was playing it cool. A testament to his fortitude. With Bible in hand, he took to his sanctuary of silence, laying low atop a summit for the time being, a broad grin engraved across his handsome face. He peered down the steep embankment from where he had paddled earlier a winding waterway, from headwater to estuary . . . hiding out, too, like his nemesis, Robert Redler. Geist turned off his Walkman and removed the headset.

No news is good news, he mused, making his way along the garden path to the fortress on the hill. In short order, he settled in for the night. *Peace be with you my brothers and sisters*, he giggled to himself. Still smiling, he fell into a deep, sound sleep on a thin bare mattress in a corner of a dark, dank room. Bible for a pillow.

The next morning, Richard awoke early within the cloistered confines of the claustrophobic space. Exercise was immediately under way. Fifteen minutes of in-place jogging to get the blood flowing. One hundred sit-ups to limber up. One hundred push-ups to get those muscles moving. Twenty-five one-arm push-ups with his left hand. Twenty-five more with his right. Next, he performed a number of controlled, deep breathing exercises, followed by a series of katas. And then it was as though someone had fast forwarded the action. Richard flew about the 5 x 11 foot area with deft precision, alternating between powerful kicks and punches. The balls and heels of his feet narrowly cleared the rough-hewn walls. The knuckles of spiraling fists marginally missed the gray-white granite blocks. Forty-five minutes later, he was finished exercising for the day.

Fine-tuned to perfection, Richard grinned satisfactorily in a dripping sweat.

He firmly believed that weightlifting as well as excessive exertion on the body—say to the tune of three full sets of ten repetitions, pushing two-hundred-plus pound bench-presses, five hundred push-ups and sit-ups daily—only slowed one's reflexes over time. Richard went on to prove the point on more than one occasion, competing—sometimes tangling—with scores of no-neck gorillas in their pretentious gymnasiums of worship as well as the more serious establishments of little notoriety. He fondly recalled a late evening many years ago when a muscular six-foot-four Mr. America type actually had the audacity to laugh in his face after witnessing a rather enthusiastic workout, mimicking then mentioning something about 'that mute's moronic drill.'

Richard ignored him, showered, then waited for the man by the doorway, handing the loudmouth a telling note stating that he was going to *drill* and *kill* him within the next five minutes, smiling and consulting his watch before snatching back the note from the dumbfounded bodybuilder. Richard turned and left the building. Seconds later, the muscle-bound he-man came bounding down the steps of the Ironsides Health and Athletic Club in downtown Newark with no less than murder on his mind.

To Geist's surprise, the giant took a good six minutes to succumb. In spite of Richard's brutal blows, his opponent had the stamina to fight on. But lack of speed led to the powerful man's demise. Richard finally finished him off on the ground with a series of lightning-fast, hammer-like chops to the throat before delivering the fatal slam with the heel of his hand, driving home the bone of the man's nose back into his brain. Deliverance from a protracted death was to be this supine superman's salvation as Richard disappeared into the darkness among his followers who had witnessed the onslaught from a distance.

As their cult leader, both fear and sheer respect were Richard's means of control over his fold.

Chapter
——>
28

Time for a shower, shave and a sermon, Richard decided, leaving the chamber to clean up and change his clothing before taking center stage. Time to change the tide of America. Time to reshape a malleable government, he yawned and stretched.

An hour later, Richard appeared before his elite corps. Silence heralded the paradoxical moment in lieu of either seated or standing applause; yet, one had the sense that his audience could feel and even peel the presence of palpable energy off the very walls. The entire amphitheater was filled with bright flowers and fervent followers sitting perfectly erect in rows of folding chairs, each worshipper energetically sending a single cupped palm rhythmically back and forth across his or her body: the sound of one hand clapping.

A large video screen stood above a young woman monitoring a projector as Richard signed, the words enlarged approximately half a foot high for the benefit of many new recruits. One to several sentences were displayed at a time.

"Friends. My Inner Circle, thereof."

The next silent and surrealistic sweep of adoration lasted a full three minutes before he could continue.

"We are on the verge of victory," Richard Geist continued. *"And victory will be ours before anyone will even realize total war was ever*

waged." Young men and women went wild in what could only be deemed a deafening calm. "*But no victory is near complete without the telltale sign of bodies in the street. No **bloody** victory, that is!*"

The multitude was on its feet, clipped tongues holding steadfastly in their brainwashed heads.

"*Three D.A.s are dead in Suffolk, Nassau, and Queens,*" he declared.

The nodding of shaven heads released a furor of jubilation, not heard but seen vividly in pairs of focused eyes.

"*I, one mortal being, have diminished their sacred security in three counties!*" Hundreds of hands reached out toward Richard from their seats. Richard shook his head with practiced modesty. "*I am but one soul and servant. You are many!*"

Chanting rose among ranks.

Ohmmmm. Ohmmmm. Ohmmmm."

"*You are stealth personified.*"

"Ohmmmm."

"*You are swift.*"

"Ohmmmm."

"*You are strong.*"

"Ohmmmm."

"*You are, indeed, brave soldiers, all.*"

You could have heard a hair fall out of place had there been but one, apart from Geist's flaming red crop paired to the dark coiffure combed straight back into a chignon of severity of his female first lieutenant, now standing at his side.

"*You are the deadliest of deadly soldiers,*" Richard signed and swore, signaling for the exercise to begin.

And with that announcement, chairs were folded, cleared and set along the walls before each warrior went into a series of katas choreographed to deliver destruction, magnified by the susurration of muffled blows amplified by the percussion of stark-white gies slapping off sound bodies.

Several minutes later, everyone suddenly stopped then faced forward. Pairs of thumbs and forefingers came together to form hundreds of sacred symbols.

"*You are the army of destruction, and Armageddon is close*

at hand," Richard revealed, holding the Bible high above his head.

On command, each soldier assumed the position, stepped immediately forward while slashing an invisible column of air, arched his or her body backward to the point where one would believe their spines would surely crack, then somersaulted forward before returning their eyes to center stage.

"*Each of you has a name and a face of an enemy fixed firmly in your mind. I will relish reading that name in the obituaries during the coming weeks and months. In time, that name and face may fade from memory while your deed and devotion will live on forever in our hearts. A new enemy shall shrink in fear before you. You will bow before no man as we, together, shall unleash a wrath that shall ring thrice around the world,*" Richard concluded. "*Peace be with my brothers and sisters.*"

Richard's lieutenant dismissed the faithful lot.

A February snow fell silently as Richard Geist's followers filed out of the auditorium. Flakes as large and white as feathery down smothered the earth while his worshippers went to prepare. From a window, their leader watched the whiteness eerily etch the tops of the tall reed marsh across the bay.

Chapter
——>
29

There were only three officials in Geist's inner circle allowed to retain their tongue. One was Angelica, his top lieutenant. First and foremost. The other two were trusted translators. Angelica was anything but an angel. Her given name and looks put anyone, good or evil, off guard. Not only was she allowed to keep her tongue, but her head of hair as well. Long and lovely coal-black hair fell past a pair of slim shoulders as she removed her combs.

"You were stupendous out there," she whispered, trailing a luscious tongue from Richard's scrotum to the tip of his penis, her eyes glued to his. "You were positively demonic," she said seductively, taking his member to the back of her throat and withdrawing it immediately. "You had them by the short hairs," she sizzled and sighed, slipping a thin, moist middle finger between his buttocks while swallowing him whole again, pushing him down upon a bare mattress, forcefully fingering his anus. "You were omnipotent," she said with a winning smile, withdrawing her finger then removing a lacy black bra and matching panties.

Her tight, entirely well-tanned body absolutely thrilled him as she rose and stood at the head of a platform bed, wearing nothing but a pair of black spiked heels. Leaning forward, she pressed herself solidly against a cold stone wall. "Fuck my ass for the best mass you ever delivered, preacher."

Richard got up and opened the drawer to a nightstand, removing a small jar of salve and a flat tin, liberally applying the ointment to his penis before working in a coarse sand-like substance from the other container. Stepping behind her, he slowly pushed the head of his penis past the sumptuous cheeks of her shapely bottom. She gasped. He thrust his tool deep within. Angelica moaned and writhed in a mixture of both pain and pleasure. A warm and steady pounding drove her flat against the cold stone blocks. Tossing her head from side to side, she cooed and cried. "Harder," she commanded, groaned, and moaned.

Richard brayed, pressing her pelvis squarely to the stone, slamming into her repeatedly. Violently.

"Yes!" she shouted. "I want cock-around-the-clock. I want your balls bouncing off the cheeks of my ass, my clit, and my chinny-chin-chin. Oh, yes! Fuck me faster," she screamed until he finally exploded.

When Richard withdrew, a thin red line trickled down her inner thigh past an indelible design, its segmented tail appearing as if hooked into her very flesh and the source from which drops of blood traced a long and shapely leg into a single patent leather spike.

Angelica went over to the bed and rolled her slim, trim figure athletically across the mattress. Kneeling up, she seductively brushed small but well-proportioned breasts back and forth along a single pillow. "Get Lether in here," she ordered, opening and closing her legs in a series of sensuous poses. "Get him in here, now."

Richard grinned and moved toward the door. "*His reward?*" he signed.

"Alas, he shall soon discover that no heaven could be more splendid than this heaven right here," she crooned, massaging her vagina unabashedly. "And here," she directed, plunging a middle finger in and out of her sensuous mouth. "Heaven's right here on earth, preacher," she swore and salivated.

We'll see, Richard thought, opening the door. *We'll see*.

Three thunderous claps brought the tall black man immediately into the room. Lether glanced from Richard to

Angelica then back again to Richard.

"*It's all right for you to look at her, Lether*," he danced his fingers communicatively. "*It's all right for you to covet lovely things.*"

The black man did not avert Richard's eyes.

"*I said, it is all right,*" Richard said through sign. "*Angelica wants you to look at her, Lether. Angelica wants you to do more than look. She wants you to get crackin'*," he assured the man. "*She wants you to become Johnny-on-the-spot.*"

Lether trailed his eyes from Richard to Angelica.

Angelica was already at the foot of the platform bed, summoning her servant with a forefinger. "Come over here, Leth. I don't want to have to say it again. In fact," she said coyly, "I don't want to have to say anything at all with my mouth full." Angelica reached for the drawstring to Lether's sweats, undoing the double knot, pulling the garment down, grabbing the black man's genitals, massaging him gently, squeezing and kneading his prodigious penis. "Take these off," she ordered. "Along with your top."

Lether obeyed, and Richard pulled up a single chair for the show. Angelica took the man's penis in two fists and put it into her hungry mouth, circling the erection with a teasing tongue. "Is this how they measure horses?" Angelica purred in question. "How many hands high?" she inquired demurely, pressing the stiff rod up against the servant's washboard-like abdomen.

"*Three hands high,*" Richard signed and snorted like a steed.

"Why, it's practically four inches beyond his bellybutton," she announced, whinnying like a mare before taking him fully into her mouth again. Pulling him down on top of her face and swallowing him whole, she gagged and writhed and moaned and would not let go, even when he picked up the pace and drove himself to what he thought was the very depths of hell's fire.

Angelica threw her legs wildly about, erect breasts heaving and falling with each and every thrust of mutual lust. And just when Lether realized he might choke her to death with his turgid member pounding away at the back of her throat, she suddenly sank her nails firmly into the soft flesh of his buttocks and held him mightily, sending him even deeper till she thought she'd surely die of asphyxiation or simply drown in his river of semen that seemingly flowed forever.

And when the act was over, it proved merely a prelude to an insatiable appetite Angelica swore would starve her if he didn't immediately mount her missionary style and have her for a month of Sundays. A quarter of an hour later, she lay kissing and biting Lether passionately.

Richard stood.

"Leave the room, now, Lether. I want to be alone with Richard," Angelica finally said.

Lether quickly gathered his clothes, dressed immediately, then left in a confused but all-fired hurry, closing the door behind him.

"If that animal had but a single thought in his head," she confided in Richard, "I'd have him lick me for a season."

"*If he had a brain just a fraction of the mass of his dick, he'd be a marvel,*" Richard signed.

Angelica laughed. "Do I detect a hint of jealousy; perhaps a pinch of prejudice?" she needled.

"*The real animal in* me *is unleashed on the battlefield, not necessarily in the bedroom,*" Richard said defensively.

"I don't know, Richard," she went on. "I still think I sense a bit of petty jealousy."

"*If I were truly jealous, even envious, let alone prejudiced, I would do something about it.*"

"Such as?"

"*Eliminate any and all competition,*" he declared quite seriously.

"But not this Robert Redler?"

Richard's grin disappeared as suddenly as if Angelica had flicked a switch.

"Oh, I see I hit a nerve," she goaded.

"*You think you know all about him?*"

"I read his book, which you keep under your mattress."

"*That's supposed to tell you about me; not him.*"

"I read between the lines," she explained. "Still, he paints you as some kind of monster. Brilliant but not crazy."

"*But I am.*"

"Crazy but in control, I'd say."

"*You would?*"

"Indeed, I would," she asserted, getting up from the bed and draping a terry robe over a pair of splendid slender shoulders. "You know something, Richard? Lether now has two masters to serve," she teased.

"*I'd make the careful distinction between serving and servicing if I were you.*"

Angelica laughed. "I think Lether should take Redler out."

"*You do?*"

"Yes, I do."

"*We don't even know where he is. But when we do, Robert Redler is all mine.*"

"Why?"

"*Unsanctioned biography,*" he answered with a grin.

"Cute," she said, heading toward the bathroom. "But I feel it's a mistake."

What Angelica *thought* was of little consequence to Richard; however, what she *felt*, was of some concern. Her feelings were uncanny. He followed her into the shower, turning her around to face him.

"*What do you mean a mistake?*" he signed.

"You will find out where Redler is because those who have him will want you to."

"*And?*"

"It will be a trap."

"*You think so?*"

She nodded. "I'd strike the home front— striking first and hard."

"*Like this?*" he said, roughly massaging her breasts before biting down hard upon each erect nipple.

Angelica put her head back, washing and massaging his raw, gritty penis with both hands. "That was wild," she sounded. "My ass is still on fire."

"*When I was five, I watched my mother take on seven men at the same time,*" Richard recounted. His mind was a million miles away.

Angelica's eyes were closed as streams of water hit her lovely face. He didn't care if she was paying attention or not to his demoralizing tale, for he knew she knew the story all too well. It was in his book and in Redler's, too. *Redler, Redler, Redler,* he thought. He could have killed him easily half a dozen times before. In the basement of Redler's own home. Upstairs while the writer lay sleeping. Off Robin's Island when he and Liza were anchored near the beach. On the dock when 'Captain Rob' was putting new canvas on his boat. Or on that sunny afternoon at Arthur Field's lawn party when Angelica had photographed them together. He, dressed to kill in a wig and sequined gown, looking gorgeous, coming up behind Redler for the pose. Dressed to kill but holding out for a more propitious moment. Yes. Robert would surely sweat bullets before he finally killed him, Richard promised himself. All in good time. But not before his highly-trained corps of killers advanced his precious cause.

"How many men have you had at one time?" Richard suddenly wanted to know, wiping the soap from her eyes, having to repeat the sign.

"Five, I think," she sputtered, pushing out the words past the heavy wall of water. "Not counting the custodian."

"Custodian?"

"Yes, the custodian."

"When and where did all this take place?"

"Gymnasium. In high school."

"What happened?"

"One of the seniors on the basketball team lured me into the locker room on a Saturday night after a big game."

"And?"

"And five of them gangbanged me. Or so they thought," she clarified and giggled.

"How did the custodian fit in?"

"War wound, so he didn't," she kidded, soaping Richard's member. "He was old and scared and pawed me while the others did their thing. He was the one who let them back into the building, cleaned and locked up after us."

"How old were you?"

"Freshman. Fifteen, I guess."

"I guess you were very popular."

"Very much like your mother, Richie, dear."

"Very much like her, indeed."

"Maybe that's why we connect."

"You know I killed her."

"I do, indeed."

"Aren't you afraid that I might kill you one day?"

"Not if I kill you first," she said succinctly behind a smile. It was a heavenly smile that could have melted tempered steel. But behind those sea-green eyes was a cold and calculated fix that could freeze hell completely over and forever.

Chapter
——>
30

Having returned from Malone Correctional Facility in upstate New York, Robert Redler was standing and holding a hot cup of coffee, waiting for Doctor Bianco in the psychiatrist's outer office. It was 5:00 a.m. A minute later, Bianco appeared, inviting the returnee inside the well-appointed space, asking him to take a seat.

"So. How was Malone?" the director asked as though a friend of his had just come off a Caribbean cruise.

Redler sat and stared around the room uneasily before answering. "On a score of one to ten, and considering that I spent yet another day on Rikers Island, I'd say Malone was a minus eight. Of course, I haven't made a tour of the other hot vacation spots in this great state. The plumbing was remarkably better than Rikers, heating adequate, but I wouldn't go back for the cuisine. Perhaps it was the off-season. I'm not really sure. But let me tell you about the game playing. Mind games you wouldn't believe. Playing for keeps as when one guard clubbed a black man repeatedly on the gourd for sassing him because he spoke out of turn. 'Coconut head,' the corrections officer *corrected* his handcuffed prisoner after each and every blow. And people wonder why they've practically got a revolution on their hands in this country and why people like Farrakhan have a fucking following. Little things like that. Should I go on, Doc?"

Police Chief Grear and Deputy Inspector Lancing walked into the main office and took a seat on either side of Redler.

"Aren't people getting just a little suspicious," Redler asked with a good degree of bitterness, addressing his question to the pair.

"About what?"

"About your visits here. I'm sure the media have *you guys* under surveillance."

"It's only natural that we're here."

"Natural?"

"Sure. Richard Geist spent the better part of a year here before being transferred to Havenwood. It's only natural that we'd be talking to Doctor Bianco about a former patient and murderer at large."

"Part of an ongoing investigation," Lancing added.

"And we're not here every day," Grear added.

"Only a few of us know you're here," Doctor Bianco assured his charge.

"And I suppose none of the staff knows who I am. None of the doctors or nurses or orderlies. And I guess no one reads the papers in which my picture is probably plastered across the page like Geist's. And an alert visitor walking by couldn't possibly make the connection and report that information to the press."

Grear looked from Lancing and Bianco. "Drink your coffee, Rob." The cop pulled his chair closer to Redler's. "Want to know a secret?"

Robert Redler sipped his coffee. "I want to know a lot of things."

"Well, we'll start with this. Outside of Doctor Bianco, here, the other doctors and nurses and orderlies you see in this wing are actually police personnel protecting you around the clock. The patients are real enough but haven't the mind to put two and two together. Newspapers and magazines carrying your picture are nonexistent on this floor. And as for visitors, the only one you'll see is Liza, who's scheduled to be here after midnight tonight when the rest of the media world is either sleeping on the job or busy following bogus leads.

"Magazines, too?" Redler frowned, shaking his head in disgust and staring at the ceiling.

"I thought you'd be thrilled about Liza coming tonight," Lancing snapped. "We went through a great deal of trouble."

"You *caused* a great deal of trouble," Redler retorted.

"Screw you," the inspector scowled.

"Listen. I am thrilled," Redler said. "I just get torn up inside when I think about what I'm putting her through."

"If it's any consolation, the worst is over for her," Grear offered.

Redler nodded. "I can't wait until it's *all* over. It's been a goddamn nightmare."

"Well?" Lancing asked impatiently, getting down to business. "Can we lay this thing out now?"

Chapter
——>
31

At a Nassau County cemetery that same morning, another meeting was about to begin between Barbara Giordano and one of Frank Demeco's intermediaries, for it was too risky for the housewife to be seen with the senator himself. The two faced one another as they sat in their respective vehicles with the engines running. Driver-side windows were sent down simultaneously.

"Well?" Barbara was the first to speak.

The man just shook his head.

"Another fucking week and no one knows shit. What the hell is going on, Michael?"

"We don't know."

"It's your business to know. You know when the governor takes a dump for Christ's sake."

Michael took his eyes off her angry face.

"Who the fuck do they think they are? What about the law?"

"They're bending it, Barbara."

"They're goddamn well breaking it, you mean. What the hell is Russo doing up there besides sitting on his ass?"

"His hands are tied."

"Don't give me his hands are tied crap. They're clamped down between his butt and a toilet seat. He's sitting on them, Michael. And I want Frank to either give him a good kick in the ass or flush him like the Tidy Bowl Man. I want pressure applied to lethal points this time. I want access to Mr. Robert F. Redler in Malone. I don't want to hear this no visitors bullshit."

"Redler is not in Malone, Barbara."

"What?"

"He was in Malone, but they moved him. We don't know where."

"I don't believe this shit! First you tell me he surrendered to Suffolk police. Then he disappears into thin air. You tell me you don't know where they're holding him. Next, he turns up in Malone. Only I hear it on the news first. Now you're telling me they moved him. And again you don't know where. So we're right back to square one."

Michael shook his head again.

"Look. I want you to check and then double-check every goddamn penal institution in this state, the tri-state, and then around the country if you have to. I read what the son of a bitch had for breakfast yesterday morning. Saw him on the eleven o'clock news last night. And you're telling me he's not in Malone? Read. **ALONE IN MALONE.** See the headline?" Barbara held up a copy of the morning paper. "*Newsday*. Note. **In Protective Custody.**"

"That's their cover story, Barbara. Our people checked it out. He was there, but now he's gone."

"Maybe they've got him tucked away in solitary or something."

"Believe me, we'd have found him."

"I think you'd have trouble finding your dick in the dark, Michael. I don't think you could find a penny in a piggy bank. You've got to bring severe pressure to bear upon these so-called servants of the people in Queens and Suffolk. All right." She calmed down and collected her thoughts. "We know that Suffolk is sealed up tighter than Casey's nuts. They feel they have free reign because the courts are upside down right now. They've got interim-acting figureheads is what they've got, and the top bananas believe they can pass the buck. Well, get busy and pass the *big* bucks around the boroughs, Michael. I want answers."

"We've already done that. We know for a fact that the Nassau district attorney's office knows absolutely nothing."

"What about this Captain Cally of the hundred eleventh in Queens? Last week you said there may be a connection."

"We'll have an answer tonight."

"And Police Chief Grear and Lancing out in the boondocks? What about those two?"

"They're another story."

"With a happy ending, I hope."

"Can't get near them."

"What does that tell you?"

"We know they're running the show. But no one's talking."

"I'm talking, but you're not listening. Those at the top are giving them the green light. They're sanctioned. Find out by whom."

"I'm telling you they got a lid on this."

"I'm telling you to uncover it."

"Barbara, listen to me. Don't you think that the senator is doing everything that he can possibly do?"

"Michael. I sleep with the senator. The man has his limitations. He's a good man, but good is not what we need right now."

"What do you want me to do? You want me to tell him what you just said?"

"Yes, Michael. That's exactly what I want you to do. You also tell him that I want Castoro's people brought in on this."

"Castoro?" Michael shook his head.

"Why do you keep shaking your head?"

"You're getting into bed with the enemy, Barbara."

"Whose enemy?"

"Your enemy."

"*Your* work force, Michael. *Your* daytime laborers. *Your* A-team. Your fucking soldiers of fortune."

"Still your enemy, Barbara. Again, to repeat myself, we have our own people out there looking."

"And again, you couldn't find shit in a stable. But Castoro's people *could* indeed find a needle in a landfill."

"And they'd whack Redler in a hot second if they knew

135

what you were up to. Listen to me, Barbara. The boys know you're up to something. Exactly what, perhaps, they haven't quite figured out yet. But in all likelihood they will. Why would Castoro's family want to help you cut their own throats?"

Barbara reached toward the dashboard and turned up the heat. "Because they would like to continue to do business with me. Because we have vested interests. Because time is running out. You have to remember, Michael, the prostitution and rackets we run are but a mere pittance compared to the drug trafficking we control. Although it's all a filthy business, it makes the dirty laundry you hand me weekly turn out snow-white. So everyone gets obscenely rich and has a good time in the bargain. So, you tell Frank I want Castoro brought in. You tell him I want Robert Redler found. Then you line up lawyers with the most strings to pull and the greater number of markers to call in. You know where to reach me," she concluded, rudely sending up her window and shifting the Mustang convertible into gear.

Chapter
——>
32

A stately figure with long coal-black hair walked into Donna Bianco's living room and life as the homemaker was busy preparing for her special day. Doctor Bianco had just pulled out of the driveway with their young son, the two en route to school and office, respectively.

"Where—who are you? What are you doing in here?" Donna asked with apparent alarm.

The pretty creature smiled broadly but didn't say a word, taking a seat on the couch and crossing a pair of lanky stockinged legs in lady-like fashion, looking around the room and nodding with approval.

"I asked you what you're doing here," Donna repeated. "How did you get in? What do you want?"

The woman sat quietly. Still smiling, she directed Donna to a chair beside her.

Donna searched for an explanation. It was her birthday today. Was this some kind of early surprise? she wondered. At eight o'clock in the morning? Some sort of perverted joke her husband had concocted?

The woman was still pointing to the chair.

"You do not order me around in my own home. I asked what you wanted."

The stranger's smile suddenly disappeared, taking in Donna rather sternly, lips set firmly with disapproval. Oddly, the unfamiliar face did not look as lovely as when Donna first set eyes on her. The woman's features darkened. Deliberately, the person smiled again. A bright, warm, practiced, winning smile. Toying with a choker in one hand, she smoothed out a wrinkle in her black wool skirt with the other.

Donna Bianco was staring through her. Beyond the artificial facade. Beyond the subtle mask of makeup. Behind the sea-green eyes. "Oh, my God!" the housewife gasped. "I know who you are."

The figure now standing before her ripped the long coal-black wig from his head, exposing a flaming carrot-red top.

Donna trembled. "Why did you come back, Richard?"

Richard pouted with feigned disappointment, removing a pair of diamond earrings from his lobes. Donna made a sudden start for the kitchen. A sudden short-lived sprint. Richard stopped her in mid-stride, the blade of his knife pointed vertically across her tightly pressed lips.

"Please don't hurt me," she whispered, knowing he'd kill her in an instant if she screamed. "I'll do anything you say. Just tell me what you want. But please don't hurt me. Plea-se," she begged. "I don't want to—to die." Donna shook, sounding out her plea. "We never hurt you. We only wanted to help you. We even prayed for you," she lied, praying that he'd drop dead.

Richard pulled Donna toward him by the hair, tearing her from the room, pushing her roughly down the hallway and into the same bedroom he had visited eighteen years ago.

"Please," she implored, shivering in her shoes.

On the bed was Donna's purse. In it, he found a tube of lipstick.

"Are you going to kill me?" she asked in earnest.

Removing the cap and twisting the base of the tube, Richard stepped toward a mirror. The same mirror on which he had scrawled a message so many years ago; a massive etched glass antique mirror attached atop the dresser.

"Where is Robert Redler?" he velarized inarticulately as he

legibly wrote the garbled words upon the glass.

Donna shook her head. "I don't know! I swear to God," she lied. "I don't want to die. I'd tell you if I knew anything," she swore, wishing to God in that moment she hadn't seen or spoken with her husband at all.

Richard threw her on the bed and tore insanely at her face and clothes. Off came her blouse on a single tear. Then her skirt and bra and panties. He pointed toward the mirror again.

Again, Donna shook her head. "I swear, I'd tell you if I knew," she quavered. "I don't know anything of his whereabouts. I can't tell you something I don't know. Listen to me, Richard. I have jewelry. And money. Over a thousand dollars in the wall safe. We have artwork that's worth a small fortune. Take anything you want, but please don't hur-hurt me. Ple-pleeease."

Richard ripped her from the bed and ran her head into a wall like a battering ram. Once again he pointed to the mirror. Donna gaped then gasped for air, swearing that she didn't know. She knew that if she told him, he would surely kill her, and if she didn't, he'd kill her just the same. It was only a matter of time.

"I swear on my mother's grave, I-don't-know. I wish to God I could tell you something, but I can't."

Richard took her up again and, from a foot away, smashed her beautiful face forcefully into the glass. Composed and supportive, he held her before the mirror and allowed her to reflect. What he wrote next hurt more than her head or face, for it gripped and ripped at her heart:

Saint Bonaventure

It was the name of her precious Timmy's parochial school. Next, Richard listed the child's schedule. Times of the first and last bell. The boy's teacher and room number. Lunch and library hours. Gym class meetings on Mondays, Wednesdays, and Fridays. Finally, he drew the route her husband took to drive the boy to and from school.

Donna knew she couldn't save herself, but she truly prayed to God that Richard would spare her son. "The King Foundation," she said, watching the blood run down her truly frightened face.

Where? he scribbled in script.

She shivered, staring down blankly at Timmy's Mr. Magic Face pieces that lined the dresser: Ears. Eyes. Teeth. Hair. Chins. Foreheads. Cheeks. Noses. "Second floor."

Secured? he scrawled.

"Yes. But you'll never get to him. Police Chief Grear is on the scene," she said with a certain satisfaction, mustering a modicum of courage.

Where on the second floor?

"Mr. Schimmel's old room," she revealed and wept bitterly as she knew he knew the former patient, for Donna had been a psychiatric nurse at the King Foundation during the period Richard was confined.

Smiling satisfactorily, Richard sent her to her death with one swift motion, which opened her throat so wide that she was dead before her eyes ever left the glass.

That afternoon, as the final major storm of February hit Long Island, Doctor Bianco was heading home through the blinding snow with his son, Timmy. The man was proud as all-get-out that he had had the foresight to install rubber-guarded winter wiper blades on his SUV, never before realizing the difference they really made. As he approached their street, his seven-year-old wanted to know what all the fuss was about.

His father smiled. "Well, with the old windshield wiper blades, the icy snow sticks to them, and you can't see a darn thing. But these—"

"Not that, Daddy," Timmy interrupted. "Over there," he said and pointed.

Doctor Bianco slowed the vehicle as he saw the cars and commotion near the end of his block.

Chapter
——>
33

S imply put, it was Richard Geist's, 'I would not ask you to do anything that I, myself, would not do,' innuendoes that contributed to the success of his reign of terror. By the middle of March, most of the team players who had been responsible for bringing criminal proceedings against Robert Redler back in 1991, or even remotely connected with his case, were found murdered. Thirty-one law enforcement officials to date. Educators at Queensborough Community College who had cost the instructor his job would soon be terminated, too. Ostensibly, it looked as though Redler himself was somehow calling the shots. But from where? virtually every concerned law-abiding citizen wanted to know.

Among the murdered had been the "monolithic old farts and fossils of the courts," the writer had been quoted in a rather lengthy phone interview some years ago, along with several other unprintable phrases directed toward one detective who had railroaded him—the cop's action having been initiated by a pompous servant of the Queens district attorney's office.

Queens Bureau Chief Eugene Hanson's sudden dismissal from the world was prolonged and made as tortuous as humanly possible. The official had boasted that he alone would decide the guilt or innocence of Liza's troubled daughter and boyfriend when the shoe was on the other foot and the pair had been defendants in a case brought by both the mother and Robert. Hanson was found gagged and hanging upside down in his garage, his naked body *power-washed* as it were. The man's big brown eyes blown clean out of their sockets. Comparable size holes were found throughout his flesh, maliciously yet meticulously bored by powerful needles of water as was the wooden overhead beam. Newspaper accounts reported that the bureau chief had held on for a good forty-eight hours before his life was finally extinguished. A cardboard sign hanging off the dead man's neck read: SUSPENDED.

The murder of the two most responsible for Robert and Liza's pain to begin with was swift and, therefore, merciful . . . unless, of course, one counted the agonizing sixty seconds that ticked off Liza's teenage daughter and her beau to the very end . . . frantically pulling and dragging the heavy unit . . . fighting the clock before the time bomb exploded as the terrified couple stood helplessly handcuffed to the handles of a sizable refrigerator/freezer.

Lether had barely made it out a back window of the modest Miami studio.

A large segment of both the private and public sector from Queens to Suffolk was citing a conspiratorial plot. Government. Geist. Geist and Redler working hand in hand. And even Doctor Bianco had trouble dealing with the facts, for he had fallen deeply into a state of denial, devastated over his wife's brutal slaying.

Police Chief Grear was completely guilt-ridden, feeling totally responsible for Donna Bianco's death. He had underestimated Richard Geist, for the plan had been to lure the serial killer back to the kingdom from which he had come: the place where he had once been confined for a period of time, the place where he had discovered who his real father was, the place where he had killed his own mother and supposedly discovered his divided selves. The King Foundation.

Although it had been the psychiatrist's call, it was Grear and Lancing's team whose responsibility it was to provide the necessary protection. Grear's mentor, Lieutenant Lark, had made what the chief felt was a similar mistake so many years ago when Richard was locked in a room at the King Foundation's infirmary. Lieutenant Lark had initially put two men at the door to the patient's temporary quarters after Richard had caused himself several serious self-inflicted wounds. But the doctors had assured the lieutenant that Richard wasn't going anywhere in his condition. So Lark had pulled one man off the door. A fatal mistake. And one that Lieutenant Lark learned to regret but never learned to live with. But what had Police Chief Grear learned? Nothing, he told himself over and over again. Grear's initial reaction was to blame it all on inadequate manpower. He had put his men where he believed they were needed most. Oh, he had put *four* men on Bianco's house, all right. Two in one car watching the front, and two in another vehicle watching the rear. None of them had seen anything suspicious. And none of them wound up dead like Lark's man had. No, sir. But Donna Bianco sure as hell had, he cursed himself. His four-man surveillance team had proved to be insufficient. *Fourteen* men should have been covering every goddamn door and window in that house, he told himself a hundred times a day since her death.

Their plan, however, had worked to a degree. They had, indeed, lured Richard Geist from his nest. A week earlier than expected, however. They knew from Richard's mirror messages that he most assuredly wanted and would risk life and limb in finding Robert Redler. For what reason, none of them really knew for sure. What they did know with virtual certainty was that Richard Geist would keep his date with destiny. At least Bianco, Grear and Redler knew it because they knew Geist better than anyone. Deputy Inspector Lancing cared little about the madman's history and was fast becoming a raving fool. *His* backup plan would have been tantamount to lighting a big fire and then running through it with a wet handkerchief. Yet, he was a good cop and a good man. He, too, was personally involved.

Lancing had lost a colleague and close friend at the hands of Richard Geist. Doctor Bianco had lost his wife. Police Chief Grear was losing his grip. And Robert Redler was losing what little freedom he had. But somehow, the four of them, working together, would box Richard in, they begged to believe. Somehow, Grear would find him and kill him, he swore, just as his colleague and friend, Lieutenant Lark, had attempted to do while Richard lay recovering in a private room at North Shore State Hospital, twenty-five years ago. Lark had tried to kill Richard there but couldn't, fighting a bout with conscience and later regretting it—before a merciless cancer took its toll—before the cop could ever enjoy the retirement of which he often spoke so fondly—about a boat and a fish and finally a very secret wish that sounded like a whisper in Grear's ear. Only it wasn't a whisper but a series of sibilant sounds of a weak and dying man who had his protégé simply listen to his plea then implore a promise.

Grear was sitting behind his desk at police headquarters, his thoughts interrupted by a dispatch. A woman had been robbed at knifepoint by a black man in back of Swezey's Department Store in Riverhead. A male Caucasian in his thirties had stopped the man at gunpoint, returned the pocketbook to the frightened woman, then made off with her late model car, New York license plate number J3X191. These were the kinds of crimes the Riverhead police dealt with occasionally. Nothing along the lines of Richard Geist. Grear shook his head, admiring the scrimshaw-handled pocketknife Lieutenant Lark had given him as a gift many years ago, a special gift that had been handed down for three generations in Lark's family. Grear treasured it.

Chapter
——>
34

It wasn't a week after his wife's funeral when Doctor Bianco was back in the fray, attending an important meeting in one of the conference rooms down the hall from his office. Grear found it difficult to look the psychiatrist in the eye, glancing up uncomfortably while wondering if the man could really handle what the police had in mind, but deciding to move ahead as planned. Redler and Lancing entered the room and took a seat, neither of them saying a word. Redler was acting jittery of late, and Lancing was becoming more impatient by the moment. Both were behaving more and more like patients with every passing minute, and Grear was growing quite concerned.

"All right. Here's what we've got," the police chief said. "At first we weren't really sure whether or not Donna told Geist that Rob was here. We never got the chance to place our story, which *The Post* had agreed to run. A story which may or may not have pushed the right buttons and lured this lunatic to us. Well, it appears that Geist is waiting us out. Even if the paper had run our story, Richard might have perceived a trap. But right now, he doesn't know for certain that we know he knows that Rob is here."

The three of them were staring at Grear as though he had two heads.

"What?" Lancing snapped. "You want to run that by us again?"

"We have a definite advantage in that Richard doesn't know we know he knows that Rob is here at the King Foundation," Grear repeated, his words making but little sense.

"We don't know what Richard got out of her before he cut her throat. Sorry," Lancing said, glancing uncomfortably at Bianco.

Doctor Bianco said nothing, fixing his eyes on the table.

"We didn't know until a few hours ago. That's why I called this meeting. We're going to box that bastard in."

"How?" Redler asked.

"What advantage do we have?" Bianco questioned quietly.

"Yeah. How did we come to learn this, and what the hell difference does it make 'who's on first?' And why am I hearing about police business for the first time in front of two civilians?" Lancing demanded.

"Because we're all on the same team and because time is running out," Grear said calmly. "This is not your run-of-the-mill psychopath. This is—"

"Don't you sit there and lecture me because I outrank the fucking lot of—"

"Don't *you* say something you'll be sorry for later," Grear barked, pointing a finger in the deputy inspector's face. "This goddamn thing has little to do with rank or years in grade or any of that happy horseshit. It has to do with cooperating with those actually in charge of this operation. Now, I just spent two unhappy hours going through the same crap with several FBI agents. There's sort of an invisible line drawn for us between *out there* and *in here*. In here, I'm in charge. Out there, they're taking over. Or they think they're taking over, depending on who you talk to. You make your phone calls and decide what you want to do. But if you're in here, it's my ball game. Out there, you can argue with the ump."

Lancing wanted to tell Grear that doing it his way already got Donna Bianco killed. Then again, most everyone connected with the Redler matter was winding up on the slab—federal, state, and local protection notwithstanding—and there wasn't a damn thing he, the FBI or any other agency seemed able to prevent. "Go on," Lancing snapped impatiently.

"We got our first break this afternoon. The Bureau picked up a young female Caucasian with a sophisticated piece of photographic equipment and night vision binoculars. She seems to fit the description of a woman seen leaving your kid's school the day of your wife's murder," Grear said, looking directly across the table at the doctor.

It was as though someone had hit Bianco in the face with a pail full of ice water. He came to attention in his seat. His voice shook. "Timmy?"

"Yes," Grear answered.

"You didn't tell me about a woman."

"We didn't know; the connection was only made a short time ago."

"What do you mean?"

"She was under surveillance by the FBI."

"Why the hell did the feds have to go and pick her up?" Lancing snapped.

"Because she wasn't returning to the nest."

"What nest?" Redler asked.

"Richard's nest," Grear replied.

"They should have let her be," Lancing carped. "Goddamn feds. She'd have led them to him."

"They don't think so. Not until she's completed her mission."

"What mission? Where?" Bianco barked.

"Right here," Grear said, staring straight ahead at Redler.

"How do they know she's connected to Richard?" Bianco pressed.

"Well, the person who left your home that morning, dressed like your wife, of course we know was Richard. The long black wig, the heels, and the clothes he left behind would fit the woman that the feds picked up to a tee. That and the fact that my men watching the house saw a woman dressed like her pass by."

"You mean, more like *distracted* by her," Bianco charged, trying to make sense of it all as well as assign blame.

"And that's when Richard slipped in," Grear conceded. "Dressed like our mystery woman going in, dressed like your wife coming out."

"But all the doors and windows were locked; Donna knew the precautions to take," Bianco countered.

Grear simply shrugged, not wanting to remind himself of the fact that locks were nothing to Richard Geist.

"Mystery woman, you said. Your men and now the feds couldn't make a positive ID on this woman?" Lancing fumed and frowned.

"Not outside of free, white, and over twenty-one."

"Fucking cunt," Lancing blew.

"That she is," Grear agreed. "When the feds grabbed her, she offered them the best head they ever had, giving her address along with assurances of freebies for a year if they'd let her go."

"Layaway plan, huh," Lancing snapped sarcastically. "What address did she give?"

"A phony one, of course. But one of the feds said they saw her on Overland Drive in Flanders."

"What's of interest over there?" Redler asked.

"She was staying in the back room of a church run by a black Baptist minister. Comes and goes."

"I'll bet she does," Lancing assured them with a chuckle. "Now, what's a white woman like that doin' hangin' 'round the dark part of town?"

Grear shrugged. "Don't know yet."

"So, where do we go from here?" Bianco sighed.

"Well, at seven o'clock this evening the woman is going to be found dead."

Again, the three looked at Captain Grear as though he had lost his mind.

"Dead?" Redler questioned with astonishment.

"Only it's not going to be our mystery woman. It's going to be one of our female detectives."

"Good," Lancing declared. "I know just the one. She's made life miserable for our office for years. Tried to bring the lot of us up on sexual harassment charges. Made Altman's life a living hell," he bantered.

Doctor Bianco found nothing amusing in the cop's mirth. Neither did Redler nor Grear.

"So you're going to stage her death," Doctor Bianco said, getting to the matter at hand.

"Yes."

"And how is that going to pull Richard out of the woodwork?"

"Well, if the feds hold her, Richard might wait around for her release. But if they fake her death to fit a rape and murder M.O., he may pick up where she left off."

"In other words, Richard will be twisting in the wind as to what to do. Just like we're twisting now," Redler said.

"Only we're not twisting any longer," Grear replied.

"I still don't understand all that shit about Richard not knowing what we supposedly now know, or why that's so important. What do we know? You haven't told us yet," Lancing queried.

"This," Grear said, opening his hand.

The three of them leaned forward, staring at the flat, thin flesh-colored piece of plastic.

"What the heck is that?" Redler asked, furrowing his brow.

"A nose."

"A nose?"

"Yes. See?" he said and smiled, sticking it to the side of his own nose for a second before it fell.

"Mr. Magic Face!" Bianco exclaimed.

"Exactly."

"Mister who?" Redler asked.

"That's Timmy's," Doctor Bianco made clear.

"Yes, it is," Grear agreed.

"Like a Mr. Potato Head," the doctor elaborated. "Only with the pieces of a face that you arrange on a magnetic board."

"And how does this tell us anything?" Redler questioned.

Grear fixed his eyes on Bianco. "Your wife had this in her hand when we found her," he said softly. "I think she was trying to tell us something. I think she was trying to tell us that, 'Richard *knows*.'"

"Jesus Christ, Grear!" Lancing lashed out and laughed. "I've seen reaching in my time, but this tops everything. I was there in the room with you. Remember? There were dozens of these scattered across the top of the dresser."

"Only they weren't scattered. They were arranged. I really didn't give it much thought at first."

"Yes," Bianco interjected, "Timmy does that! Cheeks with cheeks. Eyes with eyes. Teeth with teeth, and so on."

Robert Redler looked intrigued. Lancing was shaking his head with a ridiculous grin plastered across his face.

"And the noses were all the way over to the right side of the dresser," Grear went on. "A rather long dresser at that." He paused. "I'm going to have to get a little graphic in order to make my point, Doctor. Do you want to leave the room for a moment?"

Bianco shook his head.

"All right. Picture it," Grear said. "Geist's literally trying to beat it out of her that morning as to where Robert is. Writing on the mirror and banging her head against the wall, smashing her face into the glass. The blood is running down her face and onto the top of the dresser. Here," he demonstrated, leaning forward and placing his palms upon the conference table. "Just to her left, are the eyes and teeth. The hair and chins take up the area in front of and just to the right of her. The foreheads and cheeks are further along the line. But the noses, gentlemen. The noses are way off to her right. Yet she reaches for and clutches one nose. Not just any nose. But a nose that is remarkably similar to Richard's. Richard Geist's nose. Richard *knows*!" he concluded, holding up a blow-up of Geist's face. "Your wife was a very brave and focused woman, Doctor, who took a brutal beating before telling Geist what he wanted to know. Obviously, threatening her with your life and Timmy's as he wrote the name of his school and schedule, along with the route you take to and from Saint Bonaventure. And his accomplice, that woman in waiting, was waiting across from that school to harm the boy if Donna had not revealed Robert's whereabouts.

Lancing applauded the show, still shaking his head in disbelief. Redler was pondering the points. Doctor Bianco nodded in excitement.

"I want to share something with you," the psychiatrist said, addressing the three. "Donna spent a great deal of time with Timmy, working on his spelling, phonics and such. Like homonyms and homophones. One of Timmy's favorites was 'nose' and 'knows'. When he was two and a half, he would say, '*nose*,' and touch his nose like this," Bianco declared and demonstrated. "And then he would touch his finger to his head, nodding it up and down, *knowingly*." The doctor wept, tears running down his face as he got up to leave the room. "I'm sorry," he said and sobbed, embarrassed to be exhibiting such raw emotion in front of them. He thought he was all cried out after the funeral. But he couldn't shake from his mind the horrible moment Donna must have endured in realizing Richard Geist was about to kill her. "I'll be right back. Just going to wash my face. Don't you start a second sooner," he insisted.

Doctor Bianco left the room, and the three sat in silence for several minutes until the man returned.

"All right. So what's the plan?" Bianco asked.

"The plan is simple. We wait," Grear stated.

"For how many more people to be killed?" Lancing said scornfully. "We're fast approaching genocide here, folks. I think Geist's pretty much exhausted Robert's foes. With the exception of a detective assigned to the case, the hearing judge and the courtroom stenographer, I think you've rid yourself of everyone, Robby boy."

"Very funny," Redler frowned. "You forgot the prosecutor," he was sorry he said.

"Maybe Geist's saving Mary Lou Dillany for *you*. I remember you had a few choice words for her, too. Captain Cally's people are watching her like a hawk. Probably have a fucking fortress built around her home and office by now. Fucking remarkable how all this shit keeps piling up around you." Lancing leered.

"Go to hell."

"You know, I don't fucking like your fucking mouth."

"The feeling's mutual, asshole."

"All right, that's enough now," Grear ordered. "That kind of talk isn't going to get us anywhere."

"I'm telling you, this fucking guy's a communist," Lancing swore, shooting a thumb in Redler's direction. "He wanted Nicholas Maldonado out of prison. You read his goddamn editorials. And he's got Tony Giordano pegged as some kind of fucking saint."

"What I said was, was that Nicholas Maldonado didn't get a fair trial. Period. If they can do what they did to Maldonado, imagine what they do to others with little or no money to defend themselves. Don't you get it? And Tony Giordano—"

"What I get is, Redler, is that you're a punk. He's a communist cocksuckin' pervert. I'm tellin' you," he bellowed to Grear.

Redler flew out of his seat and grabbed the deputy inspector before the man could push his chair back. Grear and Bianco quickly stepped between the angry pair.

"All right. The two of you shut up and sit back down in your seats. Both of you listen to me. We're not here for any popularity contest. This is a deadly business we're dealing with, I'll remind you. Lives are being lost on a daily basis. That's what this is all about. Human life. Geist and his group are destroying what we consider to be one of our most inalienable rights. The right to personal safety."

"He's a fucking communist," Lancing continued, struggling, trying to reach for Redler's throat.

"He's probably a bloody anarchist," Grear shouted. "And the way things are going in this country, I myself might join the Libertarian Party. But we're not here to argue politics or persuasions. We're here to do a job. And personally, I'm getting more cooperation from two civilians than I am from you, Inspector. Furthermore, if you read Redler's editorials—I mean really read them, along with that packet of his, you'd see he was set up from the get-go and that Richard Geist is capitalizing on Mr. Redler's misfortune. And if you want me to keep beating up on you in front of these two civilians, just keep it up, Bill."

"Thank you," Redler said.

"Shut up," Grear barked angrily. "Now here's how we're going to box that bastard in. Together. The four of us."

Chapter
——>
35

That evening, the networks reported a rape and robbery run amuck. A police source spoke of an unidentified female Caucasian in her early twenties found fatally stabbed several blocks away from the Abyssinian Baptist Church in Flanders. It appeared that the young woman had put up a terrific struggle, the source said. Her assailant was still at large. A full description and photograph of the unknown woman was given, including an inset that revealed a rather significant tattoo of a scorpion located along the deceased's inner left thigh. The spokesperson asked anyone with information to please come forward. A special telephone number was assigned, and phones at one network were ringing through the night, citizens demanding to know if the woman was in any way connected to the Redler/Geist murders. By morning, one tabloid had headlined the multitude of murders as "The List of Messenger Redler," a play on words targeting a sixties movie titled, *The List of Adrian Messenger,* depicting a hit list of atrocities.

There was no question about it, Richard Geist knew. The photo and insert were those of Angelica. His fallen angel. *But is she really dead?* he wondered. Was this truly her eternal sleep? Was she really the one they picked off the pavement and delivered to the morgue? Or was this a ruse to set him into action? Oh, he absolutely loved the game. *Lunatic versus the Law,* he laughed. Easy enough to confuse the two, the madman ruminated, for the law of the land was surely lunacy in the making. It took each generation nearly a lifetime to wake up to that fact. But Redler's editorials (which hardly anyone had read until recently) were opening many eyes, the serial killer sulked. Robert Redler's coeditor at the *North Shore Towers Newsletter* had seen to that, reprinting his earlier editorials in the monthly publication.

Too, Barbara Giordano had arranged for a second printing of the writer's earlier work. Twenty thousand copies of Robert F. Redler's paperback biography on Geist were being reprinted in hardcover by Simon and Schuster.

How fucking dare he peek into the window of my soul, Richard leered, throwing Redler's book to the floor. *How fucking dare he treat me like some perverted character instead of the force I truly am. Sure, they're all screaming for the death penalty now, those simps and wimps. And Redler owes it all to me. He'll get the glory and the grave. And I? I will be sought, yet sanctioned as but a knave. But the real winner will be declared by the one who sells the most copies,* he giggled outlandishly. *And I'm certainly miles ahead. Arbor House can't seem to get the next printing off the press and into shipping cartons fast enough. Four hundred thousand copies to date and going strong. Why, there won't be a godforsaken tree left standing in all the land,* Richard roared.

Richard Geist pondered what to do next.

Chapter
——>
36

Police Chief Grear was weighing the slight advantage he believed they held, brimming with confidence concerning the clue discovered in Donna Bianco's hand, coupled with the hope that Richard Geist believed Angelica was dead. Geist's guard would be down, and he would come to them, by God, the police captain prayed. Once again, Grear tried to reassure his most impatient team.

"We understand all that, Chief," Doctor Bianco said. "We just don't understand how sitting around here doing nothing works to our advantage."

"Yeah, you dazzled us with face parts and a plan. But you haven't satisfactorily explained how we're going to take advantage of this supposed upper hand," Lancing scoffed, more than just upset as to how and why the power had gradually shifted to the police chief's corner of command.

"I've tried to, Bill. But you're not listening. Geist will make his move when he feels certain about things. He'll move, and then hopefully he'll make his first mistake."

"What mistake will that be?" Redler asked.

"I don't know. I'm a cop, not a fortune teller. But believe me; we're going to be ready for him this time."

Instead of a police chief, Grear was behaving more like a mystic.

He wasn't giving them anything substantive that could be explained rationally. Yet, his gut feeling appeared to pacify them. At least for the moment. Or so he believed.

Of course, Richard Geist put a series of possibilities through his brain like a computer, ever mindful of traps as Angelica forewarned. Few knew where Robert Redler actually was. Those who did had probably wanted to tip their hand, revealing the writer's whereabouts in some such clever way as to signal but a singular message for their intended target. But Richard hadn't given them the chance, fouling their plan early on and ascertaining the truth for himself, disguising himself as an angel before slipping through a window at the side of the couple's home while his seductive accomplice paraded past the surveillance team . . . ogling her shapely body to bits. And now the authorities figured he'd somehow find a way to Robert Redler, just as surely as he had found a way out of lockup at both private and state-run facilities years ago. In and out at will.

But what the police don't know is that I know they know where Robert Redler is, Richard giggled delightfully to himself. *So I'll just have to show them what they need to know for certain,* he grinned satisfactorily, mailing off a package anagrammatically addressed to R.F. Dreler, care of the King Foundation, A Building, second floor, front. Mr. Schimmel's old room.

Oh, Richard was *so* loving the game of cat and mouse.

Overnight delivery arrived early the next day.

"Jesus Christ," Grear gasped.

Within thirty minutes, the bomb squad had the benign package and letter opened. A caricature of Richard Geist put together with the pieces of Mr. Magic Face loomed up at them.

Police Chief Grear and Deputy Inspector Lancing read Richard's message:

Dear Doctor Angelo Bianco,

See, it's me! Please see that your patient receives this gift of Mr. Magic Face to wile away the hours while the authorities decide their next step. Things must be hard on Liza. I think about her often as I did your wife.

If it's any consolation, Donna died swiftly. She needn't have died at all if she hadn't lied to me at first. Enclosed, too, please find one additional plastic nose to complete Timmy's set at home as I'm sure Police Chief Grear needs the one he's holding for evidence as well as to advance his theory. Actually, I put the nose from the right side of the dresser into your wife's hand. Fit right in with Timmy's lessons regarding homophones. Nice touch?

Please tell Robby that I miss him and that I'll see him during visiting hours. No need for him to send a Thank You note, for I move around a lot.

Always,
Richard Geist

Later that afternoon, Lancing took Grear aside in the psychiatrist's outer office. "Nothing on the woman yet," the inspector said. "Both the bureau and our boys ran her prints seven ways to Sunday and came up empty handed."

"Angelica," Grear said quietly. "Who the hell *is* she?"

"Well, Angelica, or whatever her name is, doesn't have a record, or even a traffic violation, I'd bet."

"How long are they going to hold her?"

Lancing shrugged. "Surprisingly, she's not screaming for a bloody lawyer. One cool customer. Claims she knows nothing. Denies everything. Won't give anybody a straight answer let alone her surname or SSN."

"You see her?"

"You kidding? Feds won't let me near her."

"You blame them? They probably figured you'd kick the shit out of her."

"Listen up, Mr. Magic Face. At least, I'd walk away with some answers."

"Yeah, like Richard did with Donna?"

"Pussyfooting around with that cunt isn't going to get anybody anywhere. Plastering her picture across the state was another one of your brainstorms that's gonna backfire. Richard and his people have probably hightailed it out of the country by now. We're going to look like fucking fools the minute this bitch sets her heels on the street. Fucking newspapers are going to have a field day."

"Fuck the newspapers."

"Yeah, fuck this team of yours. When the good doctor and Robby boy finally realize that *you're* the real lunatic around here, you ain't gonna have a fucking team. Bianco's turning into a basket case, and Redler's already falling apart. I can't believe you showed them that letter. Redler's worried sick about his girlfriend, not to mention his own ass come visiting day. What are you gonna tell them next? 'Don't worry about a thing, fellows. Me and Mr. Magic Face have got this thing covered.' You gonna protect them like you protected Donna Bianco? Huh? This is police business, buddy. You don't involve civilians to the extent you have. But you got it your way because you rode in on the reputation of a real cop. Lieutenant Lark. You moved quickly through the ranks because you got lucky and impressed the downtown brass with your uptown college education and ingratiating charm. But your luck just ran out. You're only their darling while things are hunky-dory. We got thirty some odd corpses connected to this case, and we haven't got a clue where Richard Geist or his fucking Inner Circle of Friends are holed up. It's over, pal. You're practically history."

The police chief's head and heart pounded like a war drum, but he kept himself in check. Taking the inspector to task or exchanging blows would only exacerbate matters, he told himself. Still and all, he fought the urge to lift Lancing off the floor with an uppercut and land him against the wall.

Lancing left and disappeared around the hallway.

Moments later, Doctor Bianco opened the door to the police chief's borrowed office and anxiously summoned Grear to pick up the phone on 03, pointing to the flashing button. "It's Captain Cally calling from Queens," the psychiatrist said.

Grear picked up the receiver then came out of his chair as if he had suddenly sat on a tack. "What?"

"Mary Lou Dillany," Cally repeated. "It had to be at least a four- hundred-yard shot. I don't think she's going to make it."

"Where?"

"Garden World, Bayside."

"When?"

"Twenty minutes ago."

"Where is she now?"

"En route. Probably either North Shore or Long Island Jewish."

"Anybody see—"

"Nobody saw a goddamn thing. Saw her fall is all. A single bullet in her back. Hold on."

Grear waited.

"They're taking her to LIJ. That's all I've got right now."

"How are you set?"

"I've got black and whites cordoning off everything from the Queens Midtown tunnel to the Nassau County line. Everything! Fifty men on foot—several with K-9s combing ground zero."

"You need more men?"

"I've got backup flowing out of the other precincts like a river."

"Whattaya think?"

"If they're on foot, we've got 'em. If they're on wheels, anybody's guess."

Grear sank back down in the chair.

"Gotta go," Cally said. "Get back to you as soon as I can."

"All right. I'll be here."

Grear hung up the phone as Robert Redler came— uninvited—through the open office.

"What's up?" Redler asked while taking in Grear's troubled expression.

The police chief studied Redler for a long moment before answering. "Mary Lou Dillany."

"What about her?"

Another pause. "She's in an ambulance on her way to Long

Island Jewish. Gunshot wound. Doesn't look good."

"I'm sorry," Redler said, looking down and then away.

"No, you're not."

"Look."

Grear was looking. "Yeah?"

"I wish they'd have fired her or something. I didn't wish her any harm. Not like that."

"Listen, I know how you feel about the system."

"That's right. The system stinks. A system in which innocent people get shafted and sent up the river for crimes they don't commit. A system in which murderers can be set free in as little as two and a half years."

"That's not the norm."

"All right, seven to ten. Twenty on the outside. Want to argue that? Thieves and drug dealers spend more time in prison than some murderers do. Killers like Richard Geist laugh at the system. It becomes a game. The insanity plea has become a joke. I try to tell people that murderers like Richard Geist must be put to death by the state. Not locked away in some goddamn institution to be studied like a lab rat. Killers like Geist get to see light at the end of the tunnel. But the victims can't even contemplate the dark. What's wrong with that picture, Chief Grear? Tell me.

"I put my life on hold, and I put Liza in jeopardy," Redler continued. "Quite frankly, I'm scared. I'm scared for her, and I'm scared for myself. There's no longer a handful of Richard Geists out there. There's probably thousands like him. We know that Richard is highly organized, supported by his Inner Circle of Friends. God only knows how many. I want a lawyer, and I want out of here. I've tried to cooperate. I did cooperate. But now I want to go home and be with Liza."

"I'm concerned about Liza, too," Grear said sincerely. "I'm concerned that if you leave us, that is, if our people even let you —"

"Don't give me that cr—"

"Let me finish!" Grear ordered, holding out the palm of his hand like a stop sign. "If you give up on me now, they'll probably pull the plug on this operation. Right now, and until I hear otherwise, I have six good men around the clock protecting Liza. That's a lot of manpower, Rob. And lots of pairs of eyes."

"Donna Bianco had four men. Like two more are really gonna make a difference."

"Are you going to be able to provide that kind of security for yourself and Liza? Richard would just love to know you're back out in the civilian population again. He'd throw a party before he killed you. And probably Liza. You think about that for a while, then let me know what you decide."

"And what if he never comes?"

"Oh, he'll come all right, Rob," Doctor Bianco interrupted. "Believe me, he'll come. The chief is right on that account. Rest assured. I'm sure you know that, too."

Chapter ——> 37

The phone rang, and Barbara Giordano got to it on the first ring, her eyes glued to the TV.

"Hello.... Yes.... Where?.... What time?.... All right, I'll be there. Oh, and Michael. Don't be late."

She put down the receiver, watching old footage of her husband being led away in handcuffs by Nassau police. The newscaster spoke of Tony Giordano's pending release and the upcoming gala the family had planned for him at the Cafe Bella Notte in Oyster Bay.

Before getting dressed, she phoned and asked her sister-in-law to come over and watch the kids. Within half an hour, she was out the door and on her way to meet Michael.

Barbara pulled up alongside Michael's Mercedes, and the pair hit their power window buttons simultaneously. Barbara was smiling. Michael was not.

"What's the matter, Michael? You told me you had good news."

"I told you I had the information you wanted."

"Well?"

"Redler's at the King Foundation. Plainclothes all over the place. Feds as well as the local boys."

"The King Foundation. Very good, Michael. Learn anything new

Robert Banfelder

about Richard Geist?"

"Geist has quite a following. A veritable army, I'm told."

"An army? I thought he controlled some freaky religious faction."

"A splinter group called the Inner Circle of Friends. Had a foothold in Jersey, but the feds broke them up some years back. They sprang up again in the D.C. area."

"Michael, dear. Please get to the point. Ancient history I can dig up for myself."

"Geist reorganized them throughout the country."

"The country?"

Michael nodded.

"Put Castoro's people on it. I want to know everything about this Geist. I want him located."

"He won't touch it. He gave you Redler's new address and sends his regards. But he won't touch Geist."

"And why not?"

"I was leading up to that."

"Go on, dear. I do get a bit impatient with you at times. This had better be good."

"Oh, it is, Barbara."

"Do continue."

"Richard's been a busy boy for the past eighteen years. He's organized his people in every major city throughout the forty-eight contiguous states. They're fanatics."

"Tell me exactly what we're dealing with here."

"A highly-trained and motivated assassination network. Topnotch."

"Oh, I can imagine. We've been watching his work here for weeks."

Michael nodded in accord.

"How many followers?"

"We don't know for sure."

"Venture a guess."

"A hundred thousand. Maybe more."

"How many more?"

"Could be ten times that."

"A million followers, Michael?"

162

"We don't know, Barbara. It's not something you look up in an almanac."

"Let's go in the middle. Five hundred thousand fanatics who would give life and limb for a cause. What cause?"

"We don't know."

"How could you not know about a movement so large over an eighteen-year period?"

Michael didn't answer.

"What *do* you know, Michael?"

"You know the woman on the news the other night? The stabbing."

"Stabbing?"

"Over in Flanders."

"Oh, yes. Pretty woman. Killed near a church. Is there a connection?" she questioned with a smile.

"She was seen parading past the King Foundation director's home on the morning the psychiatrist's wife was murdered. Next thing we know, the feds nabbed her along with some high-tech equipment."

"Surveillance?"

"For sure."

"Redler, Redler, Redler," she fretted. "Maybe I put my money on the wrong horse."

Michael nodded. "No way are you going to get Redler out of there. No way are you going to cut a deal with the feds. And no way are you going to make a deal with Castoro's people."

"Why not?"

"Because he'd cut himself a deal with the devil before he'd cut a deal with you."

"Would he now?"

"You wanted Robert Redler so that he could do your bidding and you could sleep nights. So now you know where Redler is. Fine. Now you want them to pull Richard Geist out of thin air for you. If they could control this cult, they'd control another empire. Richard isn't undermining any *family* business, Barbara. As a matter of fact, he's clearing the playing field. If they see Geist as anything, they see him as an asset, not a liability. This Redler business has gotten too complicated. Let it go. Find another writer or another kind of insurance policy."

"And I suppose you have some ideas?"

"Frank is working on something."

"Frank is always working on something. If I waited for Frank, I could be dead next week. You've lined up those attorneys we talked about?"

"Yes, but—"

"Good. Arrange for one to see Redler. High profile. Shit starter. Contacts in Washington. Arrogant. Loudmouth. Good with the press. I want their charade exposed. I want heads to roll. I want Redler out of there. You have this counselor assure his safety and the safety of his entire family dating back to the Civil War if you have to."

"But I thought—"

"Thought you'd drag this thing out till Frank could figure out what to do."

"Barbara, please listen—"

"Get on it, Michael. Call me with a name and the particulars in twenty-four hours." She pressed the power window button, and up came the glass, sealing out a stream of Michael's protests.

Chapter
——>
38

Captain Cally tried to reach Grear at the King Foundation but was instructed to call the police chief at headquarters in Riverhead. Moments later the switchboard put Cally's call through to Grear's office.

"Yes, Captain."

"Dillany's dead."

There was silence on the other end of the line.

"She held on till twenty-one hundred hours," Cally continued.

"Give me what you got."

"One fluted casing purposely left behind. Eight lines of carbon running along the length of brass. Handloaded job. Three-o-eight caliber. Probably an H & K PSG one sniper rifle, I'm told. Two pairs of boot marks in the mud along with tire tracks. Four-wheel drive from the way the ground was torn up. Forensic boys are still there. We stopped and checked anything that looked remotely suspicious both on main and secondary roads. Nothing. Expressway, Cross Island, Belt, Sunrise, and the Southern State. Nothing. Kennedy. LaGuardia. Nothing. One bullet in her back. A four-hundred-fifty-yard shot confirmed. Two perps. Driver and shooter. Professional job all the way. That distance is what bought her time. She was with two off-duty patrolmen and her father who grabbed her as she went down. Five civilians present. Three ran for cover, and two others hit the dirt. Nobody saw shit. That's about it."

"You said the casing was purposely left behind?"

"Yeah. Stuck upright in the ground within a neatly drawn triangle enclosed within a circle."

"Christ. Their symbol. I want you to fax me everything you've got by morning. Keep me posted."

"First thing, Chief."

"Thank you, Captain."

"Good night."

Captain Cally grabbed his coat off the costumer and rode the elevator down to the lobby. Once outside, he quickly walked east along Northern Boulevard for a half a block when a dark gray Mercedes pulled up. Cally opened the passenger side and got in.

"Redler still there?" Michael asked.

"I guess so."

"You guess so?"

"That's what I said."

"I don't pay you for guesswork."

"You asked me to find out where Redler is. And that's what I did."

"You don't seem too happy to see me."

"I'd be happy if I never saw you again."

"But you don't have much say in the matter. Now do you, Captain?"

Captain Cally said nothing.

"All right, now let's try this once again. Shall we? Did you phone in the report?"

"Yes."

"And you didn't ask Grear about Redler."

"No. I assumed he was still there."

"Well, when you speak to him again, I want to know for certain. Is that understood?"

Cally nodded.

Michael smiled. "Good. Will you be speaking to Grear later?"

"I said I'd fax him in the morning."

"Then you fax him and follow up with a call. Have a nice evening, Captain."

By mid-morning, Captain Cally faxed a full report to Riverhead P.D. and followed up with a phone call to the King Foundation later in the day.

"Grear here."

"Cally."

"What's up?"

"I faxed out that report. You got it?"

"Got it."

"How's our boy holding up?"

"You got a pipeline into this place or something?"

"What do you mean?" Cally asked defensively, gripping the receiver as if to halt the answer on the other end.

"He wants out."

"Does he know about Dillany?"

"Yeah, he knows, all right. Started to fold on me. The whole thing's coming apart. He's about ready to call his lawyer. I had this fucked-up theory. Geist played me for a sucker. Fell right into his trap. Went right down to the wire on a hunch. Thought we had this edge. Made a complete ass of myself. Lancing was right."

"We've all been there," Cally said consolingly.

"Anyhow. What can I do for you?"

"Nothing. Just thought you might have a question referencing the report."

"Call you if I do. And listen."

"Yeah?"

"Thanks for keeping the lid of this thing. No matter how things turn out."

Cally wanted to confess on the spot that he *was* a fucking pipeline. But he didn't. It wouldn't exactly be his career on the line. More like his life and that of his family's.

"Right." Cally hung up the phone and felt like the traitor he was.

Chapter
——>
39

That evening, having confirmed through Cally that Robert Redler was still at the King Foundation, but wouldn't be there much longer because he was ready to call it quits, Michael swung into action. By morning, *Newsday* broke its front-page story, reporting how "Mr. Robert F. Redler had been abducted, brainwashed, and deprived of his constitutional rights by a band of rogue cops following the whim of certain superiors who believed they were above the law," renowned Texas attorney, Jonathan L. Laddington, was quoted as saying.

When asked in a late morning interview from the front porch of his home in Dallas if he planned to represent Mr. Robert Redler, the stereotypical Texan beamed the breadth of his broad-brimmed Stetson and declared that he had no such plans unless asked by the man himself.

"Then who in New York are you planning to visit?" asked a young and enterprising female reporter who held up a confirmation of the attorney's flight to Kennedy Airport.

"The wife of a man who loves snakeskin boots as much as I do, darlin'," the attorney replied, fielding the next question from a male reporter.

"And would that woman be Barbara Giordano, Tony Giordano's wife?" the young man questioned and smiled.

"Oooo-wee!" the counselor exclaimed. "You guys and gals sure do your homework," he answered declaratively. "If they had reporters like you up in New York, why, the world would have known where Mr. Redler was the day after he disappeared."

There was laughter and applause across the front lawn as reporters gave Laddington and themselves their due.

"What's the first thing you're going to do when you arrive in New York?" another reporter called out.

Jonathan Laddington was waiting for this question. Smiling slyly, he reached into his pocket and pulled out a shiny red ripe apple, bringing it slowly to his face.

The cameras moved in for a close-up.

"Why, I'm going to take a big bite out of crime," he said, sinking his teeth to the core.

Pandemonium broke out among the press people.

In New York that evening, the six, ten, and eleven o'clock news networks carried the entire interview, playing it for all its worth.

Early next morning, the King Foundation was flooded with calls. Vans and camera crews lined the lawns and walkway along the buildings. Police, patients, politicians, patrons, passersby, along with crowds of angry protesters, were all part of the mix. The crowd was growing most magically. Cameras and boom microphones were busy picking up a series of sights and sounds. The circus was back in town.

A white limousine half the length of a railway car came rolling through the main gate, parking in front of the administration building. The chauffeur came around, opened the door and took the lady's hand. You would think it was the First Lady or a famous actress arriving for her movie premier. It was Barbara Giordano, and the crowd-pleasing, well-dressed woman welcomed their whistles and applause, smiling and waving as she walked briskly toward the entrance with the Texas attorney on her arm.

"May we have a comment as to why you're both here?" a middle-aged reporter asked evenly, holding her microphone between them as casually as if she were offering up a mug of coffee.

Mrs. Giordano stopped abruptly and took the instrument from the woman's hand, leaning into the Texan as though they were about to begin a duet. "We are here today to help rehabilitate a rather sick government. Sick on all fronts; that is, federal, state and local," Barbara declared, handing back the microphone.

The applause from the crowd was staggering. It was obvious

who the plainclothes police and bureaucrats were. They stuck out like sore losers: hands jammed deep into their pockets, clasped behind their backs, or laced together as tightly as their lips. Still, others spoke with body language, saying nothing but speaking volumes with arms folded firmly across their pounding chests. The larger group was still applauding or punching the air high above their heads, punctuating the moment with yesses and yelps of support.

"We have come here to mark an era," Barbara Giordano continued, speaking slowly and carefully into several microphones held inches from her face. "And please allow me to say the following."

The reporters were nodding their heads, happy to have surrendered center stage as the cameras closed in then pulled back to where the subject was pointing. Barbara was directing their attention to the building behind her, pausing for the full effect before continuing.

"Through a man's courageous writings, although his audience was indeed small, we were reminded in editorial after editorial of just how abusive this government is. Robert Redler's plea to the police and politicians across this land fell on deaf ears. They read him, but chose to look away. He fought for himself. He fought for a little girl in Brooklyn who was raped. He fought for several prisoners who were incarcerated for crimes which they did not commit. He fought for a gangster who did, indeed, commit crimes but was denied his rights under our Constitution. He fought for my husband. And he even fought for one of your own," she added, making a sweeping gesture before the group of reporters assembled in front of her. "Troy Anderson sits in prison on trumped-up kidnapping charges: a renowned private investigator/deprogrammer who was instrumental in dismantling a cult and effecting the arrest of one of its leaders. The same cult which Richard Geist has amassed into an elite corps of assassins over the past eighteen years. A cult that is killing off your law enforcement personnel day after day. A cult called the Inner Circle of Friends.

"Now, we're going inside that building behind me to fight for a man worth fighting for. We're going in there to fight for a man our government is trying to destroy. Thank you."

"Mr. Laddington. Do you have anything to add, sir?" was the following question which simultaneously directed all microphones and cameras for comment and close-ups of the tall Texas attorney.

Laddington withdrew a big, shiny red apple from his coat pocket, took a gigantic bite, and put the remaining portion into the reporter's palm. "Delicious," he chomped, heading toward the entrance with Barbara on his arm.

The crowd went positively wild.

"Welcome to the Big Apple, Counselor," one man hollered.

"Take a big bite out of crime, Mr. Laddington," another shouted.

"Take a bite out of the government's butt while you're at it, sir," a young woman yelled.

"We aim to do just that," the lawyer concluded, removing his hat and waving it high above his head in farewell. Laddington escorted Barbara Giordano toward the administration building.

"We love you, Barbara," a woman cried out.

Barbara turned and blew her a kiss.

"When is Tony getting out?" an elderly demonstrator called through cupped hands.

"Twenty-fourth of the month, we pray."

The two celebrities disappeared inside the building, leaving their smiles and warmth at the door.

Just inside the entranceway, the pair was met by a pretty nurse.

"Where is Mr. Redler?" Jonathan Laddington asked in a disarming tone, slapping his Stetson menacingly against the side of a pant leg.

"Please follow me," the nurse said as cordially as she could. The three made their way through the lobby and rode the elevator to the second floor. "Right this way, please," the nurse directed, leading the couple around the corridor and into an outer office. "Doctor Bianco will see you in a moment," she said, excusing herself then entering the doctor's private office suite.

"Ah, the inner sanctum," Laddington remarked, stepping, *uninvited*, into the commodious space, impatiently exploring the room with his dark darting eyes. Barbara stood at this side.

Doctor Bianco was standing behind his desk. "Please. Have a seat," he said politely.

"Rather pressed for time, Doc. Unless, of course, we'll be speaking with Mr. Redler right here in your office. Meaning Mrs. Giordano and myself," he stated matter-of-factly.

"I see."

"I'm sure that you do, Doctor."

"Then, we'll just put aside the formalities and get right down to business."

"My business is with Mr. Redler, Doctor Bianco. You and I have exhausted our conversation," he said with certain disdain.

"I was hoping we might first have a little chat—"

"My chats start at several thousand dollars an hour. Now, I know that you're in a bit of a spot, but I'm sure you can find yourself a competent attorney right here in good ol' New York."

Doctor Bianco ran his eyes up and down the arrogant high-priced peddler in fancy footwear. "May I ask what those boots are made out of, Mr. Laddington," Doctor Bianco asked and smiled, taking a different tact.

"Snake," Laddington answered curtly.

"How fitting."

"Yes. Now, might we move this along? You and I have nothing further to say to one another," Laddington reiterated.

At that remark, the nurse turned and took her leave.

"Mrs. Giordano?"

"Doctor?"

"Would you mind seeing this cowboy and yourself into that outer office where you were asked to wait? I think my nurse just ran for cover. I'll send for Mr. Redler and set the three of you up in a conference room down the hall."

Barbara and the attorney crossed the threshold to the outer office. Doctor Bianco closed the door and called for one of the orderlies to escort Robert Redler to the visiting area.

Chapter
——>
40

Several hours later, Robert F. Redler surrendered to state police through his attorney, Jonathan L. Laddington. By nightfall, Redler was out on bond and in the arms of Liza, while a private security force of eight well-trained, well-armed men and women in their late twenties stood guard both inside and outside the couple's Riverside Drive residence.

By late morning, an elaborate security system had been installed; not to mention a private telephone. Three rotating teams provided around-the-clock security, patrolling the grounds and home of the couple. The only thing short of house arrest was the absence of a monitoring bracelet on Redler's ankle. No one uninvited was getting in, and Robert and Liza were discouraged from going out. For when they did, great precautions had to be taken both in the home and around the property. Getting dressed to go out wasn't as simple as throwing on a coat. It was more like climbing into a lightweight suit of armor. Kevlar at its finest.

Frankly, it was a pain in the neck, the couple complained. And there was really nothing to go out for because all their needs were attended to. Anything they required, all they had to do was ask. Besides, the bullet fired from four hundred fifty yards that killed Mary Lou Dillany kept popping up in Redler's mind. How safe, really, was Liza or he, the homebound prisoner wondered.

In addition to eight warm bodies protecting Robert and Liza, there were additional private sector cars patrolling the streets while a security force scanned rooftops for snipers and such. In fact, security was so tight within a two-mile radius that half the Riverhead police force could have taken a leave of absence, Laddington's people had jokingly assured the press.

Although Redler theoretically had more freedom and mobility at home than the King Foundation, he nevertheless confined himself to a single room, writing away fervently at his desk for Barbara Giordano as contracted. And at the end of a long day, there was Liza and a lovely meal. The two were finally home together.

Barbara made no additional demands on him, even though they had lost considerable time. She was just glad that he had the good sense not to put anything down on paper in the King Foundation, a place where undercover police had been constantly milling around. Robert assured her that he had told them nothing concerning the details of their arrangement, apart from the fact that she helped sponsor his writing. Of course, she was upset with him for not having contacted her, but said she understood the circumstances. Besides, not all that much time had been wasted because he had done considerable research in areas related to the project. The King Foundation housed a marvelous library. Barbara was impressed, giving Robert a big hug and a kiss on the lips right in front of Liza, saying that she had bet on the right horse after all.

Late that evening, after Barbara Giordano had left and security saw the reunited couple to the bedroom door, their home seemed to grow especially quiet. Robert looked deep into Liza's eyes before he spoke.

"I have a gut feeling that this is going to be the calm before the storm," he whispered softly.

Liza smiled warmly. "How long have we been together?"

"Twenty-one years."

"Twenty-two come August."

He smiled back, waiting for Liza to make her point.

"We've weathered more than one storm together. Storms

concerning my daughter and my mother's demented side of the family," she sighed sadly. "Literally storms, too, in the middle of Long Island Sound and off Block Island aboard our little boat. And each time we pulled through because we always pulled together."

Robert nodded.

"So why should this time be different than any other?"

Robert lowered his eyes. "Listen to me."

"I'm listening."

"I have a premonition."

"A premonition." She said it with contemplation rather than the mere repetition of the word. "Can you be more specific?"

"Just that . . . ."

"That what, exactly?"

"It's an uneasy feeling that things are going to get real scary before anything is set right again."

"But things *will* be set right again," she added brightly.

"I'm sorry I put you through so much pain."

Liza took his hand and shook her head. "I could say that I put you through hell with my family, especially my daughter—may she rest in peace. We had no control of the situation. We always did or tried to do what we thought was the right thing. Right?"

"That we did."

"So, here we are."

"You have no uneasy feelings about not attending her funeral?"

Liza shook her head. "A bad seed from inception. I fought against my whole family to bring her into this world. My mother insisted that I have an abortion. My relatives were behind her one hundred percent. But my Catholic upbringing told me otherwise. There was nothing to argue about; there was nothing to discuss. So I had her. A product of the man who raped me. Let my family deal with her death. It's fitting because it's like they're all dead as far as I'm concerned. I'm numb to the experience. I regret having had her but would never have known that." She brushed away a tear.

Robert took Liza gently to him and kissed her tenderly, lightly stroking her blonde hair as she wept silently in his arms. "Shh," he whispered. "God is watching over her now."

Liza picked her head up in surprise, for he had never ever before acknowledged the acceptance of God in all their years together. He was smiling reassuringly, wiping away her tears. She nodded, putting her head against his shoulder, weeping silently at his side.

Chapter

——>

41

As law enforcement personnel were swarming over the counties of Long Island, Richard Geist had, at the last possible moment, switched an important Inner Circle of Friends meeting from Suffolk's East End to the Jersey Shore. The date and time were kept the same. Heads of each state convened at the new location. Everyone was early and eager to begin. Richard was already at the podium, smiling over a sea of beaming faces. This time out, there was no projection screen with six-inch lettering, for there were no recruits or soldiers in training. Everyone assembled read sign and signed flawlessly. Everyone present was a dyed-in-the-wool shepherd who commanded others of the flock. Black. Caucasian. Asian. Indian. Each with a proven ability in leadership. All with a single purpose of mind: the complete and total annihilation of our government, setting in its stead, new and awesome forces of control. Richard gestured that he was about to begin.

"*Welcome, and sign in, please,*" he signed with a grin. There followed hearty laughter and wild applause. Richard soon continued.

"*After eighteen years, we have suffered our first casualty.*" The room grew silent. "*Angelica must be driving them nuts by now,*" he signed and winked. Light laughter and cheering came from the first few rows. "*What's the matter? You can't hear me back there,*" he signed anew, addressing the others. Everyone started hooting and laughing and applauding loudly. *"I don't hear any whistling,"* he joked. *"I heard from one of our informants that when they asked Angelica where the meetings for the Inner Circle of Friends were held, she told them, Death Valley."*

The council doubled over in their seats.

"All right. Enough nonsense. Angelica will be back with us, when?"

"Should be free by the second week of April. Maybe sooner," a man to the left of the podium signed.

"They can make it next April, for all I care," he teased. *"When I'm around her, it's like I hear these voices."*

"Boo," all the women throughout the room jeered.

"Quit while you're ahead," another communicated.

"But don't quit your day job," a man in the middle section signed.

"Okay. Okay. I know when I'm licked if you'll pardon the pun. Now, down to business."

Six rows of smiling, happy faces suddenly turned solemn; all eyes were focused on Richard.

"All of you know by now that I'm having a little fun with this Robert Redler fellow. The authorities probably don't know what to believe anymore. But he's retained a high-priced, big shot lawyer who seems to be bailing him out of this distraction I've created. So I've decided to turn up the heat."

"I abhor lawyers," Maxine signed excitedly. *"I have just the young man for the job."*

Richard was shaking his head. *"I'm sorry I'm not making myself clear. It's not his lawyer I had in mind, Maxine. More like the college administration, and particularly the chairperson who fired Redler after his initial confrontation with the law. The time is ripe. Robby boy has recently lost a battle with the grievance committee. Of course, he has more important matters to worry about than teaching. Right now Robert Redler is learning a hard lesson,"* Richard assured with flashing fingers and a cocksure grin. *"Anyhow, there's that clown at Redler's unemployment hearing in Manhattan who shot him down. Also, the decision maker at his step-two hearing. Not to mention the college president and a dean. They wanted him out so as to avoid a scandal. Redler was considered a gifted teacher, well-liked by his students and peers. Such gratitude. So. This will be one of my final gifts to him for screwing around with me. After the authorities clean up that mess, they'll put him away for life,"* he fingerspelled and laughed.

"I've got the perfect person in mind," a man in the front row signed and stood. *"Worked at a college in the faculty cafeteria for thirty years before they fired him for poisoning cats."*

"Cats?" Richard questioned.

"Yes, cats. You see, many college campuses are dumping-grounds for strays because those who drop them off know the students will care for them."

"Fine, but what does that have to do with your man and why he was fired?"

"Well, when the administration found him out, he told them he loves to poison anything with whiskers. Half the faculty had beards," the man signed with a straight face.

The men and women in the audience were practically falling off their seats.

"You better sit down before I poison you," Richard jokingly made clear.

"No, I'm dead serious. He's fantastic. I've used him several times before."

"All right. Poison it is. You have your man take care of this college matter, both on and off campus, whiskers or not. Skip will give you their names and schedules. And I better not hear of any cats or dogs lying around with their tongues hanging out. Start messing around with animals and the Inner Circle of Friends is really going to get a bad rap," he teased. *"I'm personally going to retire that detective, what's-his-name? The one from the Sex Crimes Unit who was assigned to Redler's case. Been saving him for the grand finale."*

"Detective Fork," the figure beside him signed.

"Right. Oh, and before I forget, we ought to give Skip and his team a big hand for that four-hundred-fifty-yard kill that brought down a Queens prosecutor last week. Now, that was a

nifty piece of work. Stand up, Skip. I want you to tell your crew for me what a fantastic job they did, and how very proud I am of all of them. I know it was no easy task getting out of there undetected. Again, you did us all proud."

Everyone applauded Skip and his team. Skip smiled modestly and sat back down.

"Now, I know this business of late seems like child's play to most of you as we have many more important assignments coming up in the very near future. But I want to send out a clear message to local law enforcement that their days are drawing to a close. What we did in New York this past month, we are going to repeat on a grand scale throughout the forty-eight contiguous states, twelve months out of the year. The revolution is fast approaching, my friends."

All were on their feet, and all were grunting and applauding loudly. Richard nodded his appreciation.

"Why not fifty states?" a middle-aged man signed after the applause subsided.

"Well, we have to leave two clean environments and contrasting climates to vacation in once our mission is under way. Hawaii for those of us who like it hot, and Alaska for those of us who like it cold."

Thunderous applause and laughter filled the auditorium for several minutes before Richard could continue.

"In a moment we're going to hear from our treasurer who will probably bore you with how much money we're worth collectively and how much each of you is worth, net. Now, it's been rumored that the government wants to rescind the tax exempt status that some of our umbrella organizations have always enjoyed. But I don't see how that could impact the network of assassins assembled here. I mean, if we had to, we could even deduct rope and rat poison." Several chuckles mixed with polite smiles went Richard's way. *"All right. So I'm not Jay Leno. Just remember that he's only around today because he hasn't poked fun at the Inner Circle of Friends,"* Richard pushed the envelope.

"We want to be bored silly by the treasurer," Skip signed from his seat.

And the place fell apart again, encouraging Skip to stand as Richard's stand-in. Skip clasped his hands high above his head before the cheering crowd. The council was practically rolling in the aisles.

Richard frowned, dissembling before the crowd. "*My mother thought I was funny.*"

"*Maybe* that's *why you killed her. You found out early on you really weren't,*" a young man kidded.

"*Listen, Kenny. I know where you golf. Next time you're on the fairway with a five iron, maybe your ball will explode,*" Richard kidded back.

"*I'm going to pee in my pants*," Maxine roared, her fingers dancing high above her head. "*I think we should take this show on the road.*"

Suddenly, a back door to the building flew open, and two of Richard's soldiers roughly dragged in a man they held by the shoulders. The figure stumbled and fell forward, apparently in pain.

"*We apologize for the sudden interruption,*" one of the soldiers signed, "*but we found this intruder prowling around outside. Thought it shouldn't wait.*"

Richard was staring at the familiar figure, seeming genuinely surprised. "*Oh, you're so right, David. And so are you, Maxine. I think we should take this show on the road immediately,*" Richard communicated in a calm and cautious manner. "*Anyone with him?*"

The two soldiers shook their heads.

"*How did he get up here?*"

"*On foot. His car is at the bottom of the bluff. We had it moved temporarily out of sight.*"

Richard nodded approval. "*Maybe we'll take it with us. But first let's get Carla up here to translate for this clown.*"

An attractive young woman hurried over to Richard's side.

Richard turned his attention back to the trespasser as the woman communicated her leader's sign.

"*Well, well, well. Deputy Inspector Lancing,*" Richard Geist began, dancing his fingers through the air as Carla interpreted with her thick Italian accent. "*We finally meet. Come.*

We'll converse along the way. I'm sorry you missed the main attraction. I'm afraid my audience was getting the better of me. You could have seen my human side for what it's worth. Is there something the matter with your shoulder and neck? Our people can be a bit overzealous, especially if they thought you were trying to sneak a peek without an invite. You do have a ticket, don't you? You wouldn't want me to think that you were trying to beat us on the price of admission. Do you know what the price of admission to this clip joint is, Inspector? We clip your tongue free of charge; and in return, you give us your undying loyalty and unrequited love. It's really a bargain. We retire you at age fifty with no less than ten million dollars spread throughout your golden years. That's if we recruit you by age twenty. Less of a package, of course, if you join us late in the game. You can even name a beneficiary so long as he or she is not a government employee. Full medical. Dental. Unlimited sick leave. Christ, we all get sick from time to time." Richard paused and grinned. *"A four-week vacation for starters and the privilege of working mostly in the great outdoors. And if you're ambitious, Inspector Lancing—if you serve well and reach this plateau—well, the world is your oyster. Yes, indeed."*

Along the precipice, members of the council were filing by. It was a cold but beautiful moonlit night. Inspector Lancing was being led along the path, but suddenly stopped.

"You're a fucking evil bastard, Geist. And you're going down," Lancing swore.

"Very brave, sir. Defiance in the face of death. You're quite a good detective to have tracked us here. Remarkable, actually. Are you sure you didn't have some help along the way? Such a shame. I could have used a man of your ability," Richard signed as the woman translated coldly.

"You're going down," Lancing repeated.

"No, Inspector Lancing," Richard signaled and signed for the benefit of no one save his female soldier. *"I'm afraid it's you who is going down,"* he nodded to the woman. *"Please send Deputy Inspector Lancing quietly on ahead, then meet us at the base of the cliff."*

It appeared as though the luminous eye in the night sky

suddenly blinked as a silhouetted body went sailing off through space before breaking up silently upon the rocks below.

Richard watched the cop's descent to the bottom of the sixty-foot jagged escarpment, saluting the deputy inspector adieu.

Chapter
——>
42

Detective Steven Fork was sitting in the living room of his cluttered Long Island home. How anyone could have gotten past security was beyond the realm of reasoning. But Richard had. He simply had himself delivered. Sort of like the Trojan Horse. Only it wasn't a horse at all, but a crated riding machine with a fair amount of horsepower. It was Saturday morning when the truck arrived. After being checked by security, the driver and his helper lowered the crate in front of Fork's spacious three-car garage.

"No, no, no," Fork insisted hurrying over to the two men. "I want it inside the garage, please. I left a space on the right."

The driver and helper hopped back into the truck as Fork pushed the remote, raising the garage door. The driver hit a lever within the cab, and up came the wooden container, resting solidly on the front end of a hydraulic platform. Fork directed the truck forward. After the box was lowered and perfectly positioned, the detective signed the invoice and tipped the driver.

It was noon before Fork decided to uncrate his brand new toy. Of course, there was no real hurry, but he couldn't wait until springtime to at least take a peek and perhaps sit upon his prize Red Ryder. Taking a crowbar off the workbench, he pried loose a strip of pine.

CRACK!

Two security guards were at the garage door.

"Need a hand?" one of the men asked.

"No. You guys go inside and grab some lunch," Fork insisted. "Pot of coffee is on the counter."

"Suit yourself."

"You can bring me back a cup, though," the detective called out.

"Right."

Fork removed a half a dozen slats and was delighted to see patches of shiny red metal between sheets of protective plastic covering. He was like a kid tearing open a great big birthday gift. What he saw next unnerved him. A hand. It came from out of nowhere and took him powerfully by the throat, fingers clutching tenaciously around the detective's windpipe.

NEED A HAND? was the message printed on a placard with bold red lettering, fixed to the shiny blade of a black-handled bayonet.

Fork fought in vain for his piece, holstered hopelessly out of reach at his ankle. The detective's eyes bulged in a mix of fear and hatred as Richard rose from the seat.

I'M GLAD YOU DIDN'T MAKE ME FORCE THE SPRING, STEVEN, were the words printed on the flip side of the sign that the cop never got to read, for Richard played his part to the hilt, delivering the missive smack between the man's ribs, the ten-inch dagger-like steel disappearing deep into the detective's heart. Detective Fork collapsed.

Richard withdrew the bloody blade before taking up a rather long tube taped to the floor of the crate. About to vanish through a window, he heard footsteps.

One of the security guards was heading back toward the garage with coffee in hand. As the man came around the corner, he suddenly dropped the container and grabbed the side of his neck. A tiny shiny arrow did its damage almost instantly, but Richard blew him another which struck just to the rear and below the man's left ear.

Richard was gone in an instant, leaving behind the tools of the trade: bayonet, blowgun, and a handful of deadly poison darts.

*****

The following morning, another murder story appeared in the papers. Katherine Gale, the woman who chaired the English Department where Redler had taught, had suddenly fallen victim to what associates believed was a serious case of food poisoning. However, toxicologists later concluded that the professor's death was the result of a toxic agent discovered in her drink. That afternoon, two colleagues connected with Redler's dismissal found themselves being rushed to treatment centers for stomach and intestinal problems. One poor soul vomited for several hours then suddenly succumbed. Another thought his head would split before he convulsed, fell into a coma then died.

A note was sent to college officials:

To Whom It May Concern:

Your prescription regarding the dismissal of Robert F. Redler was ill-fated.

Rx

Chapter
——>
43

At the end of March, the authorities felt they had gotten their first real break. Deputy Inspector Lancing was still missing, but the inspector's wife had told them about something that her husband had been working on. A secret *something*. Police Chief Grear was sharing that piece of information with his superiors. The trio sat and listened attentively. Three men with the power to tie a state into knots. And they were doing just that.

"Richard Geist left behind only the things he wanted us to find in his studio apartment," Grear expounded. "Evidence that would incriminate Robert Redler. And although the building superintendent said that nothing was missing from Geist's furnished apartment, no furniture or appliances or anything like that, there was an item of significant size that Richard had moved in with then took with him when he left." Grear paused for effect.

"We're all ears," a mousy-looking gentleman stated.

"A freezer," Grear replied.

"A freezer?" a second man echoed.

"Yes. An old Fridgit-King. We knew from the impression left in the linoleum that it had to be something pretty heavy."

"Is the super sure about this?" the third gentleman asked.

"Yes. The freezer didn't belong to the building. We just learned that the tenant, who gave his name as Gary Fletcher, who is Richard Geist, of course, had ordered it soon after he moved in. We have a record of when it was ordered and delivered. He had it removed shortly before he moved out."

"Why was it so important for Geist to have a freezer, do you think? Food for his fold, I'd bet," the same fellow asked and answered.

"Initially, I thought so, too," Grear admitted. "But I believe he was hibernating in that apartment. For a significant period of time, no one saw him come or go. The old woman above him always heard him though."

"Interesting."

"What's your theory, Grear?" the thin, frail figure sitting between his colleagues asked, the hint of arrogance written across his scrawny face.

"Well, it's more than a theory, now," Grear stated.

"Go on."

"Lancing told his wife that he had a solid lead on Geist. He found the freezer."

"So, Lancing was freelancing," the tallest of the three mocked.

Grear said nothing. The trio looked at one another and then back at Grear. "Where?"

"North Shore State Hospital for the Criminally Insane."

"Havenwood?"

"From where Richard escaped eighteen years ago," Grear added.

"But why would he have a freezer delivered there?"

Grear shook his head.

"There's got to be some connection."

"Maybe Geist had it delivered there to drive us all crazy. To throw us off track," the man sitting on the far end offered.

Grear was shaking his head. "Out of fifty-three patients released there in the last six months, fourteen have dropped out of sight. No one knows where they are."

"What are you saying?"

"I'm saying that the North Shore State facility, and others like it, may be fertile recruiting grounds for the likes of Richard

Geist's elite corps."

"That's crazy. Many of those patients are completely dysfunctional and couldn't follow their feet."

"Many of them are," Grear agreed. "However, I think Richard's people carefully select those who can be recruited and properly trained."

Grear wanted to use the word *cured*, but he knew they wouldn't buy it. Certainly they had to know that more than just a handful of those inmates were not at all crazy to begin with, just 'crazy like a fox' as Lieutenant Lark had believed Richard was from the start. Like the slick bastards Robert Redler wrote about. Grear also knew that the three men sitting across from him would not be able to accept the idea that Richard could successfully rehabilitate those considered beyond the hope of recovery. But Richard had a gift. The gift his father had.

But what neither Police Chief Grear nor the trio knew at that moment was the degree of success the cult leader actually achieved. For Richard was able to restore in a soul what society had renounced, thereby converting and perverting vast numbers of patients to suit his own end. He had given his following a new religion, a greatness along with an awareness that the world around them was filled with hope. He had given each of them a power and a purpose. He taught them how to love to hate. He taught them how to temper their violence and direct it to *the cause*. He provided them with lots of money but showed them how to save and use currency as a tool. And like most religions, he gave them an icon to worship other than himself. He gave them insights into an image they would not fear. Richard had bestowed upon their psyche the lithe and noble deer, instructing his worshipers on the creature's inner strengths and its ability to survive.

"So, what's your next step?" the man in the middle asked Grear impatiently.

"To monitor those patients who are close to release."

"Then have them followed?"

"Exactly."

"I see."

"And do you have someone on the inside?" his associate

189

pressed.

"We have a snitch. A black mute by the name of Alex Lether. Outpatient at North Shore State. Been in and out of institutions most of his adult life."

"How did you decide on him?"

"Actually, he decided on us. Heard we were asking questions. He told us that he'd been approached. Claims he knew someone who was recruited."

"Can you trust him?"

"I'm not sure," Grear said candidly.

"You be careful, Grear," the ferret-faced figure stated, about to leave his seat.

"May I ask you about the woman, Angelica?" Grear directed his question to all or any of the three.

"The feds are still holding her. But not for long. She's not saying a word. If she tells us anything, you'll hear about it."

"Thank you, gentlemen."

"Thank you, Chief Grear."

Chapter
——>
44

Police Chief Grear knew that a good part of Richard Geist's success had to lie in the fact that no one was talking. That is, up until now —so to speak—the cop punned and pondered, for they had Alex Lether in their corner. Grear kept running the thought back and forth across his brain as to whether or not the mute could be trusted.

Successful police work sometimes began with the furtive tip. The anonymous phone call. The paid informant. Many times it was simply a matter of interrogating people until they broke down and gave you what you wanted. Rarely did it begin with pure unadulterated police work performed with the proverbial magnifying glass and brilliant powers of deduction. Most often, those elements were brought to light and into play following a forensics lab report. Of course, the sophisticated science of eavesdropping put the police miles ahead of the game. Yet, on the streets and in back alleys, pool halls, as well as local bar and grills, where word spread faster than money or drugs, no one had ever heard a single syllable concerning Alex Lether or a band of fanatics he had supposedly worshiped. Not a whisper to either confirm or deny the man's confidential talk with police.

Why? Grear wondered.

Was Lether a patient with a fertile imagination, or had Grear's people stumbled upon sacred ground? Of all the powers of police work, in many cases, nothing proved more potent than the power of the hunch. But Grear was beset with ambivalent feelings that something was very right and, at the same time, very wrong. Even after being proven wrong concerning his theory regarding Mr. Magic Face, he had been right to a degree . . . the degree that Richard had allowed before he most magically made the Riverhead police chief appear as a fool.

For a moment, Grear had entertained the notion that Geist's people were all a band of mutes. Like Richard himself. Along with Lether. Angelica had a tongue but held it. Lether had one in his head yet couldn't speak since birth but learned to read and write, though rather poorly, whereas Richard had his tongue aborted in the booby hatch in Havenwood by Lieutenant Lark, Grear reflected. For an instant, the police chief held a fleeting thought as one might a key phrase or word suddenly lost on the tip of one's tongue. What was it? He couldn't quite take hold of it. Where did it go?

Suddenly, he was on the phone with Havenwood. Forty minutes later, he had orderlies opening the mouths of catatonics and several other patients who hadn't uttered a word in years.

"Can you tell us exactly what you're looking for, Chief Grear?" one of the nurses asked in confusion.

"Strep throat," Grear deadpanned, feeling quite ridiculous.

Once again, with the help of pen and paper, the police chief went over Lether's story. Again. And again. And again. And this time, Lether had remembered something he had seemingly forgotten until that moment. An area he had heard about along the Jersey Shore.

Twenty-four hours later, Grear's men recovered Inspector Lancing's broken and decomposed body. Lether's information was rock solid. They found Lancing's car several miles away in an abandoned warehouse. A mannequin dressed as a uniformed cop was sitting behind the steering wheel. Its arms and legs were smashed to bits. The dummy's busted head faced backward; the police cap off to the side. A cigarette hung from the shattered plastic mouth. A note attached to the coat read: Close, but no cigar.

The handwriting, but of course, was Geist's. Grear wanted

to scream. With the cooperation of the feds, every deaf and mute institution in the tri-state area had been checked and rechecked. Every adult home and house of worship had been revisited and combed for a sign or a clue: cloisters, monasteries, convents, et cetera. Any establishment where silence was considered golden.

Nothing.

Chief Grear sat alongside Doctor Bianco in the psychiatrist's outer office.

"Well, we lost Redler to that Texan in fancy footwear. Found Lancing. And now I'm afraid I'm losing you," the chief of police declared.

Bianco shook his head. "I'm afraid I'm losing my mind," he said. "I lost my heart when I lost Donna. I don't want to lose Timmy, too. I don't know how much help I can really be."

The man looked terrible, shaving and bathing every other day. His black wavy hair was greasy and matted. It appeared as though he had slept in his clothes if, indeed, he had slept at all.

"Look. Why don't you try and pull yourself together. I know—easy to say. But I need your help to beat this fucking monster. You find a way to fuck with his mind, and I'll fuckin' blow him apart when he rears his fucking flaming red head."

"You've been using that word a lot lately." Bianco managed a smile.

"Listen, I know what you're going through."

Bianco shook his head again. "I used to imagine how my predecessor felt after Richard murdered his own mother—Doctor King's fiancée. He was so in love with her. He worshipped her. Like I worshipped Donna. You can't imagine how I feel. Believe me, you can't."

Grear nodded. "Perhaps not. But I know how we'd all feel if we caught this bastard. I feel I'm missing one small piece of the puzzle. A critical piece. A piece that prevents me from seeing the whole picture."

"You're not going to go back to Mr. Magic Face, or Havenwood, now are you?"

"Oh, so you heard about my little visit."

"I was on the phone with one of the doctors. They wanted

to know what you were really after. Everyone wants to help."

"I don't know . . . I had this crazy notion."

"Such as?"

"Such as none of them have a tongue in their head. Like Richard."

"Angelica has. So does Lether."

"Yeah, but he couldn't speak from birth. Just strange that he pops up now."

"Does he sign?"

"Nope. Never learned. He has to write everything down."

"Can he read?"

"Of course he can read. If you can write, you can read. That's how we communicate with him. Can't spell worth a shit, though," he joked.

"That's not what I mean. I mean, read sign. Many mutes can read sign fairly well without knowing how to sign. Just like someone can understand a foreign language but not necessarily speak it. I speak seven different languages. I understand several others. But I can't speak them."

Grear was staring at Bianco as if the doctor had a third eye in the center of his forehead. "Thanks, Doc." Grear stood abruptly.

"Where are you going?"

"Guess."

"Back to Havenwood?"

With his back to the doctor, the police chief gave him the high sign. "But first I'm going back to school."

Chapter
——>
45

Alex Lether moved the mop and bucket wringer along the corridor as if he were sweeping a metal detector above a strip of beach instead of mopping the lengthy, expansive floor. He did his chore effortlessly, yet with set determination scored across his lips. Working his way around the corner, he looked up in surprise to see Police Chief Grear back again, this time with several police officers standing beside one of the nurse's stations. A doctor and two orderlies came hurriedly over to the counter. A woman in her late twenties and a group of students from St. Joseph's School for the Hearing Impaired were passing through the area. Grear seemed upset, excused himself then went quickly down the hall. Lether was picking up his pace, steadily mopping his way toward the nurse's station.

"What was that all about?" a nurse asked a young doctor.

"Not now!" the psychiatrist snapped, pulling the orderlies aside.

"*What happened?*" one of the students visiting from the school for the hearing and speech impaired signed.

"*Something about the FBI and a woman hanging herself in her cell,*" another signed excitedly.

"*Holy cow!*"

"All right, boys and girls. Let's all move along," the woman from St. Joseph's signed and spoke. "We're going downstairs now to see doctors and nurses work with patients in physical therapy."

"No way," one of her charges babbled comprehensibly. "I want to see doctors and nurses work with patients in *group* therapy."

"*I'm going to talk with the doctors and nurses about putting you in group therapy*," she teased. "*How many want to see Matthew in group therapy?*"

A dizzying amount of fingers went dancing through the air.

Lether put his mop aside and disappeared down the other end of the hall. He was clearly agitated as he dialed a seven digit number . . . hung up after the first ring . . . dialed again . . . then hung up. Looking nervously over his shoulder, he dialed the number for a third and final time, immediately hanging up the receiver and returning to work.

Less than thirty minutes later, Lether had a visitor. A woman by the name of Maxine Waters came to see him. She signed the visitor's log at the front desk. It wasn't visiting hours, but it really didn't matter because Lether was an outpatient who worked and resided at the hospital. A trusted individual. The doctors had decided several years ago that their patient was no longer a danger to himself or anyone, that the man was making progress by leaps and bounds, building a newfound confidence and civility which they hadn't seen before, giving themselves a pat on the back and reminding everyone of where this poor soul had been but a decade ago: at the bottom of the heap.

Maxine was listed as Lether's former landlady who had initially taken an interest in the misanthrope and would carry word back and forth to his rather reticent family. True enough in part. But if the administration had only known about his newfound family and who this woman really was, they'd have cringed.

Maxine took a seat beside Lether in the visitor's lounge and read his note, smiling and giggling, never uttering a single word. Lether communicated by writing frantically, pushing the paper under her nose. Maxine just shook her head and sighed, tapping the back of Lether's hand, insisting by nods and facial expressions that his words simply were not true. Lether was becoming more and more unsettled. Finally, Maxine took the paper and pen and wrote but a single word. Lether stared down at the paper before looking up into her round face and sparkling eyes. Maxine nodded emphatically, tapped the back of his hand again reassuringly, took the paper, and was gone.

Grear signaled for his men not to follow her.

Lether had gone to his room, feeling somewhat relieved.

"You able to trace that number, Jim?" the police chief asked a man coming down the hallway dressed in coveralls and carrying a black leather case.

"Got it," the cop affirmed with a thumbs-up.

A plainclothes detective, police Sergeant Dennis Phelps, spoke up smartly, addressing the group of excited students through a translator while several other children read his lips.

"Well, he definitely took the bait, boys and girls." Phelps beamed proudly at the two youngsters who practically melted on the spot. "You girls really pulled it off," he assured the pair. "You should have seen his face. But let me add that you were *all* great. I really mean that. And I want to hear it for my main man Matthew, here," he said, tousling the boy's hair. "Take a bow, Matthew."

There was nothing shy about Matthew, for he took a dozen, behaving like the clown he was.

The performances by everyone had been flawless, having played their roles to perfection. The part of the teacher had been fittingly portrayed by St. Joseph's drama coach, a class that all the children from the school attended. Having had but a morning of rehearsal, they were nonetheless ready and eager by late afternoon. The group felt very proud and had a perfect right to be. Even several of the doctors and nurses thought they themselves were headed for the stage.

Both Sergeant Phelps and Chief Grear sincerely thanked everyone for their cooperation before he and his men got down to business.

"So, whattaya got Jimmy?" Grear asked impatiently.

"Seven miles east of here. The Villa Immaculata," the undercover cop declared, handing over a list of particulars.

Grear smiled and nodded, thanking and dismissing the man before taking Sergeant Phelps aside.

"The Villa's the place where Robert Redler bowhunts," Phelps said. "Right?"

"Right."

"You think the cult operates out of there?"

"No," Grear said emphatically.

"Then where?"

"Where the deer run freely."

"Deer?"

"And a vow of silence is sacred."

"Like a monastery?"

"Like the one out east in Island Park."

"Or that convent."

"On the south side of Flanders Bay."

"Hubbard Hills. But our boys have been through those places. So have the feds."

"True. But you and I haven't."

"So then how does the Villa Immaculata fit in?"

"Very nicely," Grear answered enigmatically, nodding with a certain satisfaction as things were beginning to finally make some sense.

"Meaning?"

"A common meeting ground for Geist's group whenever the nuns are away visiting other retreats and the place is empty. I think Richard Geist and his flock move about like nomads."

"Come on, Chief. We'd have heard something by now."

"Heard?" Grear shook his head. "Where silence is golden?"

"But even those walls have ears. We'd have picked up something, I'm sure."

"Not if no one *says* a word."

"What?"

"What if the sect is clipped?"

"I don't understand."

"What if Geist's followers have no tongue to wag? Just like Richard. You couldn't make a slip. You couldn't spill the beans, even accidentally if you got a little tipsy from too much of that sacramental wine," he said half-jokingly.

"You're saying that Richard cut the tongues out of their heads, just like that?"

The Signing

"The Turks clipped the tongues out of the heads of the Greeks, just like that," Grear affirmed, snapping his fingers sharply.

"Well, I'm not up on my history, Chief, but I'll bet they didn't have too much of a say about it," he quipped indulgently.

"You're right. But supposing Richard *had* given them a choice?"

"You mean, his way or no way? Then I guess he wouldn't have recruited many politicians, preachers, or insurance salesmen, heaven forbid."

"That's pretty funny, Sergeant. It's one of the reasons I take you with me on these outings," he said and laughed fondly, recalling the line Lieutenant Lark had so often used whenever Grear, as a young sergeant, was brought along on assignment.

"Lillian says I'm a born comedian. Even my parents think I'm funny. But they wanted me to become an accountant. I'm really good with numbers, I want you to know."

"I'll keep that in mind," Grear promised. "Now, let's just say for the sake of argument that *your* choice was clip or be clipped?"

"I guess I'd volunteer."

"Especially if you were promised this world and the next."

"I don't know if that would make it any easier, though. I mean, you'd have to have had Lillian's linguine and white clam sauce to know what I'm talking about," the sergeant offered, still humoring his superior.

"So, why don't you have me over for dinner some evening when this business is finished?"

"You're on! So where do we go from here?"

"Island Park and Hubbard Hills, I would imagine."

"What about the Villa and that phone call?"

"An office phone with a volunteer and caller ID? They wouldn't have Lether call home away from home. All that is is an emergency number. That's why I didn't want Maxine Waters picked up. We'd have tipped our hand."

"You're sure about all this?"

"Call it a hunch."

Sergeant Phelps was tempted to ask his chief if there was

any validity to the rumors he heard tell of the Mr. Magic Face debacle, but he didn't dare. Deputy Inspector Lancing had been pissed and spread that story about like manure around tomato plants. So the sergeant tried a more logical tact.

"One thing bothers me about your theory, Chief."

"Shoot."

"Both Lether and Angelica still have their tongues in their heads."

"Yes, but Lether's a mute from birth."

"And this Angelica woman?"

"Really not much difference seeing as how she hasn't said shit so far. Besides which, they'd need at least one trusted soul in their midst to communicate verbally in a pinch."

"From what I hear, she communicates both verbally and orally," Phelps funned, driving home his point with that double entendre.

Grear smiled. "Any way you look at it, no one seems to say a word."

"But the only one minus a tongue for *sure* is Richard."

"It didn't look like Maxine had anything to say either," Grear reminded him.

"True enough. But the nurse on duty said the woman indicated she had laryngitis."

"I don't know, Sergeant. It's the only thing I come up with that would explain why we haven't heard a single, solitary word. Nothing. If I'm right, it tells us we've got a band of fanatics on our hands. The kind that would never know from Lillian's white clam sauce," he added in all seriousness.

Phelps was beginning to digest Grear's theory. Not necessarily buying into it. "So let's say we find a nest. We don't know their strength in terms of numbers. The feds say there might be other splinter groups in Jersey, Connecticut and the D.C. area. What if there are nests up and down the coast?"

"Still, the killing sprees have been confined to New York, with the exception being Lancing out in New Jersey. Who knows?"

"The real mystery is how Robert Redler really fits into all this. Do you think he could be part of this cult, Chief? This Circle of Friends?"

"I don't know. But one thing's for certain. He sure is not the one killing all those people. Not directly, anyhow."

"Got that right."

"Come on. Let's go find us some religion."

Chapter
——>
46

During the drive out east, Grear was being updated by Captain Cally as to their suspects' status. Maxine Waters booked a flight to Hawaii for that very evening, and Alex Lether kept to his room at the hospital. The feds still held on to Angelica. None of the three had a criminal record. Maxine and Lether were seen as deeply devout churchgoers. Friends and neighbors who had known Maxine years ago in Miami, knew her to be guilty of gossip. Nothing more. A nonstop chatterbox. If you had asked her how she was doing, she would have praised the Lord and bent your ear for forty minutes at a clip. One day she just upped and disappeared. Lether, on the other hand, never spoke a word in his life. That fact was checked and double-checked. He had been a janitor and handyman for several houses of worship. He never seemed to have trouble mingling with church folk or men and women of the cloth. Pen and paper was his standard means of communication. But whenever he sought work in the community at large, he would invariably find himself in trouble. Nothing serious. He just didn't like outsiders was all. As time went by, the hospital in Havenwood became his home.

Chief Grear thanked Captain Cally then called Bianco at the Foundation, discussing Waters and Lether at length. He did not need the psychiatrist to tell him that both Maxine and Alex were prime candidates for indoctrination, so long as a suitable sermon was attached. Angelica, or whatever her real name was, was another story. Truly fearless. Manipulative. Bright, if not brilliant. Dangerous as they come. Bianco went so far as to tell Grear that she might one day be Richard's rival.

Grear appreciated the fact that Bianco did not attach psychiatric labels to every mode of behavior he saw. The good doctor simply placed his patients between the poles of a little bit crazy to quote unquote, *stark-raving mad*, adding that Richard's bell would ring way beyond the boundary of the circus strongman's striker, sounding off somewhere in outer space. Grear loved that comparison, for Bianco's daily world of entertainment was indeed a series of sideshows. But Grear, like his predecessor, Lieutenant Lark, believed that Richard was crazy like a fox. Sly. Slick. Anything but sick. And what difference did it really matter, the police chief often thought. If you were evil and destructive, causing decent people pain and loss through murderous acts, you had to be destroyed. Plain and simple. Where but between heaven and hell was there any room for discussion? But the laws of the state would be carried into the courtroom if Richard Geist were apprehended. And the defendant would either be sent to prison or another psychiatric institution, either of which left no room for reasoning as far as the chief was concerned. Grear felt he knew at least one of the reasons why Richard had picked and was holed up in the State of New York. It didn't have the death penalty. Not yet, anyhow.

If Lancing had only been a team player, they would have been so much further along the line, Grear believed. Then again, perhaps the deputy inspector had found the freezer because Richard wanted someone to find it in order to limit the investigation to the North Fork of Long Island, the police chief entertained. *But then why leave Lancing's car and body in New Jersey with an incriminating note?* he argued with himself at cross-purposes. Bianco had said that it showed sheer defiance and arrogance. It was Richard's way of sending home a clear message. *Close, but no cigar.* It also sent a subtle message, for Lieutenant Lark—his departed friend—had cherished cigars.

The police chief knew that Richard was toying with him

now as he had toyed with Lark and the authorities then.

Close, but no cigar, Grear said silently. *Not yet, Richard Geist. But soon,* he promised.

Sergeant Phelps took the map off Grear's lap and pulled over. "I thought you were navigating."

"Thinking."

"Think you made me miss the turnoff. Here we go. Go back to sleep."

"I wasn't sleeping."

"Right."

Grear closed his eyes and realized he'd been to more funerals over the past several months than in his entire career as a cop. Since the beginning of March, the murder rate in New York had soared to an average of three per day. Richard's assassins were responsible for a third.

Twenty minutes later, Sergeant Phelps parked the car near a meadow, and the two began walking along the woodland, the chief pointing out deer sign along the way. Phelps was somewhat impressed.

The FBI in conjunction with other agencies had already been through every known convent, monastery, retreat, shack, shanty, and cloistered commune in the entire tri-state area. They, too, hadn't missed the monastery in Island Park or the convent atop Hubbard Hills. Nor had they missed the immediate surroundings. What they had missed were a series of signposts: telltale rubs, tracks, droppings, and scrapes found just below overhanging branches, which had been gnawed away with vigor. They missed the early sign of acorns, apple orchards, and bushes that had been replete with berries and branchlets. They missed them because they were looking solely for Richard and his band of renegades. They hadn't been looking for deer. The deer had taken to the lowlands to protect themselves from the harsh winter as high winds had sent the mercury down to the low teens and minus zero range for months on end. No, it wasn't necessarily the buildings or the immediate area where they'd find Richard and his fold. It was the lowlands and the thickets that held the key.

"I didn't know you were quite the hunter. Are we looking

for deer here now?"

Grear didn't bother telling him that he had gotten his newfound knowledge from books and scores of magazines on bowhunting. A crash course. "Probably won't see any knocking about like this."

"So why are we down here instead of up there at the monastery?"

"Because, as you yourself said, everyone's been through the place. Because we were reading the wrong kinds of sign from the get-go. Because this lowland leads to a narrow body of water which connects the monastery in Island Park to the convent in Hubbard Hills. And because there's absolutely no hunting, fishing or trespassing allowed anywhere around here as those signs over there read."

"So what are we after?" the young detective sergeant asked, looking up at the sky and enjoying the first of the fifty-degree weather.

"Sign."

"Sign of what? I gotta know what I'm looking for, Chief."

"Do you, now?"

"Yep."

"Or do you want to be a good detective?"

Phelps looked at him queerly. "Sure I do."

"Well," the chief explained, "there are times you *won't* know what you're looking for."

"Hey, I got a brother-in-law like that. Never knew what the hell he was looking for in life. Still doesn't. Think maybe he'd make a good detective? Maybe I can bring him around. Tell me something, Chief. How do you know when you find what it is when you're not exactly sure what you're looking for in the first place?"

"It fits," Grear said flatly.

"Fits, huh?" Phelps said, running his eyes along a wood line to the south, staring up at a group of tall trees. "You think maybe that fits?" he asked, lowering his voice and pointing fifty yards off to their right. "Or how about over there?" he added. "And what about over there?"

Grear stared at the tops of the trees then ran his eyes

downward until something uniform broke the irregular line of thick hoary branches. "Tree stands!" Grear remarked quietly. "About thirty feet high."

"You think maybe we found what it is we didn't know we were looking for?"

"I think maybe you really *are* a comedian. And a good detective to boot," Grear stated excitedly, breaking out a pair of field glasses. "A dozen or so platforms way the hell up there with no way to get up or down from them. Strange. I don't see any ladders . . . or tree steps, or anything."

"You're really into this shit, I see."

"You don't leave portable tree stands, namely climbers, hanging like that," Grear whispered, moving ahead cautiously, "unless someone comes by with an extension apparatus, I'll bet, deposits then later collects the band of merry souls."

"Maybe if we hang around awhile, we can arrest whoever they are for hunting out of season," the detective deadpanned.

"There's another," Grear said excitedly.

"What else we lookin' for? Oh, sorry. I forgot."

Grear spotted still another. "You know, I think we found their nest, all right."

"What's this, *we*? I point out their happy hunting ground, and all of a sudden it's *we*. A moment ago I was getting a lecture, you recall. No wonder you're the chief."

"Trials and tribulations of teamwork, Sergeant. You've got to learn to share. Come on. And keep your damn voice down."

"Yeah. More like the privileges of rank," Phelps mumbled to himself.

After a quarter of an hour, the pair made their way out of the woodlot, following a pathway through a knee-high field of grasses to a clearing when most magically the area around them turned alive.

Chapter
——>
47

Chief Grear and Sergeant Phelps withdrew their weapons as a veritable army of camouflaged figures with bows and arrows rose up from seemingly out of nowhere and were coming toward them. Grear glanced over his shoulder. They were surrounded. Fifty some-odd men and women suddenly stopped some forty yards away.

"Now I know how Custer must have felt," Phelps whispered. "Shit."

"Just stay still."

Each soldier had six arrows set in a quiver fixed to a bow. One hand held the weapon diagonally across his or her body; the other hand hung loosely at the side. Camo pants and jackets were precisely the pattern of the field.

"And I thought they had his-and-her outfits these days. Silly me."

"Shut up."

"I could drop four before they ever got an arrow on their string."

"I said shut up and listen."

"You didn't say listen, but I'm listening."

"How many clips?"

"Three, plus one in the gun."

"I got three, total."

"Either this is a math lesson, or you're going to ask me to share."

"We stand back to back."

"I wanna face the front."

"You aim for the center of the body. No Wyatt Earp crap. One shot per man. Every other one. Don't waste a round on a woman."

"But they'll scream discrimination."

Grear turned slowly, and put his back against the sergeant's, moving him slightly to the right. "If one of them makes so much as a move toward his quiver, or takes one step forward, you fire on my command. Got it? On my command," he repeated.

"Right."

"Good. Now here's the plan."

"The plan! I thought that was the fucking plan. How much more shit do you think I can keep in my head right now? I'm only a sergeant."

"The closest cover is the way we're both facing. North and south."

"Right."

"We find a hole and hopefully make it to the trees."

"Right."

"You've got the shortest distance."

"Why *lucky* me?"

"You've got more bullets."

"Right."

"You get to the car and radio for help."

"And where're you heading?"

"Toward the bay."

"How come they don't say anything?"

"They can't."

"Why don't they move?"

"They will."

"When?"

Chief Grear addressed the crowd. "All right. Here's what we've got," he said in a commanding tone. "Two New York police officers and some fifty misguided young men and women."

"Better than twenty-five to one odds," Phelps quipped nervously, sweat beading up on his brow.

"You guys and gals have several hundred arrows, but we have many clips of ammunition to put you down for good if we have to," Grear lied. "We have the advantage of firepower, the accuracy over your weapons, and therefore the capability to outdo your show of force."

"You've either got a faulty computer for a brain or a pair of mammoth balls," Phelps whispered.

"We don't want to hurt anyone. So, I'm asking you to put your weapons down, then put your hands on top of your heads."

To the cops' amazement, all fifty-six men and women lowered their weapons.

"Jesus Christ!" Phelps exclaimed.

"Weapons on the ground. Hands on top of your heads."

But they didn't listen. Instead, they all stepped forward.

"NOT ANOTHER STEP!" Grear shouted, leveling his pistol at one man's chest.

The sergeant did the same.

Simultaneously, two additional circles of soldiers, set approximately twenty and thirty-five yards out, rose and appeared before them. Over one hundred arrows were pointed at the two cops.

"This is my first standoff, Chief. Hurry up and tell me what the fuck to do."

"Lower your weapon slowly, Sergeant," Grear ordered.

"You wanna try running some algebra by them first?"

"Do it!"

Two women from the rear came forward, one of them snapping up the chief's handgun.

"Take me to your leader," Phelps demanded as the woman roughly pulled the weapon from his hand. "But before all that, you might wanna give me your vital statistics," he added, adding insult to injury as she cracked him fiercely across the mouth. "She's crazy about me," he continued, wiping blood from his lip along the sleeve of his jacket. "Well, maybe just plain crazy."

"You don't know when to quit, do you?" Grear snapped.

"Sure I do. It was right after their odds rose to better than seventy-five-to-one. Maybe if you had one of them fancy calculators you could have *really* negotiated with them. Maybe if and when we get back, I can drop that into the suggestion box. I know. I know. First things first. Perhaps I could test out that theory of yours and see if I can get this feisty one here to French kiss me. Did I ever tell you about Sarah Shimshitz from my college days? Probably didn't even know I'd been to college, Chief. One semester of accounting. Nine of them whatchamacallits to my credit. You know, I don't think I'm letting them get a word in edgewise. Lest I be shot for monopolizing a conversation. Why are we still standing here? This is not at all what I expected. I thought maybe I'd be strip-searched by that cutie over there in the corner. At worst, dragged off to their village where this giant pot of boiling water is standing off to stage right. Ever notice that in those old native movies, Chief? Never off to the left of the honcho's hut. But always off to the right."

Grear consciously looked to his right. A Jeep was heading toward them from a distant field then abruptly stopped.

"Anyhow, when we head back for my wife's linguine and white clam sauce," Phelps went on, "I might invite the one immediately to your left. On second thought, Lillian might be offended if Jungle Jane didn't lick her plate clean or I inadvertently brought up Sarah Shimshitz in conversation."

"What do you think?" Grear asked.

"About what? The Jeep? These aborigines? Or Sarah Shimshitz?"

"What the hell are they waiting for?"

"Probably the high priest. You know, I'm glad they finally lowered those bows and arrows. They were making me a fucking nervous wreck. I never thought I'd have over a hundred fucking arrows pointed at my heart. Then again, I'm sure that half of them were pointed at you. Did you ever see that Japanese film where that big bologna gets it on the balcony? Like a human pincushion. I bet fifty arrows hit him before he finally fell. How do they film something like that?"

"Here we go," Grear said, gesturing in the vehicle's direction.

The Jeep was coming toward them again. Olive green and black. Roof rack. Something atop. A good-sized deer with a rack of its own became discernible. Several of the warriors waved. One of the figures in the Jeep waved back. As the vehicle neared the edge of the adjoining field, two men got out. They walked briskly forward. Laughing. One signed while the other immediately translated.

"Police Chief Grear," one man saluted.

"Jesus Christ," Grear said softly.

"It's Geist," Phelps said.

"*Well, we finally get to meet again*," the translator spoke for Richard as the killer's fingers flashed from several feet away, signing as he closed the gap, ultimately extending his hand in welcome. "*Oh, come on, now. Don't behave like that. It's been a marvelous hunt for both of us through the years.*" Richard turned obliquely, then back about. "*How do you like my trophy? Ten pointer.*" Richard pointed back toward the Jeep. "*I take no shot under fifty yards unless it's strictly for food. Well? What do you think?"*

"I think it's out of season," the sergeant answered with a smirk.

"Down here we set our own rules and regulations and abide by limits as well as predetermined dates. You'd find that in most cases, we're even stricter than the DEC. Perhaps the two of you would like to join me on a hunt. I have several bows in the Jeep," Richard toyed.

"With no strings attached, I'll bet," the sergeant quipped.

"Very good, my friend. I wonder if your skills are as sharp as your wit."

"Well, we found you, didn't *we*?" Phelps said, glancing at Grear.

"Actually, I found you," Richard assured them with a laugh. *"But I won't take any credit away for your initiative. Deputy Inspector Lancing was a surprise, though. Now, how did he ever manage that?"*

"Inspector Lancing was a very resourceful detective," Grear stated sternly.

"Yes, but he wasn't a team player. Am I right? But of course I am. Otherwise, he wouldn't have gone up there alone. Correct?"

"But *we* didn't make that mistake, Richard," Grear stated. "We have backup on the way."

"No. No. No," the translator spoke as Richard signed. *"You have no one heading out here because you really weren't sure what you'd find."*

"We also sign out in a log before we leave," Grear added, ignoring the translator while locking his eyes on Geist. "And the duty sergeant is sending for a helicopter as we speak."

"I-don't-think-so," the translator related, punctuating each word as Richard slowly dipped and drove his digits with emphasis. *"But we'll see soon enough. Yes? Besides, we're quite equipped to handle most anything that comes our way. Please don't let these ancient weapons fool you. This is strictly for sport, you see. Oh, and I'm so glad the two of you had the good sense not to—how did you put it, Chief Grear? 'No Wyatt Earp crap.' You see, I still read lips flawlessly."* Richard dropped his eyes to the binoculars hanging around his neck. *"I really enjoyed the show. It was when you guys went back to back that I lost the sergeant's sense of humor. Anyhow, let us show you what one of our women—that you didn't want to waste a bullet on—can do, Chief."* Richard gestured to the young woman who had smacked the sergeant. *"Leave your bow with Yvonne."*

The woman handed over her bow to another then stepped forward.

"All right, now empty the sergeant's gun and hand it back to

him."

The woman released the clip into her palm and slid the pistol's action back, ejecting a bullet from its chamber, returning the gun to the sergeant. From his belt, she confiscated three additional clips. The sergeant gave her a wink and received yet another crack across the mouth.

"You're so right, Chief Grear. Your partner just doesn't know when to quit," the translator offered through Richard. *"So. What I want you to do, Yvette, is to take your bow back from Yvonne and pace off about twenty yards. Sergeant, I want you to holster your weapon,"* the translator continued.

Sergeant Phelps was staring at the two women. "Yvonne, Yvette. Yvette, Yvonne. You know, I can't keep this shit in my head. I'm only a sergeant. Can't we just kiss and make up? No, huh?" The sergeant brushed his jacket aside and agilely shouldered his empty piece.

"Good. Now face Yvette."

"Yvette?"

"And assume the position."

"Nothing kinky now."

"Sergeant, I really do admire your sense of humor in the face of danger."

"Danger?"

"Yes, danger."

"You mean she's not going to be shooting blanks?"

"No, Sergeant. She's going to be shooting a Muzzy broadhead, like the one I used on two D.A.s."

"You know, that's a confession in front of at least a hundred and fifty witnesses. And furthermore—"

"And furthermore, nothing," Grear broke in. "He's not going to play your fucking game, Geist."

"Oh, but he is, Chief. That is if he wants to live," Richard signed, assuring the chief of police. *"Now. What you're going to do, Sergeant, is draw your weapon on command, point it at Yvette, and pull the trigger before she can 'ever get an arrow on the string' is what I believe you said."*

"Did I say that? Did I? How do I know he's translating accurately," Phelps argued before turning to his captors. "Let me see a show of hands, folks. See. Not one fucking hand in the air."

"You are, indeed, a funny man," Richard signed. *"I could have used you at our last meeting in New Jersey. I was dying out there."*

"Where's that goddamn helicopter?" the sergeant stalled.

"You know there's no helicopter coming, or any kind of backup. Don't you remember your chief telling you to 'get to the car and radio for help'? Or can't you keep all that in your silly head?"

Several smiles broke out among the troops.

The sergeant smiled, too. "Listen; don't worry about them, Richard. They're a tough audience, and a Bob Hope you're not."

"But you and the chief are a captured *audience, Sergeant. And I think the real star here, namely Yvette, is rather anxious for us to get on with the show. You see, this is audience participation day. Now. What Yvette is going to attempt to do is remove an arrow from her bow quiver, nock it upon the string, come to a full draw and release it before you can unholster your weapon and pull the trigger."*

Phelps swallowed uneasily. "I don't like the *release* part, Richard, because someone could get hurt. May I call you Richard?"

"All you have to do is beat her to the draw, Sergeant. And it's over."

"Over?"

"Yes. You'll win."

"Win? What's the prize?"

"Your life."

"And if I lose?"

"You're a riot, Sergeant."

"Look. I'll make a deal with you."

"You're in no position to make deals."

"I know. I know. But just hear me out. You can always say no."

"Funny."

"You let us go—"

Richard was laughing good-humoredly.

"Wait. Wait. It gets better. You let us go, and we'll give you back Angelica."

Richard smiled. *"But I thought she was twice dead, Sergeant. A murder on your mean streets and a hanging in her cell."*

"The feds have her on ice. I don't mean ice, ice. I mean they're baby-sitting her."

"They are?" Richard signed with feigned surprise.

"Tell them, Chief."

Grear nodded his head that it was true.

"Let me tell you why you're really here, guys." Geist was facing Grear directly. *"You're here because we led you to us. Actually, we thought you'd be here a bit sooner. But I knew you'd finally figure it out, Chief."*

"Show-off," Phelps scolded playfully.

"*You're here as part of an exchange that the sergeant just suggested—in part. But I want Redler, too, in the bargain.*"

"We don't have him," Grear said.

"*I know that. But you can help us get him. You in exchange for Redler. The sergeant in exchange for Angelica.*"

"And I thought Dicky, here, had the hots for Yvette. Or is it Yvonne?"

Richard grinned. "*Ready, Sergeant?*"

Grear grew anxious. "If anything happens to—"

"*To your detective sergeant? Not to worry. We're just playing a little game. Simply a demonstration of our skill. If Yvette killed him, I'd have less of a trade. True? So. Without any further ado, let the game begin.*"

"Wait. Wait. Wait. Wait. Wait. Please," Phelps said, throwing his hands in the air. "I just want to get this straight. All I have to do is draw, aim, and dry-fire before she can get off an arrow?"

"*Precisely. Once you pull the trigger, she stops.*"

"But does *she* know that?"

"*She does.*"

Yvette nodded from the twenty-yard distance between them.

"Can I take off my jacket?"

"*You may.*"

"All right." The sergeant removed his jacket and laid it upon the ground. The handle of the weapon hung from the crook of his underarm. He looked over at his chief. "A walk in the park."

Grear nodded apprehensively.

"Whattaya gonna say so I'll know? 'Ready, on your mark, get set, go,' or what?"

"*Ready!*" Richard signed and smiled handsomely as the translator spoke.

The sergeant held his hand in front of his breast, fingers spread evenly apart.

"*On your mark!*"

Yvette was staring her rival straight in the eyes. The bow was fixed in her left hand. Her right arm hung casually at her side.

"*Get set!*"

"This bitch can't be serious," Phelps jawed.

"*Go!*"

It was as the sergeant gripped the handle of his pistol that Yvette had an arrow on her string; fletching at the corner of her mouth. As the cop leveled his piece and was about to pull the trigger, an aluminum shaft carrying a lethal four-bladed broadhead was already traveling toward its target, tearing across the sergeant's cheek.

The crowd went wild.

"*Well, what do you think of our women, now?*" Richard signed as the translator spoke. "*Pretty impressive. Wouldn't you say?*"

In shock, the sergeant dropped the weapon and grabbed his jacket, pressing it firmly against his bloody face.

Grear was immediately at his side. "Here, let me see," he said, taking the jacket away.

Sergeant Phelps shivered, spitting out a stream of blood. "Felt like she just brushed my teeth."

"She did." Grear turned around. "I want my man treated! I want him attended to **now**!" he demanded.

"*Listen to me carefully,*" Richard Geist made clear. "*I'm asking you nicely. Don't ever take that tone with me again, or it will be your second-in-command whom I'll be dealing with because you won't be around. Do you understand?*"

Grear looked away.

"*Do I have your attention, Chief Grear?*"

"I understand. I also understand that my man needs medical attention. Please."

"*That's better. You may not believe it. But we behave pretty civilly around here.*"

"I can see," Grear seethed.

"*That's only a scratch, Chief Grear. Last year, Yvette and Yvonne pinned back the ears of a dissident who wouldn't listen up. Thirty-yard shot. Isn't that right, Michael?*" the translator had to ask of himself, finding it rather strange and uncomfortable at having to speak of himself in the third person. Richard grew angry and impatient. " . . . *Hello, in there, Michael,*" Richard signed. "*The chief's waiting for your answer.*" Richard smiled patiently.

Michael wasn't smiling. "Yes, that's right," he responded. For the poor soul had been Michael's first cousin.

Richard gestured abruptly, and an older man and woman stepped forward.

"Say, Michael," the sergeant grimaced in pain. "You look and sound just like Richard when he's mad," he sputtered as the couple led him away.

Richard noted the chief's concern. "*It's all right. Really. They're medics. They'll fix him up, and he'll be no worse for wear by dinnertime. Come. You must be hungry. You really had some day. I want to know what you've been doing with yourself all these years. I mean besides climbing the career ladder to nowhere."*

Grear had the distinct feeling that Richard Geist knew exactly what he had been doing.

"Oh, before we go any further, is there something that you'd like to give me?" Richard signed as Michael spoke distinctly.

"Give you?"

"Yes. Come clean, now. What do you keep in your boot? I believe you call it a throwaway piece. You know. In case you have to shoot someone and need to call it self-defense. Two fingers, please. Nice and slow. Easy does it."

Grear stooped down and carefully handed over the weapon.

"Good boy. They're going to search the two of you anyway. You wouldn't want to give anyone the wrong impression, would you? Oh, and the extra clip for your Walther. Thank you very much. Now, follow me. Chop. Chop," he added impatiently.

Chapter
——>
48

T he convent at Hubbard Hills held an austere dining area. A U-shaped arrangement of trestle tables with wooden benches ran the entire length of the room. Seating easily accommodated over two hundred people. Every space was occupied; Geist's soldiers sitting shoulder to shoulder. In a corner stood a steam table with seven servers dressed in clean white uniforms, each stationed behind a prodigious pan capped in stainless steel. Another table for cold dishes stood along the far wall. Every warrior was seated, silent, and sipping wine.

"What's on the menu? As if I couldn't guess," Sergeant Phelps said, sedated yet alert, enunciating as clearly as he could, taking a seat as directed to Richard's left.

"*Venison,*" Richard signed as Michael interpreted, both men having changed from camo to khaki pants and matching shirt.

"Yeah, I figured that. But what else are we having tonight?" he pressed, one side of his face heavily bandaged and out of Grear's view.

"*There are other delicacies along the wall behind you, Sergeant. You can help yourself. You won't leave the table hungry,*" Michael translated, standing directly behind his leader.

"So what else is under those shiny armor covers? Can't all be venison."

Richard nodded. "*Yes, it can. And it is.*"

Sergeant Phelps scrambled his arms around. "All of it?"

"*Yes, all of it. Venison prepared seven different ways.*"

"Seven ways?"

"*Ribs. Chili. Stew. Cutlets. Steaks. Chops. And a special surprise tonight.*"

"I'm surprised already."

"*You'll love it. Have you ever had venison, Sergeant?*"

"Deer meat? Not in my wildest dreams, Richard. But not as wild as some of yours, I'll bet."

Grear thought he was going to die. Literally. The two of them. Hung from a rafter upside down and splayed with a pole or board like the deer they had seen coming through the area earlier. Maybe *that* was the surprise Richard was referring to, the police chief entertained.

"*Have you ever had venison, Chief?*" Richard inquired and saluted by raising his glass. "*To your health.*"

"Several times," he answered, ignoring the salutation. "It's delicious if prepared right. Foul if it's not."

"Fowl," Phelps chimed in. "Now that's what I could go for. But as good as Yvette and her hunting party are, I bet they couldn't hit shit on the fly with a shotgun."

"*Wing-shooting, Sergeant?*"

"Yeah, they got a name for everything, I guess."

"*Oh, I'd imagine Yvette and her sister could be matched against the best of them. Wing-shooting. Skeet. Trap. Sporting clays. That's if they had a mind to. But all of us like things quiet around here. We paddle and row instead of motor, set dry flies upon a pond's surface instead of casting lead sinkers and noisy plugs along the bay. We fell deer with a whisper rather than making a commotion and blowing half the meat to kingdom come.*"

"Sounds all very sporting," Grear said. "Not like what happened in Suffolk, Nassau, and Queens Counties. Not like what we found along the Jersey Shore."

"*A bit of pleasure; a bit of business. But I must argue that a four-hundred-fifty-yard shot falls into the category of sport, although I cannot take credit for it,*" Richard admitted straightaway.

"Outright murder is what it was," Grear growled his outrage.

"Don't you ever get tired of eating venison?" Phelps interrupted. "I mean, even seven different ways."

"*You're making it sound as though we have it seven days a week. We don't. Only for very special occasions. Especially around the holidays and certain celebrations.*"

"Such as?"

"*Such as this.*"

"And what are we celebrating?"

"*Your capture, but of course.*" Richard grinned maniacally.

"Are we really that important?"

"*No. But Robby Boy and Angelica are.*"

"Why is Redler so important to you?" Grear questioned.

"*Some wine down here,*" Richard ordered, poured then passed the magnum. "*Well, for one thing, he pissed me off, so we really have to have a heart-to-heart.*"

"Will he have one left when you get done with him?" Phelps asked. "I mean, I heard about what you did to your mother."

Grear slowly shook his head from side to side.

"*Oh, don't worry about your sergeant, Chief. If and when we trade him in, I might send him packing with a missing part.*"

"Oops," Phelps said, covering his mouth with one hand and, with the other, his private parts. "I mean, at least he keeps you guessing."

"Just stop it," Grear said with utmost seriousness. He turned to Geist. "You were telling us about Redler before the sergeant rudely interrupted."

"*You're aware, I'm certain, that Redler is working on a novel.*"

"I am."

"*Do you know what the book is about?*"

"I don't believe we ever discussed it in detail."

"*Do you know how much of an advance he's received for the reprinting of his unauthorized biography as well as the rights to a current book?*"

Grear shrugged. "Is that important?"

"*Oh, believe me, it is.*"

"How so?"

"*At this point, I have to say that I'm a bit disappointed in you as a detective.*"

Grear said nothing

"*You have so many pieces of the puzzle, Chief. But the most important one you fail to grasp.*"

"Is Robert Redler somehow mixed up in this business with you? Is that why you kill for him?"

"*I wish he were. Things would be a lot simpler.*"

"Really?"

"*I can't believe you haven't figured this thing out for yourself.*"

"Why don't you enlighten me?"

"*Why don't we have something to eat first?*"

Sergeant Phelps leaned back in his seat. "You don't mind if I order in, do you, Michael? You can even place the call if you like. Any takeout place will do. The Colonel's ribs or chicken will be fine. If they don't deliver, tell them I can be there in twenty minutes. Richard, you don't mind if I borrow the Jeep. Oh, and Michael, see if anyone else wants anything." The sergeant looked down the long line of shaved heads and ruddy complexions. "Yvonne," he called out. "You'd love the Colonel's chicken. Yvette, I ain't even speaking to you." He lowered his voice to a whisper. "Ignore a woman, and you'll have her eating out of your hand. Yvonne, I love that Sinead O'Connor look, darlin'."

"*And they call me crazy,*" Richard signed and laughed good-naturedly.

When everyone had finished eating, Sergeant Phelps received the bad news.

"What do you mean there's no dessert?" The detective was carrying on like a child. "Lillian always has dessert. Our friends and neighbors even serve dessert or they wouldn't be our friends and neighbors because we'd be forced to move. This is so unfair. I even conceded that the venison chili was very good."

"*Desserts are filled with flour, fat, and sugar, Sergeant,*" Richard explained as if communicating with a child. "*Are you looking for an early grave?*"

A line of more than a hundred fifty followers filed past the four of them, heading out of the dining area.

"Where's everyone going?" Phelps asked. "It's only eight o'clock."

"*To their rooms to read or retire for the evening. We're up before it's light.*"

"And the others in the corner over there?"

"*They'll be relieving those on watch. Now, if you'll excuse your chief and me, Sergeant Phelps, we have some business to discuss. Gary and Peter will escort you to your room.*"

"Without dessert?"

"*You may have a brandy if you wish,*" Geist suggested.

Phelps yawned. "With all the medication I have in my system? I think he's trying to kill me, Chief."

"What I think you need is a good night's rest," Grear said.

"I think maybe you're right," the sergeant agreed, gingerly

touching his bandages. "Been a long and trying day."

"*Good night, Sergeant*," Geist signed.

"Good night, *mein* host. Michael. Chief."

"Good night," Grear said. "You all right?"

Phelps nodded absently as two men led him away.

Chapter
——>
49

R ichard and Michael led the chief to a commodious room down the end of a hallway.

"Well. Here we are. Brandy, Chief Grear?" Michael translated.

"Thank you," Grear forced himself to say. He took in the spacious room and its sparse furnishings. "This is quite a remarkable study."

Richard waited for Michael to finish pouring.

"Imported marble tile and columns. The nuns had it shipped here from Italy right after the war."

"Very impressive."

"So is Mr. Robert F. Redler."

"How so?"

"You say you have little knowledge of Barbara Giordano's business in all of this?"

"Just book business from what I understand."

"That's it?"

"That's it. He's a good writer. She sees a good thing. He'll probably make it big this time around."

"But why Redler? Why not someone else?" Richard prodded.

"He did a few editorials on the Giordano/Ziegler story. Asked some hard questions. Treated the husband and his family fairly. He firmly believes Tony had no knowledge of Ziegler's intent to shoot his wife."

"*And?*"

"And that's about it."

"*And on that basis, she arranges a five hundred thousand dollar advance against sales plus a nice percentage?*"

Grear shrugged. "It's a crazy business. He probably deserves it."

"*You really are naive.*"

"Then enlighten me."

"*Barbara Giordano's life is hanging by a thread. Not only by the bullet lodged in her skull, but by a group who wants to finish the job it started.*"

"Who?"

"*La Mano Nera.*"

"Come again?"

"*The Black Hand.*"

"You mean the precursor to the Mafia. Aren't they extinct?"

"*Yeah. Like the practice of witchcraft.*"

"And who are they, exactly?"

"*The elite and elusive phantoms of our government, if you'll pardon the redundancy. Descendants of La Mano Nera. Not to be confused with the Mafia.*"

"You have names?"

"*You chew on that awhile,*" he signed, smiling up at Michael. "*Mrs. Giordano is caught between a rock and a hard place. She has so-called friends at the very top. She has these friends because she has power over them. A power that associates of the Mob tried to undermine by putting Alice Ziegler on her doorstep. She can rattle the top of the tower. And she can bring down the* families *throughout the five boroughs for openers.*"

"Barbara Giordano can do all that?"

"*She can and she will if she has to. She wants to prove it to them by having published but a part of what she knows.*"

"Like what?"

"*Like what Redler will present as fiction in his next book.*

Pension fraud. Insurance scams. Contract murders. Little things like that. Just a sampling, mind you. Just enough to get her message across."

"And what do you want with Redler? You want to kill him?"

"If I wanted Redler dead, he'd be dead before I could give it a second thought."

"Then why do you want him?"

"You wouldn't believe me if I told you."

"Try me."

"You'd think that I was going mad."

"I think you're mad now."

"But not crazy?"

"Not really."

"Nor did Lieutenant Lark. Some of the doctors think I'm crazy. Some of them will go to their graves believing that. You tell me if I'm wrong."

"I think you fooled some of the doctors."

"I did."

"I think you're crazy like a fox."

"I am."

"So where do we go from here?"

"I want Redler with us."

"Why?"

"Before I answer that, I want to give you a little test."

"A test?"

Richard grinned sagely. *"Answer this question. How could I have done the things I did, murdered all those people in cold blood, and not be deemed crazy in your eyes?"*

Grear did not hesitate in giving his reply. "I draw a fine line between crazy and slick. Your mind is as sound as your followers are silent. Your acts are slick. Not sick."

"What's your basis for saying so?"

"You're not wildly impractical."

Richard Geist was very impressed. *"Very, very good, Chief. You've certainly got me pegged. Indulge me a moment longer, please."* He paced the floor. *"Had my acts been committed with wild abandon as opposed to the soundness you suggest, what*

224

would you opt for in terms of punitive measure in either *case?"*

Again, Grear did not hesitate. "In either case, I would opt for lethal injection to be carried out by the state."

"Permit me one final question along this line. As we do not have the death penalty in this state, as yet, what would you personally do to me, or someone like me, given the perfect opportunity?"

"I would shoot you and your kind on sight."

"I would expect no less from you. You are, indeed, a wise and worthy adversary. I really do admire you, although you might find that hard to believe. But what I'm about to reveal to you, you will find unbelievable."

"I'm all ears."

Geist looked Grear directly in the eyes. *"Robert F. Redler is a prophet."*

Chief Grear paused before he spoke. "Bianco's right. You are stark-raving mad," he stated and laughed disconcertingly.

"Why?"

"Why? Because that's wild and reckless and unsound. That's why."

"I think I can prove otherwise."

"You can try."

"Have you read his early fiction?"

"Yes, I have."

"And I'm sure you read his editorials."

"Each and every one."

"So, you read his fiction and his nonfiction."

"I just said that."

"And you don't see what I see? Or what Barbara Giordano sees? Or what the government is beginning to see?"

"I see that you're starting to get crazy on me. Or maybe you've already crossed the finish line."

"Are you going to stay with me on this, or what?"

Grear hesitated. "Let me ask you this."

"Ask."

"Does Redler say he's a prophet?"

"I don't believe he really knows. But if he does, he can't accept it . . . yet."

"Doesn't know?"

"*No.*"

Grear looked over at Michael. "Michael, if I were you, I'd get my résumé in order. Maybe try the U.N. or some institution like that. I'm sure they could use a talented sort like you. I think your employer is on a very short fuse."

Richard looked up at Michael, sighed and signed.

"He wants me to tell you that it's true," Michael said.

"*He* wants you to? What do *you* want to tell me, Michael?"

Richard nodded that it was all right for Michael to voice his own opinion.

"I want to tell you that what Richard is saying is the gospel."

"According to whom?" Grear asked and laughed, thinking that enough was enough.

"*According to those who know what's going on,*" Richard signed and Michael swore.

"But you're telling me that Redler doesn't know this."

"*No, not yet.*"

"And what is Redler going to do when he finds out? Or aren't you going to tell him?" Grear couldn't help but shake his head in disbelief.

"*That's why we want him here. We want to know all about his gift.*"

"You know, I don't believe I'm sitting here. And I wouldn't be if I were free to go."

"*Well, being that you're fully aware of the fact that you're a captured audience of one, I want you to go back in time—about eighteen years ago. Do you remember being on the phone with Doctor Bianco the night after my escape from Havenwood?*"

"Like it was yesterday."

"*And do you remember Bianco telling you, and I quote, 'He's actually turning his fiction into fact,' meaning yours truly?*"

"So?"

"*Well, Redler writes fiction, too, and it somehow manifests itself into fact is what I'm telling you. Only he doesn't know the power he possesses. There are things in his first novel that were impossible for him to have any prior knowledge of. None whatsoever. I know what I did and didn't tell him in an interview years ago. Yet, it's all there in black and white. But, of course, you'd argue that there would have to be some sort of logical explanation. Well, I want you to find a logical explanation for this, Chief Grear.*" He handed over a stack of papers. "*I want you to look at certain highlighted passages in the beginning. Take your time. We have all night if need be.*"

Grear took the papers and settled back for a spell. What he read seemed unbelievable. The cop furrowed his brow. He skimmed, stopped then started again, sifting through the pile of handwritten pages—pages written in Robert Redler's script. Grear thought he had or was about to lose his mind. He read on for nearly thirty minutes before Richard interrupted.

"*Those are the first one hundred sixty-nine manuscript pages of Redler's new novel you're holding,* The Awakening, *written in his own hand. If you were to read on, you'd see he's almost at the turning point,*" Richard signed anxiously as Michael translated.

"And you want him to write *your* ending, I suppose."

"*If Barbara Giordano got him to begin her story for a mere half a mil, I will offer him a kingdom to finish mine.*"

"You *are* slick, Richard. You know that."

"*But certainly not crazy?*"

"No, I'm afraid you're not."

"*It's good to be afraid, Chief Grear.*"

Grear held his tongue.

"*Now, I want you to read on from this point. Take your time.*"

Chapter
——>
50

After another thirty minutes, Michael instructed Grear to put down the manuscript. Grear was visibly shaken.

"*I'm afraid Redler's work may be near completion,*" Richard signed without emotion.

"Then I would imagine that your fate is somehow already sealed."

"*Unless, of course . . . .*"

"Unless what?"

"*Unless Redler took a different tact like you had said before. Like those kinds of stories where you choose your own ending from a selection,*" Geist put forth through Michael. "*What I want you to do now is jump ahead,*" he insisted, thumbing through several chapters to an earmarked page. "*From here.*"

Grear pored over page after unimaginable page. He shook his head in total disbelief. He had just read several accounts and developments witnessed and investigated by police authorities over the past several months, events that Robert Redler could not possibly be privy to. It was all there, chronicled in Redler's manuscript, including the day's event with Sergeant Phelps: their capture; their courageous stand that afternoon, incorporating the elements of his sergeant's defiance and humor in the face of danger and possible death; Yvette's demonstration of her remarkable skill with a bow and arrow; right up to and inclusive of the evening meal. It was as if Redler had been on the scene, directing the action from a script. Grear thought he was going to be sick.

The police chief lowered the pages. "How did you get your hands on this?" he asked, finally looking up with an ashen expression.

"*It's called a break-in, Chief. A burglary,*" Geist further clarified, knowing the police, too, had visited both residences surreptitiously, a judge's denial of search warrants notwithstanding. "*Just like you fellows did. Initially, I made copies so as not to spook our boy.*"

"But when? Where?"

"*A few months before he and Barbara Giordano had a clandestine meeting at that Riverhead restaurant mentioned early on in his manuscript. The first four chapters were found in his Riverhead home. He retained two Xerox copies. One in Riverhead, and one in Fresh Meadows.*"

"How come our boys didn't find them?"

"*Your boys didn't know where to look,*" Richard explained. "*Anyhow, I tried to stop him.*"

"How? By murdering those district attorneys who were already murdered on these pages? He got you to do his bidding!"

Richard shook his head emphatically. "*My planning those murders began well over a year ago.*"

"He programmed you," *you sick son of a bitch*, he wanted to add but didn't. "The two of you are probably in cahoots. What the hell difference does it make when he planted the seed?" Grear was livid.

"*Whoa! You're not listening to me. I am not in bed with Redler. I haven't seen him in years. Not since that interview some twenty years ago.*"

"You're full of shit because we've got your pretty face posing with him at a lawn party thrown at Field's home two summers ago. Remember that?"

"*That wasn't a goddamn reunion. Redler didn't even know who I was. I mean, I was drop dead gorgeous, arriving in my Sunday best and on my best behavior. All the men went nuts. I had Angelica shoot several rolls of film that afternoon for laughs. Not just of Redler. But also of Maggie and my two little friends; her daughters. I'm telling you it wasn't until* after *I killed Arthur Field's family that I knew for certain that Redler was somehow turning his fiction into fact."*

"Redler had to have written this *after* the fact."

"Yes, concerning the three D.A.s. Granted that was already written. There was no exchange of dialogue. But I didn't read the chapter on Field's family until I went back to Redler's Riverhead home a second time. There it was, recorded on his desk. My deed in Bridgehampton. It was like the four of us had been through a rehearsal. Like reading a script after viewing the performance. Everyone had their lines. Maggie. Margaret. Melissa. With yours truly as the leading man. Each of us had played our parts to perfection, the way that Redler had set it down. Whether you believe me or not, you have to admit that there are facts written on those pages that only the police and I could know. I'm telling you that Redler had everything recorded before the bloody business began."

Grear wasn't buying any of it. "When did you decide to set Redler up by murdering those responsible for his arrest and firing from the college?"

"When I knew for sure. I told you, I tried to make him stop."

"Stop what? Having you fulfill his prophecy? You played right into his hands."

"We're going around in circles. Look again at the pages on your lap. Explain them. Tell me how he could have written that before it ever happened."

"You're following a fucking script. You're all mixed up on your times. You've had to have read this first. You're out of sync. Your mind is like a computer, moving paragraphs and chapters around. You're doing rewrites and revisions in your head."

"Are you?" Richard grabbed the papers from Grear, hunting through pages toward the back of the manuscript. *"Were you reading from a script when you said, 'We stand back to back,' or how about, 'We find a hole and hopefully make it to the trees.' Oh, and here. This business about white clam sauce. Were*

you reading from a script? Huh?" He dropped the papers back in Grear's lap.

"You read lips," Grear snapped. "It's in your file. You even said so earlier today."

"*I see,*" Richard signed calmly. "*In other words, I read your lips, came in here before dinner, wrote everything down in Redler's own handwriting, original copy, mind you. And then handed you this incredible story.*"

Grear was shaking his head in confusion.

"*What about your sergeant, Chief? He was facing away from me. I couldn't see a single word he was saying.*"

"Somebody on the other side could have. Somebody who could read lips, too."

"*I see.*"

"I know you're brilliant, Richard. A genius, in fact. I know you're into games. The more complex the better. But there has got to be an explanation for all this, or I'd say you pretty much met your match. What do you say? You said there were one hundred seventy-eight pages, Richard. I see one hundred sixty-nine."

"*I'd say you're finally paying attention, Chief.*"

"Meaning?"

"*Give the chief the last nine pages, Michael.*"

"I can't."

"*And why is that?*"

"Because he's sitting on them."

"*Is that a fact?*" Richard toyed and nodded knowingly. "*Chief Grear. Would you mind standing, please? And take those pages from underneath your seat cushion.*"

The police chief stood, lifted the cushion and removed the pages, handing them to Richard.

"*No, no, no, no, no. I wouldn't want to be accused of underhandedness,*" Richard punned, signed and sighed impatiently. "*You hold onto those papers, sit back down, and read them. Then you tell me. Where do we go from here?*"

Grear sat back down and began the next chapter. His hands trembled. What he read was positively apocalyptic. There was no other word for it. "Oh, my God," he whispered. Grear was reading chapter and verse of the present scene that he, himself, was in and had been sitting on, complete with words and phrases relating to the imported marble tile and columns that the nuns had shipped from Italy. It contained exact passages, line after line. The dialogue was precise, right up to the lifting of the cushion and down to the line where Richard had signed, "*Then you tell me. Where do we go from here?*"

"*The last nine pages of Redler's unfinished manuscript, Chief.*"

"Jesus Christ."

"*Nine pages, Grear. I couldn't have written them as we sat. We hadn't even had this conversation, although you could certainly argue that I knew my lines. But what about your lines, Chief? Have you ever seen this script before? Are we trying to drive the other crazy? Or is Redler some kind of sorcerer or seer. It's not the wine or the brandy. We each had but one. Or have we slipped into some sort of a dream state? Michael, wake us if we have,*" Richard ordered.

Grear turned to face Michael. "Who *are* you?"

Michael remained silent.

"*It's all right, Michael. Tell him everything,*" Richard coaxed.

"I work in Albany," Michael said. "I work for a senator."

"Which one?"

"It really doesn't matter."

"*I said everything, Michael.*"

Michael took the papers from the chief and put them aside. "I work for Senator Demeco."

"Doing?"

"His dirty work."

"Which entails?"

"Many things."

"Are we going to sit here and play twenty questions?" Grear asked.

"*Michael, open up to the man.*"

"These days I'm making sure that Mrs. Giordano doesn't overstep her bounds," Michael said reluctantly.

"*What Michael is having difficulty expressing, Chief,*"

Richard communicated as Michael uncomfortably translated, "*is that he is a soldier for La Mano Nera.*"

"The Black Hand? In Albany?"

"*No. In Macy's window,*" Richard signed and sighed in exasperation. "*I'm trying to give you a realistic picture of who's who in the capital world of captains and kings, Chief. World governments, for all intents and purposes, are one gigantic oil, weapons, and drug cartel. It's really a very simple picture with a very basic economic application. Bottom line? Money talks and bullshit walks. The rewards of those three industries are enormous. They make all other institutions run reasonably well, although the liberals would disagree,*" he added with a smile. "*For our government not to have ventured into the latter would have been capital suicide. Wealth courts power, power corrupts, and morality, as you know it, Chief, is out the window,*" Geist lectured. "*You wouldn't want it any other way. Believe me. Goodness is the luxury of undergraduates. Those with true intestinal fortitude are reshaping this nation into the great power that it once was. But something has happened in America, Chief Grear. Our government has gotten too greedy. Where's the tolerable balance? Some folks are not getting their fair share of the pie. Look at the deterioration of our goods and services. The shift in the distribution of wealth. More and more Americans are becoming angry and rebelling. Hence, we are going to have one hell of a revolution on our hands. And I plan on being there to lead it.*

"*Anyhow, to bring this business back into focus, I'll sharpen up the image. Michael has to kill Barbara Giordano. But if he kills her, he cuts his own throat in the process. What to do? Nothing, for the moment. Allow the lady her insurance policy in the form of Redler's novel. Fine. Either she has it her way, or this housewife from Oceanside—who controls the trafficking of drugs in several countries, not just a couple of counties, Chief—exposes a worldwide operation. Barbara has tapped into this Redler phenomenon. No one quite knows what to make of it. Least of all, me.*"

"Perhaps this is a warning. A sign from Him." Grear was pointing toward the ceiling.

"*God?*" Richard was shaking his head.

"How else could you explain something like this?" he asked, searching their faces.

"We're afraid that Robert Redler will publish what Barbara Giordano believes she's capable of holding back," Michael said plainly. "We'd stand to lose everything."

"If I were you, from what I see here, I'd be more afraid of losing my soul."

"*Yeah, well, from where Michael and I are standing, I don't believe we've much hope left in the department of redemption,*" Richard assured their captive with a little laugh. "*No intention of repenting, Chief. Many roads and miles to travel before we rest. Hopefully in peace.*"

"How the hell did the two of you ever hook up?"

"*Let's just say that we run in the same circles, and leave it at that.*"

"I see." Grear shifted his eyes to Michael. "And that would explain your ability to interpret sign. I take it you can sign as well."

"As well as the next," Michael signed and said simultaneously.

"*As a matter of fact, Michael taught me, Chief.*"

"I guess the two of you go back a bit."

"*Quite a bit.*"

"Strange bedfellows. An aide to a New York State senator and a cult leader. What a formidable alliance." Grear shook his head with disgust, fixing his eyes on the ceiling.

"*What's the matter, Chief?*" Richard questioned. "*You seem a million miles away. Those last pages really got to you, I see. Just imagine how I felt when I first picked up Redler's manuscript. It certainly took me by surprise. I didn't know what to make of it at first because, as I told you, I had been planning those initial acts for quite some time. How could he possibly know? I asked myself over and over again. Oh, I'd show that bastard if he thought for a second that I'd change my strategy or even change my mind. So you could say, as you did a moment ago, that I carried out his bidding. Perhaps to a point. And I understand yours perfectly. Anyhow, I finally grabbed up all those pages, then went home and read. But I hadn't read every word because I played this little game. I purposely held back part of a chapter like I did with you. Sat on it, so to speak. Didn't even peek. Then I went about my business. I made Steven Fork's death as dramatic as I could. You should have seen the detective's face when he opened up that crate. He had security all around his home. But there I was. Sitting on his brand new riding machine. The brand was Ryder. Robert, bless him—and the devil may care—even got that right. Next, I said to myself: Self, what in the name of hell am I going to do? I had already given my lieutenants their assignments at our last meeting in New Jersey. It's as if Robert Redler were in the very room. And as you know, your associate, Deputy Inspector Lancing had a most unfortunate fall. Oh, come on now. Don't give me those 'if looks could kill' dagger eyes of yours. Redler wrote it that way, and that's the way that it went down.*

"What intrigues me, though, is not that Lancing found us, for I knew he had a line on the freezer I kept in my basement apartment. It's the fact that Redler hadn't explained its significance. I don't suppose you could shed a little light on that business. Hum, Chief?"

Normally, a cop would never have shared that kind of information outside his *circle* about anything he knew or even didn't know. But nothing here was normal. And for one reason or another, Grear felt compelled to admit that he hadn't a clue.

"I can't help you there, Richard."

"Can't or won't?"

"Can't," Grear stated truthfully.

"Well, perhaps it means nothing, or maybe it's something quite significant. Anyhow, I'm sure you're going to bat this whole business back and forth tonight. I'm sure you're going to be looking for some trick to explain away this madness. But I can assure you that Redler's revelations will remain as much a mystery to you as they are to me. And I do believe we're at a turning point, like I said. Whether or not I can dictate my own ending, or must contend with Redler engraving destined events in stone, I truly do not know. The uncertainty, I do admit, concerns me. That is why I must have Redler here."

"The authorities will not bargain with you."

"*A veteran and valued chief of police and his sergeant in exchange for a couple of civilians? Oh, I think they will. Don't sell yourselves short, my friend.*"

"I'm not your friend."

"*A pity. Anyhow, I suggest that you sleep on it. I could use your help. Perhaps you'll see things differently in the morning.*"

"It won't matter how I see things. No one's going to negotiate with you for Redler or anyone."

"*We shall see. Meanwhile, get some rest. Michael, please escort the chief back to his room. Good night, Chief.*"

Grear remained seated.

Michael started for the door, stopped, then turned around. "Coming, Chief?"

The police chief got up and walked over to his captors. "Tell me something, Richard. How could you have raped and killed those two little girls and their mother? How could you have committed such an outrageous act?" he asked, standing before the two. He turned to Michael for the answer.

There was a pause.

"Richard says, 'It was very easy, Chief. They weren't very nice to me at all.'"

Chapter
-—>
51

Lying on a cot in a cell-like room, unable to sleep, Chief Grear recalled having attended a nightclub performance with his parents more than forty years ago. The entertainer was a man who enjoyed a reputation for mesmerizing his audiences worldwide. A mind reader who appeared to possess powers of the preternatural kind.

The police chief fondly remembered one young fellow from the audience who volunteered to be blindfolded, then was asked to think of a well-known person, place, and thing. The lad was given a pen and a blank piece of paper with which to record his selections before folding the sheet in quarters and putting it into his pants pocket. Then the boy was handed a beanbag and directed to throw it out into the crowd. A middle-aged man caught it and was called to the stage. The performer asked the man to write down a verb, adverb, and an adjective on another piece of paper. Lots of humor ensued over the parts of speech and those who "wouldn't know a verb from a virgin if they fell over one," the telepathist had joked. After several minutes, the two participants were told to take their folded slips of paper and place them upon the floor of the stage, forty feet away from the entertainer.

Next, the showman asked the pair to concentrate solely on the words they had written while the mind reader held a blank sheet of paper to his temple. Through the supposed power of telepathy, the performer then jotted down a single sentence. Lastly, he asked the two to repeat aloud the three words they had selected.

"Ben Franklin, Washington, D.C., and carriage," the boy recited.

"Ran. Quickly. Broken," declared the other.

Smiling out over a sea of focused faces, the superstar slowly read his single sentence aloud: "Ben Franklin ran quickly from the broken carriage while visiting Washington, D.C.," he recited, handing over his sheet of paper to the two spellbound participants who, in turn, passed it along to the mesmerized members of the audience for undeniable confirmation.

Phony! Fake! Fraud! the youngster on stage had wanted to shout after witnessing such a feat. Only he couldn't. There was no way, for he alone had chosen those first three nouns. Grear had been that young boy who had volunteered and was called to the stage.

But tonight had been altogether different. Tonight had either been a hallucination or a hellish scheme. Or perhaps Robert Redler was indeed what Richard Geist believed him to be. Some sort of seer with sight into the future. A prophet or a profiteer, the police chief pondered. His mind was reeling. He was actually afraid to fall asleep. Maybe Richard and Robert *were* on a telepathic plane. But how could they have set the dialogue, orchestrating the stage and script? Perhaps by planting subliminal messages . . . or what? Yet, like the sentence on the sheet of paper the performer had read from those many years ago, Redler's wording had been accurate. In many instances, exacting.

The police chief laid his tired body upon the canvas cot, his aching head upon the soft foam pillow. Grear felt as though he were losing his mind in that moment. Had he so misjudged the writer? Were Richard Geist and Robert Redler working in concert? Had Lancing been right all along? Or was all of this just a bad dream? Surely, when and if he awoke in the morning, he would find himself in his own bed. Like Dorothy in the *Wizard of Oz*.

Chapter
——>
52

Doctors Thomas Fowler and his wife had enjoyed an evening at Lincoln Center, followed by a late and leisurely dinner. As the two podiatrists approached the entrance to their Manhattan brownstone, a building known for housing many musicians because of proximity to the music hall, they encountered a middle-aged woman having difficulty getting her cello case past the glass doors at the threshold.

"Here, let me help you with that," Fowler offered.

The woman smiled gratefully.

"I don't know what happened to our doorman this evening."

"That's strange," Fowler's wife declared after stepping inside the vestibule and attempting to open an inner door off the lobby, then the other, as her husband maneuvered the cumbersome case between the glass partitions. "I can't imagine why they're locked. Maybe something happened."

"Let me see," Thomas said with some concern, supporting the case with one hand while angrily shaking the inside doors with the other. "I'll be damned."

The middle-aged woman began to cry, and the case slid carelessly from her hands. Thomas caught it, propped it up against a wall then tried to comfort the distraught woman.

"It's all right. We'll be in in just a minute," Fowler promised, calling loudly for the doorman while reaching for a set of keys.

"We were at the Center earlier," Mrs. Fowler remarked cordially, attempting to calm the distressed woman. "Are you in concert there?" she inquired.

In one swift motion, the woman turned away from the wife, grabbed the husband's keys from his hand then stepped back outside the entranceway, leaving the couple standing there as she closed and locked the door behind her.

"Hey! What are you doing?" Fowler demanded, rattling the front door before cursing at the top of his lungs.

From out of nowhere appeared a group of musicians carrying their instruments, standing just outside the doorway.

"Help us," Helga Fowler implored. "Please help us," she hollered.

The young men and women were gesturing for the couple to open the cello case.

The wife was shaking her head as though she did not understand.

"Open it," the group mouthed simultaneously.

Mrs. Fowler turned toward it.

"Don't touch it!" her husband exploded. "It might be a bomb."

But the group shook their shaven heads and crossed their hearts in unison, setting their own cases down upon the ground, opening them in front of the frantic couple so that they could plainly see. There were no musical instruments within. Only hardware from another era one might associate with Al Capone and/or Elliot Ness. Tommy guns for Thomas and his wife.

Doctor Helga Fowler stood screaming and pulling frantically on the inner doors. Her husband was cursing and insanely kicking them, glancing over a shoulder at the assembled group.

"Open the case," the fraudulent musicians insisted in guttural tones, reaching down and taking out a dozen potentially noisy instruments of destruction, leveling them at the couple caged behind the glass.

"Please," the wife turned and pleaded, pressing her hands and face against the tempered plate of glass. "He didn't mean anything bad," she sobbed, inching her body down the ice-cold sheet of tempered glass, polished nails tracing and prying the narrow space between the panes. "Liza and Robert ran our niece ragged through the courts. Thomas was only protecting her," she screamed. "Robert wouldn't leave well enough alone. Thomas is so sorry. Tell them how sorry you are." But Thomas didn't say a word. "Tell them how sorry you are, YOU FUCKING BASTARD," Helga Fowler shouted. "Tell them what you did and that you're sorry," she trembled. "He'll say and sign anything you want," she sobbed, kneeling before the band of Geist's followers. "He'll confess how he advised both Alicia and her boyfriend and helped set Robert up."

It was the middle-aged woman who signed, orchestrated, and conducted the bloody business at hand while Fowlers' neighbors from across the street stood off to either side of their spotless brownstone front apartment windows, peering down in horror and disbelief.

A deafening cacophony of .30- and .50-caliber bullets began the eerie show; a white curtain of glass fell like an avalanche of icy snow. Geysers of red poured from three bodies as the coffin-like case flew open and an already dead doorman toppled out. The adjacent courtyard caught and immediately released the din, echoing sounds of anything but a symphony. In a flash, the impostors disappeared into the night. Moments later, sirens were screaming in the distance.

By morning, questions were flying about the city like nasty bugs. As both husband and wife were doctors as well as prominent patrons of the arts, why hadn't anyone protected the pair? Newspapers and politicians of New York City demanded to know. On the East End of Long Island, the wives of Police Chief Grear and Sergeant Phelps insisted on knowing their husband's whereabouts. What would be the police commissioner's and the mayor's statements to the public? Their respective spokespersons simply had to know. And why was Robert Redler out on bail? Virtually every citizen in all five boroughs begged the question.

Behind the scenes, three autonomous men who controlled the window of Operation Spirit were busy putting their people into play. Those who knew them, and few did, dubbed them the 'Mouseketeers.' But there was nothing Disney-like about them.

Chapter
−−>
53

Before the police chief even opened his eyes, he knew exactly where he lay, on the cot where he had lain for several hours, having finally fallen asleep. As he awoke, he literally prayed it was all a bad dream. But last night's nightmare had been very real indeed. Grear was mentally exhausted. His thoughts turned to Sergeant Phelps.

Suddenly, Grear heard a scream. The kind he never heard or even knew existed. The sort that went beyond the definition of bloodcurdling. Seconds later, there came another. It was a ghastly shrill that chilled him to the bone and made his very marrow quake.

Men and women in white robes were moving quietly down the hall when the piercing cry sprang up again, carrying through the walls.

"What's going on?" Grear shouted, pressing his face against the tiny barred window in the door. Several familiar stoic faces filed past his cell. "I said what's going on?" Grear demanded.

It wasn't until midmorning that Grear learned about the fate of his sergeant. Michael went on to explain that Richard had sent a message to the authorities sometime during the night, hoping to strike a deal. Richard had given them until 6 a.m. to reply in the affirmative.

"The feds wanted proof that we were holding the two of you, and that no deal could be struck unless they had proof in hand," Michael explained. "So, Richard gave them what they wanted. Your gun in Sergeant Phelps' hand," he said matter-of-factly.

Chief Grear screamed and kicked and pounded on the door until he thought he'd die and wished to God he had. "I WILL, SO HELP ME, GOD, KILL THE LOT OF YOU," Grear promised, unleashing a long list of profanities he hadn't used since his military service days.

"Richard said you would probably carry on like this, so he told me to inform you that unless you simmer down and give us your full cooperation, your sergeant will positively go to pieces. He's already lost his sense of humor. Therefore, I suggest you keep a civil tongue in your head," Michael warned.

The single emotion that Grear experienced at that moment was one of sheer helplessness. His whole being could be compared to that of a clogged pressure cooker with the heat source beneath it set on high. Grear was rumbling up more and more steam by the second. About to explode anew. Somehow, he summoned forth a degree of self-control. Somehow, he drowned that doubtless din . . . the sound of the sergeant's cries still ringing in his ears. Somehow, he just stood there shaking and taking in countless scorching breaths before emitting a single, silent wail of the long and lonely dead.

"When you calm down, Richard would like to send a message to your superiors. Concise and to the point. Juice, toast, and some fruit will be awaiting you shortly; that is, if you can manage to keep it down," Michael added with a sneer.

Grear felt entirely responsible for Donna Bianco's death. He wasn't about to put his sergeant in harm's way, he swore. *In harm's way*, he laughed insanely to himself. He had already cost his man a hand, he lamented. He wouldn't allow them to take his life, he promised the Almighty. Not if he could help it. Not if he had but half a breath. God, how he would slay these monsters if given half a chance, he vowed.

"All right," Grear conceded. All he could do was buy time. "Anything you want. But first I have to see my man. I want to see that he's still alive."

"*You're such a doubting Thomas, Chief,*" Richard signed, peeking inside the cell, standing alongside Michael.

Grear's face immediately turned hot and filled with hatred,

a face he couldn't hide.

"Keep a cool head, Chief, and you'll manage to keep it." Richard glared. *"See you in forty-five minutes,"* he signed then saluted sharply. *"See that the chief gets a shower, a shave, and a fresh outfit."* Richard disappeared from sight.

Chief Grear saw Sergeant Phelps through a window in the door. A window very much like the one in his own cell. Only the detective was in a larger area, hooked up to intravenous. The man's wrist was starkly bandaged at the point where his hand had been severed. The hand that yesterday held a gun in the face of the enemy. Maybe he had called that one wrong, too, he wondered. Maybe he and his sergeant should have taken out as many of them as they could. Maybe suicide would have been better than this.

"He's resting peacefully," Michael said.

"I said I want to see him."

"Suit yourself." Michael knocked, and a guard came to the window. Michael gestured, and the man unlocked the door. "Let him see him," Michael ordered.

Grear walked around to the other side of the bed. Phelps was dead to the world, but alive and breathing heavily. His bandaged cheek was hidden by a pillow; Grear gently touched the other, turned, and left the room. The guard locked the door the second Michael stepped outside.

"He has a nurse and a doctor nearby," Michael offered.

"That's very comforting. Did they assist one another during the amputation and operation through sign?" Grear snapped and snarled.

"His color's good. They assure me he'll be fine."

"He'd better be."

"We have to protect our investments," Michael stated flatly. "Now, if you'll follow me, we have to get you cleaned up."

Forty minutes later, Michael marched Grear down the hallway and into a small chamber. Richard was seated behind a desk. He appeared vexed. Michael wasn't too surprised, for Richard had been in a foul mood since early morning. Still, Michael sensed that something new was brewing. "What's wrong?" he asked.

Richard angrily flashed his fingers.

Michael sat down and turned as quiet as a mute.

Richard pushed a late edition of the morning paper under Michael's nose.

Michael picked it up and scanned the story on page 3.

Grear caught Lether's picture in the upper corner.

Alex Lether was not what you would call photogenic in that particular shot. He was apparently grimacing in agonizing pain, his bandaged elbow held high along with intravenous tubes supported by medics as he was being wheeled away on a gurney to a waiting ambulance in front of North Shore State's psychiatric facility, en route to a different kind of hospital.

Michael read for himself that according to sources inside the state institution, the man had met with an unfortunate accident in the scullery that morning. However, informed medical sources who wished to remain anonymous had said that a so-called *accident* of Mr. Lether's nature was highly unlikely and that the loss of the man's forearm ran more along the lines of foul play. With Richard's permission, Michael set the paper down in Grear's lap.

Grear scanned the story as well as the adjacent article dealing with a double homicide of two doctors: a husband and a wife. Grear recognized the surname and was about to turn the page.

"*One story at a time*," Richard signed. Michael took back the newspaper. "*One story at a time*," Richard repeated. "*They're fucking with me, Chief*," the aide animatedly translated in the vernacular for Richard. "*They're playing tit for tat.*"

"What did you expect?" Grear barked.

"*I don't expect them to act crazy.*"

"How did you act? You sent them Sergeant Phelps' hand."

"*In a box, labeled,* Thing. *Nothing original, I must confess. I guess I shouldn't joke around like that. See what happens when you kid? No one takes you seriously. I guess I'll have to show your people that I can get a leg up on them; or should I just sit back and let them have the upper hand?*" he toyed and smirked. "*After a while, I'm going to run out of body parts. Then what,*

Chief? Hum?"

"What do you want?"

"I want you to sign this letter. It explains the terms of the exchange. No time for special delivery. I'm going to fax it to the feds who will in turn inform the trio. That's who's really in charge of this operation, I believe. Operation Spirit. Right?"

Grear ignored the question. "Why is my signature so important? It doesn't tell them whether I'm alive or dead."

"No, it doesn't."

"Then why bother?"

"Because it's still a document. Now pick up the paper and hold it high. The document, too." Richard opened the drawer to the desk and pulled out a small camera. *"At least they'll know you're alive up to this edition."* Richard aimed the lens at Grear and shot. *"Now sign."*

"Like I really have a choice."

"One always has a choice, Chief."

"To do or die?"

"Still a choice."

"Between two unsatisfactory conditions."

"The choice is yours."

"May I read it?"

"But of course."

Grear read the letter. It was simple and to the point. His safe return and the return of his sergeant in exchange for Robert Redler and Angelica. The exchange was set for Friday, noon.

"They're not going to deal with you."

"In this case, they will."

"Why don't you ask for Lether in the lot?"

"Damaged goods. Besides, he won't make it through the night."

"How come?"

"He's become a liability."

"You have people who can get to him, I suppose?"

"We have people everywhere."

"Then why an exchange? Why not have your people whisk Redler and Angelica away in the night and bring them to you in the morning. Start the day right."

"*Come, come, come, Chief. A magician I'm not. Anyhow, I want things to be nice and neat. Unless, of course, your people pull another stunt. That would be another story with a most unfortunate ending for all,*" he added most prophetically.

Chief Grear took up a pen and put the newspaper and document down. He looked Richard squarely in the eyes. "I have what I believe is a reasonable request. Especially since we have till Friday."

"*He wants to have his lawyer look it over,*" Richard signed and laughed loudly, looking up at Michael quite humorously.

Michael laughed, too, then translated.

Grear forced a smile and shook his head. "First, my request."

"*Well, what?*" Richard signed impatiently.

"I'd like to read those manuscript pages. All of them. Starting with chapter one and leading right up to the point where Redler left off on page one hundred seventy-eight."

Richard shrugged. "*I have no problem with that. But you'll sign that letter now. I'll let you have a copy of the manuscript to read immediately. This is not open to further discussion.*"

"Fine." Grear reluctantly signed the document.

Chapter
——>
54

It was a busy week for the Giordano family. Tony was getting out of the Nassau County jail on Wednesday, and Barbara was arranging for a quiet evening in their Oceanside home. The big dinner party was scheduled for the following night in Oyster Bay.

Of course, Robert and Liza were invited, although Barbara had said that she was worried sick about the couple's safety. Two security teams now had to coordinate their efforts in order to protect both families, screening well over two hundred fifty guests, restaurant employees, spectators, reporters and camera people. *A Current Affair* would be videotaping Thursday's event. Anyone present represented a potential threat.

Suffolk County law enforcement authorities were especially troubled and tried to stop Redler from attending the party with the threat of an injunction. But Laddington's spokesman reminded everyone that Robert Redler was not under house arrest, but out on bail and could come and go as he pleased, just so long as he didn't leave the state. Besides which, the man added, the couple had been going stir crazy, cooped up in their Riverhead residence virtually night and day. They needed to get out and enjoy a change of scenery. Also, Redler had insisted on covering the event.

Liza knew that the Giordano affair would be fodder for Robert's new book. He had been working feverishly, sitting at his desk for fourteen to sixteen hours a day, six days a week. But on Sundays, Liza made Robert stop and take a break. They'd have their friends over, but things were really not the same. Friends or no friends, they had to be searched no matter how many times they came to visit, regardless of how many times they had been greeted by the same members of the security team. Not that the precaution strained their relationships because Robert and Liza's friends understood fully that it was in the couple's best interest. And it wasn't because the security team didn't give the couple and their guests their space, because they did. It was the atmosphere in general that became uncomfortable, for Robert Redler had become preoccupied.

With each passing day, Robert was growing more and more intense with regard to his writings. He couldn't let go, for his thoughts consumed him. Liza was becoming worried. The novel was engulfing him like a tidal wave. One evening, after very little sleep, it was as if he had awoken in the midst of drowning, kicking for his life in soaking wet pajamas while clinging to his pillow as though he were holding fast to a life raft.

No sooner than the nightmare was over, Robert got up, spilled a can of sharpened pencils alongside a yellow legal pad, sat down at his desk quietly, and wrote, and revised, and wrote until Liza thought she'd lose her mind.

Chapter
——>
55

R obert Redler and Liza Downs arrived at the Cafe Bella Notte under heavy security and were immediately escorted inside through a door at the rear of the building. The front of the restaurant was barricaded with blue wooden horses. Security guards on foot as well as horseback and in County vehicles patrolled the entire area. Behind the wooden barriers stood a long line of spectators, photographers, reporters, and camera crews. The front of the restaurant was already mobbed with invited guests, the lobby filled with family members and personnel: cousins and distant relatives, business associates, friends (dearest and otherwise), actors and actresses, waiters and waitresses. Assembled in a large room toward the back of the building was Tony's immediate family and selected VIPs. Barbara Giordano was hugging and kissing Robert and Liza, putting the pair at ease, making them feel as though they were a very special part of the group. Tony's attorney, Nelson Miles, was standing at Barbara's side, trading mock blows with Jonathan L. Laddington.

"To-ny! To-ny! To-ny!" Miles chanted, bobbing and weaving, fading then stepping forward before landing a light but decisive blow on Laddington's chin. Jonathan threw up his hands in affected surrender.

"Nelson's way of promoting and endorsing a match between

Geraldo Rivera and Tony," Barbara explained quite seriously to the couple. "Put down your mitts a minute, Nelson, and say hello to your opponent's client," she insisted, taking hold of Miles' ear. "This is Mr. Rob Redler and his gorgeous gal, Liza. Twenty-one years they've been together, Counselor. Maybe you could learn a thing or two."

Nelson dropped his hands at his side, staring Robert Redler up and down, shifting his eyes toward Liza, then back to Robert. "You a fighter, young man?"

"No, sir," Robert said and smiled.

"Oh, yes you are! You're one hell of a fighter from what I read and hear."

"Thank you, Mr. Miles."

"You fight me over this lovely lady here?"

"Yes, sir," Robert said.

"Good man. Good man," Nelson decided, gently brushing him aside and stepping forward to take Liza's hand. "He good to you?" the attorney asked. "I mean in the Biblical sense?"

"Is that a professional question, Mr. Miles, or are you just talking trash?" Liza asked with laughing eyes.

Nelson Miles held back a breaking grin. "Young lady, when I ask a professional question, I *am* talking trash. I'm a matrimonial lawyer. That's what I do," he added emphatically. "I'm only handling Tony's case for the flair."

Everyone around them laughed good-naturedly.

"He's a damn good lawyer," Laddington offered. "We know all about him even way out west. Got a reputation far and wide."

"Yes, for lawyering and loitering around pretty women," Barbara said. "Now, you give Liza back her hand before *I* step in the ring with you."

"Not until she answers my question," Nelson insisted, putting his other hand on top of the one he held.

Liza smiled. "Yes, Mr. Miles. Rob is very good to me in every sense."

"So there's no work for me here, I take it," he said with the saddened eyes of a basset hound, releasing her hand.

"No, Mr. Miles," Liza agreed wholeheartedly. "There's

not."

"Then you may call me, Nelson. Normally, I try and keep things on a professional basis. But if there's no work here . . ." He turned his attention back to Robert, putting his arm around the writer's shoulder. "Maybe you have one little complaint about Liza, here? Does she snore? Abuse her charge cards? Anything at all? You have to realize that I lost an important client around eight a.m. this morning, Rob," Nelson said quite seriously.

"Liza and I are not married, Mr. Miles. So there's really no work for you at all," Redler clarified candidly.

"Not married? But Barbara just said— What about twenty-one years? I thought— Wait a minute." Off came his arm from around Robert's shoulder. On came his charm as he stepped back into Liza's corner. "Liza, listen to me, please. There are laws in this state. Very definite and concise laws regarding domestic partners."

"He never quits," Laddington told Redler. "That's why he's such a huge success. Better humor him. He loves attention. He'll go on like this until he has her in his office," he teased. "Look, he's already giving her his card."

Robert smiled, shook his head, turned, and tapped Nelson on the shoulder.

Nelson Miles turned around abruptly, assuming a fighter's stance.

"No más," Redler said, throwing up his hands in capitulation. "No más."

"You throwing in the towel?" Nelson asked.

"Throwing in the towel and a chapter on you in my up-and-coming novel."

"Is that how and when you get even with me?"

"You better believe it, Mr. Miles," Robert answered straightaway.

"But no low blows," he insisted, coming in low but stopping just short of Robert's groin.

"I'll tell it like it is."

"Then you may call me, Nelson, too," he insisted, smiling broadly while vigorously shaking Robert's hand.

"Now that this round is over, I want you all to let your

guard down and try and have a good time," Barbara insisted. "Liza, I want you to meet a few members of our family. They've been on the sidelines all through this fiasco, but one hundred percent in our corner from the start. Soon, we're going to have the real opponents on the ropes." She winked playfully at Robert. "Yes?"

"Right," Robert agreed, knowing that she was being anything but playful.

"Raymond. Maria. Leonard," Barbara called out. "I want all of you over here. Liza, this is my father-in-law, Raymond, and his lovely daughter, Maria. Maria is my special friend," she announced. "And this handsome fellow here is my brother-in-law, Leonard. This is Mr. Redler's special lady and longtime sparring partner, Liza Downs. Liza. I give you my family. Robert, of course, has met most everyone."

Raymond Giordano stepped forward and extended his hand. He took Liza's and kissed it graciously. He was every bit the gentleman that Robert had said he was. "Hi, Liza."

Liza liked him immediately. "Hi there yourself."

"And I'm Tony's younger sister," Maria gushed and beamed brightly, kissing Liza on the cheek.

"And I live in the shadow of my infamous brother, Tony," Leonard frowned, coming forward and giving Liza a great big hug.

Liza gave them all hugs and kisses along with her sincerest well-wishes. They all stood around chatting happily on that early spring evening.

"Now, this is just the beginning," Barbara went on. "We've got wives and husbands to meet. Lovers and friends. Uncles and aunts. Cousins and nieces. Nephews and neighbors. Et cetera. Et cetera. Et cetera. This is your extended family, Liza and Rob. After tonight, you'll never be in want of a more loyal family. Mark my words. And speaking of words, Rob, how is your writing coming along?"

"Almost finished with the first draft."

"I'm dying to see it. When do you think I can take another peek?"

"With Tony home now, Barbara, whenever are you going to

find the time?" Maria asked rather seductively, smiling from ear to ear.

"By Monday, Tony will be back to being Tony," Barbara assured her sister-in-law. "But for now, he's captivated with the new me," she declared, turning three hundred sixty degrees with poise and elegance, exhibiting a sexy sequined Bob Mackie design while daintily patting her new hairstyle.

"Speak of the devil," Maria said.

Tony came up behind his wife, grabbing her around the waist and nibbling at her neck. Barbara smiled, tilting her head back and giving Tony a kiss upon the cheek. Everyone was gawking, talking, and smiling through wild applause.

"Take notice, ladies," Barbara broadcasted, "of how attentive your partner can be after four-and-a-half months of captivity."

"After what I gave her last night, she told me she's lucky it wasn't a year!" Tony roared, pounding his chest like a gorilla.

A family member started cheering Tony on.

"To-ny! To-ny! To-ny!" Nelson Miles chanted once again, promoting his man of the hour through uproarious antics and calls of the wild.

The party hadn't officially begun, but everyone was getting into full swing. Tony put Barbara over his shoulder and made his way through the group of men and women, grabbing and shaking hands as though he were pulling himself from vine to vine, heading toward center stage with his prize. Tony climbed the stairs then put Barbara down. "Me Tarzan," he announced, pausing for the full effect.

The men in the audience started behaving like baboons. "Then who's that?" Leonard cried out, pointing to his sister-in-law.

Tony looked bewildered for a moment. "I don't know, but it sure as hell ain't Alice Ziegler," he bellowed, kissing and dipping Barbara to the floor.

"That ain't no plain Jane you're holdin' there," Tony's father swore.

The family was going wild, one trying to outdo the other with suggestive comments directed to center stage. Even the women were getting into the act. "Is she your *current affair*?" one relative punned playfully.

"Playmate or primate?" another cried.

"Show him what an animal you can really be, Barbara," a young man cried.

"Yeah, knee him in the nuts," a woman hollered from the back of the crowd.

"Go for it, Tony baby," an older man countered.

"Yeah, make us proud."

"Alice Ziegler's rookie—ain't gettin' any nookie— 'cause his client's in the can," a relative quipped in singsong, referring to the fact that Ziegler and her lawyer were caught having an affair.

"Yeah, they've got themselves a real case of the ass as I hear it," someone shouted from the corner of the kitchen.

"All right. All right," Nelson Miles called to everyone. "None of that kind of talk when the news people start clicking their teeth and their cameras. I want to see ladies and gentlemen, all. That was then and this is now." Nelson signaled to Tony. "Pick Barbara up and bring her back here, please. We're going to let those vultures in in just a minute. No, Tony. I didn't mean for you to put her in the air again. I meant help her up. You're out of the woods now, kid. So behave yourself. Raymond, keep an eye on him. Maria. Leonard. Watch your brother like a hawk. Tony, did you even bother to say hello to Mr. Redler and his charming lady, Liza? Come on over here," he said, shaking his head and removing a sequin from Tony's shoulder. "You know I hate it when you upstage me like that," he half- kidded, faking a right cross.

Tony laughed. "Lighten up, Counselor. This is supposed to be *my* party." He turned to Liza. "See, I can give him back-talk because I haven't paid the bill yet," he jawed, taking her hand and giving her a peck on the cheek. He turned to Robert. "I want to thank you for what you did. Your editorials were fair and uplifting."

"Forget the uplifting, Tony," Nelson implored. "Please. He's got uplifting on the brain," the attorney said to Robert. "He's been working out with weights for months."

"Don't mind him," Tony went on. "He's really a wreck today. Loves the limelight but sweats a lot. Listen, I also want to thank you for giving me the benefit of the doubt. Sorry I didn't write you from the country club, but I got thousands of letters. Read them all but didn't write back to a soul. Just not a letter writer, kid."

"Not important; forget it."

The two put their arms around one another, and a family member snapped a picture.

"Thanks, pal," Tony said, patting the writer on the shoulder.

"All right. All right," Nelson cried, waving a pair of meaty claws around like those of a five-pound lobster. "I've got to get back outside and organize this thing. Tony. Out back with Barbara. They've brought the limo around."

"We have to sneak out the back way and then make our appearances in front," Tony explained, shrugging his shoulders with a big smile. "It's nearing showtime, boys and girls. See ya later, kid."

Nelson collected Tony's parents, Maria, Barbara, Tony and several others. Maria's older sister, Anne, remained behind and was introduced to Liza.

Chapter
——>
56

Nelson Miles stood receiving guests just outside the restaurant, scrutinizing their invitations, checking their names off a long list, taking their right hands and strapping on either green or yellow wristbands, explaining the rules to the long lines of people in passage. Yellow gave guests up to an hour and a half in which to devour hors d'oeuvres and down cocktails and to schmooze with Tony and company before being asked to leave. Green was a permit to park or parade oneself for the entire evening.

Nelson smiled, nodded, and forced a series of little laughs, making small talk with guests while encouraging everyone entering the restaurant to "pay a toll" to the kids who held the door along with a good-sized paper bucket in which to deposit cash.

Those on the inside looking out were watching 'Fox-Five's own,' Penny Crone, scooting back and forth in a navy blue blazer with matching skort and opaque tights, standing still just long enough for Redler to size her up and down, figuring her for five-foot-three with short, frosted gray-brown hair—eyes the color he couldn't quite catch —and black flats that were immediately on the move again.

Nelson waved to her but went unnoticed, pulling back and passing a comb of flaccid fingers through way too long, dark, wavy hair that completely covered his ears. Steve Dunleavy, of *A Current*

Affair, had turned and thought Nelson was waving to him. The producer nodded politely. Penny simpered and tripped over the cable that Steve's assistant was busy trailing around the parking lot. With a hint of annoyance, Dunleavy reached down and raised the power cord, banging his gray pompadour into Penny's buttocks on the way up, both of them uttering cursory pardons and how-do-you-dos.

Back inside the restaurant, guests were staring in fascination while plates of eye-pleasing hors d'oeurves comprised of broiled baby lamb chops, stuffed mushrooms, strips of grilled chicken and sirloin, shrimp, and scallops with pimento kept arriving with most hospitable grace. Drink orders were taken and delivered at an equally welcoming pace. The cocktail hour, every minute of it, was a spectacular success. The food, it was unanimously decided, was devouringly delicious. The servers and service were second to none—the young men and women being prepared, prompt, and pleasant to look at with a pleasing manner to match. The party was well under way.

In short order, two limousines arrived in front of the restaurant. Those assembled oohed and aahed and were taken in by the showy display. Tony's parents stepped from the first vehicle, followed by several members of the immediate family. The crowd went wild as Tony, in a navy suit and matching tie, smiled and waved and stepped from a stretch Corvette, donning gray and white snakeskin boots. Barbara stepped out behind him in a black sequined sheath, matching sheer stockings and peau de soie pumps. Her blonde hair was styled in a French roll and bedecked with softly furrowed bangs. Her warm smile sanctioned her husband's shameless bravado. Behind them, demonstrators and supporters were jerking placards that read: "Tony, Do The Right Thing," as well as, "Tony *Did* The Right Thing."

Leonard and Maria were waving to their sister, Anne, inside the building. Howard Stern's *babbler* was busy making excuses as to why his boss was a no-show that evening. Steve Dunleavy's audio man was busy bustling about his boss, hooking him up to a power pack. Another member of the crew went prowling around the room with a portable boom microphone adorned with something resembling a fuzzy gray flannel sock that almost wound up in Tony's *Welcome Home* cake: a sheet cake displaying Tony's true love: his boat.

The cake sat off in a corner upon a light blue sea of frosting. The microphone had grazed the decorative radar arch, and Nelson Miles practically had a stroke. Dana, one of Nelson's secretaries, giggled and patted her employer on the shoulder, assuring him that the affair was going well and not to worry. Maria's husband, a goalie who had played hockey for some Canadian team, assessed and repaired the minor damage with a whisk of a finger across the icing, giving it his seal of approval after sampling the creamy frosting.

Hardly a soul had even noticed the telltale mark as the yellow banded guests were being asked to leave while the privileged green-braceleted were directed to the opposite corner in which sat large decorative baskets and bowls alongside huge trays of still more fare that was being uncovered. Breads, salads, rigatoni and sausage, penne with spinach, chicken rolled with mozzarella, broiled fish, eggplant parmigiana, and a mountain of grated cheese lined the wall. Practically every eye was glued to the buffet table, stomachs about to recommit sin.

Leonard Giordano was rolling and raising his eyes toward heaven, debating whether to praise or curse the god of gluttony. "*Marrone!*" he exclaimed, bunching and flagging the tips of all five fingers.

Dana stood alongside Leonard while staring down in delight, her eyes defying a usually cautious appetite. Petite, slim and pretty, she slithered along the line in a tailored ivory wool knit, scoop-necked, short-sleeved, button-down gown. Raymond and his wife, Roberta, were making sure everyone had a plate in that auspicious moment at hand.

The line outside the restaurant was never-ending. Men in satin jackets from Executive Security and Investigative Services were keeping order for the night. Nelson Miles was busy moving back-and-forth and in and out of the building—a cellular phone pressed against an ear.

Tony and Barbara were mingling among the guests. She seemed much cooler than she appeared earlier. Polite rather than familiar. Tony, on the other hand, was Tony at his best. A man's man. Circulating and joking with the men at the open bars throughout the rooms. Moving Barbara through the crowd of well-wishers. Laughing. Teasing. Yet, somehow keeping himself in check as instructed.

Chapter
——>
57

Final arrangements had been made to exchange two law enforcement officers for two cult co-conspirators. Robert Redler, of course, was not made part of any deal. Richard Geist knew early on that he would have to find another way to lure the writer to him. And as far as the threat of silencing Lether went, Geist also knew it wouldn't have been the prudent thing to do. The risk of dissension among the new recruits regarding such an act would have been far greater than the risk of Lether revealing what little he knew. Except for the abandoned warehouse along the Jersey Shore, Lether knew nothing of the cult's safe houses throughout the tri-state area. Richard's posturing had been nothing more than a negotiating ploy. The important party, for now, was Angelica, for she had grave responsibilities that lay ahead.

Chief Grear and Sergeant Phelps stood on the south side of the Peconic River in Flanders. Angelica and Lether were to the north in Riverhead. All four hostages were positively identified by respective parties on both shores. Richard Geist was nowhere to be seen.

FBI Agent Ronald Towers peered through his binoculars and told one member of his team to start the Whaler's engine. Two men brought Lether forward and helped him into the boat. The frightened figure was given simple instructions. Lether nodded, engaged the forward gear then headed steadily across the river. Before he reached the opposite shore, one of Richard's soldiers brought Sergeant Phelps to its edge. Lether put the engine in neutral, raised the outboard motor, and the Whaler sailed smoothly to the shoreline. Two of Geist's soldiers steadied the boat. Lether got out. Sergeant Phelps got in. One soldier standing behind the stern maneuvered the fourteen footer back into deeper water, lowered the unit, and pointed its bow toward the other shore. Phelps popped the boat into gear and was gone.

Angelica stepped into the water and waited. Two FBI agents flanked her, staring fixedly at the approaching craft. Sergeant Phelps was staring dead ahead, trance-like. Angelica showed no emotion nor acknowledged the savagery the sergeant had suffered at the hands of his captors: bandages covering one side of the sergeant's face and handless wrist. In a moment, if all went well, they would both be free. The two agents stepped forward to assist the sergeant and help Angelica into the boat.

"Fuck you," Angelica snapped, hopping into the craft as Phelps climbed out. She slammed the engine into reverse and twisted the throttle clockwise. The boat swerved backwards, sending an agent sprawling into the water. Swinging a hard left, she sent the boat around one hundred eighty degrees then slammed the shift forward and hit full throttle. Immediately, the Whaler went up on plane and sped across the river.

"Fucking bitch!" the drenched agent sputtered.

"Keep your eyes on Grear," Agent Towers ordered. "If you lose him, take her out."

Chief Grear was standing in plain sight. Pairs of binoculars read his serious dark eyes. A myriad of cross hairs aligned in deadly concentration lightly combed the back of Angelica's head and shoulders. Several sharpshooters who preferred open sights at close range set theirs just slightly left of her spine. As she neared the shoreline, the boat suddenly stopped dead in the water then coasted freely forward. Angelica jumped out. For some reason, Grear was standing fast.

"What the hell is he waiting for?" an agent questioned.

"Swap or SWAT," ordered the senior member of the team, steadying his field glasses on Grear.

From high above, Towers' men stood still as toy soldiers positioned on a board game, but they were very real, indeed: butt plates planted squarely into solid shoulders; elbows raised like single wings; fingers feathered to trigger action.

"What the fuck is going on?" a second in command demanded.

Angelica moved directly in front of the police chief.

"Jesus fucking Christ," another agent shrilled.

Suddenly, Grear came back into sharp focus as Angelica leaned forward from the waist, dropped her trousers down around her knees, her shapely buttocks giving those with field glasses quite an eyeful—those with telescopic and iron sights a brand new fix. Then in a flash, the target was gone and so was Grear.

On the north side of the river, chaos ripped along the shoreline. Red faces and angry expletives ran up and down the ranks. Two helicopters rose out of nowhere. A Coast Guard cutter came out of the east and headed west, converging at the point where Geist's followers had pulled their disappearing act. Members of the SWAT team were everywhere. Hand-held radios were squawking away noisily. Neither Geist's group nor Chief Grear were anywhere to be seen.

On the south side of the river appeared a rookie cop who quickly uncovered the ruse.

"Over here," he called out. And everyone in the vicinity went running over to discover a drainageway at the spot where Angelica and Grear had been standing before they suddenly disappeared. The breadth of the ditch was fitted with a plywood plank. A series of camouflaged tarps covered the entire length of passage, running approximately seventy yards further to the south. Geist's and his soldier's escape route, having taken Grear with them.

"She must have ducked under this canvas here," an agent surveyed. "They probably yanked the captain off this platform with that rope over there."

Agent Towers was on the radio. Seconds later, a chopper swooped in, hovering then covering the course along the entire stretch. Men on foot followed a series of tracks that led to a narrow inlet until there was nothing left to track.

"That's not supposed to be there," a member of the Coast Guard cried, pointing to the trench.

"It wasn't," another hollered. "Someone dug it out to connect the inlet, and it flooded over at high tide."

"They've got to be heading inland," Towers barked across a secured frequency. "There's no way for them to flee by water."

"We've got the area surrounded. They can't possibly penetrate our line," a voice came back. There was a pause and a very brief commotion. Another voice was on the air.

"This is Sergeant Phelps. Riverhead P.D. You listen to me. These people do the impossible."

"Thank you, Sergeant Phelps. Now, you put my man back on. We've got things under control."

"No. They've got *you* under control."

"I don't have time for this—"

"You don't have time, period."

"We've got it covered, Sergeant.

"I'm telling you they've got the upper hand and the hand of the devil on their side."

"Sergeant—"

"They're not concerned with your impenetrable line. They're going to cross the river and escape."

"You're nuts."

"I'm telling you, they'll cross. They want you to think—"

"Impossible!"

"Not if you're concentrating your efforts in and around Flanders. Now listen to me—"

"We've got our men up and down the river—from the bay to the center of town. So butt out, Sergeant. Crossing would be suicide, and they know it."

Suddenly, there was a commotion to the south. Agents, cops, and Coast Guard personnel were scurrying everywhere. A mass of black smoke rose in the distance over Flanders. A moment later, a tremendous explosion occurred along the northern shoreline, downriver from the Moose Lodge. Sirens were screaming nearby. The Coast Guard cutter was reported to have broken contact. Prevailing westerly winds carried the thick black mass of smoke across the stretch of river. Another great explosion sounded as though it had come from town, shaking the ground from shore to shore.

"Alpha One. You copy? Alph...." Sergeant Phelps was yelling.

"Copy," came the succinct reply.

"Off...star..."

"You're breaking up. Repeat."

"Off to starboard, shithead. Your other starboard," Phelps bellowed, watching the special agent in charge falter before focusing on the fine line of canoes and kayaks making their crossing from south to north along the black boundary of smoke. "World's smallest book, Agent Numbnuts? Answer: Blacks I have met yachting. What's wrong with that picture, asshole? That's another diversion they're creating. Clergymen and their congregation. Geist's pawns. They're leading you astray. You're going to follow them to your death."

"You're finished, Phelps," Towers bellowed.

"I'm telling you—get those choppers the hell out of there."

"Bravo One. Bravo Two. This is Alpha One. Birds down and blow those bastards out of the water," commanded Special Agent Towers.

"NO!" Phelps screamed. "They're not Geist's people. They're innocent members of the Baptist church. Stand down! You negotiate for my chief's life. Do it now! Before they blow you sky-high."

"They probably murdered your chief, jerk-off."

"You don't know that."

"Get off this radio."

"You can't cut them down like animals. Women and children are down there with them. Geist's creating a diversion, I'm telling you."

"I'm ordering you off the air."

"You're being blindsided."

Two copters were fast approaching the prodigious clouds of black smoke carried eastward by the wind.

"I have orders, Sergeant. You remember orders, don't you?"

"You're in charge of this operation. You can stop it! I'm

begging you to exercise discretion and common sense. We're talking civilians down there. Geist's followers are going to destroy you and get away. You're outnumbered and outclassed. You don't understand what's going on here."

"Your brain is fried."

"We don't have time to argue this."

"You got that right. Bravo One. Bravo Two. You have your orders. Send those bastards to kingdom come. Do you copy?"

There was no immediate reply.

"This is the FBI," a voice commanded from one of the hovering crafts. "Drop your paddles and weapons in the water and place your hands on top of your heads," a man inside the beater ordered.

"Bravo Two. This is Alpha One. I'm countermanding that order. Now blow the bastards to smithereens. Is that a copy? Bravo One...."

Scores of boats were already on the Riverhead shoreline. Hundreds of black men, women, and children lined the bank, standing defiantly with arms folded across their rising and falling chests, facing the turbulent water created by the whir of beating blades. The flotilla of black insurgents kept coming, paddling insanely to the north to join the others.

"They're not Geist's people," Phelps repeated. "They're being used. He controls the fucking church."

Those caught in the middle of the river tried to steady their canoes and kayaks, more out of concern of tipping over into the frigid waters than any fear of having their bodies drilled silly from above. Cops and SWAT teams were moving swiftly down both shorelines. Off to the east, a small vessel drifted across the Peconic River from out of nowhere.

"I repeat. This is the FBI. Put your weapons—"

It was the last word that preceded two great explosions as projectiles fired from rocket launchers hit the belly of the whirring beasts. Midday, midair wreckage filled the sky. Two giant yellow fireballs spewing metal in every direction created a surrealistic scene. It was as if a skyway had suddenly spanned both shores. Teams of FBI men to the rear of the insurgents fell as silently as late fall leaves and ephemeral flowers, a shower of arrows targeting parts of their bodies exposed just above and below Kevlar vests.

To the northeast, Agent Towers was screaming at the top of his lungs in sheer frustration, ordering chaos to conform, demanding discipline from a deserting officer already dead yet traveling twenty or so feet in the direction the broadhead was pointing him, the man's fists clasped firmly around the aluminum shaft as though he were praying. A second later, the man unwittingly obeyed the agent's command, halting and falling forward upon his face.

Agent Towers begged for backup. An arrow came from out of nowhere, striking the center of the letter **F** on the back and through his jacket, penetrating the flakless vest beneath, tearing up muscle and shattering bone before blowing out his chest. Two Muzzy broadheads simultaneously hit the bull's-eye—one directly above the other into the letter **B**. For effect, Yvette dotted the capital **I**. Sharpshooters on both shores saw their leader twist, turn, and topple but had no clue where to precisely set their sights.

Chapter
——>
58

When it was over—really over—fifty-seven law enforcement men and women lay dead. A dozen more were missing, inclusive of Chief Grear. Twenty-three black members of the Abyssinian Baptist Church had been killed as a result of midair wreckage; scores more were critically injured and arrested. Not a single soldier of Geist's cult was apprehended. The minister and head of COAL (Coalition of Activists and Loyalists) promised retribution, claiming his flock had engaged in nothing more than a peaceful demonstration.

Sergeant Phelps had been debriefed, hospitalized for twenty-four hours then returned to restricted duty. He was instructed to give a brief and carefully crafted statement to the press. Off-duty, his obsession with the case caused doctors, family, and friends great concern. But Phelps told everyone that the best medicine he could possibly receive at the moment would be to have *their* full cooperation and support.

The feds had gone back to the monastery in Island Park and combed the convent in Hubbard Hills. Both facilities were unoccupied and antiseptic, the way they had been left initially. The lowlands were as Phelps had described them, only there were no clues left to follow. Only signs of the elusive deer. Everyone had vanished without a single trace. But to where?

Phelps somehow knew that Robert F. Redler was his only hope, but none of the sergeant's messages had been returned. For the writer, too, was gone.

Laddington's office was uncooperative as well.

Phelps felt alienated from his peers, seeing as how he was assigned to desk duty. Captain Cally in Queens had given him a sympathetic ear but a cold shoulder when he started asking hard-and-fast questions. Things did not add up. *Were people being told not to talk?* he wondered. Or was paranoia taking hold?

A lawyer from the P.B.A. spoke to him about disability retirement. Apart from a consoling comment or two, no one was saying a word about Chief Grear. Had Geist made further contact with the police? Was the sergeant out of the loop completely? His debriefing had indeed been brief. There were a lot more questions they could and should have asked, he felt. About being held captive. About the prisoner exchange operation gone to pot. When he volunteered information he believed relevant, it appeared as though the department was disinterested. All they seemed to want to know about was what Chief Grear knew, thought, felt, or said.

Late that afternoon, Sergeant Phelps phoned Doctor Bianco. His secretary put him through immediately. The doctor would see him within the hour.

Chapter
—–>
59

Richard Geist and several soldiers entered an old barn. Chief Grear had no idea where he was being held. Light filtered in through the rafters.

"*Ah, there you are, Chief. I trust my angel and the others have been taking good care of you. No need to worry,*" Richard signed and Angelica translated. "*We're not expecting rain tonight,*" he joked and smiled gleefully.

Grear shifted his eyes from Richard to the roof to the woman in white whose freshly shaven head was tilted oddly to the right. She was studying him closely, like an entomologist studying an insect. In fact, he felt as insignificant as a bug, sitting there in the corner, secured in his own handcuffs.

"*Your boys were very, very bad, I've been told,*" Richard put forth with a frown. "*Not too much on the brain except water games, I suppose.*"

"What did you expect? You didn't keep your word. You had no intention of sending me back."

"*You're wrong, Chief. I had every intention of sending you home. Still do.*"

"They're not going to give you Redler. I told you that."

"*We'll see. Besides, I now have eleven other hostages to sweeten the pot*," he communicated if only to keep the police chief in the dark, having known from the start that negotiations with authorities regarding Robert Redler would simply prove a waste of time. "*I still might need you to convince Redler that a little chat is in order.*"

"You really believe Redler is just going to drop whatever he's doing and come to do your bidding?" *That is, if he isn't already on your payroll,* Grear wanted to add. For he wasn't really sure about anything anymore.

"*At the very least, I want to know all about his power. At best, to usurp it.*"

"His so-called power has got to be just one big coincidence or some kind of magnificent trick."

"*Oh, come now, Chief. We both know better than that. It can neither be coincidence nor chicanery. And what happened to that other possibility you were espousing? Hum? Or have you given up on God? I guess He let you down, too. So what do you really think? Whatever the story, I believe we both agree that Redler does possess an extraordinary gift.*"

"But you don't believe he's aware of his ability, you said."

"*Well, if he wrote off two whirlybirds before they went to helicopter heaven, I'd say he'd have to by now.*" Geist giggled like a child. "*True?*"

"If he is clairvoyant, he probably knows about this conversation we're having right now. At least your wants and wishes. Would he not? So my intervention would prove moot."

Richard shrugged. "*Nothing happens in a stagnant pool, Chief. One first has to cast a stone upon its surface in order to set things in motion. Action is the catalyst. I think it's rather obvious that Robert Redler cannot change the course of events. He can only record them before they happen.*"

"Yet, somehow you believe *you* could?"

Signing, grinning, and circling a finger through the air before making the sound of an explosion, Richard communicated, "*I could certainly give it a whirl.*"

Angelica offered a little laugh.

Chief Grear thought for sure he had entered the twilight zone. He thought it from the moment he finished reading

Redler's manuscript. Especially the last nine pages. But the whole business, he certainly realized, was very real, indeed. He wished he had had the opportunity to share the enigma with Phelps. The only thing he had gotten a chance to say before they put his sergeant into the boat was, "Go with God." He didn't know why he had said that, but he had.

Chapter
——>
60

Sergeant Phelps lay down on the psychiatrist's couch in Bianco's private office. "You don't mind?" Phelps asked.

Doctor Bianco smiled. "Be my guest."

"I mean, this is not a real honest-to-goodness analyst's couch, is it? Because I pictured something a bit more—"

"Stereotypical?"

"Yeah, you know, black leather. No back. Severe looking. Not all these plush cushions and fancy fabric."

"Comfortable?"

"Very."

"Good. So think of it as kind of a modified analyst's couch, Sergeant."

"Fine. Listen, this isn't gonna cost me a bundle, is it?" he kidded. "Lying here as opposed to sitting over there in a chair. I mean, I don't know about my coverage anymore."

"Depends," Bianco said with a straight face.

"On what?"

"On whether or not I can cure what ails you."

There was a momentary silence. "Can you cure this, Doctor?" Sergeant Phelps asked, holding up the stump of what had been his right hand.

"No. But I know you know about prostheses because you have a fireman friend who lost a leg and has an artificial limb. I also know you know about that cop out east who had most of his face blown away with a shotgun blast and is ninety percent blind but leads a productive life running a bookstore in Greenport and doing the lecture circuit. Even writes some poetry. And I absolutely know you didn't come here for me to give you a lecture on how to get on with your life."

Sergeant Phelps was off the couch and sitting across from Doctor Bianco. "You sound more like a cop who's been doing his homework than a shrink. I think maybe I need this kind of talk instead of the crap I've been getting," he said, staring down at the carpet while holding back tears. "I'm feeling very much like a cripple and very, very sorry for myself. I begged those fucking bastards to send me home with my hand so that maybe the doctors could still sew it back on. I cried like a little kid. And I'm crying now because I want my chief back. Alive. And I also want justice."

"You lost your hand, Sergeant. I lost my wife. Arthur Field lost his entire family. Not forgetting that there were other victims with families, too. We all want justice. There are thousands of Richard Geists out there. There is madness all around us. You and I see or hear about it most every day. Now, there is a kind of madness in you and me. But somehow we'll manage to control it. Somehow we'll manage to act civilized. We'll rehearse our lines and strive to play our parts to pure perfection. People like Richard can't. Not once you cross the line."

"You make it sound like we'll be reading from a script. 'All the world's a stage,' sort of thing."

"Oh, we are, and indeed it is, Sergeant," Bianco assured him. "Believe me, Shakespeare had it all figured out," he said and smiled wisely.

"Well, that I wouldn't know about. Poetry and such. But what I would like to know, though, is the whereabouts of Richard Geist and my chief. I'd also like to know how Robert Redler really fits in all this business."

"I believe Redler is simply a projection of Geist's revenge."

"A projection?"

"Simply put, Richard Geist is attributing his own feeling of vengeance onto Robert Redler. Whereas Redler, like the rest of us, wants justice, Geist seeks sheer revenge. Pure punishment."

"Justice and revenge."

"It's a rather thin line, Sergeant. A *very* fine line like we're walking at this moment. Kind of like a high wire—a tightrope. Balance will be the key."

"I don't know if I understand."

"You will. Trust me." Bianco picked up a pen and wrote down a name and a phone number. "This fellow, whose name I'm giving you, was the director of North Shore State Hospital when Richard was confined in 1969. Ask him to introduce you to the bard."

"The bard?"

"He'll know."

Phelps stared down at the name. "This Doctor Kirby is retired as I recall?"

"Yes. He retired some years ago. Still keeps active with lecturing and consulting, though. He'll show you around. Nice fellow. I gave you his home phone. His housekeeper will probably answer. You tell her who you are, and she'll have him get back to you."

"Where's all this leading, Doc?"

"I'm really not sure, Sergeant," Bianco answered honestly.

"Got any other suggestions or information?" he asked hopefully.

"Stay on the union's back with regard to the prosthesis. Go to your orientation for rehabilitation the next time they call you. And remember that psychiatrists are medical doctors, too. I'm giving you sound advice."

"But no bill?"

"Not this time," Bianco promised through a laugh, seeing the sergeant to the door. "No consultation fee. This was police business, was it not?"

"Maybe a little bit of both. Thanks," he said, extending his left hand.

Doctor Bianco took and shook it warmly.

Chapter
——>
61

Doctor Kirby was a card. The joker to be sure. He met Sergeant Phelps promptly in the main lobby of North Shore State Hospital at 8 a.m. sharp. It was Saturday, and Phelps had the morning off.

"So, I can't talk you into a Marco Polo or a Napoleon," Doctor Kirby joshed. "You're sure Doctor Bianco wanted to start you out with the bard?"

"That's what he said."

"Your funeral. Would be, too, if I put you in his cell," he summed up quite seriously. "I want you sitting in a chair or standing a good fifteen feet away from him at all times. Are you clear on that?"

"Clear."

"Good. And if he tries to coax you over with a song or a sonnet?"

"I say, 'Sorry, Mr. Shakespeare, but I'm wise to you.'"

"Good. No coy response, or he'll fly into a bloody rage. If he does one of his death scenes for you, don't get caught up anywhere near the cage, 'cause I'm telling you he'll have that other hand for breakfast. Understood?"

"Understood." The sergeant experienced a kind of phantom tingling beneath the bandages as he digested the thought.

"You'll get much further with the truth as you'll soon learn. He sees through everything. He may just sit or stand and mock you like a parrot. Or he may say absolutely nothing at all. Here." He handed Phelps a clean handkerchief.

"What's this for?"

"He may decide to spit on you or worse. Remember. Fifteen feet, and at least you'll stay relatively dry."

"Are you having a little fun with me?" Sergeant Phelps asked.

"Oh, my boy, that's for the bard to do if he so chooses. I'm just listing all the necessary precautions. I would have much preferred to start you off with General Patton. We have only one of them here. The other hung himself years ago. Couldn't stand the competition. But this poor boy has no doubts about himself whatsoever. Therefore, nothing to prove. The real McCoy. Or so you'd think. So. Are we ready to take a trip down memory lane?"

"Ready, I guess."

"Here we go then." Doctor Kirby smiled and led the way.

The two men rode the elevator and got off on the second floor. The sergeant was required to check his weapon. Actually, he had been surprised that the department still allowed him to carry one. Through locked doors, security, and gates they walked.

"What did the bard do to wind up here?" Phelps asked.

"You mean Bianco didn't tell you?"

"Nope."

"About a dozen boys between the ages of eight and eighteen."

"Sexual assault?"

"You for real? If that was all, he'd be out stalking the neighborhoods tonight. Authorities found the body parts of one child in three states along the eastern seaboard. Had to match the prints of the boy's soles to the ones on his birth certificate for positive ID. The bard would make Jeffrey Dahmer look bad at a cannibal convention. You know *The Silence of the Lambs* book and movie?"

"I do, indeed."

"Well, given half a chance as a stand-in, he'd have split that guard's chest cavity open wide and formed it into a crown roast, capping each rib with an eyeball from members of the cast."

"That's quite a vivid description."

"You spend forty-three years in this place and see the pictures you come away with. My wife, God rest her soul, thought I'd go mad during retirement, seeing as how I have no hobbies; the irony being that she was going nuts having me home twenty-four hours a day, seven days a week. So I did some lecturing then came back here to do consulting and hold onto whatever sanity I could salvage. Actually, it's not very much because my madness overshadows what little soundness of mind I have left. So much more obvious when I leave the building for the light of day. Is this talk making you uncomfortable?"

"Me? Oh, no. Certainly not."

"Good. Because if you were to give the bard the impression of insincerity, he'd eat you up alive so to speak. He senses like the animal he is."

"Glad you keep reminding me."

"Right through this door and we're there."

The similarities between the corridors they had just passed through and the cellblock they were presently in was what Phelps could best compare to some of the background settings viewed in Thomas Harris' book. If children could actually witness what he saw before him now, they'd automatically be good for life, he swore. But this was not a prison per se, he had to remind himself. *Yeah, right*, he thought again.

The steel door closed behind the pair with a sense of finality, leaving Phelps with the feeling that the place was positively evil rather than something simply sad or bad. A strong stench of urine and mold permeated the cold, old cobblestone floors and cellar-like walls. He brought the borrowed handkerchief to his nose.

"We have to pass The Duke in order to get to your poet. Kind of like a rerun. Maybe if you wrap that handkerchief around your face like a bandito, he'll do something from *True Grit*. But don't dare call him Pilgrim. Only *he* says that," Kirby warned in a whisper.

A tall figure with white whiskers stood in the corner of his cell, hands placed near his sides as if he were about to draw a pair of six-shooters. Except for the eyes, the man did not move a millimeter.

"Right around the corner and away from the madding crowd," the doctor directed.

"Somehow I get the feeling that Shakespeare isn't going to be boring. Even at eight fifteen in the morning."

"Not if you remember that this is the Globe Theater and that his cage is really center stage. Ah, good morning, William," Doctor Kirby greeted the bard.

Hardly the threat that the sergeant had envisioned. The hunched over old man turned and greeted the two of them as though he had been waiting out an intermission.

"'The play's the thing. Wherein I'll catch the conscience of the king.' Did you know Doctor King?" the raggedy figure asked, directing a scrawny finger at the sergeant. "Yes, I'm talking to you, knave. Speak up."

"I think he likes you," Kirby said excitedly. "He usually sulks and parades the stage for quite some time before he speaks to anyone," he whispered. "That is, if he even speaks at all. Answer up."

"No, I never knew Doctor King. But I heard many good things about him from another doctor."

"Then you know nothing about the man at all. For another's judgment has no value in and of itself and is but a worthless reference. Take me at this very moment. I am the window to the world, yet you see before you whatever picture this autumn clown standing beside you has painted in your mind. SAY IT ISN'T SO, SERGEANT!"

"It is so," Phelps said without hesitation, nor without taking his eyes off the man. "How do you know I'm a sergeant?"

"I'll ask the questions if you please. Yet, you had the answer before you even asked, but you were listening with your eyes and not your ears. So you heard, 'crazy old man.' Say it isn't so."

"Yes. That's so."

"So, we'll see."

"I meant no offense."

"Oh, you couldn't give a shit about offending me, Sergeant.

Tell me why you're here."

Sergeant Phelps turned to the doctor. "I'll be fine. I'd like to speak with him alone, now."

"You just remember what I told you."

Phelps nodded.

"You keep to the wall on your way back. Then pound like hell on the door. There are no buzzers or bells in this section."

Phelps nodded again.

"I'll ask you one more time why you're here," the bard insisted.

"I'm not sure."

"But you'll know when you found what it is you're looking for. Does that fit the bill, Sergeant?"

From around the hall, the steel door slammed shut behind them, and Sergeant Phelps never felt so alone in his life. "What did you just say?" Phelps swallowed, staring at the bard in disbelief.

"Through *my* questions, though however rhetorical they may seem, you may find what it is you're looking for. For you found me. All right?"

"Who are you?"

"ALL RIGHT?"

"All right."

"We'll see. How's your Lillian doing, Sergeant?"

"Oh, my God!"

"Oh, you don't know the half of it. The answer to my question, knave."

"My wife is fine."

"Is she, now?"

"Yes."

"Well, when you get home, you take her to your family physician. Line up a pulmonary specialist for some x-rays. Right lung. Two of the three lobes. Spots. Nothing to be alarmed about because of early detection. But don't let it go. Just a matter of medication. How are you healing?"

Phelps felt the goose bumps at the tops of his shoulders. "I'm going in for a prosthesis and physical therapy. It's a long rehabilitation process from what I understand," he answered, numbed by the conversation and the fact that he was even discussing his handicap and his wife with this . . . stranger.

"You're going to do all right. Now. Down to cases. Of course, you met Richard Geist. He was in one of the sets next to me many years ago. Played the part of a multiple personality. Played it to the hilt. Even wrote a book while he was here. Robert Redler wrote a book about him. A brilliant work. As you know, he's writing another as we speak. It's a most unusual manuscript. He has the gift. God-given. He can record events before they actually occur. This book will be revolutionary in every sense of the word. Richard's trying to stop him, but so far he cannot. Robert and Richard are being guided by the forces of light and dark, respectively. The irony being that Geist is in league with the devil while Redler is an agnostic who's been chosen to do battle with a single weapon. That is, the Word of God. There are several rogues out there who know that Redler possesses a certain power but are uncertain of what it is exactly or how to use it to their best advantage. Redler's first book was a signal to some, his editorials a tip-off to others. Redler is playing the role of a writer with an apocalyptic message on the horizon. It will make for most interesting theater. The drama of the century for sure. You've got branches of government, both good and evil. You've got the Mob, both the Mafia and The Black Hand. You've got black insurgents kowtowing to Geist's Inner Circle of Friends. A failing prejudicial, judicial system and an angry underdog who takes them all to task. You've got insanity, morality, brutality, sex, religion, and more. Comedy. Tragedy. A thriller with an ending that God and Satan will vie for. I am the window to this world, yet I cannot see beyond Redler's written word.

"And so, Sergeant Phelps, if this soliloquy has broadened your horizon, if things begin to fit, go play out your role as a competent detective and unravel for us this tangled web we weave."

"May I ask you—"

The bard threw up his hands. "Please. No questions. I'm in rehearsal. Now go."

Sergeant Phelps turned around and made his way along the

wall as Doctor Kirby had instructed, listening as the bard delivered a telling line.

"The web we weave is of a single, mingled moment; good and evil entwined about a gossamer thread. Oh, by the way, Sergeant," the bard called out. "While you're still here, let me have a peek at that wound."

The sergeant rounded the corner and stopped, standing directly across from the Duke. "Oh, no. I'm wise to you, Mr. Shakespeare," Phelps said shivering.

"Oh, Sergeant. Say it isn't so."

"Good-bye, William."

"Ingrate!" The bard rang the word like a bell. "Even Lillian thinks you're an ingrate."

The Duke hadn't moved the width of a whisker when suddenly he drew two gun-fingers from the hip. "Got to be pretty quick with the hardware to get the drop on me, Pilgrim," the performer said with perfect pitch and form.

"I left my hardware at the door, Duke," the sergeant said, making his way again along the wall.

"You come back and see us again real soon, son. Hear?"

"Just as soon as the cows come home," the sergeant promised, pounding insanely upon the door, truly and fully worried for a full ninety seconds that it might never ever open at all.

Chapter
——>
62

Sergeant Phelps was back at the King Foundation by eleven.

"How does he know?" the cop demanded of Doctor Bianco. "How the hell does he know about my wife? He told me she had two spots on her lung but that she'd be all right. I already made an appointment. Am I losing my mind, or what?"

"Are you here on police business or as a patient this time, Sergeant? You know it's Saturday, and I'm usually not around the office. I may have to bill you double time," Doctor Bianco kidded.

"Please tell me what you know," Phelps said in earnest.

"I can only tell you what I *believe*."

"Then that will have to do."

"I sent you to that hell hole so that maybe you, too, might come away a believer."

"Believer of . . . ?"

"Believer in."

"God?"

"God."

"That's a very hard pill for me to swallow," Phelps said candidly.

"It was for me, too," Bianco admitted. "I've vacillated between the poles of atheism and agnosticism for most of my adult years."

"And when did you see the light as they say?"

"Shortly after my wife was murdered."

Phelps lowered his eyes.

"Oh, I know what you're thinking. A horrible and recent experience of losing my wife at the hands of a madman like Richard Geist, and this old boy's susceptible to any sort of cockamamie explanation. A crutch if you will. You feel I turned to God to see me through this dark and lonely time. And the fact that I have a parochial upbringing makes it all the more easy to accept. Yes? But like you, Sergeant, I needed so much more than that. A true sign, you see. If you look around you, there are signs everywhere. Look at what just happened in Riverhead."

"That was hardly Armageddon, Doctor."

"That's not what I mean. Your chief is still with that sinking ship of misled souls. He stands alone between Geist and Redler. Between the forces of good and evil."

"He's a hostage, along with eleven others. Hopefully still alive."

"Yes, but he's seen and heard the Word through Redler. He's been given a sign. Several of them in fact. And so have you. Like the bard."

"How does that nutcase know what he knows?"

Bianco shook head. "The bard was one of Doctor King's patients at the King Foundation before being transferred to Havenwood, when Doctor Kirby took over. It's no coincidence that Richard wound up in the cell next to the poet."

"Why transferred?"

"The more severe cases eventually wind up there. Authorities didn't know his early history until after his arrest and trial."

Sergeant Phelps nodded his understanding. "But why would God give a person like the bard such a *window* as he put it. Such power?"

"We're all sinners, Sergeant. Redemption is God's thing," he explained. "To take one of the most wicked and have him repent in the final scene would be God's way."

"Why not turn Richard around a hundred and eighty

degrees?"

"I'm not God, Sergeant. But I can tell you this. Richard Geist is the personification of evil. Evil in its purest form. He killed his mother and was responsible for Doctor King's death. A man who, perhaps ironically, was the epitome of goodness."

"Yes, I heard many good things about him."

"Yet you know nothing about the man at all. He was an icon."

Phelps paused and bit his lower lip before speaking, focusing fully on the psychiatrist. "So I guess my judgment of King would have little value."

"And would be but a worthless reference. But I tell you, he walks with God."

Phelps was visibly shaken.

"Are you all right, Sergeant?"

"Did Doctor King have any children?"

"Just the one."

"The one?"

"I thought you knew."

"Knew what?"

"About Richard."

"What about Richard?"

"Richard Geist is Doctor King's son."

"Jesus Christ!"

"You didn't read Geist's or Redler's book?"

"No."

"Then I strongly suggest that you do. Not too many know the *whole* story," he added, jotting down the titles. "Try the library or the bookstore on Main Street in Riverhead. Your head will swim if it isn't already."

Chapter
——>
63

The Giordano home was a large Cape, sparsely furnished with expensive antique furniture functionally arranged across highly-polished parquetry. Barbara and Robert sat opposite one another, reclining in overstuffed chairs and ottomans set off to both sides of a prodigious fieldstone fireplace.

Tony was away on business in California, and Barbara had the kids in bed early. At her insistence, Jonathan Laddington had arranged for Redler to meet to discuss the new book. She put down the nearly completed manuscript.

"This is most intriguing, Rob. Much more than I ever expected or bargained for." She did not seem pleased. "Your first book, including your editorials, told me that you were insightful. I never expected anything quite like this." Barbara took a sip of wine before continuing. "You say things about me here regarding a reputed drug operation that I do not wish to see in print." She drew a deep breath. "Is this out of your head as a novelist? Or are you back to investigative reporting, working for someone out to hurt me?"

"I'm strictly freelance," he assured the woman, "working for the highest bidder." Robert Redler smiled, taking in the furnishings.

"You're sure someone hasn't made you a counteroffer? We do have a contract."

"This is mainly fiction, Barbara. Except for certain information that you had me include. No?"

Barbara Giordano studied her charge before choosing her words carefully. "I don't know about you anymore, Rob."

"Why is that? Is there something I happened upon? Some sort of accidental truth?"

"I think you know the answer to that."

"I write what comes into my head is all."

"Someone is feeding you information. And I want to know who it is."

"No one's feeding me information but you. That and the fact that I write around some of my editorials. Embellish here and there."

"What about the characters, Rob? Some of the characters you have in here are remarkably similar to characters I know personally. Characters other than those I discussed with you. Obviously, you're aware of that. Even the names are similar."

"I guess the editors and the literary lawyers will decide what to do about that."

"No, Rob. *I* will decide what to do."

"Be my guest."

"Your guest?" Barbara Giordano was livid. "I sponsor you. Just remember that."

"I remember everything you tell me."

"I didn't tell you about any drug business."

"Is it true, Barbara?"

"True? How could it be true if you're writing fiction? And where in hell did you come up with the name Michael?"

"The drug thing just popped into my head. Michael could have been anyone. How about Vito? Would you prefer Vito instead?"

"Don't you be flip with me," she snapped.

"Tell me what else about the story bothers you."

Barbara leaned forward, covering him completely with cold dark eyes. "Does Michael really kill me off in the end, Rob?"

"On those pages he does."

"Let's stop playing games. All right? You've written things that are extraordinarily coincidental. Things that only weeks or days later come to pass."

"For instance?"

"You wrote the scene about Tony's party at the Cafe Bella Notte days before it ever started. No one had advance notice that Howard Stern's *Babbler* was going to be there instead of Howard. Or that

Penny Crone would be wearing blue. A skort over opaque stockings no less."

"I also wrote that the family and you scooted out of the back of the building, arriving some time later in a limo. And that Nelson Miles was shadowboxing and promoting his charity match between Tony and Geraldo that evening."

"Those arrangements were planned well ahead of time," she argued. "The fact that Tony picked me up and put me over his shoulder was not," she steamed.

"Tony's rather spontaneous," Robert offered as an explanation. "Just something he would do. No?"

"You're being very coy with me, Rob. Tell me you don't write things down and that it's as though you have a crystal ball."

"I elaborate and embellish certain parts, Barbara. Mixing fact and fancy to make the action credible. I do a lot of research. Yes, sometimes I do put things down that later come to pass. But it's strictly intuition. Not prognostication."

"Intuition," Barbara said and smirked. The housewife was shaking her head. "What about your dialogue? Words that were never spoken until *after* you set them down on paper. Scenes that were acted out by those who had never before laid eyes on you or your work, moving through them as if they were reading from a script. Sit there and say it isn't so." It was as if Barbara had been jolted in her seat. "Mother of God," she said, sitting back and pushing the manuscript pages aside as if they were about to catch fire. "I don't believe I just said that. That bard character of yours gives me the creeps."

Redler smiled understandingly. "You have the manuscript there with the exception of the last few chapters, Barbara. I don't know what's really going to happen to you or me or Chief Grear or Sergeant Phelps. I don't know how I'm going to handle Geist, his cult, or any of the other characters for that matter. I won't know until I start putting them down upon the page again. Characters have a life of their own. Many times they just take over. It's the writing process. Of course, I start with an idea as to where we're all headed. That's the reality of it. I combine fact with fiction or sometimes keep them separate. Sometimes I have a block and call upon God for inspiration," he stated rather seriously. "You see, no one outside these pages really knows what's fact and fancy unless they've played an active role."

Barbara was burning. "I hired you to write a story as my insurance policy. But I really don't know about next week, next month, or next year. All I know is that some of what I've seen there in those manuscript pages has come to pass. And it frightens me."

"Then I'll tell you what I'll do and hopefully put your mind at ease. I'll write you back into the scene. How's that?" he offered.

"And what about the drug cartel?"

"There's nothing really there for anyone to note," he said. "No dates. No times. No places. And the people you're so worried about . . . well, you'll really keep them on their toes. To tell you the truth, Barbara, with regard to your insurance policy, I think I've given you extended coverage. Term life."

Chapter
——>
64

Michael and Barbara met at a secluded spot in Manorville. It was a meeting on which he had insisted. Another person was with him in the car, seated in back. Barbara put down her window.

"You're late, Barbara," Michael said. The other man said nothing, staring straight ahead. It was 2 a.m.

"Well?" Barbara snapped impatiently. She could see the set of papers on Michael's dash.

"The governor is most upset," Michael announced.

"What's the matter, Michael?" she asked, knowing perfectly well what the matter was. She also knew who was sitting in his backseat.

"This!" he said, reaching for and holding up the original two hundred and seventy-five pages of Robert Redler's draft.

"So why don't you stop it?" she questioned nonchalantly.

"Its publication? Or you?"

"Either."

"You have many more enemies now than you ever thought you had before."

"It's that kind of a business, Michael. You know. The bigger we grow and all."

"You put us all at risk."

"Ten years ago, I put you on the map."

"No one's forgotten that."

"Oh, I see. That's why Scalla had Junior put Alice Ziegler on my back stoop with gun in hand and murder on her mind."

"It wasn't Scalla," Michael said.

"That's bullshit. It was sanctioned by that weasel."

Suddenly, the figure in the rear slid over and put his window down. Barbara raised and readied her revolver to an inch below the glass.

"What Michael is telling you is true," the man said.

"And how do you know this to be so, Mr. Castoro?"

Angelo Castoro sighed heavily. "Because *I* ordered the hit."

"You?"

Castoro nodded his head most regrettably. "Yes."

"Why?"

"For no other reason than business, Mrs. G."

"You know you're taking quite a chance in telling me this."

"Confession is good for the soul," he said rather sadly. "I'm sure you want to pull the trigger on that gun you're concealing and put a bullet in my brain, too."

Barbara shot her hand through the window, leveling the barrel inches from the man's head. "Who sanctioned it?"

"Jesus Christ, Barbara," Michael winced.

"Heads of *all* five families," Castoro said flatly.

"Liar!"

"Why would I be lying to you now?"

"Why wouldn't you be?"

"Because it wouldn't be the business minded thing to do. You see, we wanted your people to believe that Scalla ordered the hit so that they would lean on Russo to remove him quietly. He was becoming quite an embarrassment."

"A liability, you mean."

Castoro shrugged. "Same difference."

"So you put that Jew in office. David Black."

"A man who went to shul every Saturday and knew how to mind his own business."

"A Jew you controlled."

"A former judge with a sense of community."

"Who was more interested in auto theft and prostitution than with—"

"Family business," the Mob boss stated, smiled and nodded smugly. "Russo will be out, too, after the next election. When Redler's book hits, the public will be screaming for the death penalty. With Russo out of office, and our man in, we'll have a bit more leverage with Albany, Mrs. G. You and I can do more business."

"You didn't need me before, but now you feel you do?"

"You didn't have Redler before."

"I don't own him like a race horse or a yacht, Mr. Castoro."

"Would you mind putting that gun down so that we can talk?"

"I don't think that either of us have anything further to say."

Castoro looked at Michael. "Tell her," the burly figure ordered.

"Geist and Redler are working together to take over the cartel," Michael said.

"You're crazy."

"No. Geist is crazy and Redler is *his* insurance policy, Barbara. They feed off one another."

"They need one another like you and I need each other now," Angelo Castoro said.

"He's been using you," Michael assured her.

"No." Barbara shook her head. "I found him and used him to keep you bastards at bay."

"No, Mrs. G. He found you, and he's not letting go."

"Geist and Redler are recruiting soldiers at the rate of a hundred a day. Across the good old U.S.A. We've managed to gather and confirm intelligence reports. Redler met Geist back in the late sixties and formed an alliance when they were working on their respective books."

"They're amassing an army against us as we speak," the Mob boss interjected.

"Geist has assumed the role of a devil, and Robert F. Redler is his leading man," Michael declared.

"Inspired by God Almighty," Castoro dramatically sounded in mock concern, laughing while raising and lowering his hands to the ceiling of the sedan and down.

Barbara swung the gun toward Michael's face. "He has you in the manuscript as part of Geist's camp," she blasted in angry words.

"Jesus Christ. What am I? The fucking fallen angel?"

"I know what you are, Michael. Now, I'm going to find out exactly where you stand."

"Mrs. G. Please. We have to talk. Geist and Redler have created a stroke of genius. Kind of like how we're in partnership with the government here and there and every now and then. You know what we are. What do scholars say? A necessary evil? We are indeed. Like government itself. More than occasionally, now, we join forces. Well, that's what Geist and Redler have done. Joined forces. But what a coup! The disciples of the devil and an agent of God Almighty Himself, he'd have you believe. A recruiter's dream. Good and evil under one roof. Who's left? You and me and a fragile government on the verge of collapse."

"And what are you suggesting, Mr. Castoro?"

"Putting that gun to better use, Mrs. G. Write Redler's epitaph."

"Kill Redler? And who'll take care of Geist?"

"Chief Grear."

"How?"

"With the help of Sergeant Phelps," Michael added.

"This is one hell of a meeting, boys."

"Everything is at stake," Castoro assured her. "When Redler's novel explodes in bookstores and libraries, he'll have parts and pieces of people in the palm of his hand. Their hearts, their minds, and their very souls."

"Geist and Redler will be raking in the green for glory and gain. And unless they're stopped, they'll put a part of the government we more or less control out of business for openers, tearing down its walls and erecting a bridge between church and state. Their church. Their Circle of Friends. Think not? Tomorrow's headline in *Newsday* is already typeset, calling Redler an apostle based on a press release your people sent the paper citing excerpts from his manuscript predicting the events that occurred in Flanders and Riverhead, confirming foreknowledge," Michael added angrily.

"Better he should be made a martyr now," the Mafia figure avowed, rudely sending up his window with a polite little nod.

"Call you tomorrow," Michael concluded. "The senator sends his best."

"Oh, I can see that," Barbara quipped. "One question before you go."

"Shoot."

"Oh, how I'd love to."

"Well, you've got your target and your instructions."

"Maybe a *pair* of targets."

"Come on, Barbara. I've got work to do."

"How can Geist and Redler be plotting anything when, in fact, he's been working on his novel sixteen hours a day, six days a week, and is virtually under house arrest?"

"Novel's not finished. And besides, was he not at your home last night?"

"Answer my question, Michael."

"The answer to that, my dear, comes under the heading of parapsychology. Not only are Geist and Redler telepathic, but they can communicate ideas into the minds of certain individuals. I'm going up to a convention in Boston tomorrow to learn more about it."

"Mother of God, Michael. And you want me to whack this guy?"

"Mr. Castoro's associates whack people, Barbara. You're a lady! We simply want you to shoot Redler in order to protect our vested interests. You're the only one who can get him out of that house of his and into yours."

"What am I going to do? Invite him into my living room, shoot him, and then swear that I thought he was an intruder?"

"Close. You're going to invite him into your living room and swear that he somehow wound up in your daughter's bedroom while she was sleeping. That's just off the top of my head. We'll talk more tomorrow. Say hello to Tony for me when he calls." Michael terminated the conversation.

Chapter
——>
65

Sergeant Dennis Phelps phoned his wife from headquarters and learned that hospital x-rays did in fact reveal two spots on her right lung. Their family doctor had already scheduled an appointment for Lillian to see a pulmonary specialist in Manhattan at the end of the week. The sergeant hung up and went back to Havenwood to see the bard but was intercepted at the front desk. The assistant director of North Shore State was anything but cordial.

"Doctor Kirby had no business taking you up there, Sergeant. I won't allow it," the man stated emphatically. "Now, if you'll excuse me. Oh, and don't try and give anyone that official police business rhetoric because the director knows that you're on restricted duty and have no business being here. I wouldn't want to have to call your superiors in Riverhead and lodge a formal complaint against you, Sergeant Phelps."

Phelps left the lobby red-faced, a blinding rage building up inside him like a furnace. Hot and as bright as the afternoon sun itself. He felt as though he was about to snap when suddenly he had a revelation. One of the biggest manhunts in recent history and no one could find a trace of Richard Geist, let alone his band of at least two hundred soldiers that both he and Grear had encountered at Hubbard Hills. Virtually all mute . . . with shaven heads . . . moving about in camouflage clothing by day before changing into white robes in the evening. But you wouldn't necessarily hunt or hide from the elusive whitetail while wearing white unless of course a world of snow and ice covered your surroundings. And the snow had come in droves all season long.

Both Grear and he knew that somehow Geist and his followers had managed to survive the horrendous winter in the lowlands, along with the noble herd. Through a blinding stark-white, *frigid* winter. Nature's own concealment. A purity that hid the blinding truth in a light that searching eyes refused to see. Phelps closed his eyes. A piece of the puzzle was right before him. Concealed so cleverly.

Had Richard Geist actually made a mistake? Had he inadvertently left behind a prodigious clue that would ultimately lead authorities to Havenwood and Inspector Lancing to the cliffs of the Jersey Shore? Or had Richard purposely misled authorities into believing that the search should be conducted in and about mental institutions and religious retreats? What was the significance of that freezer delivered from Richard's basement apartment to Havenwood?

Phelps believed he had the answers.

"That clever son of a bitch," he blew.

Geist had authorities turning every religious and mental institution in the tri-state area upside down. The freezer was Richard's subtle way of saying that the lead had turned ice cold, Phelps believed. But was it really? Just like the message found hanging from the mannequin: "Close, but no cigar." Lancing somehow had gotten a lead on the freezer. A lead that led him up the garden path and down to his death. But whose lead and lie was it? Phelps believed he knew the answer to that question, too. It had to be someone Lancing trusted. It had to be a member of the team.

Chapter
——>
66

Sergeant Dennis Phelps had Captain Cally up against the wall in the foyer of the man's apartment, the muzzle of a snub-nosed .38 pressed firmly against the man's right eye.

"I want to know everything, and I want to know it right now or your neighbors are going to see you horizontal on the ten o'clock news. We'll start with Lancing. How did he get a fix on Geist and his flock in Jersey?" Phelps pushed the barrel forcefully into the man's skull. Cally grimaced in pain. "You sent him there. DIDN'T YOU?"

"YES. I didn't know they were going to kill him. I swear it. Someone gave me the information to pass along."

"Who? You're as good as dead if you don't tell me."

"Michael."

"Michael who?"

"You met him. He's Geist's right hand. That's all I know."

"Oh, no. You know so much more than that. How do I find him?"

"You don't. He finds you. He's a go-between."

"Between who? I'm really losing my patience with you—you son of a bitch."

"Everybody. Geist. The Mob. Some big boys up in Albany. They're not playing around. I had to cooperate. They threatened to kill my family and would have. What the hell was I going to do? Call the fucking cops?"

"How long have they had their hooks into you? When did it go bad?"

"I'm a decorated cop, Phelps. I was clean for years. I made just one mistake. They wouldn't let go."

"Well, I'm not going to let go either. You're going to go away for a long, long time, Cally." Sergeant Phelps removed his piece from against the man's eye and left in a quiet rage.

It had been Captain Cally's last assignment. The last bit of information he would ever pass along in life. Phelps had been more than right. Prophetic in fact. Most of Cally's neighbors did get to see him horizontal on the ten o'clock news, for the man took his own life with his .38-caliber service revolver shortly after Phelps left the apartment.

Chapter
——>
67

"*Well, Chief, I do believe your loyal lackey will be coming for you soon,*" Richard signed, seated comfortably in a new location. He giggled in delight with Michael standing at his side.

"I thought it was Redler you wanted," Grear sallied.

"*Oh, indeed I do.*"

"Then leave Phelps out of it."

"*I'm telling you, Chief, such loyalty gets me right here,*" Richard declared sarcastically, tapping the plate of his breast.

"Haven't you caused him enough pain?"

"*We're fast approaching the final chapters, Chief. And pain is all a part of it I presume.*"

"And how is he supposed to find me?"

"*Oh, let's just say he's been helped along a bit. Given a clue in part. A bit part.*" Richard kept giggling like a silly school girl.

"Like you did with Lancing?"

"*Very good, Chief. Quite right. Like we did with Lancing.*"

"What is it exactly that you intend to do? Take over the world, Richard? Is that it?"

Richard looked at Michael and laughed loudly. He signed

something that Michael was not to repeat.

"*The world, Chief? Do I appear to you to be a megalomaniac?*" Richard and Michael were both laughing. "*Not the world, Chief Grear. Just the largest drug cartel that operates in this hemisphere.*"

"Hemisphere?"

"*You know, it's amazing to me that you don't realize what's going on right under your very nose.*"

"So enlighten me. I'm only a Riverhead cop."

"*Then it wouldn't be fair for me to assign blame. Now would it, Chief Grear? No, of course not. You belong to the Suffolk clique, while it's really Nassau that's running the show. Covertly controlled by an unlikely young woman from Oceanside.*"

"Barbara Giordano," the police chief realized.

"*You know, I think he's finally getting the picture, Michael.*"

"And who underwrites such an operation? I'm sure she doesn't operate in a vacuum."

"*Take a guess,*" Richard teased. "*Come on,*" he coaxed.

Grear looked at Michael. "Albany?"

"*Oh, come come come, Chief Grear. Are you really so naive?*"

"Are you going to keep me in suspense?"

"*The power goes way beyond your upstate capital, Chief, to the one that ends in 'o' and sits on a hill in Washington. You know, I find it most ironic that they call it the District of Columbia. You see, South America is going to be my stiffest competition. Initially, that is. After Columbia, and several other third world countries, maybe then I'll tackle the world. But for now, it's high time that the people of our land had a real government for and by the people. A government comprised of a Circle of Friends.*"

"How does Redler fit into all this?"

"*Really now, Chief. I'm not going to do all your homework for you. You must play out your own role as Chief of Police, Riverhead PD. The stage will soon be set. But for now, you can just sit back and relax and see how power is seized. Real power is not like a coat that somebody hands you to be worn for a season or so then handed over. Real power is permanent, anchored in fists and hearts of steel."*

"And I suppose you have everything solidly in place."

"Everything," Richard signed and swore. *"Everything."*

Chapter
——>
68

The phone rang and Lillian Phelps grabbed it in the kitchen.

"Hello?"

"Mrs. Phelps?"

"Yes."

"This is Robert Redler."

There was a pause as she immediately cupped the mouthpiece with her hand. "It's him," she whispered, inventing her own little dance in a corner of the room.

"Him who?" Phelps muttered, taking a spoon from his mouth and wiping the corner of his face on Lillian's apron.

"Redler."

Sergeant Phelps set the utensil on the stove then took the receiver from her hand. "Sergeant Phelps, here."

Redler laughed lightly. "You answer the phone like you're at headquarters instead of home."

"It's a twenty-four hour a day job," the cop stated curtly. "You know that I've been trying to get ahold of you for—"

"Don't say anything."

"What else do you do on a phone?"

"Just listen. I'll do the talking. There's not much time."

"So, I'm listening."

"I want you to meet me."

"Where?"

"You know The Duke?"

Phelps was staring at his wife. "Yes."

"Meet me at noon. Go right up to the desk."

Phelps hung the receiver on the wall, glancing at the clock. He had a good hour. Plenty of time.

"What? What? What?" Lillian asked anxiously.

"Gotta go."

"Go where? You know you're running a low-grade fever. But a fever nevertheless. You should be in bed."

He put a finger to his wife's lips. "Shh."

She held on to him well below the bandaged wrist. "I don't want to lose you," she whispered, tears collecting in the corner of her eyes.

"Everything is going to be all right," he said and kissed Lillian good-bye.

Chapter
——>
69

Sergeant Phelps had been driving Lillian's hatchback because his own vehicle was standard shift. He figured he'd park several blocks away and walk.

As he headed toward the building, although feverish, Sergeant Phelps felt uplifted, sincerely believing that everything was going to work out all right. He felt it in his heart. He somehow knew that with Robert Redler's help, Chief Grear and the others would return safely.

Phelps entered the rear of the building, quickly making his way across the lobby to the front desk. Immediately, an orderly approached and escorted him to an elevator around the corner.

"It's all right," the man said. "Mr. Redler called and said to take you up. Give me your gun and put this on."

Phelps removed his ankle holster and handed over the sheathed weapon. The orderly put it aside and helped Phelps into a strait jacket, fastening the straps at the back of the garment, mussing up the cop's head of slicked-back gray-brown hair.

"Is this necessary?"

"Keep your head down and talk to no one. Walk like you got a load in your pants."

Once again he was taken to the second floor and led along the corridor of steel and stone. "This jacket gives me the creeps," Phelps complained. "I feel like Houdini in a whodunit."

"I'm putting your gun behind the counter here. You know the drill." The man was all business. "Right on through this door," he said, unlocking and swinging the narrow steel door open on its creaking hinge. Sergeant Phelps crossed the threshold.

"Where's Redler?" Phelps asked uneasily.

"Just relax."

Phelps was never more aware of his handicap than with both arms bound across his chest. Down and around the corridor and past The Duke they went. The orderly stopped in front of an open empty cell. "Get in," the man insisted.

"What the fuck is going on?"

"Get in," echoed the bard from the cell around the corner. "Your reservation noted nothing about accommodations. This is as grand as it's going to get, McDuff."

"Get in," the orderly repeated, gently moving the sergeant into the cell. "It's all right."

"It's hardly that. I'd say more along the lines of inadequate," Phelps balked, looking around nervously.

The orderly locked the cell door and was gone. Phelps listened to the sounds of steel doors opening and slamming closed in the distance. Finally, the place turned still as stone.

"Yoo-hoo. Willy," Phelps called out in a quiet tone. Dennis Phelps waited, but there was no reply. "Yoo-hoo, you ol' fart. Are you pondering away in there?"

Suddenly, an evil vision of loveliness appeared.

"It's okay, Sergeant. He's only a stand-in. That's why he's waiting in the wings." Angelica smiled handsomely, hands behind her back.

She stood erect and stately in a white nurse's uniform, a winged cap pinned atop a wig of auburn hair. So magnetic was her bearing that Phelps lost himself in the moment as she moved closer to the cell, pressing her breasts firmly against the bars. Stepping back like a ballerina, she shot a leg out and up to a horizontal bar.

In shock, Phelps couldn't bring himself to say a word.

"I have a few minutes and a few little questions for you,

Sergeant," she began seductively. "Tell me. Does Lillian really want to remain with an amputee? Is it not pure pity that she feels for you? Are you sure she'll be around when you're out on disability? That's right around the corner, you know. How many times a month do the two of you do it, Dennis? Maybe once or twice?" she tormented, laughing and running her tongue languidly up a cold steel bar. Angelica put her leg back down then raised the other. "I'm surprised they still let you carry a gun. This is yours, I take it?"

Phelps saw his weapon in its holster, strapped to her slender ankle. "Where is Geist and Chief Grear?" he demanded.

"Oh, behind a veiled curtain waiting for my cue, I'd well imagine."

"Let me ask *you* a personal little question, bitch. How in hell did you ever become so fucking sick?"

"Actually, Sergeant, I'm about as sane as you. Maybe even saner if only because of all that silly cops and robbers, law and order shtick you do. Just look at what it cost you," she said, gracefully setting her foot down upon the floor.

"What's going to happen now?" he asked, wondering what she had behind her back.

"Now? Now we set this country on its ear. Now we open the doors of insanity and put the patients back on the streets. No different than in the thirties when this great state emptied its warehouses under the ostensibly noble banner of having the mentally ill assimilated back into mainstream society, when in reality, the bottom line read that the treasury was nearly deplete. New York was the forerunner, Sergeant. Other states soon followed suit, and its coffers were suddenly replete. The states were suddenly out of the red. But at what cost down the road?"

"You sound like an intelligent woman, Angelica. But I also think you're fucking nuts. You really haven't learned anything. Have you?"

"I've learned about survival through the years. I do what's good for Angelica and cause."

"Cause?"

"'Cause there's no one more important and beautiful in all the world than me," she swore.

"I see. So it's whichever way the wind blows, I take it."

"And I blow free, Sergeant." She blew a kiss his way that he thought might melt the very bars.

"You're just going to open up these doors and let everyone out, I suppose."

"Why shouldn't I? Besides which, who has time for all the bullshit paperwork?" she said through a titter.

"Violent or not, you're just going to let them flee?"

"Yes, much like Fidel Castro did in the sixties. As when he opened his prisons and sent the dregs of the earth to our shore. But first we evaluate them and hold onto those who might prove to be assets. Give them special training. Redirection and purpose. We know a valuable resource when we see one, Sergeant Phelps. I guess if a comparison could be drawn, it might be made along the lines of Bastille Day, if you remember your history like a good little boy. A revolution is on the rise. Today we throw the country into chaos."

"How is releasing some patients here from Havenwood going to impact on an entire country?"

"Oh, not just Havenwood, Dennis. You don't mind if I call you Dennis, do you, dear? You see, civilian life for you is right around the corner as I've said. No, not just Havenwood, but every major mental institutional facility in the forty-eight contiguous states. The stage has been set; the likes of which law enforcement has never seen. You should know by now that our soldiers are the masters of escape, so surely you must also realize that for them to spring a mass of murderers and rapists before guards who will unquestionably have their guard down will be mere child's play for our elite."

"And how are you going to manage that?"

"It's called networking, Den, darling. The moment is practically at hand. Oh, you just reminded me. I have a little going away present for you. I've been keeping it on ice." Angelica's hands came from behind her and presented him with a gift tied with a bright red bow.

"I guess you'll have to open it for me," Phelps said, hunching his shoulders helplessly.

"What? And spoil the surprise? Why, I should say not. You

come over here and promise me you'll be good, and I'll undo those restraints."

Phelps came forward obediently and put his back to her, praying that she wouldn't plant a blade between his ribs. He figured that if she wanted him dead, she certainly could have managed it by now.

"There you go, sport. Now step away and see if you can manage the rest by yourself."

Phelps struggled with the jacket. With one hand, it proved to be a chore. Finally, he wriggled free from the claustrophobic cloth, damning it to a corner of the cell.

He took the weighty gift and held it against his chest, working the ribbon free, fumbling with the paper, pulling the remnant with his teeth. He felt the item shift inside the white Styrofoam box. His heart began to race. He looked up at her.

So beautiful she was, nodding excitedly. "Go ahead. Open it, and then you can wave good-bye."

Phelps held the box and shimmied off its cover. He stared down at the familiar diamond band set upon the fourth finger of Lillian's left hand. A hand enmeshed in a clear bloodied plastic bag of Dry Ice. "LILLIAN," he screamed and wished to God he had two strong hands with which to bend the bars and reach out to strangle Angelica. "LILLIAN. LILLIAN. LILLIAN, "he continued shouting at the top of his lungs.

"Good grief. I'm afraid they're going to have to put you back in that horrible jacket, Denny. You're creating a terrible, terrible scene. You don't mind if I call you Denny, do you? For you're behaving like such a child."

"I'll kill you, you fucking witch. I swear to God I'll put a bullet in your fucking brain," he swore and shivered.

"Of course, they can perform miracles with microsurgery these days. Time is the crucial factor here. Do you know what time it is?"

Dennis Phelps was staring down at his wife's hand. "What do you want?"

"I want to know where Redler is. That's all. You got a call that he was to meet you at The Duke at noon. I followed you after I said hello to your wife. You're late. What are you doing *here?*"

Panic raced through Phelps' brain. Obviously, she thought Redler had meant the fleabag mid-island hotel off the Long Island Expressway. "I came to talk to the bard, first," he finally managed to say.

"Richard's old roomy? Why? What could that old fart possibly know?"

Suddenly, the bard spoke up from around the corner. "That Mrs. Lillian Phelps is in critical but stable condition over at Kane Memorial Hospital," the old man replied. "Your people, Angelica, have already informed them that her severed hand could possibly be on its way. As Lillian is the wife of a police officer, a top team of doctors and nurses are attending her, and another special team that specializes in microsurgery at nearby Presbyterian Medical Hospital is standing by."

"He has the *gift!*" Angelica cried, disappearing around the corner.

"I have bursitis, gout, and bad gums. Not enough nutrition. I could really use a hand, too, Angelica."

"Where is Robert Redler?" Angelica demanded.

"Playing The Duke," the bard responded.

"You're lying. Our people already went through that place with a magnifying glass," she cried. "He's not there. Where is he, William?"

"Tell the sergeant where to find his chief and other hostages," the bard commanded.

"Tell me where to find Redler," Angelica snapped.

"If I do, will you promise to take me with you?"

"Richard didn't ask for you." Her mind was on overload.

"No. But I know the answer to your question."

"But you choose to play a game."

"I gave you the answer, but you were listening with your eyes and not your ears, Angelica."

"There is no theater there. It's past noontime. What is he performing . . . a fucking matinee? Is The Duke the name of some ensemble, William? Is that what you're trying to say? Is Redler holed up in some second-rate club by the same name? Is The Duke a code word, Willy dear, for some other rat-infested dive?"

"Oh, I can assure you that The Duke's accommodations are a notch up the line from mine. Mind you, right about now, I'd say Redler is shaking in his boots."

"So why isn't this asshole sergeant there?"

"He told you. He felt he first had to talk to me."

Angelica went back to Phelps' cage.

Sergeant Phelps had the package secured in a corner of the cell, afraid to breathe for fear of creating the difference of a degree.

"Where is he, Denny?"

"How long does she have for the surgeons to sew back her hand?" Phelps cried out to the bard.

"Several hours," came the rather ambiguous reply.

"All right, Phelps. Listen up, and listen well," Angelica ordered. "Whether or not we find Redler is immaterial to what's in store for institutions like this across the nation. Everything is set in motion and cannot be stopped unless the clocks across the country lose their hands or hide their faces. That's a given. Got it? But what you can do to save your wife's hand and your own life is to take me to Redler. Now! We're going to walk out of here together. You and me. Pick up that jacket. The faster you move, the sooner I'll see that your precious package gets delivered." She removed a set of keys from her pocket and opened up the cell. "Leave the box there and put this back on," she insisted, assisting the sergeant with the barrel of his own gun pointed at his head. "Thatta boy. Now turn around." She strapped and buckled him back up. "There. Hold still. We got one more. Good. You're back to playing patient Phelps." Angelica picked up the box and made sure the cover was on securely. "All right. Say good-bye to your friend." She put the weapon away.

William called out to them. "Are you sure you can't give an old man a hand?"

The two moved along the corridor, nearing The Duke's cage when suddenly the figure stepped out of a shadow. "Howdy, ma'am," the man said politely and smiled, tipping an imaginary hat. "It sure is a pleasant afternoon. I can tell you where Robert Redler is just as sure as I'm standing in these boots."

"Keep moving," Angelica ordered.

But Phelps stopped dead in his tracks. "My God!"

"I said move it," Angelica ordered.

"Now, that's what I call a fine how-do-you-do. I'm trying to make polite conversation and answer some unanswered questions, and this showboatin' lady's actin' downright rude. Makes a gentleman like myself a might upset."

Angelica was staring at the figure in the cage, uncertain of the voice and mannerisms when suddenly it all clicked. But The Duke had his weapon out before should could bat an eyelash.

"Step aside there, Pilgrim. Wouldn't want the lady's blood on someone else's hand. Now, take out that gun, Missy. Nice and easy like. Make one false move and I'll drill ya inta tomorrow. The Duke wouldn't want to shoot a lady, but if I haveta, I sure as shootin' will." It wasn't a pair of six-shooters Robert Redler was holding. It was a 9mm pistol. The kind the Riverhead cops were issued even before the city boys got theirs. "The gun, Missy. Don't want to haveta say it again. Nice and easy like. Put it on the floor."

Angelica put the box down and carefully removed Phelps' gun from the ankle holster beneath her pant leg. "Listen to me—"

"No, you listen, lady. Back against the wall." Robert Redler stepped out of the cell. "All right, Pilgrim. Now turn around like so. Good man," he continued in character, capturing the slow and distinctive cadence of John Wayne's gravelly voice. Redler unfastened Phelps' restraints.

The sergeant picked up his gun and carefully cradled the box. "Got to get this to the hospital as fast as we can," Phelps trembled.

"Got to get a grip on yourself first. Now, the three of us are gonna mosey on outta here, and we're goin' to do it now. Put this jacket on, ma'am."

"You should know better than anyone that Richard has a world to offer you," Angelica said as Redler harnessed her up.

"I want to pull this trigger so bad," Phelps swore.

"Put it away, Sergeant. In here, I'm the law. When we're outside, I'll turn the prisoner over to you."

"You'll be lucky if you last the day," Angelica said through a sneer.

"You'll be lucky if you do," Phelps retorted.

"Now, I've heard just about enough nonsense," The Duke rejoined. "So the two of you pipe down. We're going out the back way once we hit the stairwell. Take her keys, Sergeant."

"You got horses down there, Duke?" Phelps asked, going along for the ride, believing they were all a bit crazy at that moment.

"Yeah. Barbara Giordano's Mustang convertible. What are you? Some kind of nut?" Robert Redler questioned, suddenly stepping out of his western role and intonation.

Sergeant Dennis Phelps sputtered a laugh for the first time since . . . he couldn't remember when. Then just as suddenly, he started to cry.

"Your wife is going to be just fine, Sergeant," the bard called out from around the corridor.

"She will," Redler said flatly, reassuring the cop.

"Tell me you know that for a fact," Phelps asked pleadingly.

"For a fact," Redler swore and nodded with a genuine smile.

Tears of happiness filled the sergeant's eyes. For the time being, those words would be enough to sustain him. He knew not to ask any more questions. In that moment, he knew to stop behaving like a cop until they were all outside and the prisoner handed over. But Phelps couldn't help but ask one more question.

"Mr. Redler?"

"I'll bring Chief Grear and the others home safely," Redler said, anticipating the question. "Promise."

Phelps nodded and said nothing further.

Angelica, too, remained quiet.

Outside the building, federal authorities immediately took their prisoner back into custody. Local police secured the area and grounds while Emergency Services rushed Sergeant Phelps and his package off to waiting personnel at Presbyterian Medical Hospital.

In a borrowed office, two men shook hands. "Where did

you stash the real McCoy?" Robert Redler asked Doctor Kirby.

"We had The Duke moved to the fourteenth floor. Thinks he died and went to cowboy heaven. And William's already complaining that he misses him.

Robert couldn't help but laugh insanely.

"I think maybe we better get you out of here while the going's good," Kirby suggested. "And by the way. That was some performance. John Wayne and William Shakespeare would both be very proud of you," Kirby assured him with the biggest grin.

Chapter
--->
70

By morning, law enforcement agencies had advised both private and state-run psychiatric institutions throughout the area of a possible revolt. Several facilities treated the warning lightly. Others exercised extreme caution. By evening, the nation was on high alert after flare-ups occurred across the country and lunatics were on the loose. Lockdowns were the order of the day—the following day—then, "Until further notice," were the watchwords. Full-blown riots broke out where security was lax, compromised, or the word had gotten out too late. Nevertheless, alleged cult members and recruits working within the walls of confinement were eventually corralled and contained after local authorities were brought in to quell the outbreaks, thereby minimizing casualties. Loss of life and limb was limited to hundreds in lieu of tens of thousands it was estimated at the end of the ordeal.

A high ranking FBI official headquartered in Virginia was standing tall before the director in Washington, D.C. An agent from a field office in Nassau County entered the room and quickly took his place alongside the man.

"What the hell do you mean, Redler slipped away?" the director snapped from behind a cluttered desk.

"Field agents on Long Island tailed him to the Giordano home," the official explained.

"Yeah. And you were supposed to notify this office of his every move," their big boss squawked.

"And I did, sir. Agent McCullen, here, had his people covering the front and back. No one saw Redler leave. Barbara Giordano drove off alone at eleven a.m., or who he thought to be Barbara Giordano."

"That's correct," McCullen said.

"So he winds up at North Shore State Hospital in Havenwood, along with Sergeant Phelps of Riverhead PD and has this Angelica person arrested," the director blared.

"Yes, sir."

"And you have no idea where Redler is now?"

"No, sir," McCullen answered. "He told Sergeant Phelps that he was going after Geist and bringing back Chief Grear and the others."

"A veritable army of agents out there, Agent Theller, and we can't find Richard Geist or his fold, or even keep an eye on Robert Redler. But this freelance writer, mind you, is going off to find Geist and rescue a police chief and eleven hostages?"

"That's what he told Sergeant Phelps," McCullen said.

"And this sergeant didn't detain Redler, or go along with him, or ask any questions?"

"He's an amputee on restricted duty. The department pulled him off the case," Theller elaborated. "He's out of sorts. Worried sick about his wife."

"I'm telling you, this Redler smells. Deputy Inspector Lancing thought he was rotten, and Lancing is rotting in his grave. You think maybe Redler is working in concert with Geist?" the director questioned, batting the theory about.

"Phelps says it was a Captain Cally of Bayside, Queens," McCullen explained. "Hundred and eleventh precinct. The man committed—"

"I know who Cally was, for Christ's sake."

"It appears Redler saved Sergeant Phelps' hide and brought that Angelica woman out of hiding. Helped put her back behind bars where she belongs," McCullen went on.

"Yeah, he also sent Phelps out to Havenwood with that phone call," the director scowled. "If Redler's so goddamn all-knowing like I hear he is, why did he have to put on that performance at North Shore State?"

"Supposedly to learn what Geist's people were up to, from what

I understand," McCullen offered lamely.

"Sounds like a lot of crap to me."

"I don't think Redler really knew who the hell would show," Theller theorized.

"How did Geist's people even know there was going to be a meeting between Redler and Phelps in the first place?" the director pressed.

"They had to have had Phelps' phone tapped," McCullen said.

"But *we* had his fucking phone tapped!" he blasted. "How come *we* didn't know about The Duke?"

"We did. Only we assumed like Geist's people that it was a small mid-island hotel, not John Wayne's moniker," Theller clarified. "How was anyone supposed to know that Redler was up there taking a patient's place, performing western shtick?"

"We're the FBI! We're supposed to know *every* goddamn thing. Everyone knows that John Wayne's The Duke," the director barked. "First thing *I* would have thought of."

"It was that business of Redler telling Sergeant Phelps to go to the front desk that threw us off," McCullen admitted. "It fit. It reinforced the idea that it was that hotel."

The director shook his head in disgust. "How did things ever get so screwed up?"

"Anyhow, that's when Phelps warned us of Geist's master plan."

"Yeah, and Albany, like the rest of them dodos up there, just sat on their duffs waiting for confirmation. Declaring a national emergency only after the first facility fell into the hands of a handful of nuts. I've got reports here of literally scores of bodies lining the corridors of our mental institutions from New York to New Mexico," the director stormed, flipping through a pile of paperwork. "Two hundred eleven and still counting."

"It could have been worse, sir. Those who took the warning seriously and acted quickly suffered fewer casualties," Theller offered diplomatically.

But the director didn't want to hear it, picking up another report off his desk. "I want to know about this Giordano dame and her connection to organized crime. A housewife with an ax to grind."

"Maybe the Mob's behind Geist," Agent McCullen suggested.

"That's an interesting notion. Why don't you work on that," he stated flatly. "And while you're doing that, here's a memo we believe is from Geist. Get this: 'Hoover may have come out of the closet, but his boys are back in the band.'"

"What's that supposed to mean?" Theller questioned.

"You're the special agent in charge. You figure it out. Oh, and one more thing," he added, staring at McCullen.

"Sir?"

"Why was Redler doing that John Wayne impersonation to begin with? Is he really a fucking nut?"

"He told Phelps it was the only way he could pull it off. He said he was shaking in his boots the whole time. Had to slip into character in order to get up the nerve," McCullen offered.

"Sometimes I'm *Terminator Man*," Theller said in deadpan.

"And I'm forever Robo Cop," the director smirked. "Now, you're both outta here. I've got work to do."

Chapter
--->
71

Robert Redler walked into a telecommunications facility in Suffolk County and asked for Operation Services before being directed to a room at the end of the hallway. Behind a windowed cubical, he was greeted by a floor supervisor who asked if she could be of assistance. Robert insisted on speaking with the team leader. He waited while the young lady placed a call. A moment later she looked up, smiled, and told him to have a seat. Instead, he anxiously paced the reception area. Five minutes later, a matronly figure came around the partition and into the vestibule. She appeared rather austere, he thought. Austere if not downright severe.

"Yes?"

Robert forced a smile. "You know who I am," he said, the words tumbling out as a definite statement of fact.

"I do?"

"I'm sure you do. A few days ago, the FBI monitored a call placed from a phone booth in Oceanside to Detective Sergeant Phelps' home in Aquebogue."

"I don't know what you're talking about."

"The trace was run from this location, and the information regarding that conversation was related to your Inner Circle of Friends at the Nassau Chapter."

"I don't know anything about a trace or a circle."

"Not many people do. You don't find them listed in the Yellow Pages. Certain people find them through you, Mrs. Tabbit."

The woman's demeanor went from one of outright restraint to downright righteousness as though someone had suddenly hit a switch. "How dare you come in here and—"

"And what? Accuse you of being a liaison for a group of fanatics? You see, Mrs. Tabbit, we're both in the communications business. You, along with several of your operators, are networking for a front. A group of assassins who you believe carry the word of God across this land in what you see as godless times. This group that you believe in is as godless as you can get. Richard Geist is not a savior but rather a sinister force."

The woman was shaking her head.

"Oh, yes, Mrs. Tabbit. And that's where I fit in. My role is to send out a message in the form of a novel I'm currently writing. A factual account that will be guised as a novel and hopefully read by many. Its message will be abundantly clear and remarkably simple. Nothing really new under the sun, for it will tell people that our government is sick, but that not *all* people in government are bad. It will tell people that the state must take the life of the truly wicked in order for future generations to take back this country. It will point to a revolution which is close at hand. It will imbue good people with the knowledge of who their enemies really are and how to destroy them as you must do immediately by sending certain signals out across this land. You and your operators will be the ears of this movement as surely as your eyes tell me that you are scared but believe my every word. Is that not so?"

Mrs. Tabbit said nothing but nodded as tears fell from a pair of decent eyes.

"And how do you know that what I'm saying is so?" Redler quizzed.

"Because it came to me in a dream last week," Mrs. Tabbit tested quietly.

Redler shook his head and laughed. "No," he said with a knowing smile. "It came to you following the eleven o'clock news last night. You had a sense of this conversation in your head but didn't know what it meant. Yet, you knew you had to note the sign."

The woman acknowledged Redler with a nod, wiping away her tears on the back of a sleeve.

"You thought you might be going a little mad," Redler said.

"Wondering, now, if indeed you are."

"I only knew that someone might come by today. I didn't know who."

"And now it's as if we're reading lines rehearsed but minutes ago."

"Yes," she said nervously.

The glass divider opened behind them. "Are you all right, Mrs. Tabbit?" the receptionist asked with apparent concern.

"I'm fine, Delores."

The young woman slid the window closed.

"What do you want me to do?" Mrs. Tabbit asked.

"You'll know," Redler said and smiled reassuringly.

"I'm scared."

"Me, too."

"What are you going to do?"

"I'll know soon enough."

"Why was I chosen, Mr. Redler?" The question conveyed neither disappointment nor delight, but strangely enough answered itself in the sense of duty that was carried by her tone.

Robert Redler shrugged. "I can only venture a guess and say that your heart had to have been in the right place all along."

Mrs. Jean Tabbit soberly put her arms around Robert Redler and just as solemnly let him go. Turning away, she headed back through the door with purpose of mind.

Chapter

——>

72

It was the first real burst of spring weather, and the buds sprang forth blossoms which welcomed seventy degree temperatures. A black man sat on a park bench reading an editorial reprinted in the latest copy of *The North Shore Towers Newsletter.*

'Not the people, but the government . . . .' was the phrase that kept oscillating across the reader's brain. The law, which the man had come to loathe as a youth, had never been accessible to his people, he reflected. 'Not the people, but the government as it stands will soon fail and fall,' he read over and over to himself.

It had always, *always, always* been the white race and a white government that had held him and his people down, he ruminated. Once upon a time—like many a fairy tale begins—he mused, he'd been naive enough to believe the lie that things were getting better. That big white lie! As sure as black lettering appeared on those white pages before him, things were not getting all that better, *motherfucker,* the man swore silently beneath his breath. But there was something in the writer's simple words that smacked of truth. 'Not the people, but the government . . . .'

Alex Lether knew full well that it was not a government 'for or by the people,' but rather a self-serving and often evil government that controlled virtually everyone. Black as well as white. One could easily strike out against whitey in the street. But not so accessible were those so-called public servants who roamed the halls of justice or sat placidly and complacently in their ivory towers. Besides which, their assassinations would only bring the heat. On rare occasions did you ever cross the line and take out the crooked cop along his beat, Lether was smart enough to know. Yet as a young man, he'd seen the drug enforcers break all the rules and show the world that you shoot down *anyone* who gets in your way. A police captain or a governor made no never mind.

Lether had spent his early years turning his hatred of whites into rage. However, he learned something along the way, something he didn't want to admit. Most white folks were really all right. It was Richard Geist who had shown the militant soul who the enemy really was. Government. Period. Not white folks in general. Richard had shown him what the government had done to Robert F. Redler as well as the people Redler wrote about.

So, like a black prostitute working for a white pimp, he had allowed himself to be recruited for 'The Cause,' 'cause he figured he'd be back out on the street on his black ass if he didn't take the offer. Besides, Maxine Waters had treated him pretty well. Consequently, where he had once stood defiantly as a black militant, he now thought of himself as a man whose enemy was all levels of government. Not white folks per se.

But why had Geist ordered the killings of college administrators? he asked himself. Or was the enemy anyone who Geist simply said it was? Geist spoke of Redler as one of them. But was he really? Why would Geist go to such great lengths to avenge the injustices that Redler experienced at the hands of college administrators? Law enforcement, yes, who had accused him of a crime he did not commit. Was Richard Geist's aim simply to parcel out punishment? Or did he have an agenda far greater in scope. Moreover, was Robert Redler truly some sort of messenger of God? An apostle? Certainly the media and the public were batting those kinds of questions around daily since the Riverhead/Flanders fiasco. Even Redler's early editorials, predicting the chaos surrounding other events that came to pass, suggested as much.

Speculation of a forthcoming indictment naming Redler as an accomplice in a conspiracy to commit multiple murders was raised daily, too. A spokesperson for Laddington's office had said that kind of rumor mongering and reporting was irresponsible and dangerous. But where was Redler? Or Barbara Giordano? Or for that matter, Laddington himself? law enforcement officials also wanted to know.

Alex Lether was poring over many such questions, staring down blankly at the newsletter.

"You have a moment for me, Alex?" a voice asked from behind.

Lether turned abruptly and put his funny bone into a corner of the bench, staring up in apparent pain and disbelief

Robert Redler smiled down sympathetically at Lether's bandaged elbow and pulled out a pad and pen. "Would you be so kind as to write down Richard's address for me," he joked.

Lether rubbed his stump, shook his head then got up to leave.

"Only kidding, Mr. Lether. But would you jot down how contact is made and when you might be expecting a call?" Redler said quite seriously.

Lether grabbed the pen and pad from Redler's hands, resting the latter in the crook of his butchered limb. *Police look for you*, he scribbled quickly. *Go way from me*, he added, handing the items back.

Redler nodded and came around the bench. He reached down and pulled up a pant leg of Lether's trousers. "I'm sure the police are looking for you, too. How come you're not wearing your ankle bracelet? Are you meeting someone here? Would you like me to wait with you? Maybe we'll wait together."

Lether shook his head angrily.

From out of nowhere, four men dressed in khaki clothing and brimmed caps entered the area. Near the boulevard, Redler could see a white van and a figure seated behind the wheel. The four approached Robert quietly, two on either side. One of them frisked him then put his arm around the writer as if he were an old friend, leading the man away. Lether followed close behind. Redler was directed to the rear of the vehicle. Its doors flew open. Robert was pulled up and put inside.

Chapter
——>
73

"Well, well, well," Michael greeted Robert Redler in a most jubilant manner, taking the man's hand firmly into his. "I'm Michael. Here, Robert. Have a seat. Please. We finally get to meet."

The interior of the van was plush and velvety. Everything about it was custom, Redler observed. Michael told the driver to go.

Five of Geist's soldiers were seated next to and across from Robert. Lether took a seat toward the back near the rear doors. "Where are we going?" Redler asked.

"To keep a date with destiny," Michael answered. "Fasten your seat belt, please. We wouldn't want to lose you."

"Are you taking me to Geist?"

"You can bank on it," Michael said with assurance. He gestured, and two men drew the blinds. "So. You have a remarkable gift, Mr. Redler."

"So they say," he said.

"But we're more interested in what *you* have to say. I think you're putting the fear of God into a lot of folks these days."

"I'm only a messenger, Michael."

Michael smiled. "That's exactly the way I see myself. So, what message do you bring?"

"I'll deliver it personally to your employer."

"May I offer you a drink?"

"I'll pass."

They were on the road for a good forty minutes before the vehicle turned and slowly climbed a steep grade, bouncing everyone about as if they were playing around with pogo sticks.

"We on the moon?" Robert questioned good-humoredly.

"No. But you might say we're on top of the world," Michael replied cheerfully. "Certainly at the edge of it."

A few minutes later, the van stopped abruptly. There was activity all around them. The back doors opened wide, and Robert could see Long Island Sound. He knew he had to be on the northeast corner of Orient Point.

"I have to insist that you wear this blindfold," Michael instructed as they stepped down to a dirt road.

Before the writer's world went dark, Robert saw a man in a golf cart approaching.

"I know all this seems a bit dramatic. And it's such a shame you won't be able to see the sights, even for someone as clairvoyant as yourself. But I do have my orders, you understand."

Robert felt completely helpless as he was being assisted into the cart.

"Okay, here we go. Hang on. I do hope they remembered to charge the battery. Once, I recall having to push this monstrosity a good quarter mile."

The ride was mostly downhill. But then the road flattened and seemed to wind forever. Robert could smell the sharp sea air. He could hear water lapping the land before the cart came to a sudden stop.

"Now, I want you to stay close to me, Mr. Redler. We're getting out here," Michael directed, helping the author make his way. "Careful now."

Robert Redler could sense the surface beneath him moving.

"Water's a little rough today, so please stay next to me," he insisted.

Robert could see nothing, but heard a boat approaching

before it gently bumped the dock. He lost his balance, but Michael held him steady. "Easy there, mate. We're going for a little boat ride. Put your sea legs on. Step up here, like so. There you go."

Within a moment, the boat was away from the dock, up on plane, and running at a good thirty knots, slicing easily through a chop.

"All right," Michael commanded, "we're going below. Keep your head down and take one step at a time." Michael pushed Redler's head down and guided him along. "Here we are. Sit down."

Robert felt comfortable cushions against his back and buttocks. "Can I take this blindfold off now?"

"No," was Michael's firm reply. "Just sit and relax and we'll be at our destination in a little while."

Robert could hear the squelch of the VHF radio from above. Indistinct voices were transmitting and receiving.

After what seemed like a good hour, the craft turned hard to port. Approximately twenty minutes later, the engines reduced their rpms. The boat was moving along at about ten knots. A minute later, she dropped to five. The vessel went into neutral and glided. Left rudders reverse. He could feel the stern come around then touch. Off to starboard she fell. Forward thrust. Finally, they were birthed.

"Home port, Mr. Redler," Michael announced.

Robert was helped out of the cabin, off the boat, and onto a solid wooden platform. The wind was at his back, and the temperature felt as though it had dropped a good ten degrees.

"Ten minutes more, and you'll see the light of day," Michael promised.

Robert could hear the patter of busy feet working all around him, securing the boat. He felt the bumping of fenders fitted firmly into place. Lines were being adjusted and readjusted, fastened to cleats then coiled. They were already washing her down. He could smell diesel in the salty air along with the fishy smell of flesh the gulls had torn asunder. He turned around and filled his lungs with the sudden gust of fresh sea air. Yes. This was Richard Geist's port of call, all right, he told himself. This was, indeed, Geist's sea of salvation.

"Come, Mr. Redler," Michael coaxed, helping him along. "Come and meet your gracious host."

Chapter
——>
74

Inside the hideaway, Redler was told to remove his blindfold. Sunlight filled the fourteen-foot floor-to-ceiling windows, the sudden burst of brightness hurting his eyes. Squinting, he turned and gradually focused on a figure sitting several yards away. Michael was standing off to Richard Geist's side.

"*At long last we meet again*," Richard signed as Michael translated. Geist noted that his guest appeared quite nervous. The killer liked that a lot. "*When you came to interview me in Havenwood, you told me it was for an article, not a goddamn book, Robby. A biography of sorts, no less*."

Robert Redler drew a breath and signed, too, raising the middle finger of his right hand high in the air. "Fuck you, Richard," Robert said, mustering as much courage as he could through silent prayer.

Richard sat quietly for a good thirty seconds, staring Robert Redler up and down. Michael darted dark eyes between them. A brown leather shoulder holster with a weapon harnessed at his breast hung menacingly. He waited patiently for the exchange of dialogue.

"*Why did you write such a book?*" Richard signed.

"To send a message."

"*To whom?*"

"To the people."

"*And what message is that?*"

"That garbage like you should be executed by the state."

"*Why don't you have a seat, Robert?*"

"Because we won't be staying long."

"*We?*"

"Chief Grear, myself, as well as eleven others. Michael, too, if he's smart."

"*I see. Or at least I think I do. You're just going to take captain and crew and cruise the hell on out of here. Is that it?*"

"I'm sure you won't make it that easy, but that's the general idea."

"*You know. I get the distinct feeling that you're a little bit madder than I,*" Richard chaffed and laughed.

Robert shook his head. "A lot madder, I'm afraid. I'm just not as slick as you."

"*Do you believe this guy, Michael?*"

"I thought he had more sense than this," Michael spoke, shaking his head in sincere disappointment.

"And I would have thought you had more sense than to betray the trust of public office," the captive responded. "But I've learned that the battle between good and evil is not one but many, fought on numerous fronts until the final hour."

"*And is this going to be the final hour, Robby boy?*" Richard questioned and grinned from ear to ear.

Robert Redler did not answer.

"*I see. Don't know everything. Do you, guy?*"

"I've come to take your hostages home. Now!"

Richard laughed in disbelief. "*Suppose I send all of you home in plywood boxes. Or we could have a burial right out there at sea,*" he remarked and gestured toward the open water in the distance. "*Would that be to your satisfaction? Because if you believe you're going to up and leave here without first sitting down and having a little chat, it's not going to be in the plumb position you're standing in now.*"

Robert went over and took a seat opposite Richard.

"*There. That's better. Now. Let's look at this together. You insult me in my home and then defy me. You and I both know you're alive because you have something I want.*"

"What?"

"*Come now. Don't be cute.*"

"I don't have anything to give you."

"*This gift of yours. This power to predict.*"

"If you believe in it, why don't you heed my words and hand the hostages over, and we're out of here."

"*Or what?*"

Robert turned toward the great windows and pointed to the sun. "Or the eye of truth will suddenly hide itself behind the clouds, yet you'll feel a heat that will surely scorch your body and set your mind afire. This place will burn from within, but the drapes, the fabric on these chairs and the very clothing you're wearing will remain intact." Robert turned back to face the two of them.

"*No shit!*" Richard signed.

"No shit," Robert echoed coldly.

Richard exerted a hearty laugh. "*Then I had better pray for clear skies. Hadn't I? Now. Enough nonsense, all right? I want you to tell me. How are you able to put words upon a page before the words are ever spoken? Hum? How are you able to set down pages upon pages of prose and dialogue, which are later recited by players who never saw the script? How do you set down events before they come to pass? I want you to tell me, Robert. And I want you to tell me now.*"

"You mean like this?" Redler said, producing a pad and a pen from his jacket pocket that Richard's crew had let him keep, jotting down a series of signs.

In less time than it took for Richard and Michael to settle into the show, the writer ripped off and handed up a single sheet without leaving his seat. Michael came over and took the paper from the writer's hand. Without reading it, Michael turned it over to Richard. Richard sat and read in total amazement while Robert was busy writing again. Richard signed to Michael, but Michael only shook his head. Richard danced his fingers then drove the heel of one hand into the palm of the other. Michael shrugged and shook his head again, staring queerly at Robert.

Robert put the pad and pen down upon his lap.

"*How do you know all this?*" Richard demanded through Michael.

"I just do."

"*You're full of crap.*"

"I've been sent here as a messenger, Richard."

"*By whom?*"

"Your Maker."

"*What's the message, Robert ol' boy?*"

"Repent."

"*For what?*"

"For all your sins."

"*Read between the lines*," Richard signed, holding up three fingers while rising from his chair.

"Then you shall surely die, and the devil will have your soul."

Richard laughed loudly. "*He already has it on layaway. I made a pact a million years ago, ol' bean*," he joshed.

"It's not too late to repent, Richard."

"*But it's getting very late for you, Robert. So I'll tell you what. I'll make you an offer you wouldn't want to refuse. Come work for us, and I'll make you a far sight richer than any contract you signed with Barbara Giordano acting as your agent for Simon and Schuster. You wish to be a successful writer?*" Richard directed Robert's attention to the two books lying next to one another atop a teak sideboard.

Robert glanced over his shoulder and noted the copies as well as his own stack of handwritten manuscript pages.

"*Of course, my autobiography far exceeds sales of your unauthorized biography of me. Together, we can change all that. Maybe even co-author a book.*"

"Maybe he'll begin to see the light," Michael spoke.

Robert Redler dramatically ripped off the second sheet from his pad and handed it directly to Michael. "Will you, Michael, see the light?"

Suddenly, a series of ominous dark clouds rolled in and blocked the face of the sun while Michael turned as white as the caps breaking upon the sea below the high bay windows. "Jesus Christ!" he cried.

Richard tore the paper from Michael's hand and read before signing up a storm.

But it was Robert Redler who translated for Michael as Michael ripped the paper back from Richard's hand.

"Richard's explaining to you how a storm system was heading in from the east and how I somehow timed it to coincide with this event. Like the eclipse out of Mark Twain's *A Connecticut Yankee in King Arthur's Court*. But if you check with NOAA, not the ark builder, Michael, but the National Oceanic and Atmospheric Administration; that is, the national weather broadcasting station, you'll learn that there is no such storm system in the area.

"Now, he's telling you that the dialogue you see is somehow all a trick, that the words I set forth evoke a natural response. Do they, Michael? You saw me write upon the second sheet while Richard was busy figuring out the first, wondering how I was able to give an accurate compass course from start to finish, complete with buoy markers, distances, and speeds. Are you going to continue the way you're going, Michael? Reading Richard's sign forever? Or are you going to finally wake up and read the sign of God?"

Richard was signing away hysterically.

"No, Michael. I know you're not going to buy into Richard's argument. You *know* precisely when I put down the pad and pen. Can you see that what he's saying just doesn't hold water? Can you see that it is he who is all wet? Like you, I'm only a messenger. What I wrote is the Word of God! But you had to see it for yourself. Well, there it is. Written in the flesh."

Richard stood and raked an anxious set of fingers through a wavy red crop, raising his hair like a host of little flames. The bushy brows upon his freckled forehead arched most angrily, his complexion turning the shade of a setting sun. Oh, he was heating up nicely now, Robert observed.

"What trick?" Michael was screaming. "Read: 'He already has it on layaway.'" Michael read, reciting Richard's words verbatim. "Listen. 'I made a pact a million years ago, ol' bean,'" Michael continued. "That's exactly what you said, Richard. How could he possibly know?"

Richard signed, but Michael shook his head.

"I don't care what the fuck he knows or doesn't. I don't know what to believe. Maybe it *is* all a trick. But if he knows where the fuck we are, maybe others know, too."

"Still possibly a trick, you say?" Robert questioned. "All right. We'll give it one more shot, Michael. Try another tact. Sink or swim. Ask me something you know I couldn't possibly know."

"The boat," Michael commanded in an instant, knowing his prisoner had been blindfolded the whole time.

"What about it, Michael?"

"Describe it. Fore to aft."

Robert closed his eyes as if he were going into a trance. He mumbled something to himself and bowed his head in prayer. "God is angry at me for trying his patience," he announced.

Richard had the gall to giggle, for he thought Michael had him good, exposing the dissembler for what he was, finally coming to his senses.

"Forty-five foot Tolly with twin 375 diesel Cats; 3208 block. Upper and lower stations. Staterooms forward and aft. Port galley down. Fourteen-foot beam. And here's a special bulletin for you, Michael. Your mother's had another stroke and is in guarded condition at Mount Sinai Hospital in Manhattan. Better hurry, Michael." Robert Redler opened his eyes and watched as Michael dropped most magically to his knees.

"Oh, please, God! No! Don't let her die," Michael pleaded.

Richard stood and delivered a roundhouse kick that sent his unfaithful player toppling across the hardwood floor. But Michael came up with his gun, leveling it at Richard's heart. The silencer was pointed at the silent one.

"Don't make me kill you," Michael said and sobbed. "I've got to get to the hospital. There are some things you just don't understand."

Richard was rolling his eyes and sending up guttural sounds from deep within his being. He tried to sign some sense, but Michael shook his head.

"You're right, Michael. There are some things Richard just can't understand between a mother and her son. A normal son, that is."

"I have to go," Michael said.

"Of course you do. She would want you at her side. So give me that gun, and I'll help you get out of here. Alive," Robert added calmly.

Richard laughed behind very angry eyes. He shook his head, and signed in an emphatic and dramatic fashion, fingers dancing away like silly little puppets.

"How many men on this island, Michael?" Robert asked.

Michael hesitated. "I—"

"Your mother is dying. Now is not the time for doubt."

"Three hundred," Michael said. "We can't get off this island without Richard. You must know that."

"We can, and we will. Chief Grear and the other eleven as well."

"You're mad," Michael snapped.

"I admitted to that before."

"Why should I go anywhere with you?"

"Because I go with God, and because it's the only chance you have of seeing your mother before she dies, Michael. She wants you at her side. Now."

Miraculously, Michael handed over his gun while Richard stood in disbelief.

"Good man," Robert expressed calmly, pointing the muzzle at Richard's face. "Is there a bullet in the chamber?"

"Yes."

"Safety off?"

Michael nodded.

"Doors locked or unlocked?"

"Both doors are secured."

"*You'll never get out of here alive,*" Richard swore.

Robert Redler turned the gun on Michael and pulled the trigger. Michael collapsed at Richard's feet. Immediately, the barrel swung back to Richard.

Richard stepped rearward and suddenly went ballistic, ripping down the drapes suspended from rods across the ceiling, flying about the room and kicking the cushions off the seats. He was bright red and in a terrible rage. Finally, he stopped and grinned viciously at Robert. In his last act of defiance, the cult leader came forward and tore open his shirt. And then he signed.

"I haven't the foggiest idea what you're trying to say, Richard. So save it. I just want you to know that I deeply regret you having interfered by killing all those public servants and college administrators who accused and abused me as well as their oath and office like Michael here. There are a lot of sick individuals out there, but none quite like you. You took care of everyone. Creatively, too, I must admit. I know now that all the writing in the world would not have brought forth the justice I wished to see. You taught me that justice and punishment collectively is something you must mete out for yourself, or simply not complain about.

"The good men and women in this country of ours have a dilemma on their hands. They feel that in order to rid the world of evil, they must become evil themselves. God, how good people complicate matters. There is such a simple solution that is staring them right in the face. It's not evil to want evil eradicated from this land. It's not uncivilized to execute that desire. To the contrary. It would be barbaric to do otherwise. But of course we must be more than sure of a person's guilt before we take a human life. The facts must extend light years beyond a reasonable doubt. They must clearly show one's culpability, Richard. The state or the individual must be able to stake its soul on it, like I must stake my soul on you. So until all fifty states adopt a policy and execute it sensibly and to the letter of the law, the responsible individual, I pray, must exercise his or her own will. It's so easy to clean up garbage, Richard. Watch and see as you sign off."

Robert Redler pointed the weapon between Richard Geist's eyes then squeezed the trigger as Richard parried and landed a blow against the writer's wrist. But the bullet caught Richard just below the ear; he stood for a good four seconds before he fell.

Robert F. Redler shot Richard Geist there in cold blood not

because Richard was a willful serial killer, but because the law of the land is weak-willed. He shot him because the median term served in prison by a murderer is twenty years. Robert Redler shot him not because the cult leader might possibly have been declared incompetent to stand trial, but because the law in its dementia grants men like Richard Geist a glimpse of light at the end of a temporary tunnel whereas the bodies of their victims behold the darkness to the end of doom. He shot him because far sicker minds than Richard's shape and write the laws and enthusiastically support the ideas of rehabilitation in capital offenses with but little regard given to the victims, their loved ones, families and friends. Robert shot him not only because Richard was as unbalanced as those who pass those laws, but because Richard was as unstable as those who uphold them. Robert Redler shot him because Robert was in his right mind in a world filled with unsound standards. Simply put, Robert spilled the blood of an evil being because nothing could have been more sound or saner under present law. Pure evil had to be uprooted then burned or buried well beneath the shallow graves of its victims.

Robert Redler eased off the trigger. "Can you hear me, Richard? I'm so sorry there's no time left for you to sign a confession," the author said without expression. He reached down and put the silencer against Geist's forehead. "Shh," he whispered, squeezing the trigger again. "See. All the garbage is gone." He went over to the door of the study and locked it.

Chapter
——>
75

Robert Redler had executed justice swiftly and mercifully. He did not in any way feel above the law, just light-years ahead of it. He felt neither elation nor sadness. What he felt was sheer relief that seemed to soothe his tortured soul. He went over to the phone and picked up the receiver. Instead of a dial tone, he got a woman on the other end of the line.

"Yes, Michael," she answered expectantly.

Robert froze momentarily. Finally, he spoke. "Michael asked me to place a call."

"May I have the number?"

"He said that you have it."

"Then may I have the name?"

"South Central; Operation Services," Robert answered, sweat forming on his brow as he gripped the receiver and gun.

"One moment."

In less than a minute, Robert was connected.

"Operation Services."

"Mrs. Tabbit, please."

"I'm sorry. Mrs. Tabbit stepped away from her desk."

"This is Robert Redler. I need for you—"

"Hold on, please."

"No, listen— Hello! Damn it." Robert waited . . . and worried . . . and wondered . . . . He waited for what appeared to be an eternity.

"Hello?"

"Yes, I want you to take a message," Robert insisted.

"This is Mrs. Tabbit, Mr. Redler."

Robert really wasn't sure. "Yes, Mrs. Tabbit. Listen, about the conversation we had today," he tested.

"You mean yesterday," she corrected and laughed.

"Yes. That's exactly what I mean."

"Can you talk?"

Robert chose his words carefully. "I'm in a bit of a predicament and—"

"No need to go into all that right now. I want you to pay attention to what I have to say."

"Mrs. Tabbit—"

"*Time*, Robert. A luxury you young men don't, but must, allow yourselves."

"Mrs. Tabbit, please—"

"Now, let's track our progress with regard to some of the things we talked about earlier. Shall we? As you might imagine, we're exploring new horizons as we speak. There's a great window of opportunity for you. But first we need to evaluate your current position closely before we can determine what course of action to take. That's what networking is all about. Remember, no man is an island unto himself. Do you understand what I'm saying?"

"Yes, I think I do," Robert said nervously.

"Good. It's important that you do. We don't want to do anything hasty, now do we?"

"No, Mrs. Tabbit," he agreed.

"So just sit tight for the time being."

"I will."

"So. Your predicament is not as difficult a situation as you first imagined. All right?"

"You put my mind at ease."

"Good. That's what I'm here for. I need you to be patient. All good things come to those who wait. As a matter of fact, I believe I've located exactly what we're looking for," she said most enigmatically in case unwanted ears were eavesdropping. "But I just want to be sure. I'd like you to remain on the line a moment while I make a call. Think you can do that?"

"I think so."

"Fine. Be right back."

A moment later, the phone went dead.

"Hello. Hello!" Robert clicked for the operator several times before putting down the receiver.

Not a half hour had passed before the door to the study unlocked behind him. Robert swung about and leveled the gun at the doorway.

"Well, what have we here?" Barbara Giordano remarked, staring at the bodies on the floor. Jonathan Laddington stood behind her. "Murder or mayhem? Intrigue and suspense, for sure. What remarkable ingredients for another novel, Rob dear. Where do you think it should all begin? Where could it all possibly end?" She turned around to Laddington. "Darling, do step in and lock the door behind you. We don't need to create another scene out there. The natives are already restless."

"What in hell are you doing here?" Robert asked, lowering the weapon.

"I came for the matinee. This is the intermission, I take it. Did you do all this by yourself? I thought the pen was mightier than the sword, Rob," she needled nonchalantly.

"You used me."

"That's a rather feminine line. Doesn't quite suit you, my dear."

"Where are Chief Grear and the others?"

"How should I know? You should have asked Richard or Michael before you shot them. We just got here a little while ago. Aren't you pleased I brought your lawyer? Don't you think that you're going to especially need one now? You ought to tell Mr. Laddington exactly what happened before you speak to anyone. Sort of get your stories straight," she made clear.

"There are three hundred of Geist's people out there," Robert said excitedly, pointing to the door. "We have to find Grear and the others and get the hell off this rock."

"Calm down, Rob. Everything is under control. Mr. Laddington will talk horse sense to them and everyone else concerned. Just relax. Richard and Michael were about to instruct the palace guards that a certain faction has finally fallen neatly into line. I guess he thought he'd have good news to give them concerning you, too."

"You want to be a part of all this?" Redler snapped.

"Yes, Rob. We're branching out, dear. Religion has always been big business."

"And you and Laddington are going to pass around the collection plate, I take it."

"So long as Richard and Michael don't object," she said with a smile, staring down at the bloody mess.

"I've made things very convenient for you. Haven't I?"

"Let's just say we hold a very special place in our hearts for you, Rob."

"I ought to put a bullet through the other side of that brain of yours."

"I'd say you're in enough trouble, son," Laddington spoke up sharply. "You know that if you shoot her, you'd have to shoot me. And like it or not, I'm you're only hope," he swore, withdrawing a handkerchief and walking over to take the gun from Robert's hand.

"Maybe you'd like to shoot me," Robert blew. "Maybe I'm the only who stands in the way of your *new* venture."

"I never terminate a client before I'm paid in full," Laddington funned.

"Besides, we need you," Barbara added.

"What we need to do is find Grear and the others," Redler insisted, moving toward the door.

"First you have to listen to me," Laddington countered. "You do that, and you'll be all right; perhaps a hero overnight. Fail to listen to me, and you'll find what seems to follow you wherever you go. Trouble."

"Where did you get that key?" Robert questioned, pointing to the item in Laddington's hand. "Huh?"

"The woman on the switchboard," Barbara answered for her mouthpiece.

The writer just stood and stared.

"Who was it you called, dear?" Barbara questioned.

"A woman concerned about the future of this country; a woman who just woke up and saw the light."

"And who exactly is she?"

"She was a recruiter for Geist's people. *Was* being the operative word."

"I see."

"Tell me exactly what happened here so that I can help you," Laddington commanded, stooping over Michael's body.

"It was self-defense," he prevaricated.

"And Richard?"

"He grabbed for the gun I wrestled away from Michael. We struggled."

"So his prints are on this weapon, I suppose."

"Unless you just smudged them with your handkerchief."

"Then there would be latent prints, Rob," the attorney argued. "Yes?" he asked emphatically, stepping over to Richard's body.

"I guess," Robert said with eyes that showed defeat.

"You better *know*, Robert," Laddington stated, bending down and wrapping Richard's right hand around the gun grip and barrel before removing it. "You better know why you shot him twice in the head," he said, rising from the body.

"All right. Let's get out of here," Barbara ordered. "We'll find and hand deliver a police chief and how many others, Rob? Maybe Suffolk will owe us one. No?" she questioned coyly.

Robert was studying the pair, wondering if he would later regret not having shot those two between the eyes. But he also knew that the authorities would try and bury him in a heartbeat whether the two were alive or dead. Somehow he'd try and manage to walk that delicate line around the garbage without stepping into it. Or was he already in over his head. *Part of the heap?* he wondered.

Chapter
——>
76

Laddington, Giordano, Redler, Chief Grear and eleven others stepped aboard a Coast Guard cutter and were whisked across Long Island Sound. Chief Grear and Laddington had words of disagreement while Barbara and Robert stood off in a corner of the armed government vessel by themselves.

"You just had to make that call," Barbara soured.

"How the hell was I going to get out of there?"

Barbara shook her head. "Laddington's going to tell you not to lie to your lawyer. I'm telling you not to *ever* lie to me."

"What are we, married?"

"In a manner of speaking, that's exactly what we are."

Robert shook his head. "Look."

"No, Rob. You look. Look around you. You're officially in custody. Fail to listen to me and handcuffs are waiting for you when we reach the other side. That's what this is all about. Sides. What side are you on? You can walk out of this so cleanly if you walk away with us. But if you decide to go with them, you're going down the tubes like garbage off the fantail of a ship twenty miles out at sea. Jettisoned goods, Rob. You'll be lucky to make it to the surface. And if you do, that's where you'll remain. Out there," she gestured. "Set adrift. Get it?"

"Then I'll just have to take my chances—wait for and ride in on the waves of truths and values. Get my drift?"

"The truth is you couldn't put a value on what we have. You have no idea how big this operation is. If you want to do some good in this world, take the millions you could be making with us and build a hospital or a school or give it all away to charity if you like. This is not a cottage industry," she actually seethed.

"I guess what all this talk boils down to is whether I'm an asset or a liability."

"I guess it does."

"You know, Barbara, there is a war being waged every day against the things you're doing."

Barbara laughed. "Rob dear, I really don't expect such naiveté from someone of your intellect. The war *you* speak of is like a gambit in chess, each side willing to sacrifice a pawn or perhaps an even more important piece in order to gain the advantage. Officially, there are rules to follow and moves to execute in a certain fashion as on some silly board game. But the *real* war—hot or cold—is being fought globally. Each and every day. There are no rules or laws to obey. Winner takes all! Wait and see where we are in a decade from now. A war for the world's resources. Oil being *número uno*. Weapons of mass destruction to help protect and/or pave the way. And then there's little ol' me. Taking care of business with certain activities to help finance the fight. If government wanted to put itself out of business tomorrow, they'd legalize drugs today. Follow? They won't. It's not a grand theater of war they're waging, Rob. It's a minor skirmish fought on a tiny stage for show. More like summer stock. Entertaining. But insignificant."

"Like I said, I'll just take my chances with Chief Grear and the little people. And maybe when this is all over, I'll find a little island surrounded by clean water and live there with Liza for the rest of our lives."

"Oh, Rob. I know you know that no man is an island unto himself," Barbara leered.

Robert looked and locked his eyes on hers like radar.

"Your Mrs. Tabbit, Robby? Such a shame. She's had a sudden stroke. It happened just like that," Barbara added solemnly, snapping her fingers next to his ear. "Not thirty minutes ago. I can pass along your condolences to Operation Services if you wish."

Robert bowed and sadly shook his head. "She tried to stop this madness, Barbara. Your madness in large part."

"She wasn't a team player. We have our interests to protect."

"Other operators are standing by."

"Those others you speak of are falling neatly back into line. You see, we've come full circle, Rob. Play's about over, and the crowd is walking up the aisles and back outside into what they perceive to be the light. So, what do you say? We need a good director."

Grear and Laddington came across the stern.

"What do you want to do when we get back, Rob?" the police chief asked.

"I want to speak to the press."

"I'm sure many of them will be there."

"I suppose you know what you're going to say," Laddington said.

"Yes, I do," Robert assured him.

"As your attorney—"

"You're no longer my attorney."

"I see."

"No. I really don't think you do."

Chapter
--->
77

Liza was standing on the pier by Preston's in Greenport as the Coast Guard vessel docked alongside the ship's chandlery off Main Street. Robert was told by a police official that he had two minutes in which to make a statement to the press. The writer quoted from memory before a group of reporters and spectators.

"'No man is an island, entire of itself; every man is a piece of the continent, a part of the main; if a clod be washed away by the sea, Europe is the less, as well as if a promontory were, as well as if a manner of thy friends or of thine own were; any man's death diminishes me, because I am involved in mankind; and therefore never send to know for whom the bell tolls; it tolls for thee.'"

"Why are you quoting Donne?" a female journalist asked.

"Because I'm finished," Robert Redler quipped, heading along the dock toward a ramp.

"Did you shoot Richard Geist along with one of Senator Demeco's aides?" a staff writer for *Newsday* called out.

Robert Redler said nothing.

"An anonymous source in Albany claims you shot and killed cult-leader Richard Geist and his accomplice, Michael Gottis, Senator Demeco's nephew," the man pressed.

"No comment," Laddington interrupted, putting an arm around

Robert in a final effort to affect a change of heart.

"Is Mr. Laddington still representing you?" a reporter hollered.

"No."

"Professor Redler. Will you ever go back to teaching?" a young man of college age asked.

Robert gave a polite nod. "I've never stopped teaching," he responded and smiled, assigning two thumbs-up as authorities put him in handcuffs.

The young man smiled, too, forming a V for victory sign with fingers held high above the crowd.

Liza came forward but was moved back by police.

Robert nodded assurances to her as she waved and wept.

Chapter
——>
78

I t was a speedy trial as far as trials go. Robert Redler was acquitted of all charges. The defense was self-defense. Everyone agreed that the court proceedings were not the sensational display they had expected, but rather a third-rate show. The state did not push the envelope. The defense, consequently, was bland. One prosecutor, speaking off the record, mockingly offered that if Mr. Redler had *cold bloodedly* murdered a million people associated with Richard Geist's cult, the jury would have demanded to see a temperature chart. The jurors had deliberated for no more than sixty minutes before returning a verdict. To kill time, it was rumored, a debate ensued over whether Coke was better than Pepsi, while the forewoman insisted that Dr. Pepper blew them both away.

After the verdict was read, and Robert found himself outside the courtroom in the midst of throngs of reporters and well-wishers, one fellow from *Newsweek* queried as to what the writer would have said had he been found guilty beyond a reasonable doubt.

Looking the reporter squarely in the eye, Robert Redler replied, "What in God's name is ever reasonable about doubt?"

It was the Quotation of the Day that appeared in *The New York Times* the following morning and, for weeks thereafter, the very question of inquiring minds.

In a television interview, Redler was asked how sure a jury should be before convicting someone of a capital crime.

"Jack Ruby sure," came the terse reply.

In a lengthy interview with *Playboy*, the author was asked, "What consideration should be given eyewitness testimony?" Holding up the centerfold of Miss July during a camera shoot, Redler laconically insisted on 20/20. Continuing the inquiry along more serious lines, the writer was questioned as to the weight that should be accorded witness testimony in a criminal proceeding.

"For the purpose of investigation, the weight of the world," Robert Redler answered. "Insofar as it translates into sworn testimony in a court of law to the exclusion of concrete evidence, not a gram," was the profound remark.

"On what do you base that conclusion?"

"Read the court transcripts in the John Lightfoot matter for openers," was Redler's pointed comment, highlighting the fact that the young woman who was allegedly attacked by Mr. Lightfoot had drastically altered her initial story to police with regard to the assailant's height and weight; the fact that the woman's girlfriend verified the first report; the fact that the arresting detective withheld exculpatory evidence following an interview with the victim's neighbor who witnessed the attack and gave a description similar to the first account; the fact that the detective claimed he had an eyewitness who implicated Lightfoot in another case, which proved to be untrue; the fact that the detective had a history of such tactics; the fact that the same detective was later implicated in the murder of his mistress—ad infinitum—before being booted off the force, albeit with full pension.

The public couldn't get enough of Redler, and Redler couldn't get his message out there fast enough. Chief Grear had questions for Robert, too. But they were of a quite different nature.

The chief of police waited a respectful period of time before approaching Robert and Liza, as the two were busy putting their lives back together. Too, the couple was away for a fortnight, having just returned from Queens for the funeral of John Lightfoot who succumbed to cancer. The innocent soul had been released from prison after being exonerated of the attempted rape of a high-ranking police officer's daughter. Reluctantly, the sentencing judge had reversed himself following new evidence that had been brought to light.

Chapter
——>
79

Robert exited the rear of his home in Riverhead, and took the police chief's hand warmly into his own the moment the man stepped from the vehicle.

"Hey, congratulations," Grear offered. "Liza tells me you're just about done with the novel."

"Final chapter. I think I'm going to include an epilogue, and then I'll finally be free of it," the author elaborated.

"I hear you loud and clear. Listen, I'm really sorry about John Lightfoot," the chief said sincerely.

Robert nodded. "We just got in a little while ago. Things getting back to normal around here?"

"Normal? If it were only that. Guess you heard that Angelica's out on bail. Angelica Manns, we've finally learned her name. Very mysterious background. Could be another book for you, I'd wager. And I'm sure you won't be surprised to hear that Laddington's defending her."

"Laddington's a piece of work, all right."

"Probably convinced the judge that he could get him elected governor if he just leaned a little to the left," Grear half-joked and grinned mischievously.

The writer laughed. "Wouldn't doubt it in the least, Chief.

"She's going to be big trouble, Rob."

"Think she'll organize them?"

"Wouldn't bet against it. Not with Barbara Giordano waiting in the wings. If that housewife from Oceanside can negotiate unity between Geist's followers and the Mob, she'll be back in the *families'* good graces; and it will be business as usual."

Robert nodded. "Liza said you wanted to talk. Come on inside. She's got a pitcher of fresh lemonade waiting."

"Let's do that in a little while if you don't mind. Why don't you show me that boat of yours back there," he asked politely, pointing toward the pilothouse tied to the floating dock on the Peconic River. "I'm a bit envious, you know. I always wanted a fishing boat. Realistically, I haven't got the time."

"Boats can be a real headache, Chief. Absolutely heaven when they're running right. Pure hell when they're not."

"That's new, I take it."

"Practically. Very few hours on it. Not nearly as big and as showy as Geist's, though. Single screw, but it suits our needs."

"Know your way around boats and these waters, do you Rob?"

"Blindfolded," Robert answered most immodestly. "Been around boats and this area most of my adult life. New York to Nantucket. Coastal waters as well as our inland waterways."

Grear nodded knowingly. "I think you know why I'm here, Rob. There are things I have to ask you; unofficially, of course."

"So ask."

"Those sections in your manuscript. Dialogue put down before the words were ever spoken."

Robert was quiet as they headed toward the dock at the back of the property.

"I know you know what I'm talking about."

"I know."

"How? I have to know."

"I don't really know."

The two walked up the pier, down the ramp, then onto the floating docks.

"Venture a guess?"

Robert stared upriver at the setting sun. "About as good a guess as who and what makes the world go around," was Robert Redler's answer.

The chief nodded politely. "Do you believe in the Word of God, Rob?" he asked straightaway.

"Let me tell you a little story about what happened back in Bayside the day after John died. As you know, the cancer ran its course and claimed him last Friday. He passed away at four fifteen p.m. He was twenty-seven years old. The following day, his father was standing off in a corner of their living room, surrounded by family and friends. He was crying and carrying on hysterically about the futility of it all. Absolutely uncontrollable. His wife was heavily sedated. Everyone was understandably upset and very concerned. Several family members tried to console him, telling him that John was in heaven now and finally at peace. The father didn't want to hear any of it. 'They killed my boy,' he went on. 'The stress of his confinement while sitting in prison caused his cancer,' the man was convinced. 'There is no peace. There is no afterlife. There is no God,' he continued. The father was really out of it. 'If there is a God, I want to see a sign,' he demanded."

Robert paused; the chief was all ears.

"On top of the curio cabinet in their dining room sits a plastic dinosaur. A brontosaurus. It was John's favorite toy as a boy. As an adult, he'd occasionally pick it up and play around, teasing and chasing his young nieces and nephews around the house. Later, they'd all sit around and he'd tell them stories about how the giant prehistoric creatures once roamed the face of the earth. Then he'd flick a switch beneath its body, which emitted an unearthly cry, and off he'd go again, chasing after the kids. The family would laugh like hyenas, one of his brothers told me, tickled pink at the children's wonder and delight. Even when he was home from the hospital for those final days, he had the toy on the bed beside to him. Point being that it was John's toy right up to the end.

"Well, at precisely four fifteen last Saturday afternoon, with everyone gathered in the living room trying to comfort the grieving father, the dinosaur sounded its cry. Immediately, members of the family went running from the living room into the dining room. No one was near the toy, which sat high up on top of the cabinet out of everyone's reach. As a matter of fact, you'd need a stepladder to fetch it. Everyone grew silent in wonder. All the crying had stopped. George Lightfoot had received the sign he had asked for. That's a true story, Chief. Liza and I were there."

"I see," Chief Grear said quietly, tapping the side of the fiberglass hull.

Robert smiled warmly. "I think perhaps you do."

The two men said nothing for a moment, staring across the river.

"Say. Can we take a quick ride before we lose the light? Few minutes," Grear coaxed like a kid.

"Sure thing," Robert said, handing him the key.

"Yeah, right. I have trouble parallel parking," the police chief swore.

"Nothing to it," Robert encouraged, directing the man to the helm.

"Don't you have to take the ropes off?"

"Lines, Chief. Gotta sound nautical if you're gonna captain a vessel," Robert teased. "And, yes, the lines come off *after* you warm 'er up first."

"Oh. Think Liza will mind? Or will she be upset that we're going for a little ride?"

"Maybe at you; not me," he kidded.

"Maybe we should tell her. Maybe she wants to come."

"By the time she gets ready, we'll lose the light. You can blame me."

"How's she doing?"

"She's fine. Really."

Grear settled into the captain's chair.

"All right. Pull the throttle out and pump 'er; she's cold. That's it. Back to neutral. Now. Turn the key. Again." The engine caught. "Good. Now bring 'er up to about a grand."

The two communicated above the sound of the engine.

"Sergeant Phelps and Lillian?" Robert asked.

"Doing fine. They ask about you two. Want all of us over for a special dinner next weekend."

"Linguine and white clam sauce?"

Grear looked up at Redler.

"Lillian called Liza just before you got here," Robert explained. "We'll be there."

The chief returned his attention to the controls. "What do you want me to do here?"

"Act like a captain while I get the lines."

"We're losing the light fast."

"Plenty of time before it's dark."

"Rob?"

"Chief?" Robert hopped back in the cockpit and brought the engine down a notch.

"I wanted to kill Geist myself. Would have if given the chance."

"I know. But it's better this way."

"What really happened back there?"

"I showed them what they were afraid to see."

"What was that?"

"The silent truth."

Chief Grear nodded and said nothing for a long moment as the sun set behind the County Center. Finally, he spoke. "Did you know that Michael's mother had a stroke and died? Same day as her son." He did not know why he asked the question but he had.

"Really?" was all that Robert offered on the subject.

Epilogue

The writer took a sip of coffee, sharpened a number 2 pencil, placed a soft eraser to his right, then stretched his arms and yawned.

"Tell you one thing, mister," Liza warned, coming up the staircase. "You're going to learn how to type before the next book. Hear?" She gave Robert a kiss good night and went to bed.

"Good night," he called after her before resuming the final scene where he had left off in his new novel, *The Awakening*:

"So. Is this truly a God-given gift, Rob? A simple yes or no will do. Let's just start like that. Shall we?" Barbara Giordano suggested.

A jade lamp lit the landing before the three. Robert Redler sat there quietly. Relaxed. Conceiving. Studying the two women seated across from him. The writer's eyes shifted from Barbara to Angelica and back.

"From God, you're asking me?"

"Yes. This special power you possess."

"I guess."

"You guess?"

"Yes. But it's not really as unique as you may think. It's a potential power existing in most of us."

"Even in little ol' me, Robby?" Barbara teased.

"How about me, Robby?" Angelica Manns mimicked.

"Ironically, I learned how to tap into this phenomenon from Richard."

"Richard?" Angelica questioned with surprise.

"Yes, your fallen leader," he declared.

"How?" she demanded.

"So simple, really. So simple and so clear that you'd never ever see it. Not now. Neither of you. That's the even greater irony."

"But you're going to explain it to us," Barbara assured him, uncrossing and recrossing her long and shapely legs. "You're going to tell us how you come to know such things . . . this phenomenon you supposedly learned from my angel's dearly departed Dicky," she swore and smiled handsomely.

Redler shifted his eyes from Barbara back to Angelica. "You could ask any member of your cult, for that matter. Any of your Circle of Friends. They'd be able to tell you had they a tongue to wag. Maybe you can have them write it down for you."

"WE'RE ASKING YOU, ROBBY BOY!" Angelica shouted insanely, bending sharply forward from the waist. "You don't mind if I call you Robby Boy, do you? Because you are behaving like such a callous child."

"Actually, you and Richard schooled them, Angelica."

"Schooled whom?"

"Your own troops. Your soldiers. It was Richard who educated me many years ago from his cell in Havenwood during our interview."

"Go on."

"Well, he went on and on forever about the brain. How and why one uses its dominant side to 'detail to death one's self silly' is what he said to me; 'analyzing this and second-guessing that.' After his escape, the two of you met and formed a coalition, later with Michael, preparing your people for combat. Teaching them how to reverse the process of thought. To unthink. To dispel from the mind cognitive action. Instructing them, instead, how to kill *instinctively*."

"He'd have much preferred the word *subliminally*," Angelica interrupted.

"Fine. Whatever you say. It's what he did so well. To take an ancient art—"

"Something mindful, mind you."

"And refine it."

Angelica nodded knowingly.

"I made note of *all* the books strewn about that cell of his," Robert continued.

"Yes. There wasn't room enough for him to breathe, let alone tear about that tiny space of his. So he flew the coop and came to nest with me." Angelica tittered. "Voracious appetite for reading and romping," she chimed in, giggling gleefully.

"I read them all, you see."

"He knew you would."

"Herrigel's, *Zen In The Art of Archery* is one that I remember well."

"No sights or lights of any sort. Yet the Zen Master could pierce the darkness and place an arrow in the center of the bull's-eye," Angelica expanded. "Insight into self is key."

"And with a second arrow, Richard, like the Master, could split the nock of the first."

"Such precision and perception encompassing the mystical mind of man."

"Mystical to the logical Western mind, perhaps. So he taught his followers the Eastern ways of the world while you gathered and coached the mentally infirmed."

"They were naturals, Robby. Fertile ground. Their minds already cleared away of all the cobwebs; for the most part anyway," she added wryly.

"Cleared of all those details that confound the harmony of mind and body."

"Precisely."

"To do your bidding."

"On target."

"With you and Richard tending to the details."

"Bravo."

"The ancient martial arts masters understood the concept well," he affirmed.

"Overriding all conscious thought."

"Delivering fists and feet of fury—"

"With the grace of feathery flight."

"Toward the target for ultimate destruction."

"For to *think* in the heat of battle—"

"Would be to declare oneself to doom."

"The proverbial—"

"Paralysis of analysis," Robert sparred.

"Indeed," Angelica wholeheartedly agreed.

"And so my so-called secret *gift* is very much the same. Simple. I cleared away the cobwebs and simply wrote. Writing without thought to subject."

Angelica understood. "Subliminally."

"Stream of *un*consciousness."

Angelica doubled over, laughing up a storm. "Oh, I like that," she said when she recovered. "Stream of *un*consciousness."

"Yes. Using the right side of the brain—"

"In right handed people, mind you," Angelica bantered.

Robert nodded. "Lending itself more to the perceptions of the whole. The essential form. The entire feeling. The complete arrangement of all things."

"Rather than putting together the pieces of a puzzle."

"Precisely."

"For one does not draw the bow."

"Or take aim technically."

"Nor loose an arrow consciously."

"No. It is the bow that draws and releases the nethermost soul into the highest state of perfection."

"Goal and target are one."

"Attaining the purest spiritual level," Robert acceded.

"Yes, Robby," Angelica agreed. "The bowstring has cut right through you, too, I see."

"That's my secret. The book? It wrote itself."

"A gift from God, you guess."

"So simple and pure."

"Simple and pure," Barbara repeated Redler's words, practically in a trance . . . suddenly, snapping out of it . . . she asked: "What the fuck is he talking about?"

"About all that exists," Angelica answered quietly. "All that is real and at the same time surreal," the perceptive and pernicious woman answered. "All."

"And that is precisely how I'm going to kill the two of you," Robert said quietly. "Simply. No theatrics. No poetic justice. No arrow loosed from a long bow. No problem. Just like I killed Richard and Michael. Cleanly."

"Really?" Angelica said. "It all sounded rather messy to me from what I heard."

Robert nodded. "Really and truly—Angelica and Barbara."

Angelica smirked. "And just how do you propose to do that?"

"By simply writing you off," the author answered calmly and ambiguously.

Angelica roared. And when she finally stopped, she abruptly turned toward Barbara. "Do you believe this guy or what?"

Barbara Giordano sat quietly by, staring past them, absorbed in frightening thought.

*****

The author put down his pencil and proofed the pages aloud. He pushed the chair back from his desk and stood, staring out the window at the blackness. Waiting. Waiting for a sign and renewed inspiration.

www.ingramcontent.com/pod-product-compliance
Lightning Source LLC
Chambersburg PA
CBHW071511260626
47170CB00002B/336